RACHEL EVE MOULTON

THE INSATIABLE VOLT SISTERS

Rachel Eve Moulton is the author of *Tinfoil Butterfly*, which was short-listed for the 2019 Shirley Jackson Award and long-listed for the Center for Fiction First Novel Prize. Her work has appeared in *Chicago Quarterly Review*, *Bryant Literary Review*, and *Southwest Review*, among other publications. She lives in New Mexico with her husband and daughters.

ALSO BY RACHEL EVE MOULTON

Tinfoil Butterfly

THE INSATIABLE VOLT SISTERS

THE INSATIABLE VØLT SISTERS

RACHEL EVE MOULTON

MCD × FSG ORIGINALS
FARRAR, STRAUS AND GIROUX   NEW YORK

MCD × FSG Originals
Farrar, Straus and Giroux
120 Broadway, New York 10271

Library of Congress Cataloging-in-Publication Data
Names: Moulton, Rachel Eve, 1975– author.
Title: The insatiable Volt sisters / Rachel Eve Moulton.
Description: First edition. | New York : MCD × FSG Originals /
    Farrar, Straus and Giroux, 2023.
Identifiers: LCCN 2022055069 | ISBN 9780374538323 (paperback)
Classification: LCC PS3613.O854 I67 2023 | DDC 813/.6—dc23
LC record available at https://lccn.loc.gov/2022055069

Designed by Abby Kagan

Our books may be purchased in bulk for promotional, educational, or
business use. Please contact your local bookseller or the Macmillan
Corporate and Premium Sales Department at 1-800-221-7945, extension
5442, or by email at MacmillanSpecialMarkets@macmillan.com.

www.fsgoriginals.com • www.mcdbooks.com
Follow us on Twitter, Facebook, and Instagram at @fsgoriginals

1 3 5 7 9 10 8 6 4 2

For Susan Streeter Carpenter

THE INSATIABLE VOLT SISTERS

prologue

My earliest memories in the house on Fowler Island are of the girls—Henrietta and Beatrice—their carnivorous joy echoing off the walls of Quarry Hollow. The sounds of their fearless jubilation would wake me from my rest no matter where they were— hunting for spiders in the extra bedrooms down the hall from their father's study or playing their monstrous games in the abandoned quarry that abutted the house. Their voices brought me forward. Their giggles and whispers pulsed through me, a heartbeat of their making.

Suddenly, with baby Henrietta's arrival, I had become grounded again in a specific time and place, something I had not realized I'd been craving. I found that I could come out of the walls, move about the house, stare out its windows. From the turret on the third floor, I could see the limestone quarry, the gaping maw in the land that marked the end of a specific pain for me that I still can't quite remember. We talked all the time, Henrie and I. Beatrice could never hear me, not in those days, but Henrietta translated for her, the three of us in conversation while Carrie and James slept in the farthest reaches of the house. We whispered about the mysteries of the island, and I told stories of their ancestors. The famous Eileen and Elizabeth Fowler—the sisters who could speak to each other without using their mouths—built the small downtown, the roads, and the Island Museum, which the girls had come to love. I told them about the arrival of their great-great-grandfather Seth Volt, and how he'd broken Eileen and Elizabeth apart. And how the sisters, even isolated from each other, planned their revenge, an epic escape that would take generations of women to complete. Henrietta promised me she'd never let anyone come between her and her big sister. Henrietta didn't, of course, know what was coming. Even when I warned her about the legend, she did not believe it. But my time with the girls was joyful. I gained substance, depth, found a solidity that allowed me to continue the work Elizabeth had started so long ago, keeping the house sealed tight.

I was in love with those girls. Still am. I mothered them as best I could, heard their secrets and their sadness. Answered their questions and traced their family tree on the ceiling of their bedroom so that they could conquer the madness, following the trail of their history to a brighter place. I wanted to tell them more, warn them, but then I would remember the smack of the water, the weight of it filling my lungs, a whimpering far off in the dark, and the monster sucking me down, down, down.

I did try. Over and over. But, each time, my tongue would become leaden, stuck ruthlessly to the bottom of my mouth. Heavier and heavier it would get until I couldn't make a sound. Couldn't warn Henrietta that the island had plans for them. That it would slowly press in on them, making the dark, sad spots in them grow. Big rotten splotches that would take over their bodies, separate them from each other. Mold over their hearts. And then, when the black and blue fuzz of it had softened their resolve, the island would offer them the perfect solution. *Jump.*

❖1❖

Henrietta

2000

I'm in the photo studio on campus preparing for my last months of college when B.B. calls to tell me that our father is dead. I haven't spoken to my dad in months—six, maybe seven. The last call was about my final tuition payment and whether he would cover it. He always came through—at least with money—but never on time and rarely without argument. He was stubborn, my father. Grizzled and aggressive and unable to bend to my or anyone else's point of view.

"Hattie"—he was the only one who called me Hattie—"college is a scam and you're paying for an entire extra year? Ridiculous."

"Well, Daddy, I thought you wanted me to spend that first year on drugs and boys."

My father chuckled at that. Sarcasm always worked best on him.

He could never abide that his daughters might lead normal lives. When I told him I wanted to join the Girl Scouts, he said, "Hell, no. Those ladies are fascists." In high school, I asked for an SAT tutor to supplement my "fancy" off-island high school, and he said, "Those tests are some extra kind of bullshit, my dear. Try smoking a little weed! Have some fun!" When I decided to switch my major to mathematics in my fourth year so I could add something more sensible and structural to my life, he told me I was going to "turn into a goddamn robot. Study philosophy or poli sci. Or better yet, don't minor in photography. Major in it!"

I've spent my whole life trying to rebel against my father by being a good girl. Stand up straight. Be kind. Live every day like it's a goddamn pop song. It works, mostly.

Now I can hear the background noise of the island over the phone—like a bundle of cats, spitting and scratching, water lapping at their mangled tails—and the sound of it triggers something animal in me. A need to run. To scream. To strip myself bare.

"I've got news, Henrie," my sister says in a quiet voice amid the island noise. There's still no cell tower on Fowler, apparently, so you have to go down to the dumb ferry dock and stand on the edge of it while pointing your body toward the off-island town of Marblehead to get a call out. I picture B.B. there, tall and beautiful. Her hair blowing in the wind.

My sister is like my dad. Quick to temper. Does what

and whomever she pleases and never hesitates to tell me exactly what she thinks of me whether I've asked or not. It makes sense, after all: she was the keeper. The one who got to stay on island with my dad after the divorce.

B.B.'s voice is different tonight though. Hesitant. She shouldn't even be on island. She should be in Boston. In graduate school. The semester hasn't ended yet. All my senses heighten at the realization that she is not all right. She sounds sad, uncertain.

I'm dressed for a date, legs shaved and covered by jeans. I have on a white tank top and a white blouse with bright red mouth-shaped flowers and thick green vines embroidered around the collar. Bluebirds dot the vines.

I came to the studio tonight to develop one more photo before heading to the bar to meet my date, but two hours have passed. He is no longer waiting for me.

"What news? I have a date to get to."

"It's eleven p.m. Jesus, Henrie. You stood him up, didn't you?"

"I can't hear you." I hear her perfectly well.

"Stop saying yes to dates you never plan to go on. It's cruel."

"I don't do that," I snap at her, but I do this all the time. When I agree to a date, I have every intention of going, but then I just don't. I lose track of time, I fall asleep, I remember he has some sort of annoying mannerism that I don't want to sit across from. B.B. thinks I'm afraid to get rejected. She always says, "You can't be afraid to get your heart broken." I never tell her that fear of getting hurt isn't the issue. Not really. It's something else. Something I don't want to explain. It's like not wanting to stand at the edge of a cliff because I'm afraid I'll jump. My brain goes to how I will mess it all up. Crush him. Stab him in the heart. Push him under until he drowns. I've never hurt anyone or anything—I move spiders outside rather than squish them—but there is and has always been this part of me that knows I'm capable of far worse.

"This is serious, Henrie." *Crackle cackle crackle*—the phone's voice is as real as my sister's, and I have a sudden memory of the quarry, the feel of it on the pads of my feet. Rock and pine needles pressing into the palms of my hands.

I tilt my head left, then right. My neck cracks loudly, my back aches. I push the paper down into the developer. The liquid swells up over the rectangle of white, and the rubber-tipped tongs squeak against the tub. Outside the small building, the campus pounds with Friday-night music—something electronic, a hundred pairs of feet jumping and landing again and again and again. That old island rage rises in me. I push it down, shove and shove until I can latch myself shut.

"You still there, B.B.?"

"Sit."

"You sit."

"No, Henrie, seriously. Sit down, then I'll tell you." I hear a new layer of noise. B.B. is crying.

I let the tongs rest in the developer and prop myself up against a metal stool as my mind races through the possibilities that would be bad enough to merit silence and tears from my older sister. I come up with nothing solid, but a vague memory of a tire swing curved around my body—the rubber smelling softly toxic, not unlike the darkroom—and a little bit of that feeling I latched shut pushes at the lid.

"Daddy died. I found him this morning."

"What? How? He's only sixty-five."

"He was turning seventy this year."

"He was?" Suddenly I feel the cold water of the quarry pond lapping at my ankles. The sharp limestone slick under my feet. I want to howl.

"We think his heart got him. But it could have been his kidneys, his lungs. His brain. All of it was fucked-up. He'd been drinking and smoking more and more."

"How long have you been on the island?" The latch pops. Anger oozes out, a slip of bile-colored cloth peeks through.

"A day, a week. Hardly matters. He wasn't answering the phone even though I could tell he had it plugged in."

"You're supposed to be in Boston." I'm having trouble keeping up with the conversation. I'm falling behind. He can't possibly be dead. He didn't call. He didn't warn me. He wouldn't do that to me. He wouldn't abandon me again.

"Henrie."

"What?"

"Dad is dead. I'm a fucking orphan."

"B.B.," I snap. She's called to share her latest problem with me. Her current sorrow. This news, in her head, has nothing to do with me. Not really. It's her dad that's dead. I want to reach out and claw her face.

"What?"

"You are not a fucking orphan. You have Carrie, and Ms. Sonia." I haven't thought about Ms. Sonia in a long time—it was too painful, but we loved her as kids. We spent tons of time with her on island, and according to my mom, Ms. Sonia helped raise B.B. after B.B.'s mother died.

"Carrie is not my mother."

That's true. My mother is her stepmother, B.B. my half sister. After the divorce, B.B. made it clear my mom was not necessary to her life. B.B. never returned a single note or phone call from her. Even went so far as to send back birthday and holiday gifts, marking them with her own bad handwriting: *No longer at this address*. I'm the peacemaker. The one who always made sure to send cards. To remind Carrie to call B.B. on her birthday. To sign both our names—mine and B.B.'s—to gifts on Mother's Day.

"And Ms. Sonia is a joke. We don't even talk anymore.

Henrie, I think Dad died a few days ago before I even thought to check on him. It was horrible. His body . . ."

"What?" I ask, this time really not hearing.

". . . like a whole separate thing had sloughed off . . ."

"I can't hear you, B.B."

"It's like he shed . . ."

"What?" An inexplicable fear rolls through me. It floods my ears and I go under. The surface of the quarry pond far above my head, the water icy. My foot caught in something, a trap tightening around my ankle. I can't breathe.

My sister is angry with me now. "Are you freaking out? I can hear your fucking teeth chattering!"

When we were kids and on island together, we would pretend we could toss thoughts between us, without speaking. Legend was that Eileen Fowler was a bit of a mind reader, so we figured that tiny piece of her could have been passed down to us. It was fun to try, and we did become good at knowing each other's thoughts. It seems silly to me now that we ever thought of ourselves as miraculously powerful or even on the same team.

"The funeral will need to be next weekend, Henrie. And it's Masquerade."

Fowler Island has its annual spring masquerade in early April. When our parents divorced, I was fourteen so I never got to attend a Masquerade. B.B. stayed on island with our dad, but I left with my mom and never went back. Not once. Still, I've grown up hearing all about

Masquerade. It's a legendary event. College students flock to it, and B.B. always calls to tell me the gory details.

"He probably did this on purpose so he could have the weirdest funeral ever," B.B. says.

I'm told Masquerade has become an important event for the economy of the island. The two ferries unload passengers who have been packed in like sardines. It started modestly—normal clothes a bit torn and bloodied, skin yellowed with proper zombie makeup, a sort of second and exclusively gruesome Halloween—but then it grew, as good traditions do, to allow for more elaborate and far sluttier and bloodier costumes. I'm told that the bed-and-breakfasts fill up with these drunk ghouls, who do shots and dance all night to music that blares out of every available island speaker.

"You've got to get here, Henrie. And come alone. Don't bring Carrie."

"What? Why?"

"I need you to myself."

"That's ridiculous. She'll want to know, and she'll want to be there."

"Whatever." The line goes dead.

The red light in the darkroom suddenly seems murderous, and I flip on the overhead, my heart beating fast, sheets and sheets of photographic paper now ruined.

I lower my body to the floor. My cell phone is held tightly in my closed fist. There are things I should now do. Call my mother. Rent a car. Talk to my senior project adviser. But the rage is growing in me. Curling my toes. Pushing my fingernails into my palms. Fuck him for dying.

"Fuck you," I say out loud. It doesn't help. The anger itches at my joints, makes me jump to my feet. Pace.

What did my father look like as he died? Did the pain show on his face? Was his mouth pulled downward by sadness? Was his face scrunched up in fear? I pause, turn to the full-length mirror hung on the back of the dark-room door, and imitate the possible expressions. I do not recognize him in me. I never have. I don't look like my father, sound like my father, or act like my father, so I keep going, stretching my face until, suddenly, I catch a flash of him. My mouth monstrously wide, my hands at my neck, teeth looking more numerous than they are as they disappear back into the dark of my throat. I see in that brief scream of an expression that I have his cheek-bones, his too full eyebrows. I see, if I'd been a boy, where my Adam's apple would protrude too short and too high like my father's. A shiver rumbles through me.

He is dead. I will never see him again. There will be no moment of reconnection. No proud hug at my senior show. No moment when he realizes that I was the more talented sister. No confrontation when I tell him all the things he's done wrong. I want to dig my teeth into his throat, rip out his jugular so he can feel the loss I've felt. Shame comes next. A rush of it so swift and sharp I lower myself back to the floor. Then I begin to cry, sob, unable to stop.

The cell phone buzzes again in my hand. I answer it, zombielike.

It is B.B., of course, her voice inexplicably clear. "I can't do this without you."

"I know."

"I haven't even cried yet. Not fully."

"Okay."

"You weren't close to him like I was. You have no idea how much this hurts." She sounds angry with me. Really and truly pissed.

Something wrenches so sharply inside me that I press my hand to my throat, as if the pressure will ease the wound. "I'm on my way," I say in a whisper.

"The island misses you, Henrietta Volt. It misses *us*."

I wish she hadn't said that. A memory surfaces, the feel of a growl, the dark of the quarry around me, and my body strong and hungry.

The café is busy for a weekday morning. I slide my body into one of the two empty chairs to wait for my mom, and the brightly painted blue wood creaks like it doesn't want me.

A little girl is at the piano. Seated on the bench next to her mother, she's leaning forward so she can pound her fists against the yellowing keys. She's seven or eight—too old to be treating the piano this way, but her mother smiles her on, as if everything she does is magic. The girl has dirty-blond hair that frizzes down her back, and her little feet are bare despite the chill of this Ohio spring. A smear of chocolate on her cheek reaches up to her temple, and when she turns to smile at me, I see she has no front teeth, just a gummy hole where they once were. She looks like an on-island Beatrice of the same age or perhaps a little Henrietta. We rarely wore shoes back then and our clothes came from Island Thrift, whose merchandise came from the 351 island occupants (of which we were 2), so any shirt or coat or pants you bought was likely an article of clothing you could trace back to friend, enemy, or relative.

Although B.B. and I were born two years apart to different mothers, people constantly mistook us for twins. And not just the summer tourists, but even the true island folk would trip on our names—the man who owned the penny-candy store gave up and referred to us as the Volt Sisters. I used to love this.

I think now that the confusion about which was Henrie and which was B.B. had more to do with my desire to belong to my big sister, to be exactly like her in every way, which made it that much worse when she and my father let my mother take me away.

We both wore our dirty-blond hair long and tangled—B.B. shaved hers to the skin in college but mine has remained long. We both have high cheekbones, tiny ears, and are naturally thin, a blessing my mother says, although B.B. has larger breasts and the potential to "fat up," B.B.'s words, if she ever has kids. We have the same startlingly blue eyes—mine are almost ugly in their paleness, more translucent than blue, but saved by a tight ring of gold around the pupil. The little girl at the piano has our elfin features. I don't like her, and I restrain myself from slamming the piano lid down on her tiny hands.

Now, sitting in this café, listening to the bang of the piano, mangled by a little girl who could have been me or my sister, I feel the weight of the surprise I'm about to lay on my mother, and I wish I had prepped her for it. For the entirety of that first fall after we left the island, I refused to go to school. I blamed my mother for the divorce. I kept my hands balled into fists with my elbows bent at my sides, as if I thought someone were about to offer up his or her face for punching.

On island my mom had been delicate, brooding, sickly, just generally in need of protecting; off island she was strong and free willed and "blissfully"—her word and not mine—single. She left my father for the mainland and made her own life. One where she was suddenly happy. A different person entirely. I was a different person too—delicate, brooding, sickly. We'd switched places, and I hated her for being so joyful. I missed my sister. I missed my father. I hated them for not missing me enough to bring me back. I missed the island. It's horrible, but I missed *her* too. The version of my mother who used to worry too much, who was always home, always fretting. Afraid of everything and nothing. It's terrible, I know, but I liked taking care of her, knowing she needed me. I got over my blind rage toward my mother, but sometimes I worry that there is something I did on that island, something that I'm missing. If I only could remember, it would bridge the gap between who we were there and who we have become.

When my mother enters the café, her presence drowns out the noise. She is vibrant, her personality big and ever present, and even as she nears her midforties, people stop what they are doing to notice her. She has recently pierced her nose, and her blond hair is curly and falls loosely around her shoulders. A purple silk scarf wrapped tightly around her neck turns the freckles scattered on her cheekbones auburn.

Before she slides into the seat across from me, my mother gently touches the little girl's head and says, "That's enough for now." The girl and her mother smile and move away from the piano. I stand and close the lid, smacking it down too loudly, and my mother raises an eyebrow at me. She unwinds her scarf, and it peels off her neck, releasing the scent of mixed cloves.

"Mom." I hear how weak I am.

"You look exhausted, honey."

"I am."

"Are you not sleeping?" she asks, but goes off on a

tangent about how she has found another house to flip—an amazing old brick three-story near the college. "Plenty of room if you want to move in."

When we lived in the house on the edge of the quarry—long named Quarry Hollow—my mom was constantly trying to fix it up. Paint and stain. Found lumber dragged in to construct built-in bookshelves.

A café table to our left empties, and the three people rise to put their dirty plates and cups into the dishpan not five feet from us. The clank of ceramic and silverware is a momentary distraction that makes both my mom and me look. For a moment, my mom stops talking, but then she turns back to me, speaking again about the beauty of the front walk and how it leads to a front door that will one day be "grand."

Dad had refused to leave the island even in January and February, when the wind blew across our four miles of rock and sand with such fierceness that we'd lose power for weeks. Mom had become determined to turn the house into something more modern, more inhabitable than the showy yet run-down Victorian that Great-Great-Grandfather Seth Volt had built. She read book after book about repairing old houses and went to the Island Museum to watch episodes of *This Old House* on PBS with Ms. Sonia, the Island Curator. Mom would come home from those afternoons smelling of sage and chamomile with ideas about which wall to knock out and how to install ceiling lights that would get rid of the constant gloom.

The house, like our father, saw no value in these improvements and resisted all my mother's efforts. Water stains bled up through newly painted walls. Unpatchable horsehair plaster spilled its coarse, pubic insides no matter how much new she layered on with her putty knife.

I once found her sitting on the floor, in the long downstairs hallway, banging her forehead softly against the house. "I was trying to hang family photos, but the wall is soft. Something must be leaking in there, but from where? There are no pipes in this part of the house."

I'd been watching her hit her head against the wall for a long time before she noticed me. The bang of her head to plaster wasn't hard, and the wall seemed to absorb it, bounce her back a little as if her skull were a rubber ball.

"It's an old house, Mom." I meant, I suppose, that a pipe, an electrical wire, an extra joist, or a beam could be just about anywhere.

"I can't stand up to it much longer, Henrietta. I'm losing."

I don't remember if I said anything after that, but the divorce was finalized within the year, and later, my mom became a contractor, eventually moving that business here to be near me while I went to college. The thrill of a project house just waiting to be saved had made her miss the sorrow in my voice during this morning's phone call and skate past my tiredness in the café.

I interrupt her. "It's Daddy."

She goes still. The flush in her cheeks disappears. Her freckles stand out like stars in a pale sky. "What's he done?" she whispers, and in her voice I hear something like horror.

"He hasn't done anything!"

"Is it Quarry Hollow?"

"What are you talking about?" My throat is suddenly thick with phlegm.

"Jesus. Now I am scared. Did something happen to B.B.?" She reaches for my arm.

"He's dead, Mama. Daddy died."

"Where?"

"What difference could that possibly make?"

"It matters." Her hand tightens on my arm until it hurts.

I try to pull away. "You're hurting me."

"Where did he die, Henrie?"

"In bed. While he was sleeping. Let go!"

She lets go. "They have his body?"

"Jesus! Of course. He was sixty-nine. That's not old but it's not young. People die, right?"

"Sure," she says, suddenly distracted. Her right hand goes to her eye. She plucks out a lash and then another, her face gone ghostly white. "People die."

My mother met my father only a year after his first wife—Olivia Rose, B.B.'s mother—died. My mother got pregnant with me right away, and they married out of love or obligation or both. The twentyish-year age difference and pregnancy before marriage were shocking to many—her own parents, my grandparents, disowned her—but my mom took it all in stride. She wanted what she wanted. Confident and beautiful and ready for anything, or so she thought.

My mother must have known early on that she and Olivia Rose shared the same long blond hair, blue eyes, and porcelain features. She couldn't have been on island long before someone gasped, mistaking her for Olivia Rose. She has admitted to me in recent years that there was a moment when she'd realized my dad was still grieving when they met and that his attraction to her was first and foremost a product of that grief. Apparently my dad had stopped her in the frozen-food aisle of a bodega in NYC where she was choosing an ice cream sandwich. She'd closed the freezer door, ice cream in hand, to see a handsome older man staring at her. They looked at each other for a while until my father said, "You look just like my wife."

My mother, thinking it was a romantic gesture and not a literal one, responded, "And you look just like my husband."

We sit quietly in the café.

My head pulses. "Mom."

"I wish that little girl was still playing the piano." She shuts her eyes.

"B.B. is already there. She is putting together a service for this weekend. She doesn't want me to bring you."

"You're going?" Her eyes open. I have her attention now.

"Of course I'm going!"

"Do you want me there?"

"I want you to come with me."

"Then I'm coming. We'll go together, but we stay at the Inn."

"It's Masquerade. We'll have trouble getting a room."

"What about those yurts at the state park? Are those still there?"

"How would I know? I haven't been back any more recently than you."

"You're right. Leave it to me. I'll rent us something. I won't stay in Quarry Hollow, and neither will you."

"Please don't start."

"Start what?"

"Acting like that house is out to get you."

"You know as well as I do that that island is a magnet for trouble. A fucking lighthouse for disaster."

"Mom!"

"Sorry." My mom shakes her head a little as if to clear it. Smiling slyly, she adds: "I shouldn't have said the f-word."

I laugh a little—I can't help it—then lean back in my chair. "It's just an island. A house. A place where we were both sad," I say, but even I know that doesn't feel quite true. I loved it there.

"You and B.B. thought it was haunted when you were kids. You used to talk with the ghosts, tell B.B. what they said. She was convinced one of them was her mother."

"I don't remember that." It's a lie. I kind of do.

"But you do remember how women always disappeared in that quarry?" The humor in her voice is already gone.

"That's gossip. If women were disappearing on island, someone would care. There would be bodies."

My mother shakes her head at me, back and forth again and again, as if offended by my naivete. "Not if they were women no one was looking for. Women who had been disowned by their families or orphaned. Women the system didn't care enough about to keep looking. Ask your"—she pauses, and I know she was about to say "dad" but says instead—"sister."

Islanders called it the Killing Pond because women would arrive on Fowler, sad and alone, then quickly go missing, never to be seen again. But items were always left behind on the quarry cliff above the pond. A necklace, a sweatshirt, a purse. Had they all jumped from that spot, they'd have hit the sharp rocks that hid beneath the water far below. Death would be immediate. But there should have been bodies, and pretty-messed-up bodies at that.

"You can see the quarry cliff perfectly from the turret on that house. In fact, it was probably built just there so that your great-great-grandfather Seth Volt could sit back and watch women jump." My mother's voice rises with the idea. She sounds fucking crazy.

"Mom, what are you even talking about? The pond wasn't there when the house was built."

She waves me off. "Point is, it's all fucking connected— that's what I'm saying—and I always thought your father knew more than he was saying. He knew where those women went. I guarantee it."

"Jesus, Mom, what are you accusing Dad of?"

"Sorry." She comes back into herself a little bit. She locks eyes with me before adding, "Nothing. Your father loved you. I just think we were lucky to get out when we did."

"If it was that bad, how could you have possibly left B.B. behind?" I regret asking as soon as it's out of my mouth.

My mother's hand reaches up to her lashes again, another small clump gone. "I shouldn't have left her. I knew better then, and I knew better all those years that I didn't go back for her. It's not something I'll ever forgive myself for."

"Sorry." I keep my voice quiet. I am sorry. So very sorry for bringing it up. Guilt for hurting my mother, for not doing more for my sister, blooms in my chest. *It couldn't have been so bad on Fowler,* I tell myself. *My mother is misremembering.* "Plus, B.B. wanted to stay. And she's fine. She got to go off island for college. Hell, she's finishing grad school now. She's okay."

I can't tell if my mother hears me. She's far away again even as she asks, "Do you remember anything about our last summer there?"

"I remember B.B. got me a dog."

"Toast. A little mutt of a dog. Disappeared. Like those women. Everything on that damn island ends up dead or disappeared."

"Stop," I say, anger creeping into my voice.

My mom puts her hands on the table, palms flat, and pushes herself to standing. "I can order us breakfast burritos."

"Coffee. I don't think I can eat."

She studies me for a while. "Fuck, Hen. We barely escaped that island."

"Coffee, Mom. Please."

"Yes, right." She steps out from the table but then turns around and leans over to put her arms around my shoulders, hugging me. "I love you, honey." I don't want to cry so I hold myself stiffly until she lets go. "How long has it been since you'd seen him?"

"We talked on the phone."

"No, when did you last *see* him."

"Five years. High school graduation."

"We will go say goodbye together. To the house. The island. You'll be free of it after that. He wanted that for you."

"B.B. was his favorite."

This, I can see, makes her truly sad. "He sacrificed a lot for you even if you couldn't see it." My mother flicks her hair over her shoulder and holds my face in her hands. Her eyes are the beautiful version of my own. She leans in closer and whispers, "With your father gone, the island is going to want you back, Henrietta. We are going to have to fight."

❧ 2 ❧

beatrice

1989

Girls. Five more minutes and we'll call it summer," Carrie says, insisting we finish a novel that's an imitation of *The Catcher in the Rye* except the main character isn't at all sexy like Holden Caulfield. Who writes this shit?

"Wait, what?" Henrie says, staring intensely at the pages in front of her before looking up. "Finny dies?"

"Yes, he's dead, dummy. The whole thing is homoerotic and Finny loves George—"

"Gene," Carrie corrects me.

"Fine. Gene. Why can't anyone write what they really mean? If Gene and Phineas love each other and that's what that dumb book is about, why didn't the author just say so?"

Carrie's smile is pulling up the left side of her mouth. She thinks I'm clever. A stranger could tell. She wears her feelings slapped up on her face—angry, happy, sad, lonely. Lonely. Lonely. Lonely.

"It's up for debate, actually," Carrie says. "Many people don't think it is about sexual love at all."

Carrie's got these freckles across the bridge of her nose sprinkled there like cinnamon. People say she looks like my mother, but I don't see it. My mother was wild and islandy, her skin clear of blemishes. And she was full of mischief, like me. Not that I remember any of that myself, but Ms. Sonia has shown me pictures and Dad loves to tell stories about her.

Carrie homeschools Henrie and me through the winter along with a gaggle of other kids whose parents refuse to leave the island even in the grimmest of months. The other kids aren't interesting, except maybe for Wilderness, whom we also call Wilde, as in Will D. He's so tall already. It's made him shy, and he never wants to make eye contact with me, which makes it more fun to try.

Winter is horrible here. The island transforms into a hunk of rock and ice, then sits so angry and scrunched up that the sun doesn't even want to try to get to us. It's like Alcatraz, not that I've ever seen it or anything besides this island and the Ohio mainland. Daddy wants to raise me and Henrie without the "interference or the influence of the greater world." No television (except when we sneak to Ms. Sonia's) and few trips to the mainland. "The world will have plenty of time to tell you what's wrong

with you when you go to college. For now, we are heathens and heretics and harbingers." Harbingers of what?
I might ask, and he will answer: "Of heathens and heretics, of course."

"I don't know what homo-rotic is," Henrie says.

"It means those two boys want to knock boots. Do
each other up and down. Fuck."

"Beatrice," Carrie says.

There aren't a lot of other die-hard families on Fowler.
Wilde's father is the island sheriff. They moved here
when Wilde was a baby. His mother died of cancer or
something, so we have the dead-mother thing in common. Then there's the Albertsons, whose son is just now
eight. Frank and Rita, whose daughter is Henrie's age,
although hardly friend material since she hates being
touched and doesn't make eye contact. The Cunning-
ham twins are ten and the Clarks, who have seven kids
between them, ranging from five to ten, all of them stupid and boring. Then there is us. Henrietta, who will be
fourteen in July, and I'm the eldest and most gorgeous at
sixteen going on twenty-five.

I got my boobs last fall and my period this winter.
Bled like mad for a week. Carrie tried to mother me with
chicken soup. I said, "I don't have the goddamn flu. Get
me some meds!" We don't believe in pharmaceuticals
around here. Only natural solutions, which I call "the
Herbs" and I pronounce *Herbs* like it's some dude's name.

It gets on Carrie's nerves something awful, but I don't care, 'cause who doesn't have a bottle of fucking Tylenol? Tell me that.

Anyhow, I am a woman now and people can't take their eyes off me. I walk around kicking my hips out and letting my breasts bounce. I'm strong. Unstoppable. I cool it around Dad though. It makes him uncomfortable. Nowadays, if Henrie and I are asking him a question, he looks at her the whole time and only glances at me if I force a burp or a fart. That still gets him laughing.

"Can we be done?" I put my hands under my chin in mock prayer, kneeling when I catch a glimpse of Carrie's entertained smile. "I'll pick you berries. I'll scoop the litter. Eat Dad's chipped beef."

"There is nothing wrong with your father's chipped beef. And you know that we don't have a cat. One of these days, Beatrice Bethany, one of these days, your big talking is gonna get you in trouble."

"I hope so." I wiggle my eyebrows at Carrie.

This family has a history of mamas too young to be mamas. Carrie is one of them—she had Henrie when she was nineteen—same as my mama. My mama was too young to die, as well, but she did both birth and death with a flagrance that calls for admiration—not that my father will ever talk about it, which is absurd since having a dead mother is pretty much the worst and most interesting thing that could ever happen to you. "Island women do things early and on their own," our father says, sometimes with pride and always with great sadness.

Carrie is not an island woman. She's always wincing and checking over her shoulder. She thinks I don't know about her and Ms. Sonia—I'm pretty sure they've got a thing going on. They've been friends forever, but recently she's always stammering and blushing anytime Ms. Sonia comes up. Even Daddy has noticed. No one gives a fuck. Carrie should just do what she wants like a real island woman, but instead, she seems even more timid, like she's either sneaking up on something or trying to sneak away. It's so damn easy to startle her. I swear, if you walk around expecting to be snuck up on, something is gonna sink its teeth right into your bones.

"I heard a ferry come in first thing this morning. Maybe your Joshua was on there," Carrie says to Henrie.

"Mom!" she protests.

We met Joshua on island last summer. He and I are closer in age, but he's got no edge to him. Superboring. Henrie can be a little like that too. She's only adventurous 'cause I'm teaching her to be. Come to think of it, I don't think she's noticed how her mom and Ms. Sonia flirt.

"So, can we go?" My voice is no longer impatient. I'm good at knowing when I've won.

"Yes. Go. Be free. School's out for summer. Watch out for tourists."

"We love you, love you, love you," I announce for both us girls.

Summer people and tourists are two entirely different groups of people. Islanders (that's us) don't officially care for either group, but if push comes to shove, we like summer people better. They own property on the island and so care, at least a little, about what happens to this rock. Tourists buy T-shirts and ice cream and pay to see Ms. Sonia's Island Museum and tour the old dock of fishing boats. They keep us islanders afloat, but we hate them. They drink too much, leave their garbage strewn all over the beach, and make way too much noise. They carve their names into trees and take pictures of us as if we are part of the landscape.

Daddy has no time for anyone except for Henrie and me. Less me than Henrie but still. He used to have time for Carrie, but now they barely speak to each other. It's not 'cause of whatever she's got going with Ms. Sonia. Daddy flirts plenty, or at least he used to. Summer people love him, and there was that whole month he went and lived in that yurt with Courtney, or whatever her dumb name was. He's not a jealous person. It's more like he's scared Carrie is gonna jump off the damn quarry cliff. Which I guess makes sense. That's how my mother left us. We say she's dead, but we don't have proof unless you count that Henrie can talk to the dead. She's heard 'em in the house her whole life, and she keeps me informed about what they say, especially the one we think is my mama.

"Where do we go first?" Henrie asks me.

"Where do you think?"

Henrie follows me to the sweeping front porch. We launch down the porch steps, past the tire swing into the road. I raise my arms out to my sides to show my wing-span and soar.

"Good morning, Ms. Penelope, you old whore." I place my fingers in the stone palm of Ms. Penelope Fowler's angel monument. One of her fingers is missing.

"Beautiful summer ahead, Dr. Archibald," Henrie says to a flat gravestone. She taps it with her bare toes.

Henrie says that touch is as important in death as it is in life. "They may not be able to feel our skin on theirs, but they can feel that we are making an effort." Henrie's heart is so much bigger than mine. It's 'cause of her that we visit each grave at the beginning of the summer, as if the dead can get lonely. Even though Henrie is the baby sister, she watches out for me. She understands that I am motherless and that such a tragedy means I'm gonna be fucked-up for life. The little rituals she creates for us are all for me, so that I don't have to feel so sad all by myself.

"We'd stay longer but it's Memorial Day and you know our ritual, Harold. Olivia Rose comes first." Henrie bends to press her palm flat to the long-neglected grass of Harold's cemetery plot. "We'll be back soon."

This is a Volt/Fowler family cemetery—the only graveyard allowed on the island—and there are 105 graves but only 95 bodies. The other 10 graves hold nothing but pretty satin-lined caskets filled with limestone. The women disappear, mostly tourists, but sometimes Fowlers and a Volt, leaving only their trinkets on the quarry cliff above the Killing Pond, and then we must "bury" them anyway, plucking up body-size rocks in place of a corpse. My mom is one of those. A disappeared islander. Daddy said he knew what the island had done as soon as he found me floating in the quarry pond. I was just a baby, but I was an island baby: "Strong and born knowing how to swim." He'd say, "Your mother was swallowed up like all the rest." He was so mad. Rumor is he pulled me out of the pond only to leave. He got on the next ferry. Left me and the island and went to NYC for a whole year. Ms. Sonia says that's not true. She says he was here, hiding in his office until she showed up. He didn't leave for New York until sometime after, but I say it hardly matters. He left me when my mom left, and he never quite came back.

My mother's is the most recent bodiless grave. There is space next to her for Daddy when he goes, and a bit more space for me, so when we all die, vanished or not, we can make sure there's a place for the living to visit. Henrie wasn't even a sparkle in Daddy's eye when he reserved these spots, and he always adds, "Seeing as how you and your sister are practically twins, we can just bunk you up. Two peas in a pod." I don't know if that's allowed in real life, but it's too sad to think of us being separated so we don't ask more questions. No one, not even Carrie, brings up the lack of space for Carrie. It is on the list of things Henrie and I call "Items *Not* to Be Discussed upon Pain of Torturous Death and Suffering." Carrie's having no family plot is item ninety-eight.

"Come on!" I holler. I'm at the gleamy tombstone that is my mother's. It is the only piece of new stone in the place, and sun glints off it, bouncing diamonds of light onto my skin. The ritual goes like this: Henrie slithers up, top of her head to the gravestone, and lays her body out over where my mom's body should be. It's an invitation, a gift. If my mom wanted to rise up, pour herself into a new body, she could have Henrie's. It's an absurd game. Mom's body isn't even down there, and Henrie knows more than anyone that Mom's ghost is in the house with the others. Still, we do the ritual every year, and I love Henrie for thinking it might make a difference. She lets her feet relax outward and places her palms over her heart. I spread her hair out in the grass, and she looks almost as beautiful as my mother would if she were down there.

"Hold still."

"I am still," Henrie says even though I can see on her face that she knows she's wiggling.

"Mother Olivia"—I always start with this—"we give you this vessel as an offer of strength and light and peace.

Summer is here and the worms are squirming. Island waters are warming. We ask that you pour yourself into our bones to give us the strength to run and jump and swim and dive. Now we each have a specific summer wish. Is yours ready, Henrie?"

"Yes. I wish that Joshua Kevin Wilson spends the whole summer on island so we can fall madly in love and take a blood oath that our souls will never, ever be separated. My second wish is that my stupid body starts to look more like a girl body and less like something that should have a penis attached to it."

I shut my eyes and pretend to listen intently for my mother's response. "Granted."

I think I will wish for what I always do, or some version of it anyway: *My summer wish is that we sleep outdoors more than we sleep indoors and that we swim until our skin pickles and that we meet three new people who change our lives.* Instead, I say, "I wish that we leave the island."

"What?" Henrie props herself up on her elbows. She squints at me. I imagine I look like Ms. Penelope's stone angel. "You mean like to Cleveland for supplies or whatever?"

"No, like we get to travel. To a different state. To real water. Like the ocean."

"But it's summer." Henrie tries to fathom what I could possibly mean by this change.

She's right. Summer on Fowler is full. We love it. If there was ever a time to run, it would be winter, but this spring is different. I can see it on Carrie. Even Daddy seems to be hiding from something.

"I've been thinking about it lately. Don't you want to travel? See California? Or how about Scotland? Paris?"

"We'd need passports." Henrie wrinkles her nose and looks toward town as if trying to figure out where we could possibly get them.

"I'm not suggesting we buy airplane tickets right this minute. I'm just saying that at some point we will want to get off this island, right? Why not start this summer? And, what if we could take our family with us?"

"But we don't leave Fowler. We don't want to."

"Forget it. I didn't mean it. Now lie back down." I see that I've messed with her world. My stomach is suddenly tight. How could I ever leave this island? If we did leave, we'd have to take everyone with us. Daddy. Carrie. Sonia. My mother. It isn't possible.

Henrie does as she's told, and the ritual quickly becomes familiar again. "We love you, Mother Olivia, and we promise to take every moment of summer and live it to its fullest." Daddy bought me a pocketknife last summer, so I take it out of my pocket, then take my sister's hand. I make a small slice in the pad of her thumb, then one in my own. We mash them together. I put a red print on her forehead and another on mine.

"Island women forever," we say in unison.

Before the slight breeze even begins to cool the feel of the blood on my forehead, Henrie shouts, "Come on! Our bell tower awaits."

Ms. Sonia runs the Island Museum, which sits at the edge of our cemetery. She's a second mother to us, or, in my case, a third, and she lives in the old island church that Elizabeth and Eileen Fowler built before Seth Volt ruined everything. The modest limestone building is two stories, although the second floor is only a loft, which Ms. Sonia has turned into her apartment. We aren't allowed up there unless we are watching movies. The bell tower is made of wood and painted bright white, stretching up higher than the rest of the building.

"I'm gonna beat you!" Henrie hollers back at me as she begins to run. She's fast, a tiny little body with no fat, but her legs are short, so I know I can catch her if I want to. I don't plan to pass her, but once my legs get moving, it feels so good that I push harder. My body flies forward.

I take Ms. Sonia's stone steps two at a time and smack my flat palm to the arched wood doors first.

"Winner, winner!" I shout.

"You are so fast." Henrie is proud of me. She's always rooting for someone else, never seeming to notice when I miss my moment to be kind or modest.

"Morning, girls!"

The voice comes from behind us, and we both shriek. Ms. Sonia's got on her jogging clothes, a gray sweatband in her black hair even though her hair is short and spikes up around her face.

"Did my ten." She's not out of breath, so she's either lying or had her cooldown already. I know she's not lying. She runs the periphery of the island early in the morning and likes to say, "Someone has to check to make sure no one broke in last night," as if the island is a house to be robbed. She always pauses dramatically, then adds, "Or broke out." Most of the time it seems like the kind of tired joke adults make to kids, but sometimes she says it and sounds freaked out. Dad says she's the latest Island Curator—Eileen Fowler being the first.

"It's summer!" Henrie announces.

"Well, technically, it's still spring," Ms. Sonia corrects. "Summer isn't here until late June."

"Summer!" Henrie shouts back in defiance.

"We've told you this before," I say. "The arrival of summer is not calendar dependent. It is based on the weather and our feelings."

"Fair enough." Ms. Sonia stretches her calves on the stairs. "B.B., you look older. Like a woman suddenly. Did you look like that last week?"

I feel myself glow with the compliment.

Henrie answers for me, "She did. The tank top just shows off her boobies. I think she should wear a bra. My mom gave her a bunch."

Ms. Sonia sends a little spray of spit out into the sunshine, taken off guard by her own laugh.

"I look exactly the same." Henrie looks down at her flat chest and her belly, which still sticks out like a toddler's.

Ms. Sonia stops stretching and takes the steps slowly but two at a time. She kisses Henrie on the top of her head. "You are perfect just as you are."

Ms. Sonia whispers something I can't hear in Henrie's ear, and I feel a flush of jealousy rising to my face.

Done with her whispering, Ms. Sonia throws open the church doors. The old wooden floor inside is beautiful. Fully refinished by Ms. Sonia, and you can still see where each church pew used to bolt into the floor. Little dark spots in the otherwise blond wood that prove this island was working at things long before I came along.

She rushes to her desk, where she retrieves two sets of earplugs and a skeleton key.

"Fit them in tight!" She hands us the earplugs. Henrie loves the squish of the purple foam and obediently starts rolling them between her fingers so they'll fit tightly into her ears. "B.B."—Ms. Sonia drags out my name—"you don't want to end up like my grandfather, deaf in the left and lazy in the right. We had to yell the simplest of statements at him. It was always 'Granddad! Your fly is down!' 'Granddad! Don't eat that!'"

"Maybe he was just ignoring you." I say it low and try to keep the words mostly at the back of my throat. I look at Ms. Sonia to see if she's heard my sass, but she's good at keeping her face still. *How much do we really know about her*? I think, but then Henrie is shouting too loudly, the earplugs already doing their work: "It's my year to ring the bell!"

"Well then, go on. You two are old enough to be on your own up there. I've got to get in the shower. Ring it as many times as you want. I'll make sure to give it a little push with my mind to get you started." Ms. Sonia likes to pretend she's got telekinesis or whatever it's called. She says Eileen Fowler could move things just by thinking on them. That might be, Eileen and Elizabeth Fowler were magic, but the only thing Eileen and Ms. Sonia have in common is the dumb museum. It's not like there is blood between them.

We head up the stairs that hug the wall of the old church spire. The stairs look old, but Ms. Sonia's rebuilt them. Carrie's been helping or, rather, trying to learn how to be helpful. She's over here a lot. Like all the time. She's got this idea that Quarry Hollow can be fixed up to be beautiful again if Ms. Sonia teaches her how to do all the things. Problem is, I don't think it was ever beautiful. Not in the way Carrie thinks it was. It's all strange angles and dark corners and too thick walls, like Great-Great-Grandpa built it special to trap the ghosts and keep out the light. Even the big front windows are covered by the roof of the wraparound porch, with shutters on the inside *and* the outside.

We reach the top of the stairs, three stories above where we started. It's the second-tallest building on the island, and through the slats of the bell tower you can see forever in all directions.

Henrie is unwinding the thick rope from its resting place. "Is it time?" She smiles.

I've left my right earplug out. I keep the left side of my body toward Henrie so she won't notice. Henrie pulls, and the sensation of the metal so loud and close is full enough to make my teeth hurt. The sun leaks through the slats of the bell tower, and a century's worth of dirt rains down on us like toxic fairy dust. Henrie's fingers do not meet on the other side of the rope unless both hands are used, so she's latched on tight before the first pull. The bell is pulling her up and down on her toes before the third bang.

The noise doesn't hurt, not really, but I can feel it hit my eardrum as surely as a slap to my cheek. It is booming— full and round in its sound. If I plugged my ear up now, the sensation of that sound might be contained in my body, where I might hear it again and again, but Henrie is looking at me and I don't want her to know.

When the bell finishes ringing and the sound of the birds outside and the rustle of the leaves come back, I point my face to the outside world and take a couple deep breaths. Through the broken slats, some thirty feet below, I see Joshua.

"Henrie, it's your lucky day. Look." I point.

"Tell me who it is." Henrie does not get up.

I watch until Joshua is gone from view, which doesn't

take long. He's running with a couple other kids I don't recognize up the steps and into the museum below. His hair seems blonder, as if he's already spent a summer on island rather than just beginning one. "Joshua."

Henrie has a weird expression on her face, a combination perhaps of wanting to throw up and wanting to look. I pick up a small pebble and throw it at her. Somewhere below us a door opens, then, after a few beats, slams.

"He's downstairs," I mouth at Henrie as if he'd be able to hear us.

"How did you do that?" Henrie whispers, as if I manifested Joshua. "I don't really like him."

"Bullshit."

"He doesn't even know who I am."

"Sure he does. We hung out with him last summer."

"He won't remember me."

"He does remember you."

"How could you know that?"

"He kissed me last summer." I forgot I had decided never to tell Henrie this, but remember as soon as her face turns all shocked and sad. "It wasn't a big deal. Like a peck on the cheek." It was more than a peck, and I'd started it. I'd been curious what it would feel like to kiss a boy, and there he was in the old bookstore on Division Street. I grabbed his collar and pulled him behind the curtain that separates the book-sorting area from the bookselling area. Our teeth clanked together and his lips were dry, yet a string of spit hung between us when I pulled away. It was the first kiss of many last summer. A sort of experiment on my part.

"Well, if he's kissed you, then he's already forgotten me." Henrie shrugs, but hurt and worry are all over her face.

"I'm an asshole, Henrie. I'm sorry. I went to talk to him about you and it just kind of happened. He likes you. He told me he did." This lie I know is too big. Too big if he doesn't like her or remember her. Too big if she believes me, but now it's out there, and her shoulders aren't as high up around her neck, and it made her face uncrinkle.

What else could I have done? I think to myself, but Carrie says this is a famous line of mine. One I should stop using since it implies my actions are not within my control. "And we both know, Beatrice Bethany, that you have full control over that body and mind." She always says "that body and mind," the word *that* giving away how much she doesn't like me.

I scramble around in my head to come up with a truth for Henrie so that the lie maybe gets smaller next to it.

"Remember that girl who summers with her friend's family? They live in the limestone house on Division Street?"

"I love that house."

"Yes, yes. The girl, Henrie, not the house. Focus!"

"Okay, fine. Was she Asian or something?"

"Japanese American. I was into her last summer—"

"Are *you* gay now?"

I picture Jennifer's dark braid, which rested flat between her shoulder blades, and her unnaturally long fingers. She's a loner. Always walking the island with headphones on or reading a book, never stumbling over sidewalk cracks or tree roots.

"Just because I made out with a chick doesn't mean I'm gay. I'm not interested in Joshua. That's the point."

"Is she gay?"

"You are missing the point, Henrie."

"Jennifer ignores me. She won't even talk to me."

Henrie's told me how she tried to make friends with Jennifer last summer. She'd walked up to her and said, "What are you reading?" Jennifer told me later that Henrie asked even though it was perfectly clear that Jennifer was reading Jane Austen's *Pride and Prejudice*.

"I did talk to Joshua. He knows who you are. He knows you like him."

"Why would you tell him that? I feel sick." Henrie flops onto her belly, pressing her forehead to the floorboards, and gives them a little pound with both fists before sitting back up to cross her legs with an exaggerated sigh.

"You're always staring at him. He wanted to know what was up with you."

"No, like really, I feel sick. My stomach is all tight and last night I couldn't sleep it hurt so much."

I look at my sister kitty-corner from me. Really look. She is cross-legged on the floor in her jean shorts, and a heavy shadow is on the seam between her legs. It takes me a minute before I realize it isn't a shadow.

"Henrie, you're bleeding!"

Henrie's hands immediately go to her ears, probably to take out her earplugs, but also with a bit of a panic. She thinks the blood may be coming from her head, the bell having liquefied some piece of her brain. She looks at her hands as if for blood.

"Your period, Henrie! You have your period!"

This time she looks down between her legs. "No way," she says in a daze.

I stand and go to her. Pull her up to her feet and kiss her cheeks and eyelids.

"This is it? Shouldn't there have been other signs first?"

"Like what?"

"Boobs. More pubes. Something. Maybe the bell shook something loose and I'm dying!"

"Be serious, Henrie. This is awesome!"

"I wished for it and now it's here," she whispers. I can see the joy start to bloom on her face. "You know what this means?"

"It means you're a woman, Henrie. We are both women!" I exclaim, then begin to howl like a wolf, which makes her laugh.

"Hen? B.B.?" Ms. Sonia hollers up.

Henrie shushes me, finger to lips.

"I know what to do, Henrie. Don't tell her. We're fine, Ms. Sonia!" I holler down, giving Henrie my best goofy grin.

"It means that my other wish might come true. The one about, you know . . ."

"Joshua!"

"Shush!"

"Oh, this is gonna be the summer, Henrie. Best ever. Come on!" I grab her hand and pull her up to her feet. We go down the old stairs, through Ms. Sonia's home and out into the yard.

"I should clean up. People will see."

"Let them see!"

"I should tell my mom."

"We will. Soon enough. Come on! Run!"

"Slow down! I feel sick. B.B.!"

I do not slow down. I keep tight hold of her hand and slowly she matches my speed, running faster, running wild and screaming away from the graveyard and the little no-more church, back down Division Street and through our yard to the quarry. We scramble down rock into the quarry, then break through tall weeds to get to the edge of the quarry pond. We take off our clothes and jump into the water. It's shockingly cold. The summer has yet to warm it. We dive down deep and hold our breath as long as we can, mermaid hair swimming around our heads, rusty red rising from between Henrie's legs.

We come up for a breath of air, then I take her back under, signal for her to follow me. Down near the quarry bottom is a shelf in the wall. A hole from which I extract a corked bottle.

"What is it?" she asks once we surface.

"It's where we'll keep our story. The summer we were both women. We'll write it and hide it down there, and in a hundred years someone will find it and know what we did. Who we were."

"Who are we?"

I smile and press my forehead to hers. "We are the Volt sisters. Think lightning bolts. Think electricity."

I look to the sky. She matches my head tilt, and we listen to the island. Birds sing, somewhere a branch cracks, and beneath it all we can hear the land groaning, rocks grinding against one another.

❖ 3 ❖

carrie

2000

Old Route 68 curves north through small-town Ohio without any irony—signs boast dwindling popula-tions and tattered lamppost banners hang over the heads of dead-eyed storefronts. Henrie is driving, so I have time to stare out the window, my heart aching for each of these places. A structure is a living thing with a history and personality worth saving and, unlike a hu-man being, can be stripped back to the studs, all the bad decisions peeled away to its point of origin, before being rebuilt.

We'll hit I-75N, which will dump us out on Route 6 long before I-75N plunges into Toledo and glides along the left side of Lake Erie. If I'm remembering correctly, we will deviate and drive due east through another run of ghostly small towns, including but not limited to New

Rochester and Fremont. The latter of which is famous for a dam built on the Sandusky River. That dam keeps the walleye from migrating, pushing them back up into Lake Erie, where they'll die come winter, washing up on Fowler shores just when the island is starting to green its way toward summer. The confused smell of decay and new growth became so mingled in my brain that I still can't tell what to feel when a mouse dies in the walls of a house I'm renovating—my body reacts with disgust and a sense of promise.

I look at Henrie, in the driver's seat. She is twenty-four and her long hair is wild over her shoulders. The set of her chin is so determined that I want to touch her, so she knows I'm here, but her body is so stiff and of one piece that I don't know where to rest my hand. We've both changed since we left the island. Her memories of Fowler are selective, and I've been mostly glad for that. I remind myself that I had no choice but to get her out of there, just like I have no choice but to take her back. It's what James and I agreed on long ago.

In my defense, B.B. had gone through puberty smoothly, or at least without island interference, and she had Sonia watching over her, training her to take over someday as Island Curator. She was moody, sure. Proud of her new body and arrogant as hell, but there was nothing more to it. No animal ferocity. No disappearances. No spaces of time lost. I'd been warned to keep a close eye on her as her body shaped itself into a woman. We argued, she hated me a bit more than usual, but all this was to be expected. So, when it came Henrie's time, I was too wrapped up in my own troubles to notice. I'd forgotten to worry about anyone other than myself. If the eldest Volt hadn't had any difficulty, the youngest would certainly be fine, right? Wrong.

Sonia assured me over the years that B.B. was and would be fine. That what we saw happen to Henrie would not happen to her. That promise, that B.B.'s fate was secure, is what kept me from going back for her. James didn't know why, and he didn't care. B.B. was fine and Henrie was free. He assured me that he was taking care of it, and all I had to do was keep Henrie away. I did try to check in with B.B. I tried to reach out, but she never reached back, and I gave up too quickly and with too much relief.

Yesterday, I found B.B.'s phone number in Henrie's cell when she fell asleep on my couch—a new number no one had bothered to give me. All these years I've told myself that B.B. was fine. That she was strong. That Sonia or maybe even her father would tell me if I needed to come get her. Henrie was the one that needed to be saved, but if I'm honest with myself, a painful thing to be, I know I sacrificed one daughter for the other.

I called B.B. after I found her new number. Over and over. The phone going to voice mail so quickly that it was surely turned off. I tried the house phone too, but it was busy. Left unplugged, I guessed, in the tradition of her father. What would I have said if she'd picked up? I love you? I'm sorry? Will it all start up all over again?

B.B. never picked up, although the endless ringing felt like her answer: *I am already long gone.* I bring my attention back to the car, only I can't think of what to say to Henrie. My brain fumbles around and I remember an on-island night with her and B.B. up in Sonia's loft. The old VCR making its ticking noise as we all cuddled together. We were happy.

"Do you remember that old movie?" I ask Henrie. "The one with the pink dragon named Falcon?"

"Falcore," she says. "It's called *The NeverEnding Story.*"

"You loved that movie when you were a little girl. You must have watched it twenty times."

"Thirty-three." A little smile catches at the corner of her mouth. "At Ms. Sonia's."

Sonia. The name spoken out loud by my daughter makes me blush, guilt blooming in my chest.

"Dad never watched movies with us, did he?"

"He hated television." Which is true. Quarry Hollow did not have a TV. James thought TV a waste of time. Why would anyone watch television when one could be reading? Or writing?

"Why didn't he ever come to Ms. Sonia's?" I think maybe Henrie is digging for information. Maybe she remembers more than she lets on, but there is no sign of that in her face or voice.

"I'm not sure," I say, hoping that'll be the end of it.

James had a strong distrust of Sonia that predated me. "She thinks she knows everything," he'd say whenever her name came up. "She treats Beatrice like some kind of artifact that's she's dusted off for study," he'd add whenever I'd remind him that Sonia had stepped in after Olivia Rose disappeared to help with B.B. James didn't like how much Sonia knew about the failings of his family or that she believed the girls when they said they talked to ghosts. And he hated how she held the history of his family inside the walls of the museum like something that needed to be guarded.

James didn't like most people, but he loved his daughters. He was so young when I met him—a good twenty years older than me but still young for his age. I look back now and see how lost he must have been. How much he did not yet know. The death of his first wife made him skinny and neglectful, his beard too full—although he assured me there is no such thing as a too full beard—and the lines on his forehead were beginning to deepen. He had ink on his fingers, which I'd later learn came from changing out and reinking typewriter ribbons, and a photo in his wallet of his baby girl. I mistook his grief for wisdom, I suppose. He was smart and funny. So unafraid to talk about his feelings, to write poems that made you feel ripped open. I was still living with my parents when, in that first month of knowing him, we stayed up all night. We talked and fucked and fell in some sort of love.

"Why didn't he like her? Ms. Sonia?" Henrie asks, not looking at me. "I never understood that."

"He liked her fine." I say it too quickly. He didn't. I know that. Or me either, in the end. For reasons that lay largely on my shoulders.

"Mom," Henrie says flatly. "I hate it when you do that. Just because it seems like the polite or easy thing to say doesn't make it any less of a lie."

That's the thing about having a daughter. They can make you feel small with no effort at all. B.B. was a whiz at it. She was the first to realize what was going on between Sonia and me. The look B.B. gave me that morning she found me in Sonia's bed. I can still conjure it, feel its deep chill turn my insides to ice.

"It was complicated, Henrie. Adult relationships almost always are."

It's a true answer if not a full one. I loved Sonia. Not as much as she loved me, but I did love her. She was the first person who told me I could leave. We were sitting together on the steps of her building. It was warm enough to be outside and the sun was high, making her short dark hair gleam like crow feathers. I hadn't slept in days. While I was glad the winter was over—the dark cold of it was almost unbearable—summer was always worse. The whole place came alive, feisty and in bloom, calling me in a thousand directions. If I stayed, I would have bashed myself against quarry rock to make it all stop. She saw that and said, "Why don't you leave? Take Henrie and B.B. and go?"

"I can't."

All she said next was "Why not?"

I couldn't come up with an answer. Not one.

"What was that dark cloud that ate everything up in that movie called?" I ask Henrie now.

"The Nothing. Why?"

I don't answer. Because it's still there, waiting for me. I can feel us wading into it the closer we get to Fowler. Not a cloud exactly, but something just as gray, inscrutable.

I reach across to my daughter and tuck her hair behind her ear. "You're beautiful, you know that?"

"Mom." Her little blush lets me know she likes it even if she doesn't want to. Henrie holds the steering wheel with both hands, and although we don't have the radio on, her thumbs jump and dance, tapping on the steering wheel in a nervous rhythm. It's not a habit of hers I've noticed before, and I want to put my hands over hers, tell her everything is going to be all right.

I look out the passenger-side window again. It's April in Ohio, and the air outside is just starting to find warmth, the sun shining more often than not. Small green buds dot tree branches, and verdant leaves push up through mulch. I loved it when I first got here, so charmed by the old Victorians and ornate post offices.

"Look at that one!" I point out my window. The

three-story Victorian has a cupola and a porch that wraps the front, curving out of view. "Do you see that porch? It's sweeping."

Henrie glances over. "It looks like Quarry Hollow."

"No, it doesn't." I speak too quickly again, giving away my anxiety, as well as the truth of her observation. I see that the house does. The sheer size of it. The clapboard siding.

The porch looks so deep, disappearing around the sides, it might as well be a moat. The giant tower of a third eye looking out over everything. It's the same as the house on Fowler. I turn away.

We cross the border of the last small town we'll see on 68, its gas station disappearing behind us, the town crumbled away at the edges.

"We'll hit Seventy-Five soon," I say, as if this information holds some value. My own mother used to read the road signs aloud on summer trips to the Finger Lakes, a habit that made me so angry as a teenager that I could barely breathe.

"Where are we staying when we get to the island?" Henrie asks. We'd both agreed that we did not want to stay at Quarry Hollow. That decision, thank goodness, had been easy.

"I got us the last room at the Island Inn. I read online that the new owner gutted it when they bought it. Bud owned like a dozen cats, and he wouldn't let any of them out. Said they'd drown. Remember that? As if cats could fill their pockets with stones and wander into a body of water." I'm babbling now, nervous at what's about to happen.

Henrie taps louder on the wheel. "I'm not sure he was worried about quite that scenario, but he did love his cats. He used to squirt B.B. and me with vinegar if we cut across his land," she says. "B.B. liked to get as close as she could without actually getting hit. It was probably a sign of his affection." It's a good memory for Henrie. I can tell by how she smiles again, slight but there all the same.

"I'm sorry I didn't do a better job getting your father to visit us after the divorce." It's true. But it's also a lie.

She signals to merge onto the highway, and the click of it takes me back to the day we left. How we sat waiting for the ferry, the dark night pushing in on the car, the rain falling in fat drops, and the sound of that turn signal clicking away like someone peeling their tongue off the roof of their mouth over and over.

"Why didn't you ever try to go back?" I know why I stayed away, but Henrie loved her father, her sister. She did not seem scared of the island or aware of what change it brought about in her.

"You used to pluck at yourself when we talked about it." Her voice rises at the end of the sentence—she has rediscovered a moment that she shelved away, and I watch the revelation of it in the profile of her face. "Once you twisted a long strand of hair around your fingers so tightly that this chunk of hair came out of your head. Right out of your scalp. Do you remember that?"

I feel myself go pale—I do not remember this—and she looks back at the road, her thumbs suddenly beating out a much-faster rhythm.

"Dad came to see us, and we all talked on the phone and wrote letters. It was fine, Mom, really."

Suddenly, just like that, I realize I've made her protect me. I was so young when she was born. James was my first love. I didn't know what I was doing, and I raised Henrie to be my friend more than to be my daughter. I regret that now.

"Do you remember the day we left?"

"Of course," she says.

I run my hand over the faded navy of the dashboard. "I called her Betsy back then. Remember that?"

"I still call her Betsy."

"You, me, this car. We fled the island and now we are purposefully going back."

Henrie lets the car fill up with silence and I count *one, two, three, four* in my head until I reach *thirty-two*.

Finally she says, "*Fled* seems a little dramatic, Mom."

"What do you remember?" I'm worried about what she'll say. I remember the rain. And that both of us were soaking wet. Henrie belted in next to me, held still against the seat with duct tape. It was duct tape and not rope. Her head tilted to the window, drool coming out of her mouth. I don't want the memory or the creeping horror that comes with it.

"Help me look for signs for Route Six. That's what we need next, right?" she asks, knowing full well that Route 6 is the last black stretch of asphalt we need to make it to the ferry.

"Do you remember, Henrietta?" I ask again.

"Mom. I don't want to talk about it. Isn't Dad's death enough, right now?"

She's right. I stare out my window. "Your dad always said the island was sad. He said it needed us to keep it warm."

"That's not what he said," she spits out, as if she's been waiting the whole ride to correct me on this point. "He said we kept its belly full in the winter."

The corrected memory hits me hard and I press back into my seat, a hand to my belly.

"As a metaphor, it's all too digestive," I finally say, trying to make a joke, but hearing this truth aloud makes me uncomfortable.

"I always thought he meant we were the things that kept it afloat," Henrie says, flicking on the turn signal again. "In the winter when it was all barren and brittle, we filled it up like air in a balloon, and in the summer when everything was green and full, it didn't need us to keep it afloat."

No, I think. *It needed us to feed it.*

James had always talked this way too: about the island as a cork, bobbing about in Lake Erie. We anchored it when it needed us. Like it was a request. Like I should be grateful to a place for holding on to me when really it was an act of violence. A prison I was supposed to say "please" and "thank you" to for providing me with food and water. I hated James for that idea, for making me feel like my unhappiness was crazy.

I haven't thought of this in a long time.

"One time I was in the tire swing and Dad kind of lay down on the ground, put his legs through the hole so they rested on my belly, and he could rock me side to side. 'Your mom is drowning here,' he said."

I'm silent for a moment. "What did you say?"

"I don't know. It felt like I knew what he meant at the time."

My eyes have filled with tears. Sudden and blinding. The world out the car window blurs, but I can still make out the bright blue of the sign that arches over the road announcing Marblehead.

The ferry is nearly full when we reach it. Several other islands are nearby, but their ferries leave from a dock closer to Toledo. Those are the more popular islands, they thrive almost all year-round, with a variety of choices. Fowler is small, a one-trick pony with little to do besides fish and eat poorly made ice cream. I'm told that the water that surrounds Fowler is somehow colder and choppier than the water that surrounds the other islands, as if Erie itself is altered by the desolate rock that is my daughter's birthplace. Growing up on Manhattan, I thought the idea of owning a whole island, even if it was off the coast of Ohio, was incredible. Impossibly romantic. A sign of true riches. I learned quickly it was quite the opposite.

We are packed between a pickup truck full of people dressed as ghouls and an old school bus painted with pot leaves. Just as many people walk onto the ferry as drive on. The walkers have already begun drinking and are in various stages of costume. Some of them carry backpacks with boas peeking out or wear belts with plastic swords. Sweatpants and glitter. Shorts and high heels, black cloaks not yet zipped, and fairy wings hooked to parkas that will be lost overboard crossing the lake.

The island is just beginning to crawl hungrily out of the winter dark, and now there are costumes and liquor to wake up the horror of it all. We stay in the car. "Windows up," I say, then I take Henrie's hand and she lets me.

I close my eyes to wait. I dream James is still alive, sitting at his typewriter in his second-floor study. On the piece of paper I can see *My Dear Carrie* and then words that are unreadable. I stretch to see what he has to say, but the words make no sense, and I am floating, peering in the window, buoyed by water that feels icy and gelatinous.

He's pounding away at the old Royal typewriter so fast and so hard that his fingers attach themselves to the keys. His flesh stretches like Silly Putty, pulling his fingertips into a viscous liquid, which he does not seem to notice. I turn away in disgust, but when I look back again, I see Henrie and B.B. inside the room too. Posing with their heads thrown back, waiting for me to take their picture with their father.

In the dream, I lift my hands as if there were a camera. I take hundreds of pretend photos before I look through the non-lens to the wall behind the girls. The old horsehair plaster bristles like the hair on the back of a dog, an angry shuffling that makes me twist to see what is sneaking up behind me. I see faces pressing through the plaster. One of them is Henrie's. The ridge of her furrowed brow, the growl of her lips, and James rising from the keys, rubber fingers dragging, as he barks back at her, trying to call her out of the wall with a guttural noise from deep in his throat.

I wake abruptly. Henrie's eyes are still closed.

I loosen my grip on her hand, and her eyes open, pupils too wide for the sun rushing in the windshield. I watch them tighten.

"Are we there?" She does not need an answer. It's easy to see that the lake is still all around us. "I need air." She unlocks her door, stepping out before I can try to stop her.

I lean over so I can watch out the driver's-side window as she gains her footing on the deck, then weaves through passengers to the balcony of the viewing deck. I lose sight of her for a second at the base of the stairs, and I hold my breath until she reappears, climbing up to where I know I won't be able to see her.

I can feel it coming. The island. Big and bad and breathy. I reach over to the driver's door to lock it.

❖4❖

sonia

2000

'm on my island run. Slower than I once was, but still strong, and the air is April crisp—not quite cold and not yet humid. My body is grateful for the rhythm, my brain for the singular focus. I run the same route every day, and I pretend the island is my dollhouse, my mind placing people and objects just so—the director of my own live-action thriller. Yesterday, for example, Mr. Cooper was out front of his store as I passed. A middle-aged tourist was driving her golf cart too swiftly toward him, her yellow sunhat flapping dangerously in the breeze, and I imagined the worst—her swerving as she tried to keep her ridiculous hat on her head, just as Mr. Cooper stepped forward to drop his cigarette into the gutter. As he leaned out, the cart swerved, the front colliding with his head, and the smash of his skull against the plastic of the frame was like a bat to a rotten Halloween pumpkin. Huge and wet and splattering.

This didn't happen. They glided past each other grumpy but unharmed. I ran by and tried not to feel disappointed. Ms. Millie, the woman who curated the museum before me and chose me as her successor, never left the museum, so certain was she that we Curators were telepathic puppeteers, capable of directing mischief and mayhem with just our imaginations. Ms. Millie was a bit on the crazy side. She said that only those prone to "a particular kind of narcissism and a tendency to self-aggrandize" could curate this island. She claimed that Eileen Fowler—the first Island Curator—was telepathic. That she and her sister, Elizabeth, could throw thoughts back and forth. Before she died, Eileen had also begun to be able to move objects with her mind. Ms. Millie believed some diluted bit of that ability was passed down to herself and to me. We were chosen as Curators not only because we were solitary people, organized, and thoughtful, but because we had this "little kernel of potential." I've always pictured it the size and shape of a candy corn lodged sweetly in my frontal cortex.

"I saw it in you first thing," Ms. Millie said to my little-kid self. "Your daddy is clueless, but you looked right at me, and I saw the island magic in you."

She was crotchety, old Ms. Millie, a little scary, but I loved her. I loved too that she saw me as special even though I didn't believe a word of it. I wanted the museum and the island. So when she said she saw herself in me, I did not immediately think of her bad qualities, nor did I bother to look up *narcissism*. I wanted the island to be mine, the pieces of it to make up a chessboard where I could quietly move the pieces.

Today I know half of what Ms. Millie said was nonsense, so I focus on my run. I need my wits about me since it is the start of Masquerade. From the museum, I head north on Division Street until I hit the glacial grooves and the surrounding state park. Then the island begins its curve east through the campsites and the three yurts the state installed to allow camping season to stretch further into the fall. The paved road—State Route 13—leads to the wealthier houses that sit out on the northeast peninsula, but I avoid these neighborhoods, having worn my own dirt path that skirts the coast before it turns south. I curve south, curling back into the island before the fence for the abandoned fun park is on my right and the land drops off sharply to my left, the lake splashing against the cliffs. The quarry comes next, although the foliage keeps it from view since I stick to the coast, and then there's the long quiet stretch of beach before the ferry dock.

Today is also James's funeral—the suddenness of his death has triggered an island change that I'm struggling to understand—and I can't say I'm sad he's gone. He and I hadn't spoken in depth in a decade, not since I found him waiting for me on the small dock that July in 1989. I was returning the fishing boat Carrie and I "borrowed" to take us off island, and I could see James standing there like a busted lighthouse from a mile out.

"You had no right," he said, waiting until I secured the boat to the dock. His hair disheveled, his eyes shot through with red. James is a handsome man, or at least he was. Tall with a broad chest, thick hair, a kind of Superman cleft to his chin hidden under an unkempt beard. He had a strong, certain voice perfect for reading his poetry aloud but obnoxious in conversation, where the patient quality of his intonation was just plain condescending. He also had, for many years, a fortitude I admired, swearing he would not reproduce, telling the Island Council the Volt line would end with him. He made it into his forties before he fell in love with Olivia Rose, a woman I never trusted, but maybe that was just because she so clearly didn't trust me. Then there was Carrie.

I wait until my feet are on the dock to say, "Where are the girls?"

"Home," he says, but I can tell he doesn't know that. "Why didn't Carrie come back with you?"

"James," I say, exhausted. His name heavy in my mouth. I haven't slept since we left the island, not really.

"Why would she do this?" He pulls at his hair with his hands. "You could have talked her out of it."

"She'd already made up her mind." I used to feel sorry for James. His circumstances seemed so beyond his

control—he didn't have the choice to step into his role
like I did—but I see it differently now. He has choices—he
always has. "Besides, you're their father. It's your job to
protect them, above all else."

"That seems a bit sexist, doesn't it? What about Carrie? What's her job?"

"Carrie doesn't have the whole story and you know
it," I snap. Once, after Olivia Rose died, James confessed
to me that he'd told her "everything." I could only imagine what he had said, since he and every Volt before him
refused to tell anyone anything. Anyhow, it was clear, at
the time, that he thought the knowledge he'd handed
her had somehow led to her death, like he was the serpent and Olivia Rose was Eve. I found it preposterous
and egomaniacal, just as I do now.

I don't need confrontation. I need sleep. I picture my
bed. The soft white sheets. The bookish smell of the loft.
I want him to go away so badly I can taste it. He takes a
step back away from me.

"*You* haven't told Carrie the whole story!" he shouts
at me, and all his fatigue goes away. His eyes clear, his
shoulders grow square, his fists clench. Fear rises in my
throat.

"I'm not allowed," I say. I know it's a weak response.

"Exactly which rules are you paying attention to, Sonia?" I know what he's implying. I'm a home-wrecker. A
borrower. A thief. A peripheral parasite. "You're the Curator. You. Your only job is to make sure island secrets

are kept on island. That, and find your successor. But you overstep every damn time."

He's right in most ways, but people have long mistaken external passivity for weakness, when really what I do is quite active. "The three Cs," Millie called them. Collect. Conduct. Conceal. The Volts—according to Millie—have long disregarded the Island Curator, but what sits between James and I is uglier than ever before.

Back when I was a kid being groomed for the job, Ms. Millie conveyed the number one rule to me straightaway and with frequency: *Never get involved.* She didn't. She stayed inside and out of trouble. Island Counsel meetings came to her, so she never had to leave the museum. I ran her errands for her—even made sure the quarry cliffs were clean of debris. But I didn't heed her advice. I got involved as soon as I was invited in. The door was open. That much I know for sure. Left wide open, and I could hear baby B.B. inside crying, wailing. I could hear James banging away at his typewriter to drown her out. The beloved Olivia Rose was newly dead, and baby B.B. was alone and terrified. Her father was distracted by a volatile and angry grief that he was trying to get under control. B.B. was screaming. I *had* to walk in. When nothing happened, when there was no zap at the entrance, no crumbling of the island, I went back again and again and again. I placed myself in the scene and moved us all about, little island puppets, imagining the best outcome rather than the worst. I dubbed B.B. my successor, getting James to agree to it at a time when he might have agreed to just about anything.

"There are consequences for changing the story," James said angrily.

"You promised us, all of us, it would end with you." I gesture at the island. One great betrayed thing.

"You don't understand the ecosystem of the island, Sonia. I didn't understand back then either. I thought I did, but I didn't. Olivia Rose thought if we had a girl, well, that we could change the course of things, but . . ."

"Ha!" I say, loud enough to interrupt him. "I call bull-shit, James. You can't plan the gender of a baby. You didn't know girl or boy until the day Beatrice was born. Maybe you and Olivia Rose decided to rewrite what you did, justify it after the fact, but I know that's nonsense. The two of you were selfish."

"You didn't know Olivia Rose like I did," he says. "No one did. None of that matters now. We know now that the girls are still vulnerable. So, this time, we would have a boy. And now the chance of that boy setting the whole thing back on track is gone. You made sure of that. And, it seems to me, that it's *you*, always directing the story. You claim you sit back, collect, do no harm, but you stepped in to try to write our story from the start. Why can't you make your own life and leave ours alone?"

It isn't as if this thought hasn't occurred to me before. The guilt of it keeps me up at night. Washes over me as Carrie sleeps, unaware, in my bed. My own happiness is a sign of something rotting, but hearing it from James does not make me feel worse. A little seed of something powerful is growing in me.

"I do my job for the island and you do yours, James. I have as little choice as you do."

"Now I call *bullshit*." He spits the word into my face. "As soon as you got your hands on B.B., came into my house, things changed. You did something. Changed the course, and now you've done it again, convincing Carrie to run off and do what she's done."

"They love me, James. Your family. Maybe more than they love you." The shock of it, of saying it and meaning it, takes the green seed of jealousy inside me and warms it, waters it, until I feel it grow.

For a second, he looks surprised, then like he's going to launch himself at me, tackle me on the dock.

"I'm as important to this island as you."

"You are not."

"Eileen Fowler was the first Curator, and I am the current. This is my story whether you like it or not, James. I choose my successor."

"You mean *our* story. Not yours and not mine. The eldest is meant to take over for *me*, Sonia, and you know it. You've done something. And what about Henrie? If B.B. is Curator, what else shifts?" He is speaking quickly, fiercely, little flecks of spit coming out at the corners of his mouth. It's less anger than it is pure panic.

"If the baby had been a girl, you'd have full-blooded

sisters. If the baby had been a boy, you would have loved him just as much as your girls and fought for him as hard as you've fought for your daughters. There's no easy out, James. Carrie did the right thing."

The anger that was rising up in him, making his body expand, is gone. He shrinks instead, and I see the old man in him again. The gray in his beard. The bruised skin around his eyes. He turns away. Moves off the dock and back onto the island.

And now James is dead. It's been more than a decade since that conversation, and I've learned to do what I was too greedy to do then. To live alone, to trudge on without expectations. To stay in my place and need no one and want less. To ignore that "kernel" in my mind that wants to move and direct and control. To be the observer Ms. Millie taught me to be. I keep my machinations hidden even from myself.

And so, I run. The island, like time, curves away from that long-ago conversation. A breeze rolls in off the water and balances the bright heat of the sun. I'm usually out for my run much earlier in the day, but Masquerade means every islander pitches in, cleaning up Main Street: hosing down vomit and piss from the night before, re-stocking shelves, helping the drunk and disheveled back to their own beds.

The weather is always kind on Masquerade weekend, as if it knows we islanders need the income. We came up with the idea for Masquerade after the island moved from undiscovered gem to a place known for disappearances—women last seen stepping off the ferry. There was one young woman who jumped, just sixteen, whose mother showed up after the fact. She was a wreck. Gorgeous though. The kind of woman people notice and listen to. She made quite a fuss before she overdosed in the Island Inn. Apparently she was an addict. Her death brought the press running. After that the tourists fell away, leaving only voyeurs who wanted to see the haunted quarry.

"What's your mile time?" Old Mr. Albertson startles me even though this holler is a part of our routine. He's putting folding chairs at the edge of his property to keep tourists from parking on the grass.

"Too slow!" I run faster.

Get on with yourself, his wave says.

The breeze shifts, hits my face, and I smell fried dough. Big greasy cakes of it with powdered sugar dumped on top. The ferry whistle blows, a boat approaching the dock. My feet quicken. I'm more than halfway through my ten-mile run. The ferry dock is at the southernmost tip of the island, then the downtown springs up along the coast with its shops that spread out into the midland. A hundred little side streets with vacation homes, some luxurious but most modest, spring out from town, but I ignore those routes most days and run north past the VFW and Quarry Road until I'm back home at the museum.

Today I hear the bang of metal to rubber as the ferry

boat settles into the dock. The second tier of the boat is packed. Playful shrieking comes next.

The ferry has been running strong since yesterday morning, dumping ungodly amounts of people onto our small island. It reminds me that we need to station someone in the quarry tonight. It will probably have to be me. I run faster.

Cars begin to drive off the ferry and my stomach tightens.

Carrie will probably be coming to the island with Henrie. I am prettier than I used to be. More confident, leaner. My skin pale with the island winter but also smooth and clear. I was still very much a kid when Carrie knew me. Old enough to rent a car but not old enough to know better than to fall in love with someone else's wife.

Things I remember about her: blue eyes, sad stare. She loved oranges, her fingers were always sticky with them—the skin of the fruit caught under her nails. In her final island years, she spent more time with me at the museum than at home. How will it feel to see her again? I head up Division to my museum home, using every piece of my body to push myself forward. I stayed with her off island for three days and four nights. She didn't want to be touched, but I stayed close. Curled on the bed next to her or resting on the sofa across the room.

When I reach my lawn, I drop onto the grass. I often

allow myself this indulgence at the end of my run. On my back, I close my eyes to the sun and try to find my breath. I imagine her shoulders, the soft white skin, the round bump of a scar where she'd fallen from a tree house as a kid, a nail sliding in to nick her clavicle.

"Hey." A figure stands over me, looking down. I'm startled, my skin fizzing against my tired muscles, and I sit up too quickly. The world blurs for a minute, but her voice pushes on. "I don't want you there today."

Beatrice. I work my way to kneeling. The individual blades of grass pressure their pattern into my kneecaps. Beatrice is tall as a tree from this angle. More beautiful than Olivia Rose ever was. When B.B. was just one year old and newly motherless, I moved into Quarry Hollow to take care of her. It was only for two years—the years before James met Carrie—but it was the best of my life. She was already walking, already talking. Her blond hair was curly then in a way that wouldn't last but bounced around her face and wisped in front of her eyes. She loved stuffed animals, her favorite thing was putting them to bed, singing them a little song, then covering them up with a dish towel or Kleenex. I'd find these little lovelies all over the house, resting peacefully wherever she'd tucked them in.

"Are they here? Henrie and Carrie?"

B.B. shakes her head no. "I told Henrie not to bring *her*."

I wrinkle my brow, a question.

"Carrie didn't love James. Not anymore. What could she possibly want from the funeral?"

"To see you," I say, no question in my voice.

"Fuck that."

Little B.B. was a caregiver. She adored her stuffed animals, her father, and her sister. There was even a time when she adored me. She had this fierceness, and it felt good to be included in that bubble with her, like she was your shield. The woman in front of me is using that same strength to keep us all away. I want so badly to hug her, to make her remember that there was a time when I got to play at being her mother and when she wanted to be with me, like me.

"If you don't want me at the funeral, I won't go."

"Thank you," she says, but I hear doubt in her voice. I've agreed too quickly.

"How are you?" I ask her as I get to my feet. It's hard to reconcile how much she hates me with the little girl I once knew.

"How do you think I am?" The anger is back, perhaps never gone.

"You're going back to Boston after this?" My voice rises too high at the end.

"They said I can finish up here. I don't have to be on campus."

"You're still writing?" B.B. had long wanted to be like

her father, but she's more like me. Her writerly voice is strong and consistent. She conveys story competently, but it isn't poetry. She sets the stage, moves the pieces, but the voice is not unique. There is no flare. She is a perfect Curator.

"Of course, I'm still writing. It's a fucking MFA."

Even when she was tiny, tucking in her stuffies, B.B. would sit outside James's office door and pretend to type when he typed. Her little fingers punching at the floor, a secret smile on her face that meant she was onto something good. "You used to let me read your stories. Do you remember?"

"I was a teenager. Of course I remember."

"I'd love to help again. I could read your thesis for you. We could even clear the museum. You could have a reading." I dust off my knees, as if the impressions there are grass clippings.

"Don't be desperate," she says. Her disgust so well played that I shrink a little. "I do have a question for you, though."

"Okay." Something in her announcement makes it clear she's been working up her nerve to ask me.

"My mother. Does she have to stay here?"

I laugh loudly. It is the wrong thing to do so I say, "Your mother is dead." Another wrong thing.

"No shit," she says, like I'm the dumbest person she's ever met.

"Wait," I say. My brain is slow but a new worry blooms in me. "Can you hear her? And the others? Are they talking to you now?"

"Forget it." She starts to walk away so she won't have to answer my question.

I grab her arm, and in that moment of touch, I feel a decade of space burn between us. She rips herself away.

"Hold on. What are you asking and why are you asking it?"

"Mom is in the house, like the others. We used to talk to her all the time. Well, Henrie was the one who could hear her, but I know she was . . . is there."

We've never discussed this. I've told them the stories, the legends. But James never wanted them to know what really happened to Olivia Rose. Their whole childhood was spent visiting an empty grave, and then, when he did tell them, he did a shoddy job. A story half-told. Details never expressed or explained.

"You shouldn't trust her," I say, and immediately regret it. Olivia Rose was loved by everyone. Tall and calm. She took to the island immediately. Knew everyone. But there was something I never liked about her. Once I hinted at this to Carrie, but Carrie only laughed at me, saying, "You sound as jealous of her as I am." And that is likely all it is. Jealousy. "I shouldn't have said that. I'm sorry. But, B.B., has something changed for you?"

"Fuck you," she says, turning to leave.

A little desperate part of me panics. "Yes!"

"Yes what?" She's stopped moving away from me.

"I believe the ghosts are there. And if Henrie said so, then Olivia is surely one of them."

"That's not what I asked."

"You want to know if she has to stay in that house? I don't know. Honestly, I have no idea."

"But what's your guess? You know this island as well as anyone. Tell me what you think."

"I think you are capable of just about anything, Beatrice. Like me, if you want something, you can make it happen."

"When have you ever made anything happen?" B.B. asks me.

It's cruel, but maybe she's right. Long ago I saw myself as defiant. I was taking the gifts passed on to me by Ms. Millie and using them to define the world around me. But how long ago was that? What am I now?

"I'm going to ignore that bit of meanness, but I do believe you can do whatever you set your mind to."

"Really?"

My compliment means something to her even if she won't apologize for being cruel, and I let myself feel that for a moment. The warmth of it floods me with a brief but all-consuming joy.

"Your mother may have left you. But I never did." It is more than I meant to say, and I see I've lost her again.

"My mother never left me, the island took her, and so I won't leave her." It's more a statement than a question. B.B.'s back straightens, resolved.

"You could always just give the house a shove, push it right over the edge into the quarry. It's headed that way anyway!" I force a laugh and it sounds so insecure—she *should* hate me.

She stops, spins on her heels, and marches back up to me. Her face to mine. "You think I haven't tried destroying it? Burning it down, for example? Do you realize it's been a decade since Carrie and Henrie left?"

"Yes."

"Do you remember that night?"

"What night?" My voice sounds feeble. Of course I remember.

"You were there. I'm sure of that now. We were in the quarry. You, me, Henrie, Carrie. Henrie was drowning. *I* had to pull *her* out of the water. Or I tried to. Or something. I can't remember the details, not exactly. It's a big gray, rainy fog. But they left. Without me. Dad stayed, physically, anyway. But he would never talk about that night. No one would. They all left me so they wouldn't have to."

"That's not true, B.B. I tried. You wouldn't talk to me."

"But you were the adult. I was the kid. I needed *you* to try harder." She spits the last sentence, and the anger is wet and hot on my cheeks, hitting in a dozen small places.

The job of Curator is passed down from woman to

woman—Ms. Millie trained me, and before that there was Alice and before that Nora, all the way back to Eileen. We are meant to be trackers of island history, dispassionate observers. All except for me. I broke that barrier, rewrote it, pushed on it to test its give. I broke it for the first time when I fell in love with little B.B. I let myself believe I was her mother. I started breaking rules a long time ago. I took a break for a while there. Stayed in my lane. Maybe it's time to bring the old me back out. Maybe it's time to stop censoring myself.

"Beatrice Bethany Volt. You listen to me," I say and grab her right wrist, tight enough to make her jump and pin her in place. "I love you. I always have and I always will. It's unconditional, so it doesn't matter if you hate me. I'm done sitting back and watching you flail. There are things you need to know. Your father's dead. He had his chance to teach you and he didn't do it. It's my job now to give you what I know, and if you don't let me help you, you'll all be in danger."

"You're full of shit," she says. "Let go of me." It's a hiss that leaks out from between her teeth, but I don't let go. I study her face.

"I'm serious, Beatrice." We are in uncharted territory. James is dead. B.B. is the first female heir, and Henrie is on her way back.

"Okay," she says softly, and I see now that her eyes are filling with tears. I let go of her wrist. "Later. We'll talk later. Right now, I have to go."

"I want to teach you everything I know. I've been saving it for you." My power is fading. "I love you, Beatrice. Like my own."

"I heard you." Her voice is soft this time. Absent of anger and accusation, and I tell myself it's a victory. She turns away from me, heading in the direction of Quarry Hollow.

✦5✦

henrietta

2000

I dream of the quarry pond. The deep blue of its center and the way it eased out green to itch at the limestone shores. Those rocks were slick. Our small, pink feet could never find their grip. We'd crawl into the pond if we had to, like dogs with our chins lapping at the water and our bare asses stuck up toward the sun. Beatrice and I with our elbows at too sharp angles, sliding into the water with only our shoulder blades peaking, finning like sharks. My mother at the top of the tallest cliff. The one with the sharpest rocks lurking below. She is weeping up there and we are circling. She is clothed, wrapped up for winter with her big work boots, and I know, if she falls or jumps or is pushed, she will drown, and we will eat her up. I keep swimming, licking at the pond water with a hungry tongue. B.B.'s body slides next to me. I can feel the scales of her lower half, gray and rotting.

My mother's scream starts before her feet leave the cliff. Long and piercing and taking on the pulse of an ambulance siren. The splash of her body wakes me.

"You okay?" she asks, but I'm still half in the dream and can't answer.

"I need air." I push hard at the car door; the wind is fierce coming off the lake. It takes effort to open then slams itself shut behind me.

I can smell the island. The wind whips across the limestone and carries the scent of woodsmoke from fireplaces, of the soft green moss that grows at the edge of the quarry pond, of the rot of the unfortunate fish that wash up on seldom-visited beaches, particularly this month, when the island is still undecided about whether it wants to boast winter or spring. My heart races at the scent.

The image of her body way up high on that cliff, weeping like she had no choice but to stand there, makes me feel like she is wise to be afraid, and I wonder, *Am I afraid?*

The stairs to the upper deck are crowded, but it feels suddenly urgent for me to get to the highest point I can. The smell of the island is moving toward me rather than me toward it, and this little loss of control makes it hard for me to breathe.

I push through people using my elbows, my hips. Someone says ouch and I do not apologize. Finally, at the top, I hold tight to the railing and find fresh air. I am shaking. *My father is dead*, I think. *Dead. I barely knew him.* I'd thought maybe I'd go back to stay with him for the summer. My lease is up June 1. I had not asked him or told my mother; I knew what she'd say, and just how she'd say it. "Do you think that's wise?" she'd ask, straightening her spine. "Have you asked your father if he wants the company?" And finally: "Having an alternate plan would be best."

Below me, Lake Erie gushes and splashes against the boat with such force that drops hit my neck, my chin; one lands cold as ice on my forehead. I breathe in deep, lean out, let the water reach as many places on my skin as it wants. The smells of home are brighter, fresh and full and rushing at my face, as if those scents too had the shape and weight of water. The feeling growing in my stomach is not fear. It's anticipation. And joy.

"You aren't dressed up." It's a man's voice, and I know he must be the body pressed up against my right shoulder because of the clear, crisp sound of him in my ear. He smells like that too, bright and fresh and warm, a blanket I'd wrap myself in. "Unless you think 'sad girl on boat' is a costume." He laughs. It's a genuine laugh, sudden and charming, as if he's truly taken by his own cleverness.

I turn my head to get a look at him.

He's got an arrow through his heart, fake blood dripping from the shaft. "I've never been here for Masquerade," he says. "I'm not here for it this year either. Just my luck that it coincides."

"You wear that arrow always?" I look him in the eyes. Wind hits my left cheek, hiding, I hope, the flush that comes over me as I see him. He looks familiar. Blond hair, short but long enough to whip and curl. Brown eyes that look gold in the sun. One of his front teeth slightly shorter than the other, and a pockmark of a scar on his upper lip. My body recognizes him first, heating up my middle, my palms beginning to sweat. Joshua Kevin Wilson. I remember the smell of him, like citrus mixed with soil. The soft pink burn on his nose from the island sun. The way he'd trip a little when he walked, as if too caught up in his own thoughts to lift both of his feet properly off the ground.

Shit, I think.

I turn my face back into the full force of the wind, hoping that it will hide my shallow breathing. It does and I calm myself. He is just someone I once knew.

He is talking, and I've missed something but maybe not much. "Some woman gave me this. She said I was underdressed. I think she was drunk. Invited me to 'check out the potty' with her. And now that I'm saying it out loud, I wonder if she is from back East and was trying to say *party.* I assumed she wanted to make out with me in the ferry toilet. Either way, do you think she was flirting?"

"*Potty* is the word I use when I'm feeling sexy," I say, and am surprised by my own effort to be funny and even prouder when he laughs.

"She gave me a blood capsule too. And I can't seem to get the taste out of my mouth. It's nasty." He puts his hands on the railing and leans out, spitting into the water. The spit is frothy and pink; the fake blood disappears as it hits the ferry-churned lake, and I imagine my dream Beatrice and Henrietta rushing up from lake bottom to swallow that slush of red.

"They didn't have this Masquerade when I was a kid," I offer. "Halloween was always big. There was that weird parade."

"I remember that!" He looks at me now. Really looks. "Hey, you're B.B.'s sister."

In the darkroom, negatives are powerful, they create the space for the real image to emerge, but I don't want to be B.B.'s negative, a raw space only there for some other image to shine through. I will not be that again. Not for my sister. Not for the island. Not for anyone.

I decide right then not to let him know that I recognized him first. Or at all.

"Yes, that is one of the things that I am."

"I'm sorry about your father," he says. Of course, he knows.

"It's fine," I say. "The funeral is this weekend. It's gonna be a shit show."

"It's why I'm here, actually. Your father was a mentor to me."

"I don't remember that."

"Do you remember me?"

"Not really." The lie is so dumb anyone could detect it.

The first time I saw Joshua he was sitting under a tree, carving something in the bark—maybe his initials. Didn't he know that tree was alive and could feel the hurt he was digging into it? I got so mad. I ran straight up behind him and hit his shoulder blade as hard as I could with a rock I picked up off the ground.

"You and your sister were always together. Do you still take photos?"

The irritation I feel for him calling me Beatrice's sister fades a little with this question. "I do."

"You and that camera were inseparable."

"I suppose that's true." Someone jostles me from behind, and Joshua puts his hand on my lower back to steady me. It feels good. Melty. "Are you a writer?"

"I used to write. I liked to tell stories, but it's been a while. Your father read some for me. Marked them up with his red pen. Mostly, I worked in that bookstore that used to be at the back of Island Thrift. You remember? Your dad would order books like every week. He taught me about first editions and what was valuable. I read everything he recommended."

My father loved his books, his pens—green and red and blue but never black—and his typewriter. He'd refused to own a computer and so his poems were typed out one at a time. He said he liked his words to be "easily lost and easily found."

I drag myself out of my bullshit reverie. "What do you do now?"

"Just quit my job actually. My mother was diagnosed with early-onset Alzheimer's this winter."

"I'm sorry. That's awful."

He nodded. "I quit my job so I could be here all summer with them. She's been wandering. My dad can't figure how she's getting out. Anyway, I want to help out and enjoy time with her."

I feel a twinge of jealousy. But would I really have done anything differently if I'd known about my dad? "That's kind of you."

"It sounds noble, doesn't it? For a twenty-six-year-old? Well, to be fair, I hated my job," he says. The clouds thin in the sky and the sun shoots through bright and full of potential. He puts his hand up to block the light and tilts a little more toward me. He has light freckles on his cheekbones. "Marketing and social media for a chain of restaurants. Total bullshit. So, quitting my job, if looked at from another way, is just a way to freeload off my parents. How about you? Will you be here this summer?"

"No, I don't come here anymore," I say too quickly. "What I mean is, I'm just here for the funeral, then I have to go back and finish my degree. I graduate in June."

The ferry whistle blows loudly. Once, then two more times. We are almost there. The sun slips back behind a cloud. We both lean out over the railing and look toward the small brown crop of land. Spring hasn't reached the island yet. The trees reach up, naked, their gnarled fingers scratch the sky, groping for sunlight.

"You should come back for the summer after you graduate. We can drink mimosas and sunbathe."

We both laugh a little at the image. The Fowler Island beaches are mostly shaded, the lake is cold much of the year, and the water is rarely clear. Some islands in Lake Erie boast fancier houses, strips of upscale bars and restaurants, and sandy beaches where loungers take up permanent residency in June, July, and August. Fowler is not one of them.

"I vacation on island in the summer," I say in a mock-haughty voice.

He laughs. The ferry whistle blows again. I know I should head back to the car, but I don't want to leave him.

"Will I see you at the funeral?" He looks immediately embarrassed. "What a stupid thing to say. I'm so sorry."

"It's fine."

"I guess I meant we could maybe get a drink afterward or something."

"I'd like that."

He nods his head yes, as if to mark the making of our plan for a postfuneral date, then looks out at the water before speaking again. "I remember your name too, you know. Henrie. You were just a kid back then. You were so serious. Always paying attention. I always wanted to know what you were thinking. B.B. would say exactly what she was thinking—"

"She still does that."

"Your dad filled me in over the years. He was proud of you." Joshua reaches out his hand as if to touch me again, maybe to turn me toward him, end this meeting with a hug, but it is too awkward, our bodies smooshed between too many other bodies. He rethinks the gesture, puts his hand back on the railing. "I've been visiting on and off. Mostly off, but my parents are here each summer, so I'd check in on your dad."

"And B.B.? Do you check in on her?" It comes out nasty. I am wondering what to say next that might be funny and light, but the ferry hits the dock with a thump and the ride is over. "I should get back to the car," I say. "You don't need a lift, do you?" I am pushing back from the rail before he answers.

I elbow my way down the stairs and through the crowd. The ferry attendants hustle to steady the boat, lowering the metal plate that will allow us to drive off, one car at a time. The noise of that lowering, how it protests its own hinges then bangs against the dock, is a sound I haven't thought of in ages.

I unlock the car and the door opens with ease, happier to let me back in than it was to let me out. Mom is pretending to sleep, her head tilted back, her hands clasped in her lap, her body rigid. I start the car, let it idle, then reach out to put my hand between hers. She lets me, but her body only relaxes enough to make room for my fingertips. Her palms are clammy.

We wait our turn to drive off the ferry in silence, and eventually my mom opens her eyes and sits up straight, picking at her lower lip, then pulling her hair back into a ponytail, her palms smoothing her skull over and over before she finally puts the hair elastic in. Her T-shirt has dark sweat stains under her armpits. I take note of my own body, head, neck, shoulders, stomach. I scan for nervousness or sorrow. I find nothing. No joy or excitement.

We'll attend the funeral at the VFW later today—our father wasn't a veteran but it's the only large hall on the island—but maybe we don't need to stay for the reading of the will. My father didn't own anything. There can't be much to it. I'll see Joshua, give him my number.

It's our turn to ease off the ferry, but as I go to release the emergency brake, my mother grabs my wrist.

"Look at me," she says. She sounds different. The person she is now and has been for quite some time is gone. She looks pale, fragile. "Promise me you will not go near the quarry. Not in the house. Not to the cliffs. None of it."

"I can't promise that," I say. "We'll need to sort out the house." I do not say that I can feel the rock of the quarry under my feet already. The pine needles pinching my skin, the cold water folding me in.

"I don't want you going in there. If there is stuff you want, stuff of your father's, we can have it sent to us. Sort through it back home. I'll pay for it."

"Fine, Mom. I won't go in the house." I honestly don't know if I'm being truthful or just trying to be kind. It's an awfully big ask. I grew up in that house. It was ours. It was mine. Dad's stuff is in there. His books. The water glasses we bought at the dime store with old island-restaurant logos and the bunk beds with our secrets carved in the footboards. The moose head originally hung by Seth Volt above the living room fireplace—a gruesome, moth-riddled thing by the time it got to us, but B.B. used to shove M&M's and little notes up its nose to brighten my day.

Mom lets go of my wrist suddenly, with a sigh, as if she's given up. "I know you're lying." She pauses. "And I know it's too much to ask. I just have such a bad feeling."

"Of course, you do. I don't blame you for hating this place." I hold my hand up in thanks to the impatient ferry crew. We drive off the boat and onto the island, and strangely, the rocking doesn't stop as we pull onto asphalt. The horizon dips a bit deeper and my stomach drops. It's an illusion—it must be—but my mother seems to feel it too, her hand rushing up to rest over her heart.

"Yes. It's all those things, but . . ." A strange noise comes out of her, a kind of hiccup, then she is saying, "Stop the car! Goddammit! Stop the damn car!"

I am going so slowly already that it doesn't matter when she opens the door and spills out before I've completely stopped. I put the car in park and pull on the emergency brake. The cars behind us honk. As I run around to the front of the car, at first the sight of her body is blocked by the car door, so all I can see are her hands pressed to the pavement and that she's thrown up. The mess is draining away from her down the slight slope to the lake. As I get close to her, I see too that her body is still heaving, as if it has more to give up, but nothing comes.

I squat down and rub her back.

"Make it stop moving," she groans. Cars continue to honk behind us.

I've found my steadiness. The vertigo of driving off the ferry and onto land is gone. "You're just not used to the ferry," I say.

"I was fine on the ferry." Her body has stopped heaving, but she keeps her eyes closed with her face tilted down toward the pavement.

"Well, you're fine now too. I should get you back in the car."

A driver behind us lays on his horn.

"I'm not fine. Everything is rocking."

"If you feel seasick, you should open your eyes, find the horizon. Let me help you stand."

"I'm not getting in that car," she says. "The inn is close by. I'll walk."

"Let me park the car and get these idiots to stop honking at us. I can walk with you and come back for it later."

She waves me away, a gesture of both acceptance and

dismissal. I shut her car door and get back in, pull the car into an empty space at the edge of the lot.

I walk back to her, and she has taken my advice. She stares out at the horizon where water meets sky, the island behind us. She puts her arm around my waist.

"This place makes me sick, Henrie."

"That's a bit harsh, isn't it?"

"No, it makes me sick. Literally. It makes me feel like I have no center, like gravity is a thing that can choose to hold me or not. And on top of all that, I feel like there is something I should remember. Like I've forgotten some crucial thing and the forgetting of it is going to somehow hurt me. Do you feel it?"

I rest my head on her shoulder, look out at the horizon with her. "I'm sorry, Mom, but I don't get it."

"It's okay. You don't have to. I'm here for you. I can do this."

We walk together out of the parking lot. The Masquerade crowd is swelling around us but not intruding on our small space. Ahead is the inn. I can see it already. Tall and proud. Its wide windows facing the lake, watching every ferry come in.

"Just the two of us for the next few days," my mother manages when we reach the inn.

We've walked into the front hall, a dining room on our left and a living room on our right. In front of us the old wooden stairs stretch up to the second floor. The wallpaper is aggressively floral. A plush carpet has been installed over what are surely beautiful wood floors. One of those singing-trout toys that you can buy on QVC is above the fireplace, and figurines are everywhere, most of them rose-cheeked and winged. A kind of Victorian era meets haunted house meets dollhouse. The renovations are recent, yet they still seem to suffer from a degeneration that feels wholly unique to Fowler.

"I have you in the front room. Great view of the water. Have you been here before?" says a beautiful woman, maybe a decade younger than my mother, with wild flames of curly red hair shooting out around her head like a halo before streaming down her back. Freckles riddle her face, so many that I wonder if she hates them. The way they've gathered high on her forehead and again on her cheekbones is charming, a starry sky of beauty marks. "I'm Gwen. Or Wally if we end up friends. The place was decorated this way when I arrived. I added the fish. It's supposed to be ironic."

She hands me one of her business cards, clutched between her first and second fingers (Guinevere Rose Wallace), but more than the card, I notice she is missing a large part of her right thumb. A soft stump of flesh, still pink enough at the end to make the injury appear new. She sees me make note of it and puts her hand behind her back, nodding her head in a way that says, *It's okay. Head on upstairs.*

I help my mother up to our bedroom. It's tiny, the

view of the water minimal. There is an old dresser and one double bed. The handles on the dresser have clearly been replaced: dark squares around the porcelain hearts hint at a former, much more utilitarian feel.

"I reserved two beds," Carrie mumbles, slumping against me. "I swear I did. Don't get mad."

"Mom, I don't care. Truly."

She is already crawling under the pink floral comforter. "I just need to shut my eyes for a minute."

"I'll go get the car from the dock and bring our stuff up."

"This is so stupid. I'm supposed to be here to take care of you," she sighs, already going under.

I head back downstairs, each step creaking loudly under my feet. Perhaps the wall-to-wall carpeting is a good idea after all. I see the innkeeper hovering in the living room before I'm halfway down.

"Breakfast is at seven and lasts until nine." Her words come in a torrent, as if she has reason to think I won't stand still for them. "I just can't keep it up after that, so no exceptions. Also, please respect the curfew. Come in by midnight and no later. I have to lock the door at some point, and the other guests might want sleep. I do not drink—recovering—but I know people do, and it's fine if that's why you're here, but please don't get so wasted you can't be in on time or find your own room."

"Don't worry," I interrupt when she finally takes a breath, "we're not here because of Masquerade."

"No? That's a relief. This is my first Masquerade. It seems pretty messed up in terms of celebratory events, but what do I know? I just bought this place last summer."

"How are you liking it?" I ask, although I don't really care what this woman thinks of the island or how her business is doing. I just want to move the car and get back up to my mom. The funeral is this evening, only a few hours away. "Too many drunks?"

"It's not that. Have you been on island before?"

"Yes," I answer simply, and hope she doesn't ask for more.

"I came once or twice as a kid. I loved the butterfly garden on the east end and Fun Land Park. Do you remember it? The big green dinosaur is still there."

I do remember it. B.B. and I would sneak under the fence and wander the tacky exhibits. It was full of oddly colored sculptures of extinct species meant to invoke terror. We loved the tyrannosaurus. Her fangs were glorious, too long and sharp for her to ever shut her mouth. I took photos of B.B. next to Gloria Gloria Glorious—that's what we named her—B.B.'s mouth just as wide, her elbows hugged to her sides with her fingers clawing toward my camera.

The innkeeper—Wally or Gwen or Guinevere—coughs. "I bought this place after . . . after my other life kind of blew up on me."

A look moves across her face, and I feel it like a breeze

through the room. My mother had that same look in the parking lot. This woman is scared. Lonely and scared.

"People still treat me like I'm visiting. Like there is some big secret I'm not allowed to know. They have island meetings." She whispers her last sentence and waves her hands in front of her, drawing my attention to her absent thumb. How does one lose a thumb? I imagine it being bitten off by a hitchhiker or sliced off in a bizarre deli counter incident.

"Most small towns have councils," I say. "Meetings. Things like that for planning. Do they not let you go?"

"Oh, I go. They talk about potholes and ferry maintenance, but I swear they talk about other things after the meeting closes."

"Like whether to raise the speed limit or allow another hot dog vendor on Main?"

"No!" she snaps. "Like what happened to that woman."

"What woman?"

The stairs behind me creak. We both jump. Another guest is making her way toward us. She's carrying a plastic ax, and rubber cuts are fashioned to the front of her shirt as if she's sliced herself open.

Gwen puts on a full smile and tucks a strand of unruly hair behind her ear. It bounces back out almost as soon as it is tucked.

"I love it here," she says to me with false joy. "I hope you enjoy the inn. It makes a lot of night sounds, but that's just settling. Don't worry a thing about it."

I let her talk with her other guest. The gory woman doesn't seem to invoke the same level of introspection in Gwen that I did. I step out the front door and the lake is ahead of me, stretching out flat as glass, the ferry dock empty now, and I hear it almost right away, a low girlish whistle and the bark of a dog. Laughter echoing up from the interior of the island. B.B. calling my name, the way she did when I was little. I can feel the clank of a camera on my thigh as I run.

My eyes are closed. I open them and the long-ago sound is gone. The water remains calm but brushes up against the shore as it should. Little ripples of waves. A family rides down the road in front of the inn on rented bikes, all of them bright orange.

I can see my car from where I stand. Parked alone on the edge of the ferry lot.

I repeat "Get the car" over and over as I walk. The sidewalk under my feet is bumpy with tree roots, cracked with lack of care. I can hear us everywhere—little B.B. and Henrie, alive and thriving. We know every sidewalk crack, burl, and building.

The inside of the car is already hot. I fit my body into the driver's seat. My feet leave island, and there is a small relief in this. I shut myself in, lock both doors, and breathe.

When I finally park the car behind the inn and load up with our two backpacks, purses, and my camera, the innkeeper is nowhere to be seen. I climb the noisy stairs, drop our bags on the floor, and slip off my shoes. When I join my mother on the bed and pull the covers up high over my face, the world is dark enough for me to shut down. I float there in the dark, the bed easing itself along the shallow coast of the island.

My mom and I walk into the VFW holding hands. She hasn't recovered from arriving on island, although the nap helped a little, and the nearer we grew to the funeral, the shakier she became. The sun is just setting outside, and inside, B.B. has decorated with thousands of twinkle lights wrapped around the rafters. With the hall lights dimmed, it looks like the night sky from the quarry floor.

It's a wide room packed with people; the noise of them all gathered is overwhelming and nothing like a funeral is supposed to be. People chat, talking over and under one another. Laughter prevails. Acoustic music is playing over a loudspeaker, but a woman is also wandering around playing a guitar and singing faintly, almost uncertainly, as if she has mistaken this for a music lesson. And, yes, someone is crying, a loud and impolite snorting sound that isn't that much different from laughter.

It is a Fowler tradition to bury people on island with a rock resting heavily on their chest. A tradition that goes way back to my great-great-grandfather and maybe further. The rocks are culled from the quarry, and our father was among the men who would go into the quarry to find just the right one.

"It has to have the right story," he'd say, "and heft. If it can't speak to who they were on island and keep them from floating back up, what's the point?"

Once I feel less overwhelmed by the noise and crowd, my eyes find my father's rock. It sits under his silver casket. Big enough to break all his ribs and, alternately, ready to be pulled out as a footstool, as if he might sit up, swing his legs out of the casket, and share a joke with the crowd.

I can tell by its color and shape that this particular rock has been chipped from the edge of the quarry, up high at the lip. Glaciers made Lake Erie, as they did every one of the Great Lakes, and Fowler is grooved deep where the ice slid across, cutting its path. While the quarry itself is a man-made hole, the limestone at the top shows evidence of the Pleistocene Ice Age. The rock B.B. has picked for our father is from the edge nearest the house where we used to enter the quarry as a family. I imagine our bare feet on this stone just as B.B. must have when she chose it. Island limestone is soft and easily scarred. This rock is scratched from the years of us going into the quarry, chalky with recent wounds but also marked with a few deep grooves that turn the top of the rock into something ruffled.

The room is loud with people wandering with cocktails in hand. Against the wall to my left is a small bar with a meticulously dressed bartender mixing martinis for our father's admirers—colleagues, former students, and other assorted wannabe poets. The islanders themselves are few and far between but recognizable by the way they've gathered on the side of the room opposite the bar, pale and wearing too many layers as if waiting for a guarantee that winter is over. I spot my sister right away. My stomach tightens, and I put my hand to my gut. She is in her element, moving from person to person, smiling but not so much as to hide her sadness.

"This doesn't feel like a funeral," my mother says. She is standing next to me, staring at my sister too. B.B. is solid as anything, and I love her for it. "It feels more like a book launch."

"I think that's intended."

"He hated those events," she says. "Part of why he lived on this island was to avoid shit like this."

"Really? I didn't know living anywhere else was an option."

"You're right." She sighs. "This just feels weird."

"It is weird."

I can see B.B. trying to get away from the young woman she's talking to so she can come greet me, but the woman has begun to cry. Big fat tears rest on her lovely cheekbones. She grabs B.B. by the elbow and pulls her in close so she can say something emotionally urgent.

"Do you think any of these people actually knew him? Like as a person and not an idea?" my mother asks.

I know the answer is no. My father had become a recluse. He could turn on charm if he needed to, give a great speech if asked, but more than anything else he wanted to be left alone.

I don't say anything, but my mother nods as if I'd spoken this aloud. "It's sad when I think about it like that. I didn't even know him."

"Sure you did." I touch her arm. "He loved you."

"How about a martini?" She's still staring at B.B. "She sure is something to watch, isn't she?"

B.B. is wearing a short black dress. Her breasts swell out of a low neckline just below a scarf, and her short blond hair is spiky and sun bleached. She is tanned, despite the gray spring weather, and her long legs brag of the same mystery sunshine.

I see her look up, wink at me, then gesture for me to wait as she accepts a cigarette from a young man I don't know.

"I'll let you talk to her alone," Carrie says. "I'll be fine."

As my sister gets closer, I see that she looks too skinny and her fingers holding the unlit cigarette are stained with nicotine.

She reaches in her bag for a lighter. Then tilts her head back and blows smoke toward the ceiling before she leans in and puts her forehead against mine. It's an old gesture between us, our foreheads resting against each other so that our eyes slide shut. As girls we thought we could read each other's mind. I still think it's possible. I let my jaw soften. I concentrate on B.B.'s hot skin against my own, on B.B.'s smell—cigarettes and sandalwood soap—and I block out the sound of the crowd.

"He's gone, Henrie." Her voice is raspy, thick.

I have a sudden flash of our father as he looked one summer out in the garden, my mom by his side. His hair growing long breaks loose from a ponytail at the base of his neck, and his jeans are covered with dirt. He surprised us all by saying he wanted to help in the garden. Mom teaches us how to lift the sprouted tomato plants out of their plastic bins and fit them to the earth so the roots can stretch out into new ground. My father's hands twice the size of mine, his knuckles filled with dark soil. I open my eyes, forehead still pressed to B.B.'s, smelling the tomato leaves begging to turn into vines.

"You should give Mom a hug." I nudge B.B. Mom has moved off in the crowd, closer to the casket.

"You mean I should give *your* mom a hug?" Her laugh is harsh, tight. "Sure. I'll put it on my list. Didn't I tell you not to bring her?"

I open my eyes. B.B.'s long fingers have elegant fingernails, so white as to fool one into thinking she's had a manicure. "You've stopped breaking your nails." I pull away from her body and her question.

"My girlfriend doesn't like them jagged." B.B. shrugs. "Speaking of special friends, why didn't you bring one?"

She pulls on her cigarette and searches the room. "Oh, right. You still don't have one."

"Mean."

"I'm sorry." She sighs. Dropping the cigarette on the VFW floor and grinding it out with the toes of her high-heeled shoes.

"When did you start wearing heels?" I glare at her.

"You know I just want you to be happy, Henrie."

"And a boyfriend would do that?"

"Or a girlfriend."

"I met someone on the ferry," I say, then wish I hadn't. "Where is your girlfriend?"

"It's impossible to get a cheap enough flight on short notice. Plus, she's not a keeper."

"She's not a fish, B.B."

"Who'd you meet on the ferry?"

"Didn't get a name." Without breaking B.B.'s gaze, I change the subject. "What do you think Dad would say if he knew we had to have his funeral in the VFW on Masquerade weekend?"

"He'd say, 'Goddammit, girls. I've been avoiding the damn military my whole life, and you're just gonna offer up my carcass like it's nothing?' You want to see him?"

I nod yes, and we are standing together, hands on the coffin edge, before I am ready.

Our father is appropriately dressed for the occasion and his skin is smooth, as if the uppermost elderly layers have been scrubbed off. His costume is not ghoulish or whorish like the ones on the ferry, but he looks in costume. He looks as if someone—probably B.B.—said, "He wants to be an academic for Masquerade, a world-renowned poet."

"Didn't they do a great job?" B.B. asks me.

"*They* could have shined up his hair a bit." Our father has long gray hair pulled back into a ponytail. It is not at all the desirable silvery hair owed to a poet laureate. His fingers are short and squat, and even though he is horizontal, it is still somehow clear that he is a tall man. They've shaved off his beard and put so much makeup on his face that it's hard to tell how old he is. If not for the hair, he might be thirty or forty or sixty-something.

"Do you think I could take some pictures?" I ask.

"That's kinda twisted, don't you think?"

I shrug.

"You brought your camera?"

"It's in my backpack."

"So weird. Go for it," B.B. says, taking a glance at the milling crowd. "He made me promise I'd throw him a party, not a funeral. He wanted cocktails and famous people. So here we are." B.B. digs a cigarette out from the small black purse that hangs off her shoulder, while I get out my camera.

"When did you talk about his funeral?"

"It's just one of those things we talked about," B.B.

says, lighting a match, then her cigarette, then, not bothering to make sure the match is blown out, she drops it in the casket. "We talked about everything."

"You should give those up," I say, frowning at the dead match resting near our father's knuckles.

"You're right." B.B. drops the newly lit cigarette and stomps on it. "There they go. Given up. I'm gonna make a round. I'll see you soon. Love you."

The door opens as she walks away from me, so that when Joshua enters, B.B. is already walking toward him as if she somehow knew he would walk in right at that moment. He looks handsome and tall. He almost looks right at me, his eyes lifting so that they will land on me, but then B.B. swoops in. They hug each other. They hug for too long, too tightly. He shuts his eyes as he holds her, and I feel rage. Anger and embarrassment melt together, indistinguishable. I turn back to the coffin.

The camera lens shapes my father into something I can look at without the anger or the hurt in my chest growing. I snap no pictures, but I focus and refocus on his ringless fingers, on the way the buttons on his white shirt are just visible underneath his navy tie. The satin of the coffin shines in contrast to the chalky makeup that coats his skin, and I follow the creases of that satin into the dark under his body, and that's when I see it, the slosh of it, the faint swish of water as if displaced or rather splashed up by movement. It eases up, liquid darkening his already-dark jacket, his body seeming to sway as if it could be more than a puddle beneath him. The lower half of the casket is closed, and from under there where his legs must be, I hear a faint smack like water up against the side of a boat.

I focus the lens, zoom into that dark space, and the black stares back at me, forming a presence of its own. Breathing fast, I drop my camera. It clanks against the coffin even as I jump back. Luckily, it's attached to my neck, so it doesn't hit the ground, but my heart is thudding and I back up farther, smashing into someone I don't know.

Without the camera as my eyes, the casket is just a casket. My father's suit is dry. He does not float or bob or slosh. But I can still hear the lake roaring in my ears.

+6+

sonia

2000

I'm outside the VFW dressed in the darkest outfit I could find—black jeans and a gray T-shirt. My glasses—thick and plastic and black in a way I hope is ironic and sexy—keep slipping down my nose. Funeral appropriate, I thought, until I stepped out into the evening light. The jeans are too long, and I hadn't noticed a spot of something is on the shirt. My hair isn't even fully dry, and I'm sweating enough that dark circles are forming under my armpits. The perspiration is certainly more about seeing Carrie than the temperature. *What will I say? What will she think of me? Will Henrie be with her?* I want to see them separately, at least for the first time. The idea of seeing them together is somehow more terrifying, because I won't know whom to focus on or how up-front to be with my emotions.

When I was a kid, my father visited this VFW weekly. He worked for the USPS and delivered the post and other goods from off island to Fowler. My mother, a former islander, died when I was young, and my father became lonely. The island, this VFW, was his happy place—old men drinking and talking about their one bad knee.

I grew up on the edge of the mainland in a small blue house bleached lighter on its face by the wind and whip of Lake Erie. My father bought it for my mother, who was the one who wanted to leave her life on Fowler but was also not willing to let it out of her sight. There were winters so cold we could walk across the lake, hiking backpacks full of supplies. I loved those winters—the idea that the world could turn from liquid to solid, that everything below our feet was fixed in time. We'd spend the night on island on occasion, especially when the weather was harsh, borrowing a bed from someone my father knew, or we'd just roll out cots at the VFW.

If the day was long, and it always was, my father would manage the deliveries on his own and leave me with Ms. Millie. She would brew me the same loose-leaf tea, lend me books, ask me to move boxes. She loved to gossip. She was full of island stories. She'd settle into her fading-pink armchair and drink tea until she seemed as drunk as my father.

"Seth Volt was a horrid man. An invasive species. He cared only about making money and creating a world in which his name would be associated with success and power. He's the one who opened a hole right through the damn island. That first stick of dynamite went so deep it woke the devil."

Back then I only knew *of* the Volts, like everyone else connected to the island, and I liked to walk by the house called Quarry Hollow. The huge old Victorian teetered on the edge of the quarry, fierce and precarious, as if daring someone to push it over.

"I don't believe in the devil." I was ten years old and just noticing that adults knew far less then they pretended to.

"Child, he doesn't give two shits about your belief. And you shouldn't be so literal. The devil can take many forms. It's just a nice, short word pulled together to get the feeling across. *D-E-V-I-L.*"

"I don't believe in God either," I said. I was stubborn back then, and I know my father would have smacked the back of my head if he'd heard me. But he is the one who made me look at my mother in her casket so that I could see her one last time. I imagine he meant well, but when I looked, I saw that my mother was just a carcass, like the shell of a peanut or the peel of a fruit—the goodness eaten, gone.

"Well, child, you're gonna need to believe in what I tell you. You've got work to do, and I'm not always gonna be around for it."

The VFW doors snap open, startling me from the memory, and a young woman rushes out. An unmistakable flash of long pale limbs, blond hair, and a camera swinging from her neck. For a moment, I imagine a small dog at her heels.

"Henrie." My voice is too small. It doesn't register with the blur of a woman speeding past me, and before I've even stood up, she's gone, heading up Division toward the state park. My heart aches, a throbbing that comes so strong and sudden that I now know it's been there since the day Henrietta left.

"Sonia?"

And just like that, I'm in the moment I've been bracing for.

"Yes," I say, as if I'm answering a phone call or indicating I'm present in class. She has stopped midstride to look at me. She is as beautiful as I remember. Her blond hair past her shoulders, lightly curled and spilling over a red scarf.

Those clear blue eyes flash above her cheekbones. She says my name a second time, and I wish she wouldn't. The feeling rising up in me is old—the madness of young love. It once took up all the space in the world. The freckle in her left armpit. The scar on her upper thigh from the time she took a hammer to Quarry Hollow and it fought back. The deep dimples in her lower back that peek through the space between T-shirt and jeans. The way we'd spoon, and I'd practice sending my thoughts to her, catching hers when she sent them back.

"You look good," she says.

I've loved you for so long, I want to say. Instead, I say, "Henrie looked upset."

"Which way did she go?"

"Toward the grooves."

Suddenly Carrie bends at the waist. Puts her hands to her knees as if she is going to throw up. I wait. Say nothing. Slowly she rights herself. "Sorry. I haven't felt right since I stepped off the ferry. I don't want her going in that house alone. Or in the quarry for that matter. You'll help me find her?"

Someone watching might mistake us for friends.

"Carrie."

"Fine," she says, as if I've always been a disappointment. She is moving away from me. So swift it tears at my gut.

"Wait! I didn't say no. First, you need to know something." Even as I holler this, I know it is not true. It's not something Carrie needs to know. Not yet. I should be telling B.B. Telling Carrie is all about me wanting to keep her near, but she is the only person that could hear my thoughts, would let me root around in her brain, explore. We were connected for a time. Really and truly. Body and soul. It was a time when I felt my true purpose, my calling.

She stops, turns, walks back to me. "You sound scared."

I step closer. "When they dug the plot for James, it filled with water."

"So?"

"It's been happening all over the island. I dug a few holes behind the museum, pretended I was building a fence, and those holes filled too. Lake water."

"How could you possibly know it's lake water?"

"I know this island."

"Please."

"Listen to me," I say firmly, and she flinches a little. "I know this island. I know its waters. I know that when I look into one of those holes, stick my arm down into it, I can't touch bottom."

Saying it out loud makes the sensation come back. Evening light and my body resting on its side against the cooling grass. The water is cold on my fingers, my wrist, my elbow. I reach in slowly until I'm in up to my shoulder, my fingers stretching down into the dark.

"Where will they bury James?"

Her mind is moving too slowly. She doesn't get what I'm driving at, but then again, who would? B.B. would. I should be telling this to B.B.

"Listen to me." My voice is steady. It doesn't reveal my frustration. "Something's happening to the island. Started the night James passed, but I didn't notice right away."

"Like it's sinking or something?" she asks, incredulous.

"Thinning, maybe. I run much of the perimeter

every morning, but it has a frailty to it. Like it will snap away if I put pressure too close to the edge."

"That's sand, Sonia. The tide. The moon. Jesus. That's how an island works."

"You aren't listening."

"Oh, I'm listening. You're losing your damn mind. You need to get off this island. Trust me. I know."

"Look at me."

She does. We've been standing right next to each other staring at the ground, but now her blue eyes lock with mine—I concentrate on an image, the beach that's begun to thin and then the water filling up the holes I dug farther up in the sand. I don't know if she catches the image or is just convinced by my steady stare, but she nods her head, once, agreeing to listen.

"Who else knows about this?"

"James knew. The Island Council knows."

"You're making this up."

"Follow me."

I grab her arm. She makes me drag her at first. My palm to her bare skin feels good, but soon she is walking with me and there is no reason to hang on. Our pace speeds up. When we see the museum and the graveyard, she trips a little but catches herself. I wonder if she remembers how happy we were here in my house. Curled up through the winter, researching the island, making plans to build and reshape. Playing with the girls.

As if she can catch my thoughts, she asks, "Why didn't you leave with me?"

Our pace makes her words breathy, and I have a sudden flashback to a night in the quarry, her last night on island, the girls soaked from the quarry pond. Carrie too. Water gushing out of her mouth, an endless river of it coming up, up, up.

You know why I couldn't leave, I think. *I had to stay for B.B. For the island.* Letting Henrie go meant the ecosystem rested on my shoulders, on James's.

We reach the plot that belongs to the Volts. James's gravestone is already here. His birth year clear but his death date not yet carved.

The hole is still open. Dirt piled high next to it. Water up to the lip.

"This doesn't prove anything," she says, but I hear in her voice a new nervousness.

I bounce up and down on my toes. The earth squishes like a sponge. I picture my arm down there in the hole, reaching. Why was I slipping my body into this unknown space? Why wouldn't my first instinct be to find a stick, a tree branch? In my dreams since, there is, of course, always something reaching back. Its ivory teeth are sliding over my fingertips when I wake up. Sometimes this creature is Millie's devil, or, more disturbingly, Millie is the creature. Rising up out of the under-island swamp, her fading pink chair a raft, her jaw thick with teeth, and I know, in that dream of a moment, that I had no choice but to stay on island. I was where I was always meant to be, and if all I knew was right and the end point was coming, I'd need Carrie and Henrietta and Beatrice on my side.

⊹7⊹

henrietta

2000

The sun has already set—the daylight barely lasts until five thirty in the spring here—when I burst out of the front doors of the VFW into the darkening island. The streetlights on the north end of Division are few and far between, but the ones that are there light up the bumps and cracks in the sidewalk so I can run without tripping. Partygoers whoop and holler—their sounds coming from everywhere and nowhere—and groups of them pass piled high on golf carts, headed in the opposite direction, toward town. The headlights are small and blinding. I look away as they pass.

When I reach the campground, the streetlights disappear altogether. I weave through the park and find a dirt trail that skirts the coast. I don't know where I'm going, but I keep moving. For a while, I am lost, following deer trails, and trying to keep the lake on my left. My eyes adjust again to a much-darker world with only the moon to light the coastal path. My camera bounces on my lower back, my breath catches in my throat.

An hour must pass before I realize I am at the north entrance to the quarry. I am unsure of how I got here, but I am wheezing and sweating and more than a little glad to recognize where I am. I wipe at my cheeks with the backs of both hands and wish I were wearing something other than tights and a dress. I push my sleeves up above my elbows. I don't stop moving to catch my breath but instead search for the slim dirt path that cuts through the massive snarl of honeysuckle toward the quarry.

The path is muddy with the thaw of spring, and I walk slowly toward the obscured quarry entrance. Tendrils of honeysuckle reach out and grab hold of my dress, my tights. They tug at me, pulling me back from where I want to go. I swing my camera to the front of my body to make sure the lens cap is securely on—an almost unconscious habit that I've developed over the years. It's darker than the road but I know this path. It may have grown skinnier, but its twists are familiar, as are the spots where the limestone pokes up to trip your toes. If I got down on my hands and knees, I'd be able to find our old footprints with my fingertips, follow the drag of our heels, the rush of the pads of our feet as we ran in and out—B.B. and Henrie forever.

Japanese honeysuckle is not a native island plant, but

once it found Fowler, it thrived. It can root anywhere, even in the shallow soil atop the limestone, and its roots weave baskets under the ground, stretching and growing to thicken the land. B.B. calls them carnivorous plants, but they are evergreens, conifers of a sort. Their green leaves linger on into the winter, lending color to an otherwise dying rock. My mom taught me how impossible they are to kill. She went after them as if it were war. Pulling young ones up, their long hairs holding on tight to the ground, spilling soil in trails and tendrils as she insisted. She'd cut the older ones close to the ground, then paint the stubs with poison so the plant would drink it into its roots. I understood her desire to eradicate them, especially when I saw them reach out greedily to strangle trees in our backyard. They are beautiful though. They burst yellow, white flowers in the spring that smell like vanilla, like hot sugar cookies.

My gaze is on my feet as I try to keep my face from being scratched by branches. We used to use this path to exit the quarry when we didn't want Mom or Dad to know we were heading to town. It was the long way around, the farthest entrance and exit from our house and from downtown, but you could get to the dime store and buy loads of penny candy without anyone being the wiser. And, back then, we had nothing but time.

Because my head is bent, because I am only looking down, I don't see the fence until something cold and solid and sharp slices my forehead. A small warm cut that I dab with my palm.

Chain link. Old enough to be a little rusty. A sharp pain cuts across my chest, enough to draw a gasp, and I press my palms to my chest, curving my fingers over my clavicles. The pain recedes but the feeling is still there, as if something thinks it can keep my head from my heart.

"What the fuck," I say.

I loop my fingers through the fence, stare up at its height. Seven feet, maybe eight, with a curl of barbed wire at the top. A serious fence, the kind meant to put the fear of god into trespassers. The honeysuckle has already begun to wind itself through the metal, melding with it in some spots. The fence doesn't belong here. It deserves to be ripped up, shredded with force, and left to melt back into island skin. There is no way my father would have let anyone build a fence on his property. The rage bubbles up in me. I wrap my fingers around the mesh and pull. It barely moves, so I pull again. The mesh twangs back into place. I kick at it, push my whole body into it.

You can't keep me out! A waft of the cool air, the kiss of the water somewhere beyond and below, reaches up to twirl through the octagons of the fence, thick and certain as the honeysuckle's vines.

I imagine how the limestone stretches out into nothing. It's the highest point in the quarry. A jump from that spot into the pond means death. The thirty-foot drop is only part of the problem. What lies beneath the water at the base of the jump is the other. Down there the rocks poke up, spiky and ragged, ready to pierce. Something the innkeeper said flits through my head: "Like what happened to that woman."

I put my camera on my back once more so that I can keep my belly close to the fence as I follow it. I move sideways, ducking over and under branches, raising my feet high over vines. The fence makes this dress even more foolish, and although I don't look down, I can tell my black tights are shredded. If it were later in the season, I'd be worried about poison ivy, another plant that thrives here, but today such things are still slumbering.

I find a spot where someone has cut the wire down low and peeled it back a bit, a triangle that I can lift farther to squeeze through. Beer cans are on the other side, and I imagine island teenagers coming here at night, risking the edge of the world.

I move to the edge. Let my toes pair up with the dark that stretches out past the limestone and look down. The drop is steep. Bottomless. B.B. and I would come here, dangle our legs over the edge, and put our backs to the rock. This spot made us feel like queens, brave enough to tease the drop but not dumb enough to plunge, yet I can feel what it would be like. To leap. To point my body to the water. To hit rock and somehow still swim out.

The moon is bright now. The clouds clearing. I swing

my camera around to the front and remove the lens cap. I look out over the land through this third eye. The tear of land is like a long snake, the pond its head, stretching out in front of me. The pond occupies the north side, below my feet, where the quarry is at its deepest. This is where Seth Volt and company started digging way back when, and when they got so far down that there was nothing left to find, they started digging southward toward where he built our grand house. By the time they were done, the house, meant to be some distance from the pit, sat at the edge of the shallowest part of the dig, precariously perched above the last efforts of the Volt dynasty.

The pond water shines up like a big black mirror. Farther out the quarry is dry—the Flatlands stretching out for a while, only interrupted by the tall jut of the rock we call the Watch Tower—the shadows of plants there push up, shallow and starved toward the moonlight.

The faint background noise of masqueraders finding their way to the bars on Main hits the quarry floor and bounces around before finding its way back out. The quarry itself gathers all the island noises but remains strangely empty of people. Then again, it always felt empty when we were kids, as if we were the only ones in the world who knew it was there.

The soft lull of the water, the echoes of parties gearing up, the frogs moaning. I'm beginning to shiver. My sweat has dried a salty layer on my skin, and the chill will dig deep inside me soon. I'll be dangerously cold, but I can't stop now. I need to touch the water, the place B.B. and I would wade in. The run from the funeral, from that frilly cocktail-party version of B.B., will only be over once I've put my palm to quarry floor, dipped a piece of myself into the icy water.

I put my camera behind me again and use my hands to hold on to rock as I make my way down. At first, I only hear a soft whistle above the other sounds, and I know it immediately, the noise the wind makes as it moves through the quarry and hits the cliffs.

I've arrived at the quarry floor and the water sits in the dark, reachable with one shift of my feet. The tiny indents and ledges and cliffs are visible in the moonlight, more velvet black than the rest. I watch. Listen. Stand still.

The pond is murky from winter, full of leaves and branches, swarming with the detritus of the previous seasons. It won't be clear until late May and not warm until July, but we would have gone swimming as soon as we could.

I squat down, reach out my hand, and touch the edges. The water feels like ice and the rocks underneath are slippery with slime. My teeth are chattering, but I hold my hand to the water. I know I need to get back to the inn, take a hot shower, get back into my present life.

I know too that leaving my mother behind was unkind. I'm sure she is worried.

But, instead, I close my eyes. Feel the cold and the camera on my back. I listen. With my eyes closed, the whispery noises disappear entirely, and no matter how I strain to get them back, it is only me and the island. Birds cawing, wind through tree branches, far-off music. The chill of April.

I open my eyes and I suppose it is the moon and the shadows and my tired brain, but the water seems to be moving away from me, sucked inward toward the cliff wall, then lapping up it as if trying to reach the cave. My eyes follow in the dark, up from the water to limestone.

The moon lights up the edge of the cave, and I use my camera to zoom in; threads of something soft hang from the cavern toward the water. I see a full white shine that it takes me a minute to recognize. A face bent back, eyes pointed in my direction, neck at an impossibly sharp angle. A body.

My breath makes a sucking sound against my teeth. I lower the camera, clench my eyes shut, open them again. Without the zoom lens, I can see the shadow of dark hair moving in the breeze, her face, round like the moon, pointed toward me, eye sockets hollow with dark. Her arms are stretched out in a *T*, the rest of her body in the cave. A smell of rot that I had not noticed before or had mistaken for quarry life seems so strong now that it's hard to believe it wasn't all I could smell as soon as I arrived. My stomach grumbles. I feel weak. Hungry.

I raise my camera to her face once more, zoom as close as I can get, and think I see the shine of her white teeth through parted lips. She hangs there, a sacrifice, twisted and grown out of rock. I open my own mouth, stretch my jaw. The world goes black.

8

beatrice

1989

My eyes fly open with the first ring. *Daddy is gonna be so fucking mad*—this intrusion into our calm, dark night. He hates that telephone and would have gotten rid of it if not for our begging to keep it. He doesn't sleep well, sometimes not at all, so if this wakes him up, we are dead. All of us dead. This is bad. Henrie's birthday is only two days away. Carrie is still missing, and we can't have things more fucked-up than they already are. We cannot.

The question is, *What the hell do I do?*

My body is rigid with the urge to rise and rush down-stairs. I need to make the ringing stop.

My toes push into my mattress, palms hover at my sides to lift me, but, lately, my first instinct is not always correct. So, I wait.

The third ring trills, long and rattling, the handset

humming against the cradle loud as a fire alarm. It's a rotary phone, rust red. Old even for this island. With a dial that clacks as it spins, slow and ancient. The air outside is summer hot, dark, and still and humid between the rings, seeping in our open windows as thick as mist. This wave of humidity began eight days ago, the day Carrie woke up, poured us some shitty, stale cereal, and said she was going for a walk. We haven't seen her since.

Whatever. Everything is fine. *Everything is fucking fine.* As I shut my eyes, I hear the fourth ring.

My sister rustles in her bed. Downstairs the kitchen floor creaks. Dad is already awake?

I sit up in my top bunk and turn to look at Henrie on her top bunk. She is sitting up too. We each have our own set of bunk beds, and in the winter, we turn the bottoms into warm little caves, but now, in the summer, we sleep on the top to be closer to the ceiling fan. Henrie is looking at me. She's always looking at me, and I feel a flash of irritation. What if I wasn't here? What if I wasn't paying attention? I push the irritation away. I do not mean it. *I love you, Henrie.* I send the thought through the air, and I see her catch it. Smile.

Five rings.

Two nights back I went down to the kitchen for water and found Daddy standing in front of the phone, staring at it, as if he didn't trust it. I backed away and drank water from the bathroom faucet upstairs instead.

Six rings.

I gesture to Henrie that we should sneak downstairs. She shakes her head no, but I give her a hard look, and we begin lowering ourselves from our creaky upper bunks without making any noise.

In the kitchen doorway, we freeze. Our father stands with his back to us, staring down at the phone. The fingertips of his right hand brush the receiver, but he doesn't pick it up.

"Daddy?" I ask.

Henrie inches up behind me, presses her cheek to my back.

Our father shirtless, wearing his lucky blue jeans. He's been wearing them for days.

"Should I answer it?" Henrie asks in my ear.

"Go to bed," he says, but we both stand as still as we can. One statue.

"I can do it." I step forward.

"Go to bed."

"Daddy, let me—"

"Now!"

We turn in unison, running up the stairs, and have already climbed into our individual top bunks when we hear Daddy pick up the heavy receiver. He does not say hello. He does not say anything.

Carrie is just taking an off-island break, he's told us, but she left the car, and from what we can tell, all her clothes are still here.

Then from downstairs we hear, "Carrie? I can't hear you. . . . You did what?"

A sound comes next. A screaming, a rumbling that feels like it comes rushing to our bedroom. It crashes against the frame of the door, angry and loud. It sounds like *Noooooooooo*—a gut-wrenching scream of rage that comes up from the roots of the house. The pain of it vibrates my teeth. I taste blood and clamp my hands over my ears as hard as I can. Our bodies rattle, so I start to scream back. I pull the sound up from my belly and open my mouth wide. I sense Henrie is doing the same thing. We roar until our vocal cords ache, loud enough to set the house on fire.

I hear the clang of the receiver being slammed back down and it's suddenly quiet. My hands come away from my ears, blood under my fingernails from where I've dug into my scalp.

We do not breathe. *I hate this family.*

The phone rings again. He picks up right away.

"Carrie, you're scaring me," he says, quieter this time. "Come home."

My sister's eyes are dark, her body shaking. I breathe in, breathe out.

It's okay, Henrie. We're okay.

She nods to show that she's caught the thought.

"There is no way you'd do that. You don't have it in you. . . . I love you. I'll fix this," he says. "Tell me how to find you."

Silence.

"Why the fuck would you do that?" He is angry now. His voice sounds loud and suddenly convinced by her confession. "This was your home. We had a plan.

"Don't you ever come back here! You hear me!" We hear the receiver smash down on its cradle, then Daddy is ripping the phone from the wall.

"Daddy!" Henrie wails. She is sobbing, and I am off my top bunk and onto hers. In the kitchen, things clatter and bang and crash.

"Play dead, Henrie," I hiss as I hear this new sound from the walls, and next to her I begin to transform myself. Lying flat on my stomach with my face to the plaster. My shoulders relax, my arms drop into the mattress, my body puddling. I feel her do the same next to me. The two of us letting it all go, my left leg flopped over the two of hers.

The noises downstairs stop. He is done and his feet are heavy on the stairs. Thumping toward us.

He reaches the second floor, pausing before his study door, then his feet shift over the boards toward our room. Quickly, I turn my face to the doorway. He always pauses there. Touches the doorframe on either side with his palms, a gesture that may be entirely involuntary, like someone testing for a shock. He starts to cry, deep sobs as if he can't breathe, and he sinks to his knees.

I'm up and off the bunk before I can even think if it's the right thing to do. I wrap my arms around him.

"Daddy. Daddy. It's okay." Henrie leaps down too and wraps herself around the both of us. For a second, in this hug, with our father gasping for air, we are all safe. We need one another and that will make everything okay.

"What's happening?" I ask.

"Is she dead?" Henrie asks.

This makes him stop. "Jesus." He wipes his face. "No. She's not dead. Do you think she's dead?" The last question is not reassuring.

"She's not dead," I say with authority. "She needs a break from us. That's all. Come on, Daddy. You need to sleep."

He shrugs me off, but when Henrie reaches for him, he doesn't fight. He lets her lead him down the hall to his study as I think, *Fuck both of you.* Then I remind myself it isn't Henrie's fault. I shouldn't be mad at her. I shouldn't.

"She killed it," he whispers to Henrie, his voice thick with mucus, but I can still hear it.

"Killed what, Daddy?"

"This family." I watch as he stumbles and puts his weight into Henrie to keep from falling. She almost drops to her knees, but she rights herself at the last second.

"You need to sleep. Tomorrow it will make more sense," Henrie tells him. "Mom will come home."

"I can't stop. I've tried. I've tried to stop it."

"I know, Daddy," Henrie says.

"Promise me."

He wants Henrie to promise something she doesn't

understand, and I will her to do it, but she doesn't. She doesn't know what he wants her to promise, and honestly, neither do I, but she could at least fake it. I will her to fake it. I almost jump in and holler it from our bedroom doorway: *We promise, Daddy. We are strong!*

"You're hurting me," Henrie says instead.

"There won't be a choice, Hattie." He's weeping again, a quiet sound. "Not if you stay here. Maybe, just maybe, it will end with me if you leave."

They disappear into his office, and I imagine Henrie as she sits him on his old green couch. She is getting him to lie down, covering him with that ugly afghan—the one we call the beehive—and she is telling him everything is all right.

"What did he say to you?" I ask before we are even back in our room.

"Nothing. He isn't making sense."

"Was it about Carrie?"

Henrie says nothing, and I'm so fucking tired, I don't know if I even care.

"I'm scared, B.B. Something is different. Something is wrong."

I want to tell her to shut up, my head hurts, and I'm scared too, but I manage to keep quiet.

"Will you sleep with me in my bed?" she asks.

We climb into her top bunk. My body curls around hers, our backs are to the door.

"What happens next, B.B.?"

A voice cackles in my head, *Tell her, B.B. Tell her what's next. Tell her to jump.*

The suggestion is unkind. Dark. I will not offer it.

I wake up late, our legs twined like tree roots. Henrie is snoring lightly, her lips barely parted. She smells sour. I breathe it in, then untangle my body from hers, lie faceup on her bunk, and look at the ceiling where she's scribbled notes on the bumpy plaster. Her name. Printed and in cursive. *Henrie Volt. Hattie. Hen. Henrietta Sophia Volt. THE VOLT SISTERS.* There's also a family tree of sorts with all the names of our ancestors, but it spirals out from the center rather than branching out like a tree. In the tiny middle she's written *Elizabeth Volt* and *Eileen Fowler*—the original island sisters who made the downtown area and the Island Museum and even commissioned the first roads before our great-great-grandfather Seth Volt showed up and started blasting away, stealing Elizabeth from her sister. He was the cause of the rift between the two, and after Elizabeth gave birth to their son and our great-grandfather—James the first—folks say she jumped off the cliff, the first woman to disappear in the Killing Pond.

Next to our names, there's a space for a third. A little

blank spot where a sibling would go. I look at my sister. Her eyelids are still closed, and I wonder what she is keeping from me and if it's more than I'm keeping from her.

Henrie wakes up, tilts her head toward mine so our skulls touch. We listen to our father downstairs in the kitchen. He's cleaning. The sound of glass being gathered into piles, then dropped into trash bags. The back door opening and shutting; the bags slung outside make hard *thonks* on the porch boards. We do not climb down out of Henrie's bunk until the smell of breakfast wafts up the stairs.

In the kitchen doorway, we watch him cook. His back is to us. A hole is in his white T-shirt near his left shoulder blade and another along the hem. The phone is gone from its spot on the small table where we usually keep it; a chunk of plaster is missing from the wall where he's ripped the cord free. Most of the cupboard doors stand open—not unusual for us since no one but Carrie sees any point in closing things you are just going to open again—and the shelf where we keep our drinking glasses is empty. Not a single glass left.

"Morning, ladies!" he says. It's false cheer. "Let me pour you some juice."

We take our seats across from each other at the table. Henrie's chair wobbles under her in a new and precarious way, but she quickly compensates. I nod at her: *Good job.*

Daddy stares for a beat too long at the open kitchen cupboard where the glasses should be, then reaches higher and grabs two coffee mugs, fills them with juice, and puts them on the table.

"Did I ever tell you how I met B.B.'s mother, Olivia Rose?" He looks to me for a response.

If you were watching us from the outside, our little fucked-up family, and you'd caught the midnight show when the phone rang and our father had a tantrum and two little girls went back to bed scared, this would seem a strange question, insensitive perhaps, and maybe it is. There are other things we should talk about. For us, however, the topic is normal. Dad loves to tell us the same stories over and over, none more than the ones about our mothers.

I used to worry that the stories about my mom made Henrie feel bad—Carrie can worry about her own damn self—but Henrie told me once that when he tells these stories, she likes to pretend we are the same person, she and I. She falls into my rhythm. Her head nod is my head nod. Her bite of soaked pancake is my bite. We play it often, this game where we morph into one, or better yet, we are Siamese twins, attached by the head and the heart. We put on one of Dad's large shirts and try to maneuver about the house as if separation were not possible.

"I was just returning to the island from graduate school. I didn't want to be here, but I had to move back. My father was sick. There was no choice. He needed me, and if he died, I knew the island would need me next."

Legend says that our great-great-grandfather made a deal with the island when he began digging into it. He promised that in exchange for the island's limestone—and the creation of a big unscabbable hole—there would always be an heir living in Quarry Hollow to look after the island. That little blank spot in Henrie's family tree pops into my head.

"I'll die in this house at my desk," my father says. "You can bury me under my books, lock the door, then throw the key into the quarry."

"Where's Mom?" Henrie interrupts.

"Your mother . . ." He turns back to the stove. Pours pancake batter onto the skillet. Watches it for a while before flipping it too soon, its underbelly raw.

"Wait, Dad," I say. "Finish telling us how you met my mom."

"She was beautiful, your mother. Our Olivia Rose. Perfect feet. Little toenails like half-moons. She hated wearing shoes. Rarely wore them, in fact." He slaps a pancake on each of our plates. I poke at mine, gooey in the middle. "On that day, we were on the ferryboat. She was coming to the island for the first time, and I was returning. I didn't have a car, so I'd walked onto the ferry and was watching the water when this woman beside me throws up right over the rail into the lake. Vomits, but then stands with her hands on the railing and her eyes closed for so long that I think she's passed out standing there. I put my hand on the middle of her back and said, 'Are you okay?'"

"You called her 'miss,'" I say, knowing my lines, "and she corrected you. She turned her blue eyes on you and said, 'Ms.'"

"That's exactly right, B.B. I said, 'Excuse me?' And then she said, 'My name is *Ms.* Olivia Rose Mitchell. Not *Miss* or *Mrs.*' I'd made her mad, so I tried to change the subject and asked, 'Your first time on the island?' And she looked at me like I was a fool! I got so nervous, I could have thrown up right alongside her. Can you imagine that? Your daddy nervous?"

"No," we answer, and Henrie shifts a little in her chair, making an awful squeak. I shoot her a look.

"I managed to say, 'How long are you planning to stay?'"

"And she said, 'I'm seasick, so I might be stuck forever.'"

"And I said, 'Don't joke. That's how my family came to own half the island.'"

Henrie interrupts, "Then you said, 'I'll gladly show you around your new home.' She laughed at you, but you were inseparable after that."

"She made me feel coming home was the perfect thing."

"Two peas in a pod," I say. The phrase our father uses to describe us as well.

"Olivia Rose was the strongest woman I'd ever met. I never thought the island would eat her."

My spine straightens.

"Daddy," Henrie says softly.

"She dove in. Just like the others."

I picture my mother. Her body long and lean. Her blond hair falling thickly over her shoulders. Her arms raised over her head, ready to point into the water, her direction already determined. A woman that brave, that beautiful, would know how to dive, she'd have a plan. She'd shoot for the center.

"I hear her sometimes. She talks to me from the walls," Henrie says. "Maybe we can still pull her back to life!"

"Don't be stupid, Henrie," I say. Her enthusiasm also cruel. "Carrie dove in too, didn't she," I spit it out. "She's dead and you just won't tell us." I want Henrie to feel the hurt. I want our Siamese selves, one big, bruised heart. "They both killed themselves. They didn't love us enough."

This gets my father's attention. He looks at us both, settling his eyes on me, coming back from Middle-earth.

"No. Your mother loved you."

"You don't jump off those cliffs unless you are ignorant or want to die. She knew this island. She knew the quarry. She wanted to get away from us!"

There is silence in the kitchen. Outside the birds sing, their voices muffled by the thick of the house. The ghosts in the hallway have begun to wake up, I can hear them holding their breath. The bright heat of the noon sun barely makes it into the kitchen, the never-cleaned windows covered with quarry dust.

"I never wanted kids. I had a plan. But then I met

Olivia Rose . . . and then, when you were born, well, I thought, maybe, just maybe . . . and it seemed okay, so Carrie had you, Henrie."

I will Henrie to stay quiet because it is such an odd thing to say. He sounds so sad. Regret dripping off him like lake water.

"I love you, Daddy," she says, all desperate, and I am so mad at her. Dumb, dumb girl.

"I love you too, Hattie."

"Is what B.B. said true? Did my mom jump?"

"Oh, sweetie, no." He pauses, looks somehow even sadder, then adds, "Carrie is just leaving me. She's not leaving you, Hattie."

"It's Henrie's birthday tomorrow," I offer, gathering myself together.

There are little family traditions to uphold. There are fireworks that we pretend are meant for Henrie and store cake—the kind with thick, sugary red and blue roses and colored confetti. The island bakery always rubs out the *4th of July* part of *Happy 4th of July* and replaces it with *Birthday Henrie* so that the remnants of the wrong holiday can be seen as a red-icing stain on the fierce white of the cake. The whole family sleeps together in the quarry on the night of the Fourth, and at midnight, Carrie wakes us all to say, "Henrie, you are fully here now, sweetie. Present and accounted for."

"Fourteen is a big number," our father says, but no joy is in his voice. The pan is starting to smoke.

Daddy, pull it together. Don't mess this up. "Tell the story of the day Henrie was born."

"I should," he says, but then nothing.

Our dad has a graying beard and mustache. Today the hair on his head shoots out from his scalp and his chin in wiry, electric bolts. He stands over the hot skillet with the spatula raised, then reaches out and picks up the ladle, pouring the batter into careful shapes. But what began as another *H* for "Henrie" oozes into a swollen capital *A*. And I can smell the butter under it burning.

"Carrie's decided to move off island," he tells us. "And I agree it's for the best." He puts the shapeless pancake on a plate with several slices of bacon and sits at the table, the gas burner still on.

I reach my hand out and hold on to Henrie's upper arm. The ghosts hold their breath.

"Henrie, your mother has found a place on the mainland. Great schools and all that. You can summer on island." He has a piece of bacon stuck in his mustache.

"I want to stay." Henrie's voice is barely a whisper.

"We will still be a family, but Carrie and Henrie will live off island."

"Let's all go," I say too quickly. "We can get an apartment on the mainland and go to school, and you can get a teaching job and we won't complain about anything ever. You can write."

"You know we can't do that," he says, and his eyes flit to Henrie.

Jealousy flairs in me. It is red and hot and angry.

Breathe. I move my gaze to Henrie, realizing three important things: (1) there will be no rubbed-out holiday birthday cake or quarry slumber party; (2) she is moving off island, but even off island she'll still be his favorite; and (3) we will no longer live together. Three is the most impossible to swallow—I can feel my mouth fill with saliva, my throat refusing to open. I know that for the rest of my life I will associate that combination of sticky syrup touching the salt of bacon fat with sorrow.

"I won't go. I won't," Henrie tells me later that night as we lie on a ledge of the quarry, looking down at the dark water, using each other's bodies as pillows.

"It'll be okay," I assure her. "I have a plan."

"What is it?"

"I mean, I *will* have a plan. I need to think."

"When?"

"Soon. Tomorrow."

Henrie trusts me. She always has. Still, something sits uneasy with us both, and so to keep from thinking, Henrie asks me the question she loves to ask me: "What happens next?"

This time I do not miss my cue.

❧ 9 ❧

beatrice

2000

Quarry Hollow called me the night Daddy died. My cell phone ringing and ringing. I was off island, trying to figure out if I had enough credits to wrap up my graduate program, and when I picked up, there was only that *scritch-scratch* you get whenever you are trying to use your cell anywhere on the island other than the dock. The ringing went all night, and I picked it up about a dozen times, listening to the fuzz on the line. I could picture the old phone in the kitchen, the big plastic weight of the handset on the table. I screamed into my cell, yelling for Dad to pick up. Hollered at the house to stop calling.

There was nothing to be done until the sun came up besides play the game. Finally, at first light, the noise took on a shape that I, not just my dumb little sister, could hear. A reaching out from the walls that changed light and sound into my mother's voice. *Come home*, she said. A breath of wind she'd finally managed to shape into a plea. I understood then that it hadn't been the house calling—not that big, wicked thing—but my mother gathering shape and strength to lift the phone, form her voice. "Mama," I said back, and the line went dead. It did not ring again.

I've been sleeping in the downstairs hallway since I came back. Even passing by Daddy's locked office door is a challenge, especially at night. The state of him, of his office, when I finally made it to the island, was not a thing one wants to remember. The body itself repairable enough to fool a whole funeral crowd.

I can see the rust red of my sleeping bag from where I'm sitting now at the kitchen table. My pillow with its tiny blue flowered case reminds me how safe I feel right there on the floor. The wall next to me warm and giving off a kind of midnight rhythm like the plaster has a heartbeat. My mother hasn't spoken to me again—not since the phone call—but I feel her in the walls, one of the huddled masses. At night, I can hear the ghosts search about with tired fingers. Stretch their arms high. They like to huddle together between lath and plaster, gathering their strength for the next day's noise and sun. Scritch-scratching at the wall to wake me each morning. It's like those years of watching Henrie be special, be different, are over. I don't need her to translate for me anymore. I can hear them for myself, and my body feels different.

Stronger. More confident. Wanted. Even after Henrie left the island, I couldn't hear the ghosts. No matter how much I begged. It was just me and my sad father and a great big silence. But the minute my father passed, the minute I put my feet on Fowler soil, I could feel that things were about to change.

"It's good news," he says, this off-islander who wants me to call him Dennis, who is here to read me (us, if Henrie would ever show) Dad's will. He saw the pile of my bed when he came in but then kindly sat with his back to the hallway so we wouldn't have to discuss the strangeness of sleeping on the floor in a house full of empty beds.

He smells of coconut, and he's forgotten an undershirt. A dark tuft of hair pushes through the gap between the second and third button of his shirt.

"How did my father find you?"

"He phoned. Plus, I summer here."

"He hated summer people."

I'm resting my elbows on the table that has sat in just this spot for longer than I can remember. As with much of the house's furniture, the wooden legs are nailed into the floor under our feet. Still, I like the table, its Formica top, and its curved metal edges. I like knowing that if I lie on the floor under it, I can look up at its underside and with my finger follow the paths that Henrie and I drew to represent our island.

Henrie was supposed to be here an hour ago. It's not

like her to be late, but her behavior yesterday wasn't much like her either. It hurt to see her walk into the VFW with Carrie. The two of them one solid front while I was wandering around, falling apart all alone. After the divorce, Henrie never came back. Not even once. Not on my birthday. Not on Christmas. Frankly, I didn't think she'd come back for Daddy's funeral, but then there she was, and I started to wonder, *Why is she here? What does she want?*

"Do you want me to keep waiting for your sister? I can give you the gist and then she can come see me when she's back on the mainland. Paperwork can be signed later."

I want to say, *If I fucking thought it was okay to read it without her here, I wouldn't have wasted an hour smelling you sweat through your sunblock.*

Instead, I say, "We don't have to wait."

He nods, clears his throat. "Well, your father has left you the house and the quarry and a significant portion of the land on the west side of the island not connected to this land. That includes the old Fun Land Park, which you'll need to do something about soon. It's a hazard. There is a big hole in the fence on the west side and—"

"I'll put it on my to-do list," I say flatly. "When you say he's left it to me, you mean to me and my sister, right?"

"No, I mean *you*. He was quite clear about you being the one to inherit and not your younger sister."

"I don't understand."

150 RACHEL EVE MOULTON

"All I can tell you is what's on paper." Dennis clears his throat before continuing, "Good news is that your father has left funds to manage the house. I don't imagine living on this island is very lucrative, so this will ensure you won't lose the property. Half the funds are in your name and the other half is to be split between Henrietta and Caroline."

"Carrie," I say flatly.

"Henrietta's mom and your stepmother."

"I know who she is. Why would he leave *her* anything at all?"

"Well, let me see." He shuffles papers, as if the answer is there in the legalese.

I realize he's afraid of me. Dark circles of sweat yawn out from under his arms, and it's not even hot in the house. I stare right at him and give the Formica tabletop a smack with my palm. He jumps about a foot, with a yelp so hilarious I have to bite the inside of my cheek to keep from laughing.

"Forget it," I say.

"I'm sorry?"

"I don't need to know why my father did what he did. The house is in my name?"

"All yours. If Henrie decides to push things, argue for her half, it could get messy, but he very clearly states she is to own no part of the island, so she will have trouble contesting any of that."

"What if I don't accept it?" I ask, teasing Dennis but

also asking loud enough so the house will hear me playing hard to get. And, deliciously, the house sloshes and grumbles around me like an empty stomach. Like the thought of me leaving has taken it from full to starving.

Then I remember my father's body tilted over his typewriter, his forehead pressed into the keys as if he were momentarily frustrated. I told Henrie he died in his sleep. Cozy in his bed. No point in telling her he'd died at his desk, writing some sort of messed-up instructions on the care and feeding of Quarry Hollow. Nothing about disconnecting the hose for winter or changing the furnace filter, things any normal twentysomething would need to know. Instead, it listed rooms and times and specific areas of wall that needed "communication." Things like:

Piano room needs tending twice daily. East wall: apply pressure.

Ceilings must be watched at all times. If they begin to weep, spend time in attic.

Reseal turret but allow access to interior for emergencies.

Do NOT pound on hallway walls.

It was a goddamn gizmo list, so I crumpled it up and threw it away. Every time I shut my eyes, though, I see it, that salutation to me and only me with the colon punched so hard it ripped the paper. And the shed layer of him on the floor, as yellowed as his typing paper, which I shoved under the couch.

Time has passed since I arrived. A day? A week? I

haven't kept track, but the house has had only me in it since they took Daddy away. The walls have begun to slush, the ceilings drip, as if thawing. The house shimmies during the day, a ship already out at sea. It makes me wish I'd kept my father's note. Feed the house. Talk to it. Stay close. This swell and sway is new to me. Maybe I'm not ready for this.

"Accept what? The house?" He stares at me like I'm crazy.

"Yes, the house. The land. The quarry. Can I say, 'No, thank you'? Is it like when you buy a car and you sign the title over? Can I just not sign?"

"I'm sure there are options," he says, gathering his papers, "but I always suggest folks wait until they've stopped grieving to make big decisions. And I'll warn you. Your father tried for years to sign over the land to the state. He wanted it to be made into a park. I had been helping him with it, but there are so many restrictions on this land, dating back to—"

"My great-great-grandfather," I say, bored with this conversation.

"Why yes. The majority, even the quarry, isn't allowed to be used for any sort of future business. The house itself isn't up to code so would need to be gutted and rebuilt even if it could be sold. The Fun Land Park is actually an extension of the glacial grooves so shouldn't ever have been built on in the first place. I won't bore you with all the details, but it became impossible to imagine another use for this land. The state refused to take on the burden as long as there are living heirs." He waits for a *Thank you*, but I don't give it, so he clears his throat and continues, "Here, you keep this copy. Go over it with your sister. Here's my card."

He's done now. Shuffling papers with a purpose.

The house groans and a fat drip of liquid hits the table, resting on the surface like a bead of glass. He stares at it, reaches out one pinkie to wipe it away, then looks at the ceiling. Another drop hits his forehead. Right in the middle. He flinches.

I laugh.

"It's hot!" he shouts, upset. "What's up there?"

"My father's office. Rotting corpses starting to bloat."

"You know"—he pushes everything into his leather satchel—"you're lucky. You're young and you've been left an opportunity. Do something with it." His fear of me has changed to disgust. It is not nearly as pleasing.

Something thuds on the floor above us. The sure sound of feet being planted on the floor after they first swing out of bed; it sounds like my father, and it reminds me of something. A night long ago that I can't remember. It makes my brain feel itchy. Dennis looks up again, then quickly backs up. Another drop hits the table, missing him by maybe an inch.

"I didn't know anyone else was home."

"Someone is always home," I say, meeting his eyes, my voice deliberately sinister.

The silence feels so awkward even I want to break it. But I manage to stay seated and say nothing. The fear is back. He's scared of me. Of the house. I might spin my head clear around like an owl.

Somewhere, not too far off, a car horn begins to blare in an erratic rhythm every islander recognizes. Dennis the Lawyer uses this opportunity to push through the kitchen door and out onto the porch. The new punch and blare is not the house or some sound I've made up but the island cop car.

"Shit," I mutter.

The honking has made the turn onto our street.

I walk along the wraparound porch to the double front doors. I am standing there when Sheriff Wilderness Conway turns off his siren and puts his feet to the sidewalk.

"Someone called in a jumper." His voice is gravelly yet sure; I've heard it most of my life.

I lean on the railing. "You better hurry then."

"Not an *active* jumper." He clears his throat. "They claim to have found a body part."

"Then there's time." I try not to show my surprise. An actual body. Or at least one of its parts. That's new.

I've known Wilderness since before his facial hair and badge. He's island born, like me.

I walk down the porch stairs to stand in front of him. He is tall, weedy, with a beard that hides much of his face. But in the years I've been away, he's grown handsome.

I take a step closer. He smells good. Clean. His finger-nails precisely trimmed. He swallows. He looks away, and his Adam's apple, clumsy in his throat, swims up, then down.

"Who reported it?" I ask. People disappear from Fowler. People flee. They do not leave their parts in the quarry to be found.

"To be honest, Ms. Sonia found it on her rounds, but I know you two have trouble, so I was gonna skip that part. She may still be out there."

"She would be the type to guard it, wouldn't she? And we don't have trouble. I love everybody." I smile, mischie-vously enough for him not to mistake it for anything else.

"Anyhow, I thought you should know I'm going in to check it out."

"Do what you need to do."

"That fence needs to be finished."

"Jesus Christ, Wilde. You and I both know that won't do shit."

Carrie used to teach his math classes back when she homeschooled most of the island. One summer I worked ahead and in secret so I could be at his math level when our little school started up again in the fall. I had such a crush on him. I knew my work ethic impressed him by the lift of his right eyebrow.

But the eyebrow stays steady now. He shrugs at me.

His shoulders slump. He's always tried to hide his height. "You coming with? It's your land now, isn't it?"

"Fuck." I left for college when I was eighteen. It felt good to leave. Like my head was clear for the first time. Suddenly I could sleep. Really rest. Laugh. Listen to what other people had to say, like actually listen. It was like all these foggy holes that had been in my brain since Henrie left got filled in. The hole in my gut, the one that migrates hurt to my heart, never left. It may even have opened a little wider when I was off island. It was a loneliness and guilt I had assumed was island made, but even off island, surrounding myself with friends and lovers and classes and a delicious assortment of drugs, it remained. Clarity of mind did not touch it.

I expected my brain would feel foggy on island. The sheer everyday dizziness of it, like being unable to rise without a head rush blurring your vision. But I also thought the hurt in my gut might go, especially with Henrie on island again. I put my hand over my gut, push in a bit, and feel the lonely hurt. Like a bullet hole, it goes straight through.

"The funeral was nice yesterday."

"I'm glad you were there," I say, testing out a little bit of flirt.

He showed up, we did the obligatory chat. He sneered at my cigarette. Somehow, I didn't notice how broad his shoulders have gotten or, as I see following him now, how strong his calf muscles are—so bulked up and tight I wonder if they will burst.

We walk through the narrow backyard and the high weeds that flank the quarry. When we were kids, he was shy. He'd climb trees whose lowest branches couldn't be reached by anyone else just to be alone. He would swim in the quarry with us if we begged him to. He liked our attention.

"Why didn't you ever leave?" I ask.

"I leave all the time."

"No. Not like for groceries or whatever."

"I went to the academy. I traveled around Europe. I've hiked a bit of the Appalachian Trail."

"How did I not know that?" It has always seemed to me that islanders were islanders. Since I am one of them, it doesn't feel bad to say that they are generally sedentary creatures. Undereducated. Easily lulled. Horribly behind in fashion. And stuck. Not here by choice but largely from lack of imagination.

"You've always been . . . involved in yourself."

I laugh. It feels good. I am egotistical. Wrapped up in my own life. Loud and certain. People usually are too afraid of the show to notice what a total piece of shit I really am.

"I'm just saying you've got a full plate."

"It's okay. I appreciate that you've noticed I'm a bitch."

"I didn't say that word. I wouldn't."

He turns to help me manage the boulders that act as a loose stairway to the quarry floor. I take his hand, not because I need help, but because I want to touch him, and sure enough there is a zing. A flash between us that makes us meet each other's eyes. A spark.

"You're a good-looking man," I say to him. "I've always had a bit of a crush."

He reddens.

I push on. "We've known each other a long time."

"Beatrice." He pauses, as if gathering his next words. "This could be a bad scene. Maybe you should stay back."

"Wild things always happen over Masquerade?"

"I had a bad feeling last night."

"Is that how they taught you to do cop work?"

"I've been keeping watch. We forgot to post someone last night. I thought Ms. Sonia was doing it. She thought I was. With the funeral yesterday. Something's different. Not right." He rubs the side of his face with one big hand. "Keep thinking it could be someone we know this time." The red on his cheekbones is stretching down to hide behind the dark hair of his beard even as he's warning me of something. What though? Then it hits me. Like a punch.

"Henrie?"

He shrugs.

I think of her fleeing the funeral the day before. Of how lonely she's been.

"She wouldn't . . ." I stop myself. The sentence should end *hurt herself.* But I know it would be dishonest.

"I'm coming with you," I say, definitive now.

Wilderness nods agreement, and I put my hand in his, raising the blush again in his face. His hands are big, calloused, and rough. I can feel how he might lift me up, carry me out. The very idea that he's gone out and done things, then still decided to live here is intoxicating. What could this island be if I wanted it to be home? If I filled it with my people?

❧ 10 ❧

henrietta

2000

Get up! Up!"

I am aware of the voice and of the gentle shoves to my shoulder long before I open my eyes.

I rise from a deep dark place, breaking through the surface of sleep, and the light rushes in, crashing over me as my mom pulls back the curtain. I feel sluggish, my brain is heavy, and the headache is still there, not bad but lurking, as if it will creep up on me when I least need it. I pull my legs up tight to my chest. I'm sweaty. The sheet under me is moist.

"We're late." She tosses a throw pillow onto the foot of the bed.

"Where are we going?" It comes out in a slur. How long has it been since I woke up on this island? More than a decade. I miss B.B. so fully and so suddenly that I gasp and pull my legs even tighter to my chest.

"Henrietta Sophia Volt. You missed most of the funeral, and you cannot miss the reading of your father's will. Get up."

Then I remember: *Was there a body in the quarry?* The lake outside waits for me, licking at the shore as if for a taste. The sweat-soaked sheets slip away, and I begin shivering.

"Do I have time for a shower?"

"You do not have time for a shower. I will go downstairs and get you some coffee, even though it's way past the time when Ms. Innkeeper said she'd feed us."

My mom is about to head out our bedroom door when she stops. "Are you okay?"

"Not really."

"Sonia missed you last night. She wanted to see you." She keeps her eyes in my direction, but I can see her looking through me. "I was worried about you." Now her eyes are on me, fully looking me over. "You look rough." She walks away from the door to kiss me on the forehead. "And you've got a little bit of a smell to you. Maybe a shower is a good idea."

"Thanks a lot," I say, pretending to be offended, but shaking so badly now I can hardly hide it.

She places her palm to my forehead, an absentminded but motherly gesture, and I can see she doesn't even take the time to process what she feels before she is headed back to the door.

"Get clean. Get dressed. Whatever you have to do but

do it quickly," she says as she slides out the door. "If we left right now, we'd be five minutes late. And we're meeting at Quarry Hollow. Location change."

I stare at her. *Quarry Hollow?*

"B.B. texted you. I read it, sorry." My mother isn't sorry. She's too flustered to be sorry.

"Mom, you don't have to go."

"Oh, I'll go." She plucks at her eyelashes. "Your dad promised me he'd make sure the house was left so it wasn't your responsibility, but I'm sure there are other things to settle."

I rise slowly from the bed, my head thick from the sleep aid I took, but the bad feeling is fading. I flex my toes, stretch my calves. I walk to the small window and look out at Lake Erie. The sun is high and bright. People walk down the street. A ferry is emptying. I smell the diner's pancakes. The island is warm and happy this morning, and that feeling eases into me as I open the window a crack and breathe in the fresh air.

The old firepit is there in the side yard surrounded by Adirondack chairs. The gravel drive is paved now. I park on the street near the huge old tree in the front yard, where we once hung the tire swing. The tire is gone, and instead, there is a dimple in the ground, an indent like a deep hole covered with a blanket of grass.

I wait for the dread of the house to set in. I can tell it has a hold on my mother. She sits quietly, arm raised to grab the oh-shit handle in the car. Her knuckles gone white. I feel something else. Anticipation? Giddiness?

"This is it," she whispers to me.

"It doesn't bother me like it does you."

"But it should."

We sit in silence. I am holding the steering wheel, gripping it with both hands. I let go. Rest my hands palm up in my lap. There is a big blank spot in my memory from last night. I thought maybe it would become clearer as I woke up fully, like the blur of it would gain focus given a little wake-up time. It hasn't. Not really. But I know too that this isn't the first time I've seen the house. That it's seen me.

"I was here last night," I say, trying out the statement to see if it is fact.

"I figured as much. Did you go in?"

"No," I say, but that answer doesn't feel entirely honest. I don't tell her that I *did* go in the quarry. I remember that wide white face, staring up at the sky. How my mouth had filled with saliva. My stomach growling.

"Mom, I'm getting out."

"Okay."

"You gonna be okay?"

She shakes her head no. "You know how when you go back to places where you were a little kid? How they seem super-small?"

"Sure."

"It's the opposite here. This house makes me feel like I've been swallowed up. Even from out here."

I reach my hand out to hold hers. We sit together like this, waiting for a sign that it is time to get out of the car, but I realize that it's up to me. And I am very, very late.

"Let's go together," I say, and let go of her hand.

I stand on the sidewalk to look at the house. She's right. It's huge—literally and figuratively. The biggest on the island. Seth made sure it was the tallest as well, its third floor topped by an attic and a turret on the backside that hangs out over the quarry.

I climb up onto the porch and rattle the front door. It's locked. I cup my hands to the glass to peer in the window. The front room is full of familiar furniture but not people. I follow the porch to a side door, my mother now on the front steps, holding on to the white railing as tightly as she can, as if we are still on the ferry. I peer in a kitchen window, and I can see the old Formica table with its four chairs. It was too small a table for my mother's India-import tablecloths, and the fabric would hang all the way to the floor, tangling with your feet as you tried to rise to clear your dishes. B.B. and I would hide underneath. On the top of the table are two coffee cups and a pile of papers.

I turn the doorknob and the door swings inward. Something skitters out from under the table. It's too big and loud for an insect, but I can't catch its shape or features. A shadow that makes *scritch-scratch* noises on the black-and-white tile floor, noises loud enough to make me jump back, then arms are around me, enveloping me from behind, and I scream.

"Henrie!" It's B.B. "Where the fuck have you been?"

I lean forward against the doorframe, breathing heavily. I can't answer right away.

"Morning, Beatrice," my mother says, walking up to us both. She is no longer holding on to the porch railing, but her left hand is flexing and unflexing at her side.

"It's not morning anymore." B.B. keeps her body stiff, far from my mother. She doesn't want a hug. Mom doesn't try. "You were supposed to be here this morning but now it's afternoon. What the hell happened to you?" B.B. is trying to act lighthearted, playful, but she's mad at me. For being late. There is something else too. She's agitated.

"Nothing happened. And what's all over you?" I brush at the left side of B.B.'s face. "Spiderwebs? Why are your shoes all wet?"

She leans in, one side of her mouth climbing higher than the other and says, "As if you don't know."

"What the hell does that mean?" I ask. It's a test of some kind. Like she is making sure I don't know what she thinks I don't know.

"Ahhh, nothing." Her voice is back to its normal

volume. "We'll get into all that later." It's a threat but I don't understand what kind. "You left me alone with the lawyer, you bitch!"

I tell myself that's all she means. It's enough, isn't it? I fled the funeral. I missed the meeting with the attorney. It's enough to make even the most loving sister mad.

"B.B. This is all a bit overwhelming. Give me a break."

"Well, I managed it without a break." B.B. snorts a little as if I'm ridiculous.

I suppose I am. "I said I'm sorry."

"Actually, you didn't."

"She's right," my mom says. "You haven't apologized."

I glare at my mother. A WTF look even though I know WTF. She's trying to get on B.B.'s good side, a useless effort.

"I had a hard time at the funeral and had to take care of myself. I'm sorry I overslept."

"That's a suck-ass apology," B.B. says.

"It's what you're gonna get." I shrug. "Where's the lawyer?"

"He left, but we talked since you didn't show up." I try to read my sister's expression. Her voice, deepened by cigarettes, sounds grave.

"You don't seem happy."

"Oh, I'm happy. Thrilled even, but happiness is hardly the point. Do you want to sit down to hear this?"

"I have no idea. Do I?"

"For years, Dad was trying to encourage the state to

reclaim the island. He was working a deal to turn our land into an extension of the state park, tear down the house and repurpose the land, ever since he decided not to have more babies. Carrie, you remember?"

I look at my mother, whose face remains drained of color.

"Well, hold on to something," B.B. says. "The state doesn't want it. Any of it. I guess they researched the cost of turning it into a state park and rejected the proposal. Dad didn't have time to rework it so . . ."

"Fuck," my mom says. "Shit."

"So . . . ?" I say, unable to process what has gotten B.B. excited.

"It's ours!"

"What's ours?" I ask.

"All of it. The house, the quarry. Turns out we even own Fun Land. That creepy old park is ours too. We own forty-one percent of the island."

"You and me?"

"The Volt sisters back in the black." She is happy, yet there is a coldness to her that I don't recognize.

"That motherfucker," my mom mutters from behind us.

"Hey now!" B.B. says.

"Look"—my mom locks eyes with me—"he wanted you to have a different life. He didn't want to leave any of this to you. Let me see the will."

"Are you accusing me of lying?" B.B. spits out. It's so

full of hate that my mother takes a step back, hits the porch railing with the backs of her thighs.

"No. I mean, I'm just saying he promised me."

"Oh, and those are the promises we think he should have kept? The ones he made to *you*?"

"Stop it," I say. "Both of you. It is what it is."

"He also had a shit ton of money. He raised us like we were poor, but there was money all along. Of course, the deferred maintenance is astronomical. . . ."

"Deferred maintenance?" My brain is not moving very fast.

"The work that hasn't been done to the house that will have to be done before you *sell it*." My mom emphasizes the last two words, as if that's enough to convince B.B. of the next best step.

"Henrie," B.B. whispers to me. "We can live here together, like before."

"Jesus," my mom mutters. She lowers herself to the porch.

I'm stuck in the doorway, and the skittering inside the kitchen has started up again.

"He left you money too, Carrie," B.B. says. "I don't know why. Maybe because he made you live poor for so long. Or maybe so you'll go the fuck away and leave Henrie and me alone here where we belong."

I am about to ask more questions when the porch creaks. A tall man, the sheriff if his outfit isn't just another Masquerade effort, is on the first porch steps and waits for me to see him before taking one step up, then the next. He's wiry, his legs long enough to leap the whole house, so his care with each step strikes me as funny. A giggle starts in my chest, but then I realize he's familiar.

"Wilderness?" I say.

"Of course." He gives me a little half smile that reminds me so much of the little boy he once was that my heart aches. B.B. and I grew up with this man. This sheriff. The kid we'd make kitchen concoctions for—throwing together anything we could find, baking it, then inviting him over to eat.

"You're still here."

"I left briefly."

I notice for the first time that his long brown pants are soaked to the knee. Puddles form around his large-booted feet.

"Why were you in the quarry?" I ask, turning to B.B.

"Oh shit. You don't know? Ms. Sonia found a body. I thought I said that. Didn't I tell you that?" She turns to my mom to ask the last question.

"A body?" I taste blood in my mouth, as if I've bitten my tongue.

"Just a foot actually," Wilde offers.

"Did you call the dock?" Wilde asks, and B.B. stops her secret telling to look sheepish. Wilde gives a heavy sigh. "I need to use your phone, Beatrice." He steps forward toward the kitchen door.

For a moment, B.B. looks wild-eyed, and I wonder if she will block him, but I watch her, and she stops herself. Takes an intentional breath and waves him in.

She keeps her eyes on me. "An actual piece of the body was left behind this time, Henrie. Sloppy, whoever or whatever it was. Not jewelry or clothes. Not a purse or a backpack. An actual body part. Gnarled and bloody, ripped from some poor girl. No pretending something bad didn't happen there last night."

"Jesus, B.B."

My sister seems excited by the find. More alive because of its existence. "For a moment, I was scared it might be you."

I feel startled by this.

"Come on. Don't look so surprised. You disappeared yesterday and were late today. Plus, you tried to kill yourself out there when we were kids."

"That's not true," I say. I know what she's saying isn't right. I never tried to kill myself, but there is also so much I can't remember. "Mom, tell her she's wrong."

"You're wrong." My mom's voice is flat, emotionless. The words are unconvincing.

"Whatever," B.B. responds with a bright smile. "It hardly matters right now. We're both here now, and we, you and me, can take over where Daddy left off."

A memory surfaces. My body strong, thick with muscle, running like an animal through the quarry. So hungry, drool drips from my mouth.

"What do you say, Henrie? Let's stay on island and live the life. I can tell you want to."

I should say no, turn on my heels, and head to the ferry, but I don't. I should at least tell her that she's wrong; I don't want to stay. I want to have never come back at all, but another part of me knows that this decision, the one to stay or go, was made a long time ago. I am my daddy's baby girl. Some ugly, angry piece of my insides belongs here with my sister. The two of us already growing hungrier and more feral.

·11·

henrietta

1989

Wake up, Little Wing."

The quarry floor is solid underneath my right side, my upper arm my pillow. If not for the sleeping bag we unzipped and opened wide beneath us, it would have been the ground versus the Volt sisters.

I didn't sleep well last night and not just 'cause of the hard ground. Something is different in me. My mom says its hormones. "It isn't just your body changing," she likes to tell me. "It's your brain and heart too." B.B. wouldn't let my mom go on about it when B.B. got her period, so Mom saved up all her you're-a-woman-now talk for me. I liked it at first, the attention, but she keeps saying it with worry in her voice, like she's a little scared of me. Dad seems to be weird about it too, in the opposite way, like he's afraid simply looking at me is gonna make me change into something he doesn't recognize.

"Time is it?" I ask.

"Time to get up. Don't make me lick your eyelids."

I flutter my eyes open but do not otherwise move. B.B. has carefully paralleled her body with mine so that our noses almost touch.

"Liiiiittlllle Wing," B.B. sings. "Rise and shine. No time to be grumpy. You're fourteen today. This is gonna be your year. I can feel it."

"Every year is my year," I say, but my body is aching. Lately, I wake up feeling like I didn't even sleep. My joints hurt and the soles of my feet are raw. B.B. says growing pains, but I say growing pains shouldn't make new calluses form on your fingertips or split the skin at the corners of your mouth. Today my jaw is throbbing all the way up to my temples. I run my tongue over my teeth, and they feel sharper, more distinct—my molars little landscapes in my mouth that fill with saliva.

"I'm ignoring your attitude because I have a super-amazing, best-ever day planned for you. It's an island scavenger hunt, and you're gonna get everything you ever wished for, including the planet Saturn shrunk down small enough for your pocket."

"I hate Saturn."

"No one hates Saturn." She leaps to her feet and, in her best circus voice, shouts, "This is the first day of the rest of your life, and it's going to be stupendous! Magnificent! Lion-taming big! Plus." Now she drops to her knees and gets close to my unmoving head. "At the end of this day, I will tell you my plan for getting Carrie and James back together for some rekindling of passions."

I open both eyes. She's just inches away. "Gross." I sit up, but the scared little grump in me is already leaving. I try to get it back, screw up my face until I'm all wrinkles and squints, but B.B. has that magic, a way of making every moment other than the one we are in silly.

"Love is never gross. Up you go!"

I let B.B. pull me to my feet, and she gives me a full kiss on the lips that clanks our teeth together.

"Cut it out!"

"This is going to be the year for you. You're already bleeding, you'll get the boobies; you'll make your first great work of art. Joshua will fall in love!"

"B.B.!"

"You love that boy."

"I only love you."

"True, true, but this is the year you're gonna get noticed. Are you ready for it?"

"No, not at all."

But B.B. is already reaching out her hand and tugging at my shirt, pulling me toward the quarry pond, and before I can think, I am running, leaping over rocks, and holding my sister's warm hand in my own.

"Almost ready?" B.B. asks as the blue-green water of the quarry comes into view ahead of us. "It's gonna be cold!"

"No colder than yesterday! Ready!" I scream, my voice banshee wild. We are climbing and will come out above the pond—maybe ten feet above the surface of the water. It isn't the most dangerous point, that one is twenty feet up, but you still have to be careful and know what you are doing to not hit vicious underwater rocks. I catch when B.B. looks up at the highest point, and I wonder if she is picturing her mother up there. What kind of woman disappears when she has a little girl at home? A weak one, I conclude, and my mouth fills again with saliva, little killing ponds lined up in a row.

B.B. is already stripping off her clothes. The sun is just reaching its highest point, and my skin is sucking it up, greedy as I take off my shorts, then my shirt. The sun feels good on the top of my head and the back of my neck—my long hair pulled into a low bun. I'm hungry. My belly greedy for anything. I want to lap up the water, lick chalk off the limestone, shove the leafy green of the quarry pines and honeysuckle vines into my mouth.

Ahead is a large pile of rocks that angles up, creating a loose path, to the spot from which we can safely jump. A boulder is halfway up—before you get to the terrible top—a flat, gray plateau perfect for sunning or jumping.

"Ready?"

"Ready!"

Naked, we race to the edge hand in hand and leap into the air. The fall breaks our hold on each other's hand,

and I go deep. I love how quiet the world is underwater. I stay for as many breaths as I can hold and watch B.B. do the same. Our hair floats around our heads, our legs push together in imitation of mermaid fins. B.B. is sexy at sixteen. Even I can see that. She is all curves, her pink nipples bigger than mine and her hair blonder. Time is what stands between me and sexy, at least I hope that's what it is, but I can't help but hate my body when it's next to B.B.'s. The straightness of my hips, my boyish chest.

I wait until my lungs burn, a surprisingly long time, proving I can stay under longer than my sister, before I surface, gasping.

"You trying to pass out?" B.B. splashes water at me with a flat smack of her full arm.

"Of course not."

"You scared me." Her voice is edged with anger.

"Don't get mad about it."

"I'm not mad. Just don't play that trick on me. That's our game. We do that to other people."

B.B. and I like to play dead. We position ourselves in the road or crooked at the bottom of a tree or floating facedown in the water. Islanders ignore us, but sometimes tourists get fooled and try to save us. One time this older woman dragged us by our arms back to the house. When Dad answered the door, he shrugged and said, "They do what they do." He was more irritated that she'd interrupted his writing time than concerned about our games.

"I'm sorry." I am sorry that B.B.'s so angry with me,

but I also like it. She wouldn't be mad at all if she didn't love me so much, if I wasn't so good at faking my death.

"I don't want to lose you, Henrie. That's all. Not even in my mind. Not even for a second." She's talking about the separation. At least I think she is.

"You need to shave your armpits." I feign disgust.

B.B. smiles and pushes through the water to grab me and put me in a headlock, but I dive fast. I swim deep, marveling at the clear water, how it shoots down sudden in the center and never seems to end. It's at least twenty feet, and at the very bottom there is a hole big enough to poke an arm down into Lake Erie.

There is a layer of warm water as definite as the rock that cradles it. I pierce this layer, passing into ice-cold water, then my fingers stretch down to touch the quarry's deepest point. My eyes rest on something B.B. has left me, a little present wedged in so it will not move. It lies, I assume, just where B.B. has asked it to—a green beer bottle with its label peeled off. I rock it loose.

We reach the surface at the same time. Wipe our eyes and catch our breath, treading to stay steady.

"What's in it?" I ask.

"Your first clue, of course. Want to open it?"

On land, I remove the plastic and rubber bands B.B. has wrapped around the bottle. I can see a scroll of paper inside, dry if not for the drip that rolls in off my eyelashes. I try to get the paper out by shaking it, then by inserting my pinkie.

"Here, give it." B.B. throws the bottle a little ways away so that the green glass shatters on rock, little emeralds reflecting the sun. I step forward to gingerly reach into the mess and find a piece of Dad's typing paper filled with Beatrice's handwriting. I start the first page: *Henrietta and Beatrice Volt were the bravest sisters the world had ever known.*

"Read it aloud!"

"'Beatrice and Henrietta taught themselves how to appear and disappear. They knew how to fold themselves into two tiny fists that could be palmed and hidden in a pocket when necessary, or to blow themselves up so big they stretched as rubbery and invincible as the island monster. Most of all, the sisters—one called B.B. and one called Henrie—practiced how they'd float away, but on their birthdays, they'd come back to Fowler for a fantastical scavenger hunt. The first present was always tied to the choking tree.'"

The choking tree is a huge old oak with a ring around its trunk where a rope dug in years ago, scarring it and making us feel so, so sorry for it. Sometimes we bandage it just to make Daddy laugh. The note means a surprise for me is tied to our wounded tree.

"Get dressed, you fool!" my sister says. "There's a present to find!"

My legs stick to cloth so that I have to hop and struggle before my shorts slide back on.

—◦❖◦—

Tied to the tree is a small dog that looks wild, although he does not bark or howl or even pull at the long rope B.B. has fashioned into his leash. It's his matted yellowed fur, I decide, that makes him look wild and not his posture or the way he pants.

"Where did you get him?" There are few pets on Fowler and none allowed on the ferryboat. A year or so back that was not the case. The tourists would show up with their pets for the summer, and some were left behind. Our dad dubbed these animals "the Intentional Lost Boys." There got to be so many strays that they took to roaming the island together in a pack. They killed Ms. Sonia's chickens and attacked the island dump, spreading everyone's balled-up secrets along North Island Road. That's when they banned pets on the ferry.

"I found him! He was in the quarry, wandering around with cut paws and no tags. He showed up just in time for your birthday, so I knew he was your present."

"Dad won't let me keep him," I say.

"I told Dad you'd take care of him no matter what."

"But Dad's allergic," I say. Nothing domesticated appeals to him. He likes nature. Things that roam.

B.B. shrugs.

"He must belong to someone," I say, locking eyes

with the small dog. I want him. Still, I hold back, and the dog does too. Both of us stand at attention as if the introduction is meant to be formal. *How do you do?* I think.

"He belongs to you! He's half-starving and way dirty. He needs you."

As if trained to confirm it, his tail wags.

"Hey, good boy." I hold out my hand and get low to the ground. He licks my palm, digging for salt between my fingers, then going for my wrist. The formality is gone.

I sit and he climbs into my lap, still tied. His ribs are outlined as if he's holding his breath. His white fur is yellowed, and the pads of his front paws are badly cut.

"He won't run now that he's with us," my sister says. "He's very loyal."

Untied, the small dog walks stiffly like a soldier over to B.B., until, it seems, he realizes he can hop more efficiently. He leaps up, shooting himself forward in short spurts. "He looks like a piece of bread popping up out of the toaster," she says.

"That's what I'll call him. Toast. His name is Toast."

B.B. picks him up in her arms and delivers him back to me, where Toast begins to lick my face as avidly as he licked my hands.

"Do you love him?" B.B. asks.

"I do."

"I want you to love him."

"I do!"

"Is he the best present ever?"

"Yes, B.B."

"Say it!"

"He is the best present ever, and I love you, sweet sister Beatrice, for rescuing him for me."

"You're welcome! We can bathe him later. I already fed him this morning so he should be okay while we scavenge."

"Can he come with us? On the hunt, I mean."

"Of course! Let me show you the next clue. You are gonna love this. I got everybody to participate."

I think, *Who's everybody?*

I scoop the newly named Toast up in my arms, and the small dog licks under my chin as I follow my sister's bounding hop to the side of the house. A rope hangs from our bedroom window to the ground, attached to a pulley, and at the base of that rope is a woven basket, big enough for a pillow and a blanket.

Toast wiggles free and runs to it, curling up in the basket, then rolling over on his back for his belly to be scratched.

"We can pull him up at night to sleep with us, then lower him down to go poop in the morning. I rigged it up myself. Do you love it?"

"I love it," I say, and I do.

"He's rolling around on your next clue."

"Well, get him off it." I laugh at her and she grins back. "I want more presents!"

I leap forward. I pretend to dig around under Toast's

warm body for the clue, but really, I am scratching Toast. I put my face to his belly; he smells of the quarry. It is a strong, almost human smell, like our dad after he'd been cooped up too long in his study.

"Silly dog. Silly, silly dog." My hand brushes the paper clue as Toast flips to standing. "Found it! Clue number two!"

"What does it say?" B.B. asks, clapping her hands.

"You wrote it!"

"I know but I'm so damn clever. Read it aloud."

"'Henrietta and Beatrice Volt came from powerful women. Women so powerful that men had to keep finding ways to keep them small. The Volt sisters, however, were different, more powerful than all who came before them. They could not be broken up or broken apart. They used their magic to make art. They painted glittery pictures with stardust and cowrote novels with fairies. They dove with mermaids and came up with photographs of monsters gone Loch Ness. They were wizards and witches, painters and writers, and blower-uppers of rock. The youngest and most insatiable of the Volts was born with an artist's eye, so her older sister climbed the magic mountain, called up to the yellowy clouds until they dropped low enough to hand over another, even more magical eye. One crafted by rainbows and angels and sky. A manufactured pupil that the girl could place to her own, and what she saw would translate, groove to paper, frame to walls, float livid with its own magic, and always show her sister's true heart no matter what devil tried to come between them.'"

"Do you know what it is?" B.B. asks.

I picture a Polaroid camera, probably shoplifted from an island drugstore.

"Bet you don't." B.B. smiles. "Come inside."

"Stay here, Toast." I kiss him on the top of his dirty head and place him on the deck, where he sits panting up at me. He looks disappointed or maybe a little nervous, like I'm another owner who is abandoning him. "All right, come on." He hops into the kitchen, delighted.

Inside, B.B. is standing at the kitchen stove, the gas turned up high so that the blue curves up like spider legs.

"What I'm going to do will hurt," B.B. says, heating the ladled edge of a soupspoon over the front gas burner. "But it will be worth it. Get the bottle of gin out of the liquor cabinet."

"Where's Dad?" I ask.

"In his study. Like always."

I used to love the storm of his typing, but since Mom left it's been thunderous. So loud and certain I've made a habit of checking his fingertips later to make sure they are not bloodied. In his office are objects gone missing from the kitchen. Plates with hardened goo coating their surface—evidence of a yellow yolk or the sugar red of ketchup. Glasses and mugs with dime-deep liquids drying in them.

"It takes a whole army to get his attention when he's

writing," I complain. "Why does he use that stupid type-writer? He could get something quieter."

"It's romantic. He says he'll buy me one when I get my GED."

"Why would you want that?"

"I just told you! Romantic. I'm going to mark us and it's our secret. You should be glad he's busy and won't notice what we are up to."

"What do you mean 'mark'?"

"Like a tattoo."

"That sounds ouch."

"We need to *mark* this day."

"Why?" I ask, but even as I ask, I'm standing on a kitchen chair to retrieve the bottle of gin from the cupboard.

"It's the first step of my plan. Now shut up and take a gulp. It'll help with the pain."

Sometimes we sneak sips from the liquor bottles. Our parents never seem to notice. I like the way it makes my insides warm. It only takes a few gulps to make things seem fine. On a few occasions, we snuck a bottle out to the quarry and drank until we got silly.

"Here." I hand the bottle to B.B. She takes the hot spoon to the sink and pours gin over it.

I'm still standing on the chair when I feel B.B. tug down my shorts and press the spoon into my left leg. The pain is sharp and sudden, and I suck in my breath, counting as B.B. taught me: *One Mississippi, two Mississippi, three Mississippi* . . . At four, the spoon is gone. B.B. is already reheating the spoon for her own thigh.

"Put some ice on it." B.B. nods at my skin, harsh with pink. I leap from the chair and try not to let the canvas of my shorts brush up against the burn, but this is difficult. I put a cube of ice in a kitchen towel and hold it to the wound.

The scar will be small, a crescent moon no bigger than a fingernail on the upper thigh of my left leg. Its edges are blistering.

B.B. drops her own shorts and holds it to her thigh without even a flinch. Toast whines and hops, launching himself up to our knees and down again to get us to stop what we are doing and pick him up.

"There, now we can't be separated," B.B. says proudly. "We will always be linked. The identifiable Volt sisters. Like a birthmark. The day of your birth! We are twins now. Born together."

I jump down off the chair, and B.B. wraps her arms around my neck. "I love you, B.B., but you're weird," I say. "Where's my present?"

"Upstairs," B.B. says. "With Dad."

We are not allowed to interrupt him when he is working.

"But . . ."

"I've arranged everything, little sister. Trust me."

B.B. grabs my hand and we head for the stairs. Banging up them in a way that would usually make our father holler, "Girls! Girls! Be quiet, girls!"

"We're coming in!" B.B. calls to Dad.

He swivels in his desk chair and smiles at us. The desk is cluttered with glasses and discarded shells of sunflower seeds.

Toast has hobbled up the long staircase behind us, but he stays standing at the study door as if a gate separates him from the room.

"Come on in, Toast. Meet Daddy," I say, but Toast will not come.

I think of the bumpety ghosts in the walls and know they are strongest when our father is working. Slamming about, trying to disrupt our father's thoughts. Toast is smart for staying out.

"Now, why are you girls interrupting me?!" he says, feigning anger.

"It's a very special day, Daddy," B.B. says. "Remember?"

"Is it my birthday?" Dad strokes his chin and looks perplexed.

"It's Henrie's birthday, Daddy! She's fourteen. It's gonna be the best year ever. It's gonna be her year of discovery."

"Henrie who?" he teases.

B.B. stands on her toes and points both her fingers at the top of my head.

"My birthday," I say.

"What? Whose birthday?" He puts his hands behind his ears.

"Mine!" I say a bit louder.

"I'm confused. Is it your birthday, B.B.?"

"Daddy! It's my birthday!" I can't help but giggle. Our father has eyes flecked with the blue B.B. and I inherited, and when he's happy and looking at me directly, I feel like I am sitting on the lakeshore looking out at the blue-green water.

"Your birthday? Yours? Huh. I'm pretty sure you were born in July."

"It *is* July!"

"Daddy," B.B. says, "quit teasing. Give her the present."

He walks to his bookshelf. I cannot see what he's reaching for, but I might know, and I feel nervous, wanting so badly to be right.

"Well, since I forgot it was your birthday, I don't really have anything for you. I guess I'll just have to give you something of mine. Let me see here. . . .

"All I have is this old camera." He holds his 35 mm with a red ribbon tied around it. It's the one thing he never lets us touch. He takes it on his island walks. "I don't suppose you'd want it?"

"Serious?" I want it more than I ever even knew.

"It's for you, my girl." From his pockets he pulls two rolls of black-and-white film.

"Thank you!" I say and throw my arms around him.

"Time for you to be an artist." He smooths my hair.

Olivia Rose was a sculptor. She liked to work with nature best and could make anything emerge from the center of a rock just by slowly shaving away the outside. Her sculptures still litter the island. We find them sometimes, unexpectedly. B.B. wants to write, like our dad. My mom is a builder, which is art. I want to be a photographer.

The camera is heavy. I hold it to my eye. The lens sets a frame that makes the day, the year, the news, manageable.

"Come here," Dad says. He is sitting on the pea-green couch, patting the cushion next to him. "Let me show you how to load it."

I already know. Ms. Sonia has let me use her camera on numerous occasions, but I let my daddy show me. He opens the back of the camera, and a folded piece of notebook paper falls out.

"It's the next clue," B.B. says, snatching it up for me. "You can read it in just a sec."

"You have to thread the film carefully to not waste any frames. There you go." He lets me shut the back of the camera myself once the film is loaded. "Now, once you take both rolls, I will pay to get them developed. If you still want to take pictures after that, I will give you all the darkroom equipment I have."

"Really?" I feel almost breathless.

"Really."

I imagine us in the darkroom, talking for hours, thinking about art, making it. "I'll make good pictures. You'll see."

"We'll make sure you know what you're doing before the summer is up."

And there it is. The end point.

As if B.B. can feel the dread in me rising, she says, "Read the note, quick! Our next stop is almost here." She presses the note into my palm, and I unfold it to find a short clue.

"'The sisters loved to eat off-island foods. Star-shaped fruits, grape leaves stuffed with rice, pickles to make your face go sour, and bars of chili chocolate to set their throats on fire.'"

On cue, Toast begins to bark. A car door opens and slams outside.

My heart thumps in my chest, and for one glorious moment I know it is my mom and that she has been gone all this time because she went out into the real world to bring me back all my favorite things. She would be the best present I could get, better than the camera, better than the dog. B.B. would know that. B.B. would make it happen.

I see the glance that flashes between B.B. and Dad. My heart sinks down sad into my stomach.

"Henrie?" a voice calls up to the house. It is not my mother's. I rush down the stairs toward the front door.

Ms. Sonia covers her squinting eyes with her hand as

she looks up at me. We hug awkwardly. She kisses the top of my head, then scowls at Toast in my arms. "That dog stinks."

"He's my present. From B.B."

"He looks a bit used." She laughs, ruffles my hair. "And you look a bit sad for a birthday girl."

I shrug.

"Fourteen! It's a special day, no time for worry." She takes my face in her hands, staring into my eyes as if my mom is inside of me in a real and physical way. She leans in to whisper in my ear, "I can't tell you where she is, but I promise your mother's okay."

I pull back. She's not lying. She is waiting for me to accept what she's said. I nod.

"Now where's James?" The question is rhetorical. Ms. Sonia knows Dad's inside. "I bought you guys some goodies. Made a special off-island trip just for you, my girl." Then back in her whisper she adds, "And your mom helped me remember all your favorites."

"So, it's kind of from her too," I whisper back.

"Absolutely."

And the joy is back, filling my chest, making my legs want to hop and run and leap. *I love you, Mama.*

B.B. comes forward to help carry in bag after bag. Ripe strawberries and blood oranges. Cashews and yogurt pretzels and green leafy vegetables like small green bouquets of flowers. Fancy chocolate and my favorite kind of potato chips.

I think of how my mom sometimes says, "Remember, Henrie, it doesn't take so much effort to be happy. Even when things are horrible, happiness can come on sudden."

"Does your father know about the dog?" Ms. Sonia asks as she unpacks a bag.

"Yes, he says it's fine."

"Good. Come here. I have your next clue." She hands me a tightly folded piece of paper.

I read, "'Eileen and Elizabeth—their great-great-aunt and -grandmother—were the original island heroes, and the reason the island had a Main Street, where groceries could be bought, letters could be mailed, and treasures could be exchanged. Deep in the dark of the thrifted treasure chest were back rooms of books, used and new, of which the youngest Volt had once swore she'd read every word. Within the shelves and shelves of browning books on which lives unstrung themselves, the littlest Volt would find love.'

"The bookstore!" I holler, looking up at Ms. Sonia. B.B.'s tiny smile tells me I'm right.

I lead the way with Toast at my heels, B.B. quickly catching up. We race past tourists in rocking chairs on rented porches, maps spread wide on their laps.

We run past the now-defunct Fantasy Land—a place that could never decide what it wanted to be, part haunted house, and part putt-putt course. We run past the diner and the ice cream shop and into Island Thrift.

The back rooms are wall-to-wall books; a small sign above the curtained doorway says THE PANTRY.

Mr. Cooper knows it is us. "Good morning, girls!"

We shout a greeting back and are past the curtain and into the must of ink and pages. It is dark—the windows are covered with newsprint so that the books won't fade any further.

My chest is tight from running when B.B. says, "Don't be mad."

A figure steps out from the back, and my heart slams to a halt. It's Joshua, walking toward me.

"Henrietta Volt," he says. There's a lift in his voice as if he's glad to see me.

"Are you my clue?" I ask, and immediately wish I hadn't.

"Do you need help?"

"No."

He looks good, different. He's holding a pile of books. "You work here?"

"Summer job. Mr. Cooper thought I could help him get the place organized."

He's wearing a small golden name tag clipped to the left side of his shirt that says CLARENCE. He sees my look. "Sometimes I'm Tod. Or Larry. Sadly, none of the tags say Joshua."

I love this bookstore. I love closing my eyes in the fiction room and imagining the dialogue stuck between the spines of each book. They talk to me, these books, whispering into my ears just like our Quarry Hollow ghosts, teasing stories that make me pick them up and take them home. Even now I can hear the clamor of all those characters. But Joshua's being here changes all of that. I feel my face flush and am glad for the dark space.

"Is that your dog?" he asks.

I'd forgotten about Toast, hiding small and stinky behind my ankles. "My sister found him."

"B.B.?" I notice she's disappeared. And I don't like the way he says her name, as if he's picturing her, liking the different pieces of her even as I'm standing here alone.

"It's my birthday," I say too loudly. "My father gave me this camera." I weave my arm out of the strap and hold it out. "It's the one he always uses for his nature walks. It's mine now though, and I'm going to be a famous photographer."

"Famous?" He finds a rare empty spot where he can put his books down. "Can I see?"

I hand the camera to him.

He points it at the floor, at a pile of books. Focuses and refocuses. He lands on my face. "You have beautiful eyes," he says and snaps a photo.

"My sister is the pretty one," I blurt.

Joshua lowers the lens and hands me back my camera. "She's pretty but she's not prettier."

The compliment feels so good, taking the warmth from my face and spreading it down into my body. I grab his hand and kiss his cheek. I have to stand on my toes. Behind me, Toast barks at us—once, twice.

Then I turn on my heels, dashing out of the dark store and into the sun. B.B. is waiting and all I can do is grin at her. I know I'll be embarrassed later, but right now, I feel brave and proud and loved.

B.B. grabs both my hands and pulls me to her. "Did you do it? Did you erase my kiss with yours?"

I nod, gleeful.

"Happy fourteenth, Henrie!" B.B. shouts so that the street will hear. "Ready to hear my plan?"

We are running again, my big sister leading us to a new spot.

In the cemetery, we sprawl over bodies above Olivia Rose's grave. The sun shines hot on our faces, burning our retinas. We hold hands—my right in her left. The grass underneath us itches my bare skin.

"Want me to tell you more of the story?" B.B. asks.

I nod my yes, my head rocking up and down against the grass.

"The fabulous girl magicians were also descendants of the infamous and stupendously terrible Seth Volt. A man who arrived on island with nothing except the name of his family's excavation business, his massive ego, and his crippling fear of open water. He crossed Lake

Erie only once, and he did it with his eyes shut as a storm rocked the boat that had agreed to carry him. As he crossed, the boat filled until he and the sad old fisherman who'd agreed to take him were up to their britches in storm water and fang-toothed walleye.

"Egged on by his own stupid survival—he was too much of a baby to possibly cross the lake again—Seth began excavating limestone and building an enormous house on the edge of his newly minted quarry. The house was meant to woo Elizabeth Fowler and drag her away from her sister, Eileen. She was beautiful, our Great-Great-Grandma Elizabeth. A tall woman with blond hair and blue eyes. She always said what she meant. She warned him of the island monster, and of the absurdity of arriving in a new world only to immediately dig a hole aimed at its heart. Maybe if Eileen had been with Elizabeth that day, or if there hadn't been something like an electric current that flashed between Elizabeth and Seth, he would not have been so successful at winning over Elizabeth and then her father, making them both realize the island could or should be dominated."

"This story is too sad," I say, interrupting B.B.'s reverie.

"This island is sad." In B.B.'s voice, I hear that she is, deep down, scared. "Ms. Sonia says a male heir always has to live in Quarry Hollow. A male. That means not you and not me."

I squint at her. Light surrounds her hair like a halo,

and it's hard to see her eyes. "Those are all just stories," I say.

"We can't stay here, Henrie. We are stronger than our ancestors . . . stronger than my mom or your mom, but we have to convince Dad and Carrie that it's time to leave. Break the curse."

"Leave?" I have a bad feeling in my tummy at that word. It feels heavy and then sharp, pushing against my skin from the inside, pulling me to the island. I groan. It feels loud, odd in the brightness of the day, but B.B. doesn't seem to hear it.

"We are going to pretend that the island tried to eat us too!" B.B. says.

"I don't understand what you're on about," I say, trying to act like this is all still part of the game we've been playing for my birthday and that my body isn't aching, as if it is being stretched apart.

B.B. sits up on her elbow. Her silhouette blocks the sun and she is a dark shadow over me. I still cannot make out the contours of her face, and I wish she was still holding my hand.

"I've thought a lot about this. We'll jump. From the highest point! And then play dead when we hit the water. It'll be easy to make it look like we hit the rocks. I know how we can carry something on us that will turn the water red, and you are excellent at holding your breath. We can make it so Daddy is there, so he saves us. He'll know we have to go if the quarry tries to get us."

"But the island would never hurt us," I say.

"Henrie," she says, "you know it already has."

"I do not know that."

"Where do you go at night?" she asks. "I wake up and you aren't in your bed. What about those blisters on the bottoms of your feet, remember those? They were fucking gross, like you burnt them somehow."

"It's summer," I say weakly. "We love summer."

"Something is happening, Henrie. We have to plan our escape. You get that, right?"

I can hear in her voice that she is serious. That she is excited about her plan. That she is certain in a way I am not. I do not want to fight with her. Not on my birthday.

"Sure. I get it."

"Good. Thank god. So here is my plan." She is impatient with me but also too thrilled by her idea to notice that I am lying, playing along just to keep the day going. I know in my heart that I will never leave this island. It is my home. "We know the quarry better than anyone ever. We can figure out how to jump without hitting the rocks. We'll jump together, and when they save us, we can act disoriented, scared. Not ourselves. They'll know the island has turned. We'll get out. You. Me. Daddy. Carrie. My mom."

"Your mom?"

"Maybe," B.B. says. "Do you think we can take her?"

"Toast?" I ask.

"Toast can come." B.B.'s voice is stern now. "Henrie, this is gonna work. We won't be separated, and we'll break the Fowler Island curse. It's had a hold on our family for generations. I'm gonna get us out. Jailbreak Volt-sister-style!"

She reaches down and begins to tickle me, but her fingernails are too sharp in my armpits and under my chin. I sit up quickly, pull my shirt down. I try to laugh. I try to tickle back. I try to pretend that I am normal, that something fundamental hasn't changed, but I'm angry. I push too hard, dig my fingernails into her upper arms. The tickling quickly turns into wrestling. Me rolling over her and then her over me. She thinks it's still a game, but that anger writhes beneath my skin. I can feel it wanting to wrap its arms around her. Hurt her.

Finally, I dig my teeth into B.B.'s forearm. I stop before I break skin and the anger eases off.

"Ouch!" she yells. "Jesus!"

We pull apart. She points at her arm. I see the delicate shape of teeth. My teeth.

"Sorry," I mumble.

We've wrestled our way under the old cemetery elm. I can see my sister's features now. Her need for me to agree. Her hope and love and excitement. She is my everything.

"This is the plan," she says. "Our best bet. Are you in?"

"I'm in," I say, quiet as I can.

"Say it again!" she shouts.

"I'm in!" I scream so it tears at my throat.

✦ 12 ✦

carrie

1989

I stepped back onto Fowler yesterday, after weeks away. I missed my Henrie's birthday by a week, and yet she forgave me instantly, like I hadn't done anything wrong. Her forgiveness made me feel worse.

Yesterday, like today, the sun was high, the island green. The morning could have been mistaken for beautiful. I walked from the ferry to the house—the tourists ignored me, but the islanders stared. They are connected, the islanders, like the invasive honeysuckle that chokes out all the other ground cover on the island. They whisper about me, about how I never belonged here, and send their secrets underground through their interwoven roots. With each step, I felt myself sinking, falling below the surface of things. The closer I got to the bottom—to the twined roots—the more the likelihood of me ever being strong enough to swim back up lessened. I kept walking anyway, pushed myself deeper in, deeper down.

"Be safe!" I shout as the girls pound out into the island this morning. A silly thing to say—as if they won't be careful if they aren't specifically told. What I really mean is "I love you." And I do love them. Both of them. We slept in the quarry last night, just the three of us, to make up for the birthday tradition I missed. It makes my womb ache to look at them, my body missing a time when we were one. Sometimes I think it remembers B.B. just as much as Henrie. An impossibility, I know, except I *have* felt B.B.'s body grow as it curled into mine, resting in my arms instead of my belly, stretching up so that her head knocks the bottom of my chin when I pull her close. They can't feel that longing in me. It doesn't translate or leave the body, and I know, in addition to that, I've held it too close. B.B. does not know all the ways in which I count her mine.

Fowler has a way of making me pick at myself, dig at my skin and poke at my flesh. It is as if my body is the house I'm trying to renovate. I am stuck forever in the demolition phase. A dangerous place to be when the house is made of flesh and hair and blood and bone. You can dig only so deep before the structure is too weakened to ever suffer repairs.

I am allergic to this place, or maybe it is allergic to me. The soil, the sun, the rock, and sand. It rejects me. The same is not true for Henrie and B.B. They are islanders, like the rest, and on that walk from ferry to house, I realized the faulty nature of my plan. What if my girls cannot be plucked from this place? Sonia and James are like this. Stubbornly rooted. Maybe, when they say they can't leave, it isn't metaphorical or emotional. Rip them up and they will die.

The arrangement with James was this: Henrie would live with me, and B.B. would stay here, with him. Biologically it makes sense, and Sonia promises to keep educating B.B., not just about the island but about all things until B.B. earns her GED. The plan was that James or Sonia would put Henrie on the ferry, so I would never have to step foot on Fowler again. I'd simply wait in Marblehead to pick her up, and we'd drive south to the small apartment I've rented. B.B. could, of course, visit anytime, but she'd have her father and her island, and she'd be fine. I told myself that a lot. How fine she'd be.

But then I couldn't sleep. Not for several nights. Then a week went by as I sat alone in the dark worrying, thinking. Until I was blacking out, losing time more than I was sleeping, and I knew that the only way to rest would be to go back for both girls—my Henrie and my B.B.—no matter what James said. They were both coming with me.

The girls were happy to see me walk up the driveway. They squealed and nearly knocked me over. Or at least Henrie did. B.B. hung back at first, and James took one look at me and went inside. I had formed a hundred arguments, things I would shout at him in anger, and the things he might shout back, but he has yet to come out of his office.

With the girls gone, the house yawns around me. I imagine the walls stretching, pushing back from one another until they bow and bend into a new shape, accommodating the returned rock of my body.

"Fuck you," I say to the empty hallway, the stairs on my right, and the heavy front doors that swung shut only minutes ago behind Beatrice and Henrietta, sealing me in.

I picture myself swimming to the surface—a ship capsized but whole, ready to be righted. I will not be swallowed.

"One. Two. Three." I turn on the pads of my feet and walk toward the kitchen, counting until I find air. I've gotten them out of the house. "Four. Five." I have a plan. "Six. Seven. Eight." The studs crackle in this house. Like a child's cereal drenched with milk. It's one of the things I used to love about an old house. Its clatter. The ways in which its settling tells the story of everyone who came before. This house, however, makes me crazy. The floor tilts side to side along the passageway. At the far end is the deep shadow of the kitchen, a huge bulky space with a dark doorway waiting to pull me in.

I go willingly, and once in the kitchen, I start making coffee.

I crush the pills left over from my procedure into a coffee mug, add a seventh, grind them into powder, waiting for water to boil.

The girls were wild with me gone, their unbathed bodies messy with dirt, marked with the festival of my abandonment. Earlier today, when B.B. leaned in to Henrie's ear to whisper her secret, their faces disappeared behind a mutual mane of tangled hair—a joined ecosystem that only confirmed for me that I can't take one and not the other.

This morning, after breakfast, I handed them each a twenty-dollar bill. "Don't come home until evening."

"Can we buy ice cream?" Henrie asked.

"If that's what you want."

"With toppings?"

"With toppings."

"Can we go to the candy store?"

"Buy all the junk you want and maybe some new markers and construction paper. Make something while you are out and about."

"We aren't little fucking kids anymore," B.B. blurted. Then her cheeks went red, as if she'd just broken whatever promise she'd made to herself not to be mean to me.

We stared at each other for a long time after that. "I know, Beatrice." Her eyes looked too blue, not dulled at all by the dark of the house, not flinching away. I knew then that James had told them that we planned to separate them.

"What if we want to buy something for Toast?" Henrie said. "A toy, maybe, or a treat."

"That's fine, but I want you to go to Miss Rose's

Butterfly House. Rent bicycles or one of those golf carts. Make a day of it. Don't come back until dark. And then knock. Wait for me to answer."

"Is it a special project?" Henrie looked excited. "Like a surprise?"

Before I could answer, B.B. leaned in, whispered into Henrie's ear for far too long.

I suddenly wanted to hiss at B.B., *It'll happen to you too. You'll be in your thirties and sad, your loneliness a cage built up around you. You'll have grown things inside of you that never even asked if they could come in.* I felt a distaste for B.B., whispering under the surface of my skin, like the island was trying to convince me I didn't want her.

"We need more money," Henrie announced after B.B. was done whispering.

I handed each girl another twenty. Watched them leave.

Now, in the kitchen, I pour water over coffee grounds, dump in the powder, and stir before letting it set.

It's been hot these past nights—hotter than usual for July—and I slept with the girls in the quarry last night. We layered the blankets up underneath us, but even with all those layers, the limestone made for an impossible bed. The skin of the quarry pushing up into my hip bones, my spine. I thought it was the house that scared me most, but it's not. I am most scared of myself.

I woke up by that pond just before dawn with a feel-

ing like rock in my belly, as if I'd decided to emulate
Virginia Woolf, only instead of filling my pockets with
stones, I'd filled up my insides, my abdomen full of limestone, the chalk of it still thick in my throat. In my
dreams, I had been on all fours, gnawing at the quarry
walls, digging fingers into the quarry floor so that I could
fill my mouth with island. And some part of it wasn't a
dream, because when I came to, my fingertips were raw,
and my jaw ached. My mouth felt gritty, and my gums
bloodied. Pine needles were stuck to my tongue, having
flossed their way between my molars.

Full pockets or a full stomach, the goal had seemed
the same. I'd planned to walk into the water and sink.
My sleepy brain told me it was the perfect solution—why
hadn't I thought of it before? The heaviness would carry
me lower and lower. There would be no jumping. No
body smashed against rock. No ugliness or drama. I
would simply wade in and let myself go under until I was
so deep in the cold dark that the air would empty out of
my body, and I'd stay down there. Floating below the
reflection of the moon and constellations. It would be so
peaceful. I could feel the steady eternity of it, and I was
so close to stepping in, to giving myself over.

But then I saw something down there in the deep
dark. A shape floated, waved like seaweed. I watched for
longer than I should, the blackness rising until I could see
it was made up of fine, hairlike tendrils that spread out in
the water. Poison. It looked like me. What I would turn

into if I went in. A big inky puddle. Something lonely and hungry and cold, and aching to wrap itself around others, pull them down. I felt a new warmth on my upper lip. A flood of it. Blood, although when I wiped my hand across my nose, my fingers came away that same inky black from the pond. I let the blood run, down my face, the taste of it choking me.

I spent the rest of the night sitting near the girls. Too afraid to get close to them. I did not trust myself.

I depress the plunger on the coffee press and pour James a full mug.

When I was off island, my mind was sharp. I could see it all clearly for the first time in my life. This house. My relationship.

Coffee mugs in hand, I take two stairs at a time, and I swear something rustles close to me. Like the wallpaper is trying to get my attention—I imagine skin being pulled back from an open wound—but it's only my imagination. I do not look. I reach James's office door and knock. There is no invitation to come in, so I shift both mugs to my left hand and twist the old brass doorknob.

James is standing at the window that overlooks the gravel drive. He looks too skinny, his beard too long—touching his sternum—his hair wild even under his faded knit cap. It was once red but now is a rusty orange that boasts at least three holes. I picture little moths eating away at him as he sits at his desk.

"I brought us coffee," I say.

He turns to me, and his pupils are too wide. Big inky puddles.

"You okay?"

He smirks at me, a hurt look that makes me feel as stupid as I am.

"I suppose we should talk," he says, and walks toward me to take his mug.

"You start."

"What do you want to know?" He looks at me steadily, his pupils tightening as I watch, transforming to pinpoints, his irises streaked with yellow.

There are too many questions and too much I don't know and too big a part of me that still wants to ask, *Why don't you love me?* So, I leapfrog over all of it. "I should take Beatrice too. Both girls should come with me."

"Okay."

My heart stops.

He takes his first sip of coffee. He purses his lips in a strange way as he swallows, and for a moment I think he tastes the sedative. I picture the poison threading down his throat. A snake twisting down, down, down—I recall my monstrous self at the bottom of the quarry pond, the tendrils of a dead me—and wonder if I've already gone too far. I fight the urge to warn James. To tell him to spit out the coffee I've given him.

"What did you say?" My brain is too slow.

"Carrie." When we first met, he'd say my name, and it felt like he couldn't believe he'd found me. Later, I thought, he was just trying to remind himself that I wasn't Olivia Rose. "I told the girls. Henrie will go with you and B.B. will stay here. I told them and they can't take it. It will crush them. I saw that when I told them."

"Oh."

"Are you prepared for that?"

"For what?"

"To raise them both?"

"I'll do what needs to be done." I should stop him from drinking the coffee. I thought I'd be met with resistance, but here he is calm, already sedated.

"It's time."

"For what?"

"To get the girls out of here. I've noticed changes."

"What do you mean? Changes in the girls? They're both turning into women, James."

"I don't mean that."

"Then tell me what you actually mean." I hiss my words at him. An old rage coming back. "I was a kid when you met me, James. I fell in love with you so hard. I left New York. Pissed off my parents. Made your life my life, and you never loved me or told me who you really are."

"That's fair," he says, and his calmness makes me angrier.

"Damn right it's fair."

He takes another drink of coffee. "I meant to say, it's almost fair. You know me, Carrie, and even if you don't think that's true, you should know that I loved you. I love

you now, and I swear I didn't know the quarry was pulling at you. Hell, I didn't know it was calling to Olivia
Rose until it was too late."

"You're a liar."

"Why would I lie about any of that?"

"How could you not know I wasn't safe? How could
you think any of us were safe here?"

"Do you really think I would just let these things happen to her, to you, to the girls? I know I was self-absorbed.
Too focused on myself all the damn time, and I regret
it. I wish I could have been more present, I do." He steps
toward me and I flinch, a reaction that surprises him. He
stops. Takes a breath, then a sip of coffee. "Let me ask
you this, Carrie. What's worse? Pretending to love someone before you really do or quitting on someone and
never telling them you've quit?"

He's wrapped both his hands around the coffee mug
and is gripping it tighter and tighter. I worry he will
smash the ceramic, but then he sighs and relaxes,
adding, "People do a lot to hide truths, especially from
themselves. You've been in love with someone else for
years, and you've certainly never told the truth about
that, have you?"

"I never hid my relationship with Sonia."

I remember all the years of silence after we got to the
island. All the times I asked him if he was okay. If something was wrong. If there was something that I could do
to make him smile. All the times he told me he was fine

when I knew he wasn't. All the times he disappeared in the night only to come back dirty and exhausted, unable to function the next day.

"I know you think I kept things from you. But I told Olivia Rose everything. I showed her all of myself, my history. And look what happened."

"What happened, James? You mean she killed herself? Tried to kill her daughter too?"

"She never tried to kill B.B.," he says. He is really angry now. This suggestion is far too much for him. For a moment, I think he will throw his coffee mug at my head, but he calms himself. "She was not on that cliff by choice."

"I shouldn't have said that," I offer.

"Don't say it again."

"Fair enough. . . . How's the coffee?"

"It'll do the trick."

I realize it swiftly and with a punch: *He knows I'm drugging him, and he's letting me do it.* And now the anger leaks out of me.

"It will just make you sleepy."

"I figured." He takes another big drink and moves to the green couch that is so old the velvet arms have worn down to their linen threads. He lies back and puts the mug on his chest, preparing for sleep.

"I didn't want you to stop me." I sit down on the edge of the sofa. My hip touches his hip. "From taking her."

"Do you remember the day you told me you were

pregnant with Henrie?" His question feels like a non sequitur, but I nod that I do. "I was so relieved."

"Relief is a strange reaction to news of a baby, and I don't remember that. I do remember telling you, though." We were in bed. Still in New York City. We'd had sex and taken a nap. Fallen asleep above the covers with sun coming in the window. "You ran away," I say to remind him of reality.

I'd woken first and watched him sleep. He'd never been one to sleep well, but he'd slipped under easily and stayed deep for a good hour. When he'd opened his eyes, the first thing he saw was me, and I'd told him, suddenly having no doubt at all that the baby was a good thing. That feeling had lasted only a second, because as soon as I told him, he'd risen from bed, propping himself up in a sitting position, then blinking before swinging his legs off the bed. He put his pants on and walked out. Left the apartment without a word. I'd spent the day sobbing, and when he came back after dark, he was drunk. Drunk but happy or pretending to be. He told me we needed to get married. We'd raise her on island.

"I never wanted kids. I knew it was irresponsible, me having kids," he says, and I want to ask exactly what he means by this, but he is on the verge of telling me something important, so I don't interrupt. "I'd already broken my promise to myself by having Beatrice, and I thought suddenly that a second baby, Henrietta, would keep Beatrice safe. Sisters are powerful, and Beatrice would no longer have to carry the legacy of my family all on her own. I'll admit that it was easier at the time to think an unnamed, unseen baby could take on the burdens that I didn't want my sweet Beatrice to have to face."

"What burdens, James? Tell me."

"It doesn't matter. I'm just trying to say that I'm sorry I saw Henrie as less than. Even for a second. I saw her as a solution rather than a child, but as soon as I held her, I knew I'd been wrong. I loved her just as much as I loved Beatrice. I saw myself in her too. Like looking in a mirror. I love them. Both my girls. The island has always been jealous of them."

"I don't understand you, James."

"Maybe the island would still demand to come first, but I would have loved the new baby too. If you hadn't gotten rid of it."

"Don't start," I say, meaning it.

"Do you remember the first time you saw Quarry Hollow?"

I do remember. I remember how huge it looked. How clean the windows appeared. I could see clearly inside all the way from the road. The water was still in my ears from the ferry and the sun was high in the sky. The whole place felt like magic.

"I saw it the same way that day. It had been a long time since I'd seen it that way. You helped make me feel things were possible again. That's a kind of love, isn't it?"

"I guess."

James peers at me through shutting eyes. "I see now that I need to do this alone. A new baby certainly won't fix it. You did right. You and the girls need to leave and never come back. I'll make sure the house is left to the state. When I go. Not the girls."

"Is that even realistic?"

"I'm doing my best, Carrie. No matter what you think of me, please know I've tried. And whatever you have to do, I'm so sorry I can't help."

A strange sound comes out of me then. Almost a sob. Not quite a hiccup. The surprise of this generosity.

"I love them, James. Both of them."

"I know," he says, and I swear there is peace on his face. "I trust you."

I met James in Manhattan, an entirely different kind of island. His new book of poetry was not his first or his last but certainly his best. The lore surrounding him, his island in Lake Erie and his motherless baby daughter, traveled to Manhattan long before he arrived. I was nineteen and totally out of love with my parents and my fancy school. My world felt too small. I went to his reading, then followed him back to his hotel. The next morning when he stumbled out into sunlight for cigarettes, I was waiting outside the bodega. He looked at me and went pale. I knew I looked like his dead wife. I'd seen the photos.

I lied. Told him I was older than I was. I was pregnant with Henrie within weeks, and I was on my way to the island. James was waiting on the porch; Beatrice at two standing straight up and down next to him, her left hand in his and her right holding on to the big, beautiful, clear-eyed house.

"Thank you, Carrie. For loving me. For taking care of my girls."

"James." I say his name one more time, but he has gone under. Happily submitted, and it is hard to look at this tired man on an old green couch about to lose his family and know that I am doing the right thing.

I take the mug from his hands and shut his office door behind me. I stand at the top of the stairs. A hollow. I don't trust my legs to make it down, and I remind myself of why I'm fleeing. I think about the mornings I found him on the floor of his office, his breath smelling of booze but under that something worse. That islandy-death smell, like he'd swallowed the bloat of a rotting walleye or something worse. The missing girls. How often I thought he might know something. The blood under his fingernails. If there had ever been a body, a found girl—alive or dead—I might have turned him in, but in this house with its stubborn walls and talking shadows, I always felt so unsure. So confused and malleable and afraid.

I hear a car in the driveway and hold tight to the railing, making my way downstairs.

Sonia is in her old Chevy Silverado and stepping out onto the gravel before I've made it off the porch.

When James found out about us, he told me I was being manipulative. That Sonia was lonely, and I was preying on her. I told him he was wrong. I ran to Sonia and told her I loved her. Declared it like I couldn't hold it in anymore, and in that moment it became exactly what James had accused it of being. A big, awful lie.

"You're back," she says. I can see that she wants to hug me, but she holds back, as if touching would be painful, and in her voice there is a question, an unsaid *Will you be staying?* She doesn't ask, but the hope is in her, a small spark of it even though she knows it's an impossible idea, so I speak as quickly as I can.

"He says I can take them. Both girls." It's a kindness, offering something that makes my intention clear but doesn't humiliate her.

"Both? That's wonderful." Sonia swallows the word *wonderful*, the *ful* part barely leaving her mouth as she realizes how false it is. "Do the girls know yet?"

"No, I sent them off for the day with that musty dog. How did you know I was back?" I know the answer. I picture the various eyes of the islanders watching me yesterday as I walked off the ferry and down Division.

"Grapevine," Sonia says. "And the dog's name is Toast." She moves to the back of her truck. I hear the squeak of the tailgate. "You'll take him too?"

"Of course," I say, but in truth I haven't thought about it. I don't even know if the building allows pets. "What are you doing?"

"We lost another girl last night."

"What do you mean?" I ask, but I can see by the tightness of her shoulders, the grim line of her mouth, that someone new has gone missing. Sonia has always spared me the details, but I know she's head of the Island Council. I know they watch the island, monitoring the history of the disappearances.

"A guest that checked into the Island Inn yesterday left her room after midnight and never came back. Got the call this morning that her bed was found empty, and the front door of the inn was left wide open. We found her sandals and her skirt at the quarry cliffs."

"I was there last night," I say too quickly. I can picture the skirt blowing in the wind. "The girls and I slept in the quarry."

"Where was James?"

"I don't know. His office, I guess."

Sonia nods her head sagely. "We cleaned blood off of the rocks this morning."

"Jesus."

"Also, I found something in the archives."

She rolls out plans, blueprints it looks like, for Quarry Hollow.

"Where did you get these?" I put my hand on the paper, feeling the age and brittleness of it. I recognize the lines of the front porch and how it wraps the front of the house, disappearing around the sides. Sonia flips the page, and the next rendering is of the interior, the first floor. The basic rooms are there: living room, front room, kitchen, music room.

She points with her forefinger to the first-floor hallway.

"What am I supposed to notice?" I ask.

"There is a huge space under the stairs. No entry. No closet."

"What do you think is in there?" Sonia has my full attention.

"Now look at the second story," Sonia says, flipping the page. "Normal, right?"

"That looks accurate," I say. Four bedrooms on the second floor. A fifth that has now become a bathroom. She turns the page again, and we are looking at the third floor, where the turret juts out above the quarry and the unfinished section of the attic stretches out dark and skeletal.

She turns to squint at me. "Do you see it?"

I want to nod, but I don't know what I'm looking at.

"The ceiling in the attic doesn't match the pitch of the roof," she says. "You know how when you are up there, the ceiling is curved?" The attic spaces are finished. The ceiling is a beautiful oak that curls slow and round away from the spinal ridge of the roof. Quite a feat of architecture, that attic. The otherwise straight boards manipulated into shapely curves.

"You're right," I say and think about all the noises the house makes. The creaking and moaning and shifting. I always thought of that attic as the rib cage of the great big beast of a house. "It makes no sense. There looks like there is a ton of unused space between the pitch of the actual roof and the ceiling Seth Volt constructed. Why would he do that?"

"Why would he do anything? And let's not forget that there are stories about how he kept Elizabeth locked up there, and *she* was the one to finish the attic," Sonia says.

I think of the unforgiving plaster and the way it all crumbles and fades whenever I try to update it. Like its own failing organ. "Regardless of who did what, are you saying these are all purposefully hidden spaces?" I shudder at the thought. A vague image of people living in the house, pushing back at my nails, pressing their bodies to the walls, the heat of them permeating, sweating through wallpaper.

"Seth Volt built the house to win over Elizabeth, and then he imprisoned her in it. I've always wondered if there were secret storage spaces, especially in the attic, where she spent the remainder of her life."

I turn back to look at the house. A weathered structure but solid as anything. Huge and thick, throwing a shadow over the whole damn island.

"You think James knows about this?" I think of that old story—"Bluebeard's Wives." How the wife is warned to never look in that one room, and when she does, she finds the bodies of the wives that came before her. James never told me not to look. It isn't the same.

"Is he inside?" she asks, and I can see there are a million things she's not saying.

My face immediately goes red, the heat of it too much to not notice.

"I drugged him," I whisper.

"You what?"

"I gave him pills, okay! I thought he'd never let me take B.B. so I gave him something, and then I was going to pack up and get the girls out of here tonight. Don't judge me."

"Carrie," she says, suddenly so serious. She wraps her hand around my wrist and squeezes. "You were gonna take the girls, both of them, without telling James? Or me?"

I step closer to Sonia. She has a cowlick at the back of her head, a sweet spot where the hair will not lie flat. I reach out and touch it, smooth it down with my hand. We stare at each other. Eye to eye.

"You could come with us." This is not the first time I've asked her.

"This is my home," she says and clears her throat. "And I need your help before you go. We probably won't find anything, and it will just be a therapeutic send-off of sorts." She hops up into the back of her truck and pulls forward a sledgehammer. She hops out and opens the passenger-side door, pulls out an ax I've seen her use to clear a tree from the road after a storm or honeysuckle vines from a forest path.

"Here," Sonia says, handing me the ax. "Let's bust it open. See what's inside."

I test the weight of the ax in my hands. The wooden handle feels smooth, the dark metal of its head dumb with heaviness. I can feel the way it will swing. The twist that will begin in my shoulders and wind me up as it moves down to my lower back. The splash the tool will make as it hits plaster, sinking in to make hole after hole after hole. The house whimpering, bleeding, begging.

"I know where to start." A sudden grin is on my face.

✣ 13 ✣

henrietta

1989

didn't think she'd ever let us go. We've got big things to do today, Henrie. Big things," B.B. says, but her usual authority isn't there. She's been weird all day. The skin under her eyes looks all plumped up and purple, and she's been chewing on her lower lip so much it's gone bloody on the right side. It keeps trying to scab up, but she won't let it. It's kind of gross, and I'm tired of telling her she has blood on her chin, so I'm just not gonna say it anymore. I've also asked her about a hundred times what's wrong. She says "Nothing" or "I'm just tired," and I hate that too. She's lying, and I just want to be with my mom today, who also doesn't look good, but no one is telling me anything about why that might be, and Dad won't come out of his stupid office. Even Toast is acting wrong, like he's hurt his ribs somehow, because whenever I go to pet him, he growls a little like he might nip at me or something. I keep searching for a wound, but he won't let me get ahold of him long enough to really look. It all makes me wish I could just disappear, but then I feel guilty for wanting to be gone from them, so here I am doing nothing at all that I want to do, letting my sister act like things are the horrible same even though I know damn well they are not, and honestly, I'm getting a little angry about all of it.

"We should talk to Mom before we do anything else," I say.

"We have to practice. It's dangerous, and we're out of time. Tonight is the night," B.B. says.

"Wait. What?" I ask. Panic rears up in me.

"*The* plan," she whispers, then blinks a whole bunch of times, like a whole bunch—it's what she does when she just doesn't get how another person could possibly be so dumb. "To get us off island, as a family. I told you all of this."

"Yeah. Like once. I didn't know we were doing it for sure."

We're sitting on the curb in front of the dairy bar with our butts on the sidewalk and our feet in the street. It's way too early for ice cream—the Tastee Freez wasn't even open yet, but Mr. Grote was prepping for the day and made us free cones—"breakfast cones" he called them. We both got the same thing—chocolate dip with zebra ice cream. I don't even like the dip. It's that kind that hardens right away and tastes like plastic, but B.B.

insisted we get the most for our money, which doesn't even make sense because we got them for free, but whatever. B.B. is eating her dip in small smooth chunks without any trouble, but mine has cracked, splintered by some kind of earthquake, and big waxy bits of chocolate keep hitting the blacktop. It's making me feel super-grumpy and kind of ugly, like I'm some big toad who can't even eat ice cream properly. The only good bit is that Toast keeps eating the dropped bits, then looking at me with such joy and expectation that I just want to go ahead and drop the whole thing.

"I don't even understand the plan," I say. It's a lie. I get the plan, but I've been trying to work up the nerve to tell B.B. I want to adjust it. "And I don't feel good. I don't want to do anything tonight."

I haven't felt good for days. Sleep has been superbad. The other night I woke up with my feet all messed up—my ankles scratched like I'd been running through rocks. Plus, when I woke up, I wasn't in my bunk anymore. I was on the third floor, all curled up in the turret room, and for a minute, I thought I was gonna puke. Like I had something huge in my belly that needed to get born.

I take a big bite right off the top of my ice cream like the big old lying toad that I am, and the whole thing, ice cream and dumb waxy shell, topples off, spreading out like a broken egg between my two feet. Toast is on it before I can consider scooping any of it back up.

"Chocolate is bad for dogs," B.B. says, then takes a delicate bite from her ice cream.

I am done pretending not to be grumpy. "Mom is home now, and no one has brought up the divorce thing since Dad was all half-asleep and weird, so I don't think we even need a *plan*."

"Are you kidding me with this?" B.B. asks. She's squinting at me, her lip pulled up on the right, as if it's hoping disgust will reach right on up her nostril and into her brain.

"I'm not kidding, B.B. I'm tired of all this."

"Of what exactly are you tired?" B.B.'s adult tone is meant to make me feel even more like a little kid. I'm *not* a little kid.

I throw my empty cake cone into the street. It doesn't go far before it starts rolling back to me, and Toast pounces on it, fitting the whole thing in his mouth. It is gone immediately, like it was never there.

"Henrie." B.B. says my name all serious.

"What?"

"She's *packing*. Why else would Carrie want us out of the house for the whole day?"

It hits me so hard and sour that I can't breathe. I try, I do, but a wheezy noise comes out and is sucked right back in again. I try again, and this time the same noise happens but shorter and squeakier and with less air involved. The island moves under my feet, shudders and shakes. I look to see if B.B. feels it, but she is steady. The island is not talking to her.

"Put your head between your knees. Do it now."

I do it. I see the asphalt. The paling black of it, and how it is made up of millions of tiny pebbles all glued together by tar. All those little bumps laid flat. How many times did they roll over this, push it down, so that it would be one smooth thing? Over and over and over. Smash and cram.

"Breathe. In and out. In four. Out four." B.B. counts for me. I don't want it to work. I want to keep the panic until I run out of air. If I died, I would never have to leave. They'd dig me a big old island hole and sink me deep with a rock on my chest, then, when B.B. died, they could drop her down right on top of me with another rock on top to keep us both floating down there in the warmth of the island.

"I need you," I whimper. The *I need you* is so small and pathetic and true that I say it again and again and again. "I need you. IneedyouIneedyou."

"Shhhhh. I know. Henrietta. I know. I need you too. And I won't let you go. We'll stick together. I promise. You just have to trust me. We can go to the quarry this afternoon and practice. You are supergood at holding your breath, and I've figured out just how to jump so that we don't hit any rocks."

"From the top?"

"The very top."

"You've done that?"

"Well, no. But I have it all mapped out. Wilde helped, and it's physics really."

"You told Wilderness about our plan?"

"No! I mean, no. I told him I wanted to know if you could jump from the top and not die. He just helped me figure out all the calculations and stuff. He was really nice about it."

"B.B.! Don't mess with Wilde. He's a nice guy. Sweet."

"What? I didn't do anything. I didn't touch him. And why can't I have a sweet guy? I'm sweet."

"You are *not* sweet," I say, and it makes her laugh.

"Listen, we can use some time this afternoon to knock the sharp spot off that one big rock, but even if we didn't do that, it is still totally possible to jump and not die. Who knows the quarry pond better than us? And I'll be the one to jump. Just me. You get to save me!"

"No way. What if you get hurt? For real hurt." My breath is coming even and steady and the sun is high and bright on my head. My blond hair shining. Her blue eyes are lit up in that same sun.

"It'll be safe," B.B. assures me. "We'll practice the jump today after we prep the area. If you and Dad save me and Carrie sees that, and we tell them the island made me do it, and then I say I jumped 'cause I can't bear to live without you—which, by the way, is true—we can work on making them like each other again. We can do this, but you'll have to be superbrave tonight."

"I can do it." I know I am mostly telling the truth. I can do all of that up until the bit where I blame the island, and even if I do go through with that last bit, Dad will know it isn't true.

Sometimes, when my dad is working in his office and the door is open just a crack so we can sneak up on him and watch him watch his typewriter, I feel like I can see the big blankety roots of Fowler laced up under his skin. I tried to tell B.B. about it once, but she rolled her eyes and told me they were just his veins. "Everyone has them." She held her pale arm out to me. Her veins stood out like big blue tunnels at the bend of her elbow. I stopped trying to explain it to her after that, but I still see it sometimes, the ivy of it running up his arms, weaving and connecting through his neck. The dark shadows reaching up through his skull. It rests behind his eyeballs, and I know that someday he will die, and we will put him in the ground and those dark roots will push out through his eyelids and grow up and up and up until they find me for real and make their home under my skin, and then Fowler will never let me leave. Lately, I can already feel them there, and it feels good. Hot and real and whole. The parts of me that are Dad are waking up, itching, reaching toward the dirt and rock and water of this place so that when they need to burrow in, I'll be ready.

"Come here," B.B. says and leans toward me.

We press our foreheads together and shut our eyes. I can smell the ice cream on her breath, a soft milky scent. I see what she wants me to see. Beatrice Volt at the top of the tall, tall cliff. Hair long and waving in the wind, arms stretched out. Below there is a crowd. Our parents weeping. Our father reasoning with her, his words barely reaching. Joshua is down there too, so worried, looking up at her and then at me as I prepare to dive in and pull her out of the water. His curls nearly cover his eyes. I am tall and brave and beautiful. I am island.

"It'll work, Henrie."

"I know."

We break apart and I feel certain.

Toast pushes into my hand so that I'll scratch his head. He only flinches away when I try to scratch his shoulders. He leaves a little melt of chocolate on the back of my hand.

"Want to head to the quarry now?"

I nod my yes.

"We need to go to the hardware store first. We need like a pickax and a sledgehammer." B.B. has worked her way down to her cake cone and takes a crunchy bite as she talks, chewing through her enthusiasm.

"Maybe they'll sell us dynamite," I say, and her eyes flash up at me and she sees my smirk, and she smiles back at me. "Sure, you ask for that, and I'll ask for a machete and some rubber gloves." She takes another bite of her cone. "Where did you go the other night?"

"What do you mean?" I know exactly what she's asking.

"I woke up and you weren't in our room."

"I was probably peeing."

"Henrie."

"What? I have to pee. Everyone pees."

"You know what I'm talking about."

I know that there was that morning I woke up in the turret. I know there was another morning when I woke up in different clothes from what I went to sleep in. I know that my calves ached so much that next day that I thought I must have had charley horses in the night that didn't wake me up.

"Have you ever noticed that Daddy sleepwalks sometimes? Like leaves the house and everything?" B.B. asks all purposefully casual while giving me side-eye.

"Are you trying to trick me into saying something?" I ask.

"What?" She looks genuinely surprised by the question. "No. Why the hell would you think that?"

I almost say, *I'm the one who's been sleepwalking. Why don't you ask me about that?* Instead, I say, "I have no idea what you're on about, and shut your mouth when you chew, you big, old horse."

B.B. gnashes her teeth together more dramatically

and then opens her mouth wide so I can see the chocolate mashed up with the pale cone bits in her molars and on her tongue.

"You're gross," I say, and I reach out and smack the cone out of her hand with such ease that it flies up in the air above our heads high enough to give Toast time to launch himself up and fit the whole thing in his mouth.

B.B. howls with laughter, so much so that I can't help but join in.

"That damn dog is gonna be so sick," B.B. says through fits of giggles.

"What's so funny?"

Our laughter has attracted a viewer, and before I realize who it is, I make this snorty laugh sound that is so stupid little kid that I laugh even harder.

"Joshua!" B.B. shouts. "Want to come fuck up the quarry pond with us?"

"Sure." Something about his answer is so swift and genuine, like he's been waiting for us to ask, that it gets us going all over again, and we are rolling into each other and falling backward so that the warmth of the concrete is nibbling at my arms.

"Are you guys being mean to me?"

Toast barks what sounds like a yes, and we laugh some more.

"Fine. Whatever. I have to work at the Pantry anyway."

My eyes are blurry with laughing, so I can only see

the idea of him walking away from us, a daytime ghost. "Wait!" I holler, but even that comes out sounding sarcastic, so he doesn't stop. Just keeps walking, disappearing into a storefront.

I have time to hiccup, and then, all of a sudden, the feelings in me shift, and I am crying. Crying before I know that's what I'm doing, and the panic attack is back. B.B. takes hold of me, stands me up, and walks me down the street away from the shops and into this little green patch of park that no one ever uses. She sits us both down on the concrete picnic table and pushes her forehead into mine. I calm down.

"We have a plan, Henrie my Henrie. They will realize how much they love us and how much we need to be together. We will get far away from here. By tomorrow, things will be better."

"Okay." I wipe my snotty nose on her shirt.

"You got boogs on me, you jerk."

"I want candy."

B.B. shoves the candy bag at me. We bought candy first thing and filled up a huge plastic bag. Little box candies—Lemonheads, Boston Baked Beans, and Gobstoppers—and I can hear them all rattle in their cardboard as she tries to get me to take the bag. I peer inside. Laffy Taffy, Smarties, those big chewy sweet tarts that crack your jaw when you try to eat them. And candy cigarettes. Several boxes of candy cigarettes. I love the soft, chalky melt of them in my mouth, and the dust that blows off 'em that's meant to look like smoke. Sometimes, if I hit it just right, it actually does look real.

"Just don't smoke those dumb fake cigarettes in front of me. I've got the real thing if you want."

B.B. is annoyed with me now, and I don't even believe she has cigarettes, but then she's pulling them out of her pants pocket or maybe her waistband and holding them out to me like it's no big thing.

"Excellent. I love a good cigarette."

"You do not," she says.

"How would you know?"

"I would know if you smoked. We're together, like, all the time," she says.

A rush of heat goes through me then, like the shadow island vines have been inside me all along, climbing, climbing up into my brain, sitting behind my eyeballs, and they are dark and shriveled and they make me yell out loud, "You don't know everything about me either." And then: "Maybe it wouldn't be so bad to live without you."

That second shout comes out of me with spit and sizzle and an image of me in our tire swing, alone, reading a book. Swaying in the warm island air. There is no B.B. Just me and Mom and Dad and the house. The water making its calm *lap-lap* noises in the distance. There is no sister in this dream. No sister at all, because she's at the bottom of the quarry pond, her body pushed snuggly into the deep, dark hole, dead down there where I've put her to keep all the bad just where it is meant to be, and in this dream, I am not lonely or sad or guilty. I am happy. I am fine. Fine, fine, fine. The best daughter. The most loved. The only.

Then, almost as quickly as I see and feel the happy singleness of me, it is gone, and the truth of it hurts so much that I feel like throwing up.

"Let's go now, B.B. Let's go plan your jump. I'm ready."

"Fuck you," she says, not at all ready to forgive me.

"Don't do that!" I shout. I throw myself around her. "I'm sorry. I mean it. I love your plan and I love you."

"Fine." B.B. shoves me off her. I let her push me away. She's still mad, and I don't blame her. Some twisty part of me isn't right today.

I resolve to do whatever B.B. asks of me next. I will be the best, most kind sister. We will make sure her plan works.

—✦—

In the dark of the quarry cliff cave, we sit crisscross applesauce, and I pick at the dirt under my too-long toenails. If my mom were truly herself, she'd say, "Those are too ugly for real life." She'd clear her throat in mock disgust and say, "Clip those gnarled masses or they're gonna grow right into the ground." Instead, she said nothing at all. B.B. is right. She's in the house, packing to take me out of here. She thinks she can take me from my home like it's nothing. Like taking my heart out of my body wouldn't kill me. B.B. thinks it too. Like I can just walk away and live off island. Like a home is a home is a home. What bullshit that is. What utter nonsense. My heart burns in my chest, fires up my throat to my hot tongue and makes me think more bad words. Worse than bull-shit. And Daddy. That asshole. He says nothing. He doesn't fight for me. He isn't even fighting for me or the island. He isn't listening to the house. He just lets it all happen. I press my spine to the cave wall. It hurts.

I press harder and harder still until I feel myself con-nect, as if I am the blasted-away rock. Each knuckle of my spine fits into the curve of the cave, clicking into place. I am a piece of the great big gears of this place, a working piece. I cannot just be taken away. A cocooned Henrietta splitting silk to wake up a new and more terri-ble thing.

"Henrie!" B.B. is shouting. It's possible she's said my name more than once.

"What?" I snarl.

"What the fuck are you doing?"

The cave is small, shallow, so the two of us fit like yolks in a shell, but I'm at the back, and I've elevated myself by pushing my ankle bones into the floor. I relax and B.B. pulls my leg over hers so she can see my ankle.

"You've made yourself bleed. What the hell."

"I wasn't doing anything." I make sure the base of my spine is still connected to wall. Skin to rock through my wet T-shirt. Connected.

"Looked like you were seizing up or something."

"Don't be dramatic." I resist the urge to ask what she means by *seizing up.*

"You're being creepy."

"Am not."

"Whatever."

We sit for a moment. A bit of my anger has separated from my body and floats between us, its own hot thing.

"You know you can tell me anything, right, Henrie?"

"Shut the fuck up."

"Mean."

"You are," I say, thinking it's gonna be funny, but it isn't. It's just more nasty, and I find that I don't care. I don't even care when B.B.'s eyes start to look all watery like she might cry.

B.B. clears her throat, the noise loud in our little cavern, and looks away from me. "Look at Toast."

I look. He's sitting out at the far edge of the water next to our cameras and much of our discarded clothes. From that spot he can keep an eye on us even when we are up here in our high cave. He does not like the water, at least not the pond water, so he sits nervously at the edge of it, taking breaks from watching us to kick at his new green collar. We bought the collar at the hardware store when we bought a trowel and a hammer—the hammer has already dropped to an unfindable portion of the pond bottom.

I watch Toast swirl his collar, kicking it with his back leg. It was in the dusty two-dollar bin at the back of the store, and B.B. has dubbed it Emerald City Green because it is loud in color and boasts way too many rhinestones. It spins under Toast's paw, giving off little sparks of light in the sunshine. Our little disco puppy.

My big sister isn't used to having her plans not work. We are both in our underwear, T-shirts sticking to our skins. To get into our cave you have to swim, then climb, and sometimes we talk about how cool it would be if the cave was bigger—it's more of a belly button than a cave—but secretly, I like it just as it is. B.B. isn't wearing a bra and her shirt is all clingy, and she doesn't look like a little kid at all, barely like my sister, and she isn't paying attention to me, and I can feel in my arms how good it would feel to shove her out. Push so hard that her body would fall, fall, fall. It's not far enough to kill her on the rocks, but she'd hit. Maybe her stupid, stubborn skull would knock a rock or two loose.

"Your plan isn't going to work," I say. The mean feels kind of good, so I add, "It wasn't ever gonna work. So stupid."

"Got any other brilliant ideas?"

"Nope."

"That's hurtful, Henrie."

"Okay. I mean, sorry."

"So?"

I can't really think of an answer to *So?* I say nothing.

"I'm cold. I'm gonna swim."

B.B. has left the cave before there is any time to come up with something else mean to say. The space she's left looks warm, the rock shiny from where her cotton shirt and underwear touched it, but when I touch it, the rock is cold. I push back farther into the cave. I can still see Toast and the edge of the water, and I can hear B.B. splashing. It all feels so far away. I shut my eyes and the rock begins to hum. A soft lull into vibration. Such a small, kind motion that I could easily fall asleep.

When I open my eyes, the light outside the cave looks different and the cave seems longer, tunneled. The splashing has stopped. There is no noise of Toast rubbing at his collar or whining for us to come out of the cave to play. It's like I am looking through my camera, with a zoom lens on and the world is moving farther and farther away, the cave walls closing in like a warm blanket. I curl my body smaller and the rock moves in to meet me, pressing, pressing, pressing. I can feel the weight of the quarry on me. How the rock will crush me, my lungs tight with want for air. This great big body of an island is taking me in to make it strong.

"Henrie!" my sister calls.

I push out of the cave and tumble down toward the water. I hit the cliff wall. I flop onto the surface of the water with a sting on my belly and then my shoulder hits the rocks underneath. I am going under. Falling so fast under the water that it seems I must have dived from the top. I must have jumped or there would not be enough momentum to take me down through the top layer to the chill underside and farther down past our secret-story hiding place and farther down until the quarry pond begins to narrow into a cave. I am in the funnel of it, my butt falling faster, my legs and arms reaching up to the surface. I am not falling. I am being pulled.

Then it stops. It is just me. My body floating exactly where it is, not moving up or down, and I squirm around to look, kick my legs, and I see it. The opening at the bottom of the island. The unplugged hole. A dark squirm of a thing sprouts from this spot, like seaweed. It weaves and sways and notices me. Stops in its sway and begins to reach for me. It wraps my arms in its thick tangle, and some part of me thinks I should fight. Pull. Tug. Swim. The rest of me. The rest of me wants it. This was always meant to happen. I starfish my body and the dark tangle breaks into a thousand dusty pieces, swarming around me. It feels good. Like warmth. Like love. Like legacy. I am ravenous.

The dark is gone, and I swallow, breathe like I am in the air and not in the water. My insides are stronger, hardening into rock, but I still rise to the surface. As I go, I run my tongue over my teeth. They are sharper, fuller. My skin glints like Toast's collar in the underwater light.

Blinking with a green scaly tint. I feel it. All of it inside me. I own it.

Before I can pierce the surface, B.B.'s arms find me, pull me up. She is hollering, making a fuss. Toast is barking.

"Leave me the fuck alone!" I scream. I hear the anger and force in my voice. The sheer violence of it, but it does not surprise me. It was in me all along, and if Beatrice didn't know that, she's the dumb toady fool.

B.B. moves back, away from me. She is scared of me, and I like it.

"You don't look right. Something's wrong."

I turn away from her and open my mouth, suddenly so thirsty that I can't believe I haven't already swallowed up the whole pond.

My tongue forking in my mouth, I glide toward the shore. The scales of my skin soak up all the water they can, my body thirsty, as I walk out of the water and begin to run back to the house, my sister calling out to me from the water.

⊷ 14 ⊷

sonia

1989

I haven't stood in the turret in over a decade, and the last time I was in this spot, B.B. was in my arms. Her little body hot and sleepy. I knew then that she was neither an Elizabeth nor an Olivia Rose—no woman so easily trapped by a man. Nor would she be her father— the Volt men are evil in ways even I don't understand. In this spot, a smoothed indent in the wooden floorboards where insistence found a place to wait and watch, I swore to Beatrice that she would inherit the fortitude of Eileen Fowler. The sister who stood guard. Kept an eye on the island. Did what was necessary to keep its secrets hidden.

The quarry would have looked so different to Eileen Fowler. It would have been alive with workers. Men hollering, dynamite blasts rattling glass. Eileen was said to sit on the Watch Tower, the tall stack of stones off in the distance and to my right, every evening after the workers left—as regular as my run—so that her sister could see her from just this very spot.

After marrying Seth, Elizabeth had gotten pregnant almost right away, disappearing into the house. Eileen had gone to the front door many times, knocking and asking for her sister, begging for Seth to let her in or Elizabeth out. Begging Elizabeth to fight. Seth had turned Eileen away every time, offering little to no information. It is said that one night Seth woke, unsure why, and wandered to a window. Outside in the dark, Eileen stood with lantern held high as if waiting to lock eyes with him, and when she did, every window in the house shattered, as if Eileen had willed it so. Seth blacked out, glass cutting his face, and when he came to, Eileen was on the third floor, her knuckles raw from trying to reach her sister under the thin crack of the door. Elizabeth would not come out.

The woman that went missing last night was in her twenties. The younger they are, the more it bothers me, and this was a sloppy job. Different from usual. There isn't usually so much blood to clean up. I traced her footsteps this morning, as I always do, cleaning up whatever I found along the way, erasing her wherever I could. The harbor master said she was crying as she stepped off the ferry, and the innkeeper says she didn't offer much besides a first name and some cash. The dead should be remembered. But not here. Not on Fowler. Here it is my job to help them fade, and it isn't usually hard, making the sad and lonely vanish.

This is what I know. The island reaches out, sends its echoey call like a heartbeat to the mainland. Someone catches that beat. Sadness attracts sadness. Women arrive. Women jump. Their bodies are never found.

Their remnants are kept in the basement of the museum—earrings and flip-flops and sweatshirts. The things they leave behind, the identifying pieces like wallets and photographs and journals, are burned in the quarry, and the ashes spread into the Killing Pond. The best funeral I can offer. These women show up on their own. Their commonality a sadness and loneliness that predates the island and makes them delicious. Grief is very filling.

"Sonia?" Carrie hollers to me from the first floor. Her voice floats up the stairwell, sounding as if it is coming from a much greater distance than two flights of stairs. I imagine the sound of her, my lover, skittering across the surface of water. A smooth rock in flight just before it sinks. She thinks she can take both girls from me. Leave me here all alone. She's stronger than I thought, but she is still stupid enough to underestimate me. She does not respect or understand the bond I have with Beatrice or how much I want to be a part of this house even if that means destroying it.

Of course, I have underestimated Carrie as well. I see that clearly now. She is no trapped woman—she's taken care of her body, her life. She was ready to wield the ax I

brought her, no questions asked. She poisoned James before I even showed up—he's passed out in his office.
I peeked when I first arrived. He was snoring, still is. If I
focus, I can hear him even now. His ragged breath in, like
he's not getting enough air, and the slow whistle out. I'd
thought I was using her to get back inside this house, but
she was already ready to open the door to me and hand
over the keys. I didn't even have to ask.

"Sonia?" she calls up to me again, her question skipping around Quarry Hollow before it finds the attic. I
recall all the times she's whispered to me in the dark. Her
body warming my bed. Her giggle, never frivolous, always a victory. The times she let me comfort her, her
breath short and shallow before the calm.

"Are you ignoring me?" Carrie asks, starting up the
stairs.

"I'm coming down," I say. "Wait."

"You have to see what I've found . . ."

For years now, I've watched Carrie try to love this
house. To convince herself she could. That she's meant
to. I wonder how it never occurred to me that the house
and I have this in common—Carrie's desire to love us is
stronger than her actual love. If that's true, the house and
I deserve each other. I could be queen of this castle.

"This porch is great, don't you think?" Carrie asked
me that first day I met her.

I had not planned to be seen. I'd done a good job
steering clear once James arrived back on island with a

new wife. I walked away from B.B., knowing that I'd seen in her what Millie saw in me. I'd connected with that tiny part of her brain that would grow into Curator, make the island her dollhouse. Time apart from her, from the house, could not break that bond. So, I let her go as best I could, but on sunny days, when the island had grown beautiful and restless with spring, I would run by Quarry Hollow, even get as close as the sidewalk, waiting for the day Beatrice would ask for my help. On this day, it was Carrie who waved good morning and stopped me in my tracks.

"It's original to the house," I offer. "The porch, I mean." A silly thing to say, so clear is it that the house has been built to show off this very porch. Plus, nothing about Quarry Hollow looks new or fresh or otherwise renovated. If I wasn't feeling so tongue-tied, I'd point out its faults, like how the porch roof was built too high and too wide, resulting in a first floor that is far too dark.

"I'm Carrie by the way," she says and steps down to shake my hand.

"Sonia." I don't want to touch her, not yet, so I wave at her instead, staying where I am. She accepts this bit of awkwardness with grace. "I jog past here a lot. Also, I run the Island Museum."

"You helped with Beatrice. I've heard about you."

"Ahhhh," I say. I have never known what to say when someone says they've heard about you. It's a strange thing to offer, as if you are automatically supposed to get what it is they understand about you.

"Beatrice talks about you. Calls you Ya-Ya. James had to explain to me that comes from trying to say Son-Ya."

"I've tried to give you space. I didn't want to intrude or confuse things."

"You wouldn't be intruding." She laughs. The laugh is tight. A little stress in it, and I feel proud to notice. "Beatrice doesn't much like me, between you and me. Also, this house is haunted." Her face turns red. I study her eyes, her embarrassed smile, and see that she isn't serious. She hasn't heard the ghosts. She is just afraid of the old house. Unnerved.

"B.B.," I say.

"What?"

"We call her B.B. for Baby Beatrice or Beatrice Bethany. She likes the nickname 'cause she can say it."

"See! B.B. and Ya-Ya. You should come by."

"I'm here now," I say, and gesture at myself like I am a letter Vanna White is about to turn on *Wheel of Fortune*. The silence between us is momentarily nice, but I can feel it growing too wide, so I add, "Come by the museum."

"Really?"

"Of course! I can teach you about this island. The house even, and I'm renovating the museum—it was the first meetinghouse on the island—so we can talk about house projects too."

"James doesn't like to talk about anything like that."

"Like what?"

"The island. History. His ancestors. I don't know. Any

of it. Anyway"—she clears her throat and points up at the porch ceiling—"I read that porches like this should have a light blue ceiling, to emulate the sky."

"We could do that." I immediately go red. I've said *we* as if there is such a thing. "I mean, the island hardware store carries paint. And I could help."

She looks at me, surprised. I think, at first, that she is mad, but then she smiles and I know. I know that I'm going to fall for her. That she will be my first love. Her blue eyes almost clear in the sun. Her hair flouncing around her, and her small white teeth. I want to leap forward and begin, but I remember she is married. She is not mine. Not yet.

"I got to go," I say. I wave her away this time and turn on my heels. I am gone without looking back.

When I first knew the house, Beatrice was my focus. My everything. That love affair also began on the front porch. James answering the door, B.B. in his arms, her face covered with tears and snot. He looked ragged. His face not so different from his child's.

"I'm here to help if I can."

James smelled terrible, unwashed; his breath was so fierce I could smell it with his mouth closed. "What do you know about babies?" He was too tired to be as fierce as he wanted. "And since when does the Island Curator come in the house?"

"Rules are made to be broken," I offer lamely.

I was too busy trying not to look eager to step into the

house to be clever. It had always been a dream of mine—to get in that house—ever since Ms. Millie told me it was off-limits to Curators: "Eileen was the last of us to go inside, and it weakened her, took away much of her strength. No one has dared go inside since." I could see the dullness of the house behind his back. The drab wallpaper, the unpolished floors. I could smell the dust of it all, a smell that comes from windows always staying closed.

"I don't know anything about babies, but I'm smart and kind and no one else is gonna offer."

We set up a crib in the piano room, and I cared for B.B. more than anyone else, including James, in that two years before Carrie arrived. I learned to love the sound of James's snoring, because it meant I was still needed. That I could stay in the house bundled up with B.B. for a while longer, whispering to her the island lore so that it would live inside her, connect to her on a cellular level.

"It's insane! You have to see," Carrie says, pulling me into the downstairs hallway and away from all my memories.

The ax lies on the floor, covered in white. I can see where she swung so hard that it hit not just the wall under the stairs but also behind her. I notice the wet rings of sweat under her armpits. The dampness of her shirt under her breasts.

"It goes and goes," she says, but I haven't finished processing how large a space she's opened up. The horsehair plaster pokes out from behind the wallpaper at the edges.

It's a wide space too, as if she's expected us to walk through it, side by side. "There should be a stud or a support beam here," she says, pointing to the middle of the wide space. "It's not like Sheetrock. Horsehair plaster has to have something to stick to. None of this should have been able to stand on its own."

"Have you stepped inside it yet?" I ask her. "Like actually looked around in there?"

"I tried. But I can barely bring myself to keep my eyes on it. Let alone step through."

"I don't understand."

"It's not that I'm afraid. I mean, that's not what's stopping me. It's that I can't go through. My body won't do it. I don't know. Try it."

"Fuck that," I say, already daring myself to look. The blackness is thorough, infinite, as if the light from the hallway can't even touch it.

"Before I broke through, I swear I heard water. Like I was about to hit a pipe or something. Now though . . . nothing."

And "nothing" seems right. A big black hole devoid of color yet full of depth.

"Come on." I latch on to her arm, maybe a little afraid that she won't follow me if I don't hold on. "Let's try to go through."

"I'm telling you, we can't—"

Before she can finish, I step through, and it is like the sensation of dropping into the quarry pond. The water warmer at the surface but cold coming up from the underneath. My right hand is still on her arm. My skin burns a little, the bit that is out in the hallway, but I'm scared to let go of her, and I can hear her far away telling me to come back, asking me what I see, telling me she can't follow.

In the dark, I hear voices. The whisper and swish of people talking over and under one another, a cascade of eager words, and none of them are for me.

I let go of Carrie. Her body is so far from mine, and I feel myself a part of the house.

I turn my body in the dark, float, breath held.

"Hello." It comes out of me a burble, like I am deep in the quarry pond, and my word is bubbling up toward the surface, dead before anyone will hear it.

Hundreds of voices reach for mine, screaming and begging and rushing at me. They know my name. They scream it: *Sonia! Sonia! Sonia!* They are angry with me. They say, *We know what you did. You hid us away. You burned the last bits of us when you could have told our story.* I want to tell them that isn't what I did: *I cleaned up, kept the island safe, and I hid your shame! Your final weakness erased.* They do not like this. They scream at me louder. They shout in anger at me, at Millie, at Alice, Nora, and Eileen. They want to be pulled free, but they are on my back, pulling at my short hair, begging me to get them out, and I am going down, down, down. I cannot breathe. Somewhere below me I feel an opening. A

250 RACHEL EVE MOULTON

drain that will pull me in. If I sink that low, go through, I will never come back. My hand swims away from me, my arm reaching for Carrie, but there is no surface. Only swamp. But, suddenly, through the screams and pleas and panic, I feel Carrie pulling me toward her. Out into the hallway, the house solidifying. All of it real again in the right ways, and I am on the ground, on my hands and knees, spitting up water. Gallons gush out of me.

"Sonia," Carrie is saying. Her right hand is on my lower back, and her left hand around my arm. The feel of the wooden floorboards under my palms is cool and solid and strong, and I never, ever want to stop feeling it. So much so that when the water stops coming up, I push my belly down onto the floorboards. Lay my whole self down and turn my head away from the black pit so that I can rest my cheek on the floor.

She has kept her hands on me, one finding an opening between the waist of my jeans and my shirt. Her warmth is keeping me present. "I couldn't get in, it wouldn't let me through, and then all of a sudden it did, and I just stepped through, and it was like I was walking into a closet, nothing weird about it at all, and you were just standing there with your back to me, your head kind of tilted into your chest, and I kept saying your name and you wouldn't move. You wouldn't."

"I was in there with something. With a thousand somethings. They wanted me to pull them out, but they were pulling me under," I say, and sit up slowly, risking the loss of her touch.

"Sonia," she says. The concern on her face is mixed with fear. "You were gone a long time."

"I walked in. You pulled me out. A minute? Five at most, right?"

"Well, I was freaking out, so I didn't time it, but it was more like half an hour."

My heart hurts in my chest, all those screams still inside me. *What have I done?* I ask myself. A different interior voice answers, *What you had to. What you'll do again.*

And then B.B.'s voice. Familiar but also snarled and new and too loud, shouting, "What the fuck did you do?"

B.B. is in the doorway. Her little-girl body shaking and wet. Water drips off her hair and clothes. She is barefoot, half-naked.

"Beatrice," Carrie says.

It all happens so quickly. The rage. B.B. in the doorway with a sky behind her that is darkening, moving past evening. Her breathing the word "Run" just before she launches herself past Carrie and me, toward the kitchen. She must pass the dark hole of the hallway to get to the kitchen, and Carrie and I watch as the darkness stretches toward B.B., reaching out with dark arms, and Carrie gasps, reaches toward B.B. too, as if to save her, but I grab on to Carrie's arm and hold her still. The darkness is not a threat. Not to B.B. I don't know how I know this, but I know it means to save her. But in that moment, two things happen. First, the darkness misses B.B. as she moves into the kitchen, and second, something horrible and darker than the hole in the house looms.

It's Henrie. She fills the front doorway. A good distance behind her, Toast is barking, a noise too loud for his little body, and I know right away he is barking at her. At Henrie, who doesn't quite look like Henrie. It looks like some warped version of her. Some version that is so full of anger and wrath that all her edges have sharpened. Her cheekbones like blades. Her mouth somehow too full of teeth. Her elbows twitched out from her sides at harsh angles.

"Henrie? What's going—"

Carrie is midsentence when Henrie flies forward. Leaps. Launches off her back legs. On instinct, I pull Carrie to the floor with me, and Henrie is in the air above us, somehow leaping through the hall toward the kitchen, graceful if there wasn't something so grotesque about the length of her limbs.

The darkness that had been reaching out from the house to cradle B.B. is still there, and it hugs itself around Henrie instead, yanking her from midair and sucking her into the hold under the stairs. Her body slipping through and under like all those winter nightmares I used to have of dropping baby B.B. under the ice of Lake Erie. Her little body slapping through a weak spot only to begin to slide away underneath, clawing to get to me as the water moves her back and forth, just out of reach.

Carrie is about to follow Henrie through. Drop her whole body in. I know, somehow, that it will let her through this time, so I focus. Picture the wall solid again, begin with the dust and mess on the floor around us and reassemble it. Will the tiny pieces back into place until the wall is back. Fully formed with its yellowed flowers and ugly blue background. There is no sign of Carrie's work.

B.B. rushes forward, back into the hall from the kitchen, pressing her palms to the solid wall. Carrie does the same, wailing.

Inside the wall, I hear something that sounds like Henrie. A long cackle, a gurgle, a swallowing of plaster and blood and decades of disappearance.

❧ 15 ❧

henrietta

1989

As soon as I pass through the wall and into the dark, the muscles of my body and the roar in my chest fade. The taste of blood, that delicious drip of it down my throat, is gone. My jaw melts, and my teeth shrink to small little nubs in my mouth, little kernels to pop and chew. My legs lose their distinguishing parts—no more thigh into kneecap into calf—too tired to hold me up. Pathetic little noises come out. Snuffles and sniffles. Fear noises until I realize I am nothing. I am air.

I fill my torso with breath and float through this new-found space like a stringless balloon. I am in the heart of Quarry Hollow. I remember that now. I've splashed through its walls, and it will contain me. I point my tired eyes into the dark before me and stare until lines of structure emerge. A loose sketch of the backside of the hallway.

Stairs above my head. Big blocks of shape, an idea of something, more than the thing itself.

I move closer to them. The house stretches, moving away from me. I find a turn, a new space. I am above the kitchen now. I float upward. I pass the bedroom I share with my sister. I move sideways and feel my father on the other side, resting on his couch. I move up to the attic, into a space more recognizable. The light of the moonlit quarry comes into the space, but I am no different. I do not return to my skin. I breathe in, try to inflate my belly to find my girth, my gravity. Nothing. I sink back down to the first floor.

A symphony of voices is all around me. The people I've been talking to my whole life. Our ghosts. The wall no longer separates us. They are timid at first, holding themselves back from me, wondering what I will do, but they smell my familiar scent and grow brave. They move in closer. Some of them laughing. Some weeping. The sound of them becomes a rhythm, a *lip-lap* of water to shore. Their velvet skins gather around me in the deep dark, and at first, they feel warm. A soft comfort. I wrap myself in them. Hug them as close as I can until just a sliver of me is left, and I feel how easy it would be to live here in the blank space. Safe. The alternative feeling comes on quick. We are stuck, all of us, and suddenly, I smell the staleness of them. The empty rot of a thing gone to bones. They are trapped here. They do not wish to stay. They want to climb inside me and find their way to the light. Their moans suffocate me now, move into my throat, their tiny velvety hairs grow long, and I choke. I tell them, *I am drowning.* I tell them, *Stop.*

"Henrie," says Beatrice Bethany. My sister. Her voice filters through a wall that is only real to her. Her full white face is clear to me, here in the dark. Her forehead pressing forward, her eyes shut. She wants me to lean into her.

"How do we get her out?" My mother is weeping.

B.B. stays. The ghosts find me again, nuzzle into my translucent parts. I let them.

Without warning, the space around me gains depth and texture. It makes sense of itself, and I see what B.B. would see if she were on this side. A long, thin tunnel. Spiderwebs. Plywood under my feet. The pink of insulation. The only breathing room is up, so I tilt my head to catch air.

"Tell me where you are?" B.B. asks.

Restless, I find my body across from hers, my sister's. This time I press back too, our foreheads together, and through the lath and plaster and mysteriously infinite darkness, we touch. Skin to skin. Mind to mind. I see her. I see her heart. In it, she is begging for me to be free. For this island to separate from me. Let me go. Where would I go? Who would I be? I am here. I am the next generation. The mean and nasty burns in me again. My gums itch in my mouth. I want to bite through, chop off her head, swallow her up, and spit her out into the walls of the house so she can stay here forever with me.

Tell her, they say. *Tell her you love her.*

And I do. I send the thought to her through skin and distance and time. And there is still truth in it. The memory of the inseparable us is close. She feels all of its honesty and none of its venom.

Meet me in the quarry, the voices say.

I show my sister the quarry. I show her the cliffs. I say, *Remember our plan.*

I use my upper body to pull myself up and out of the structure that is the house and back into the dark place where the shadows shrink from me, murmur their ghost pleas under their breath. I push with my legs, up and up and up. I grow bigger. I change into something so monstrous that no one will recognize me. I am big and beautiful and unstoppable.

I howl as long and loud as my body will allow and leap from the house. The quarry floor welcomes me. Through the dark I glide, then it is beneath me. My humanness back. My bare feet tearing through the dark.

✦ 16 ✦

beatrice

1989

The house moves with my sister's exit. A long shudder rolls through the floorboards and rattles the doors in their frames. We all feel it. The motion of it is sickening. I shut my eyes and press my body to the wall, soften my knees to ride it out. Aftershocks come next. The house contracts, beams and joists tightening into a fist, balling up around me until it feels as if it will crush. Then release. Air whirling, space opening up.

Toast barks from the front lawn, smart enough not to come inside. His voice grows hoarse.

Loneliness is left. A deep hurt of a thing that knifes into me and wiggles around, trying to open me wider, and I wish for the contraction again, the closing up that felt much more like love.

The house groans and then is still.

"Where is she?" Carrie asks. "B.B., where did she go?"

The answer hits me like another earthquake: *She's gonna jump. That's what's happening next.*

"She's going to the Killing Pond," I say to Carrie, who is holding on to the newel so tightly her knuckles have gone white.

"Why?"

The question comes out of Ms. Sonia, but I can tell that neither she nor Carrie needs an answer. Carrie, in particular, doesn't need to know how much of Henrie is now monster. A mother will die for her baby.

It occurs to me then—still in the house, across from the spot where it opened up to swallow Henrie—that maybe we were always leading to this, and maybe it will work. Henrietta will save me from drowning, tell them all that the island is toxic, and that we will leave as a family. It is the hope that my plan of escape is somehow working that gets me out the front door and into the dark.

Carrie and Ms. Sonia follow me. Toast runs beside me. They know this land and the quarry, but not nearly as well as I do. They fall behind. Inexplicably, the night has come. It has gone from daylight to dark with no moon or stars in a matter of minutes. Like whatever sucked Henrie into the wall has taken on the whole world. I cannot find the moon even though I know it is supposed to be there. There is texture to this dark, like trying to part a curtain.

I cling to the fact of the quarry all around me. The scrape of rock on my legs as I climb down into it. The limestone sticks out shard-like and honeysuckle twines into loops that catch on my feet. I fall, palms and knees hit rock.

"B.B.!" Carrie calls in the dark.

"Keep up!" I shout back, and rise to my feet.

I run. My muscles remember the land. I move quickly through the dark, knowing that if I fall, I will get back up no matter what. The water is on my ankles before I realize how far I've come. The cold soaks into my sneakers, and I reach my hands out into the dark as if there will be something or someone there to feel. There is nothing, but the sky brightens as I reach for it, as if I've caught my fingers on a string, switched on a light.

"Where is she?" Ms. Sonia is next to me now, out of breath. Carrie is holding her hand.

They break from each other to stand apart.

Toast barks once, and I point before even looking, knowing Henrie will be there, and she is. High above us on the quarry cliff. My vision becomes focused. Clearer than it truly is. I can see my sister up there so crisply and clearly that our distance from each other shrinks. I can see her legs slightly separated, her toes just over the edge. Her hair parted so it falls over both shoulders. As I watch, she raises her arms into a T.

"Oh my god," Ms. Sonia says, seeing Henrie and Henrie's intent all at the same time.

"She won't," Carrie offers.

"She's going to," I say.

Carrie calls out Henrie's name. I want to tell her to shut up—*You don't know Henrie*—but I can't get the words right even in my head, and I know too if Henrie jumps, she will hit underwater rocks and she will die.

"Fuck," Ms. Sonia is saying, and she is off. Moving to climb the cliff, as if there is any scenario in which she has time to reach Henrie before she jumps.

I watch Henrie bend her knees. I see her ready herself. There is fear in her. It is tiny, but I see it there all the same. She raises her head to the sky and howls away that tiny bit of fear, lets it fly up to the moon. My own knees bend. I wade in, knowing I will swim to her, wherever she hits. She will be broken, but we can heal her. Lungs can be cleared. Bones can be mended. We are the Volt sisters. The two of us more powerful together. It can be done.

When Henrie jumps, I start in.

The splash of the water around Henrie's body is barely a sound.

Toast and I paddle forward, our heads above water. My feet kick rock. Behind me Carrie is wading in, crying, hollering. Useless.

I find Henrie's hair first. Long and tangled and so like my own that I am momentarily disoriented. Toast scratches at my arm, and I have to push him back so I can catch my fingers in her hair and pull. I find her shoulders next, her arms. She is facedown in the water and I fight to flip her. At least get her eyes to the sky, her nose to air. But I can't do it. I can't get enough of a grip on her and stay above water. I'm tired. So tired. My feet pump harder to keep me upright, and below us something is rising up. A thick dark thing that has threaded up through the hole at the deep bottom of the quarry pond. If it reaches me, whatever it is, before I can get ahold of Henrie, we will all die.

I grab Henrie's wrist—I'll drag her to shore. Carrie thrashes just behind me, her words shallow with panic, asking, "Do you have her? Get her behind the shoulders."

"Get out of there!" Ms. Sonia screams from the shore. She can see what's coming, feels it as it begins to rumble the island.

Henrie's fingers twitch. Her arms adjust in the water. And then her head begins to rise out of the water. Slowly at first. Like maybe it isn't really happening. Just the back of her head moving until her eyebrows are up, arched over liquid. She keeps coming. Her pupils above the surface next, looking at me through thick strings of hair. Her neck bends at an impossible angle, arching long, as if it isn't dependent on her still flaccid and floating body. She raises up until her mouth is out of the pond and moves to Toast, who is still paddling in the water. She sucks him into her mouth, shutting it around him, and before I can shout *No!* she is spitting him out. His body is limp, lifeless in the water. The dark thing just under our feet stops rising, pauses to give my sister time to shine. She is grinning at me. Her teeth are big, sharp, and rowed up against one another. A girl gone shark.

Her hands clamp over my wrists, and her mouth opens before closing over my shoulder. Like needles going in, and I whimper. I hear Carrie call my name this time, then Henrie and I are gone, so far underwater that I can't see a thing. I only feel the tangle of her. I taste blood. She is pulling me down, down, down, into the deep dark of the Killing Pond. Down into the hot dark arms of the creature that has risen up to thicken the water. I claw and fight and scream. The scream lets water into my lungs, and I sink faster. She is whipping her legs around, a giant tail, and we are past the shelf where we keep our secret story, swallowed up by the dark thing that seems as easily adaptable as the water itself. Shadows slip around us in the water, breaking into sleek long bodies that circle like vultures. The rock has narrowed all around us. V-ed into the deep. Below me is the narrow hole that connects the quarry pond to Lake Erie—the devil's doorway, bubbling up cold from the dark, and the thing that is Henrie pushes me hard toward it. My foot goes through, twisting to fit through the harsh space. She gives me another great shove and my calf goes through into lake water.

Pain rockets through me and Henrie lets go. Turns and heads to the surface in a hot flash. I am stuck. Left to plug up the island. My uninjured leg dangles somewhere out there, a worm on a hook. Panic rises up over pain. I twist and push and kick. I use my arms to pull at rock around me. But I am stuck.

I am fading. The water lives around me and in me now. Carrie is coming. I know Henrie has gone to get her and is dragging her down, readying to shove her next to me. Stick us where we can rest. I am thinking of Ms. Sonia, whom I love. She may make it out of this. She climbed the cliff. She is out of reach. Henrie is back again with Carrie held tight to her chest. Carrie does not struggle, but she is still alive and awake in her daughter's arms. Our eyes meet. Then, in the dark water just above our heads, there is a new monster. Made of hair and teeth and muscle, and it swims faster than Henrie.

The big thing that is not Henrie or not fish, not human, not a creature I could even have imagined, snags Carrie away from Henrie, then dips down to pull me free. My leg rips from the rock, skin left behind, but I don't care. We bullet to the surface. The thing growls at the circling shadows, and they shiver and regather into one great dark that pools back together. The lava in the lamp.

Carrie and I are on dry land, coughing water. Objects follow liquid and come up from deep in our guts. My body hurts everywhere, but then there is air, and I suck it in. When I can, I look up. Henrie is onshore with us, looking sad and small and bedraggled. Carrie is weeping. Ms. Sonia is dry, climbing down toward us.

"She tried to kill me," Carrie says.

It's a stupid thing to say, and so I want to say something snide in return: *Yes, Carrie, I was there, and she tried to kill me first.* Who the fuck does she think she's talking to, but then I see my father. Somehow, he is here. With us. He is almost naked. Water falling off his body. His beard wet, his arms shaking. He stands next to me. Puts his hand on my head.

"You pulled us out?"

He nods and asks, "Carrie, can you walk?"

Carrie doesn't answer.

"Carrie!" he bellows, and she says something that sounds like "Yes."

"We have to get Henrie away from here. Now."

"Okay."

"I'm serious. Far from here. Off island. You cannot come back."

Carrie nods.

"Beatrice." My father kneels down to wrap me in his arms. It hurts, but I don't say anything. I don't want him to stop, although I don't fully understand what's about to happen. "You and me. We'll stay. Watch the island. For your sister. Can you do that with me?"

I nod.

"Good girl. We all need to forget this. All of us." His voice has gained volume so that Ms. Sonia and Carrie take notice. "Agreed?"

Everyone nods.

My father moves to Henrie. He whispers in her ear. She does not move. She stays bagged into herself, blankly staring.

Out in the pond Toast's body floats swollen.

"Come." He gestures for us to gather around Henrie. "She needs you," he says and shows us how to put our hands on her—skin to skin—and then he moves back, away from Henrie and away from us. Carrie and Ms. Sonia shut their eyes. I do the same and a warm breeze begins to whip around us, cozying up under our arms, easing through our fingers, settling into our laps until it feels like there are more of us. Dark, warm woman shapes, dozens of us, covering Henrie with our hands, our hearts. I am sure, suddenly, that my mother is among them, next to me, her body warming my side.

We pour ourselves into Henrie. Our memories. Our strength. In the cold gloom of the quarry, that curtain I felt us pushing through earlier turns into a blanket that drops down over us, warm and soft. Our muscles relax, loosen, and readjust. Minds grow fuzzy. I try to grab on to the fear, the memory of Henrie in the pond, but the image won't stay. Toast. His fuzzy little body runs across the quarry floor, happy and alive. Away from the water. I try to conjure up the worry, the terror, but as I grab hold of its tail, it slips out of my fingers. Gone.

Henrie's body loosens under our touch. I open my eyes to see that she is looking at me. Eyes open, blinking. I lean in to press my forehead to hers.

"B.B.?" she says to me.

"I'm here," I say.

"What's going on?" she asks.

I search for an answer but find that my brain is sleepy. One thought won't connect to the other, and I wonder if we are all asleep, dreaming, even though that idea doesn't make sense either.

Our father steps forward to gather Henrie up in his arms. Carrie stands.

"Daddy," I say, but he is looking down at Henrie as she rests her head on his chest.

The moon slides its light down on all of us as we move into our different dreams. Even when the rain starts, dropped in handfuls from the barely born morning sky, it is easy to see our individual paths move away from one another, and part of me knows we are doing something wrong. Daddy means well but he's got this part wrong. We need to stay together, our hands on each other, warm and bright. But the night is blurring and the pain of being alone cuddles into my rib cage, too strong to fight.

⊸17⊷

henrietta

2000

I am following my sister Beatrice through the house, trying to listen to her as she gushes and tumbles over herself, pulling me from room to room in this bizarre reunion tour of our childhood home.

"Honestly," B.B. says, "I think you should have the whole third floor. The turret could be your . . ."

I'm having trouble listening. A low fuzz in my head makes it impossible to hear anything else. The house is bigger and emptier than I remember it. Each room cavernous, the furniture exactly as I left it, as if the house was staged (quite poorly) to sell some eleven years ago and has been waiting to boast about itself to a never-arriving viewer.

Somewhere down the hall I can hear Wilderness on the phone—a man I should probably call sheriff if only to convince my brain that he is an authority figure and not just the acne-covered boy I once knew who used to sit quietly at that same kitchen table looking over a math book while B.B. argued with Carrie over how many pages B.B. had left to work.

B.B. and I are moving down the hallway from kitchen to living room. The space feels tall but tight, and a sleeping bag and pillow are shoved to the side.

"Have you been sleeping down here?" I ask.

"Makes me feel closer to my mother."

What is that supposed to mean? B.B.'s boldness, leaving the evidence of her slumber like that, makes me worried. What else will she tell me if I ask? Am I ready for any of it?

"You have to consider the bones of the house and not pay attention to this shitty furniture." B.B.'s begun to sound like a Realtor. I'd mock her if I had the headspace to do so. "A lot of it is screwed to the floor. Do you remember that? We used to have to clean underneath the couch by lying on our tummies and sliding a broomstick with a rag attached to it. Fucking weird, right?"

The sofa in the living room is a scratchy brown, and hung above it is the old head of the moose that Seth Volt supposedly killed; although, now that I think about it, there have never been moose on this island. The story is unlikely, yet here remains Kind King Ferdinand with his rickety antlers and brown marble eyes. His lower lip drooping and losing its stuffing, begging to be allowed to decompose.

"Why didn't we throw this away?"

My sudden interruption startles B.B. a little. The conversation has not been interactive. "It's always hung there behind the couch. We just never used this room."

"It's awful." I'm unable to take my eyes off it.

Awful is an understatement. Ferdinand's shadow is wide and long enough to darken the whole room. The dingy brown of his hair makes the couch look new. When the island was too cold or rainy to let us leave the house, we would inevitably get in trouble with our father—for laughing too loudly or using our sleeping bags to ride down the stairs like giant worm girls. He would emerge from his office and point to the living room, bellowing, "Girls! You sit here until you've calmed down!" The moose head wasn't meant to be part of the punishment, but it would loom above us with its great snout and its rigid ears.

"It's rotting," I say.

"It is."

"Taxidermy rots?"

"Everything rots."

I don't have to touch the couch to remember how much it itched. How, when we were told to take a timeout for whatever we'd done, the old fabric would print waffles into our thighs.

"I don't like the couch or the head," I say.

"Then out it goes! We can put every goddamn thing on the curb if you want to. Let's go upstairs. I'm so excited to talk it all through." She is chattering again, talking even faster now that she's gotten me to react in some way.

"Are you on something?" I ask before following. "Too much coffee? Speed?"

"Shut up."

I didn't realize until I walked back inside Quarry Hollow that I was missing the sensory memories. I could have told you which doors stuck (all of them) or which floorboards creaked and which keys on the piano no longer worked (most of them), but I couldn't have told you about the smell of enclosure in the air—as if there isn't a single window that has ever been opened—or the way the ceiling fixture in the bunk-bed room fills with dead bugs so much that the carcasses block the light and rattle around like peppercorns when the winter wind finds its secret ways into the house. I hadn't forgotten the soft give of the floorboards, but I didn't remember how their bounce feels less like rot and more like wanting. A desire that is echoed by the rush of the toilets when flushed, as sudden as airplane toilets—the handle opening up the throat of the beast—seemingly powerful enough to suck us down.

"I'll clean up the bedroom Dad used and share that with my boyfriend. There is already a bed on the third floor, and I'm sure we can get a new mattress in there ASAP."

"Wait. What boyfriend? I thought you had a 'maybe'

girlfriend?" The sensation of being back in the house is still distracting. My brain is cutting in and out on B.B.'s monologue.

"I don't have one yet, but it's only a matter of time, Henrie," B.B. says, and her eyes barely have to flash back toward the stairs for me to know she means Wilderness.

"No, B.B. Not Wilde."

"I do what I want. Now keep up."

B.B. makes room for me to peer into the second-floor bathroom. It's an unremarkable room, although quite big once you make it through the doorway. A claw-foot tub with a shower curtain hung around it across from a white sink and toilet. The white tile floor is chipped, yellowing near the baseboards. I haven't thought about this space in years, but it's all exactly the same. Even the too-long shower curtain. B.B. and I used to take baths in that tub. Our parents' jojoba shampoo could be used for bubbles if necessary, and we'd spend hours in there, draining a little bit of cold water to layer in hot until the water heater gave up on us. The towels always hung in bunches—the damp of those wrinkled folds never losing the cloying smell of mildew.

"The turret is above here so you could easily extend the pipes up."

"For what?"

"Are you not listening? For your darkroom. We could cover the windows, and I bet Carrie would know how to extend the pipes."

"You *are* fucking crazy."

"Why would you say that?"

"We aren't staying here. We have lives off island. We both do."

"We can bring our lives here. What's stopping us from doing that? You can't be a photographer here? You can study with Ms. Sonia. Learn island history. I can take over for Dad."

"What does that even mean? Dad was a recluse. You gonna shut yourself in his office and write poems?" I don't mean it to come out as nasty as it does, an insult somehow to both her and my father. My sister glances in the direction of my father's office. She looks nervous.

"It means nothing. Just that I'd keep up the house and the land we now own. And I'll join the council."

"Jesus, B.B."

"What?"

"That sounds . . ." I realize I don't know what to say. Terrible? Wonderful? Possible?

"Carrie would never let me stay and you know it."

"Aren't you twenty-four? Does your mother get to tell you where to stay and not stay? And isn't your lease up on your apartment in June? Is someone giving you a free place to live? I mean, someone besides our dad, who has left you your own island house?"

"B.B., this place is . . ."

"Is what?"

"I don't know. Dangerous!"

"I knew you weren't listening. We will make this a new place. A new house. A new island. We will be like Elizabeth and Eileen Fowler *before* Seth Volt showed up. They were pioneers, those two. Strong women who were going to make this island a town. That's us! Volt sisters unite!"

"Don't be such a dork, B.B."

"Yes, maybe, but they were the ones who made it a home. Settled in and tamed it."

"I think the word you are looking for is *colonized*."

"Henrie, don't be difficult."

"Me? Difficult? This place is not safe, B.B. That's fact."

"What you're saying is all negative bullshit. We've been left this house. Me *and* you. It's our responsibility."

"B.B.! It's called the Killing Pond for a reason, and not just because we named it that in one of our games." I suddenly realize there is a blank spot in my memory from last night. A gap between seeing the body in the quarry and waking up in the Island Inn—my brain and body separated for a time. The realization makes me feel uneasy, out of control.

"You can't just ditch me *again*."

The use of the word *again* hurts, and she knows it.

"What makes you suddenly want to stay?" I realize she has not made this change of heart clear, and it *is* a change of heart. As soon as college became an option, she left too.

"Well"—she smiles so wide that it verges on crazy—"I feel different since Daddy died. Sad, sure. But, also, more powerful. More certain. We aren't the same girls who were separated way back when. We are new! We can be better than our parents without making their mistakes, their decisions. Plus, I know several people who are going to be homeless postgraduation. I'm thinking that, at least for the summer, we could fill this place up. Fill every room with someone we know and give it back some life."

"Carrie would never live here."

"Good! I don't want her to."

"But I do."

"Fine, whatever. I don't care. Just think about this, Henrie," B.B. says, grabbing hold of my wrist. "What has this family never tried? Never insisted on when things got rough?"

"I have no clue, B.B."

"Staying together! As soon as things get weird, we run our separate ways. Daddy thought he could handle it all on his own—"

"That's not true! He kept *you*."

"Yes, but he didn't tell me anything. He didn't ask for help. He tried to farm me out to Ms. Sonia so I could be the stupid keeper or whatever. I said, 'Fuck that,' and was really damn lonely for a long time. You and me, we are the Volt sisters. No secrets. No shame. And we can do anything together, right?"

B.B. is staring at me, begging me to agree with her,

and all I can think of is that body in the quarry, my camera closing in on her. The emptiness of my stomach and then a blank stretch of time.

"Carrie would never go for it."

"She would for you," B.B. says.

There was a time when I couldn't fathom wanting anything other than this island.

We are passing by our dad's office door, and I hear the first rustle of voices from beyond it. A low whisper, the murmur of the ghosts shushing me. They do not want me to dig through my memory, they do not want me to tell B.B. that I have lost time. *Shhhhh*, they say. *Sweet girl. It is not her business.*

B.B. slides between me and the closed door, like she wants to make sure I don't go in. I don't say anything; I let her think this sly move has not been noticed. We stare instead at an old portrait of our great-great-grandfather— Seth Volt. There were never many family photos in the house, but this one has always been right here.

"Do you remember what Daddy used to say?" Beatrice startles me with this question. It's off topic and she sounds genuinely sad.

"Every man for himself," I say, sarcastic.

"Shut up. What he used to start all his stories about Seth Volt with."

I do remember.

"'When your great-great-grandfather first got to Fowler,'" B.B. starts in a purposefully deep voice, and I join in, "'there were so many trees you had to suck in your stomach just to make it from spot to spot.'"

"'A squirrel could cross from beach to beach without ever touching ground,'" I continue alone, doing my best imitation of my father's gravelly voice, and it sounds nothing like him, but B.B. still laughs.

"Do you remember the pipe Daddy smoked? Smelled so good."

"God, yes. Did he ever give that up?"

"He did. Caught me smoking cigarettes when I was a teenager and told me he'd quit if I quit."

"But you didn't quit!"

"Nope, but he didn't know that! Do you remember how he used to leave us those notes?"

"All over the house!"

"Yes!"

"Rolled up and stuck in the keyhole of our room! What was it the notes said?" I ask, feeling uneasy.

"You remember. They either said nonsense things like 'Green is the color of the day' or they assigned us chores—'Clean stove inside and out'—or they were commands."

"I can't remember those."

"Yes, you do. He'd tape them to the back of soup cans or put them in books to mark a certain page: 'Always stay outside after dark' or 'Learn how to walk on tiptoe' or 'Risk a little death every day.'"

I remember suddenly a note taped to the mirror in the bathroom. Small and typed, it read, *Smile, no one else is going to do it for you.* Had that been from our father? His paper. His typewriter keys. So, yes, probably. What B.B. is referring to, however, seems like a whole different life. A catalog of a time when I wasn't aware or even here, and it hurts. Burns in my belly.

"He was crazy," I say, and know there is truth in those three words, but they also imply that I am on the same page as my sister, that her memories are mine, which isn't at all true. It's a big lie. Fat between us.

"That's us. Fowler Island's weirdest. Better than boring."

"Is it?"

"This portrait was one of his note spots! Want to see if there is still one left?"

B.B. is already moving the painting off the wall so I don't bother answering. Something about her holding it, awkwardly, makes me realize in a new way how big the picture is. The dark spot on the wall where it hung reflects the same surprisingly wide and tall space. A bit of wallpaper is almost pretty, another spot of brightness our family has covered up. I wonder if B.B. is right. If we unloose the furniture, pull down the moose head, and clean out all the cupboards, will there be so many bright, fresh spots uncovered that the house will find a new life? A healthier version of itself?

"There." I see a small scrap tucked into the frame. I pull out the yellow paper. It's Daddy's for sure and his handwriting with its mostly capital letters. I read it aloud: "'Beatrice was never lonely.'"

We are both silent. B.B. hangs the photo back on the wall. Some of her joy is gone. She looks angry. That tiny blip of hope that B.B. made me feel is gone now too. Dread floods in.

"Daddy left us the house. The two of us. Together. He'd want us to do something good with it." Her voice is somber. Her mouth downturned. She's lying about something—that much is easy to tell—but I don't know what. "Now is our time, Henrie. I'm telling you. We will make you a darkroom. You can fill this house with family pictures. Not Volt family. Not that old sad shit, but new shit. New family. Who we are now and who we bring here to be our family. Let's throw away this painting! And the first picture we hang will be a photo you take of us. We'll frame it and put it right here."

B.B. yanks Seth's grimy portrait off the wall again and hurls it down the stairs, the cracking shards spilling out as it skids down the stairs.

"B.B.! You can't just throw that away."

"Why not? It's my house." B.B. stops abruptly and turns a little pink before she adds, "I mean *our* house."

"We should give it to Ms. Sonia or something. It's historical."

"Fine. But you have to agree to stay and live here with me. We will fix this old place up."

"Don't you remember Mom trying to fix this place up all through our childhood? It never took."

"Henrietta Volt! Stop avoiding the question. Besides, *your* mother, Carrie, is no Volt."

"Fine. I'll stay for the summer. We'll fix it up, but you have to agree that we are fixing it up to sell it."

"Can we invite in our friends for the summer if they are willing to help?"

"Sure," I say.

B.B. spits in her palm and holds it out to me. I raise my eyebrow in disgust. "Shake on it. Spit pact."

I spit and shake. The slime of us, at least, is agreeing on something.

"Henrie!" Carrie yells from the kitchen. "Henrie! Where are you?"

"Coming," I call. The next step is breaking the news to Carrie: *Mom, I won't be leaving with you. I'm staying on.* It sounds nuts even in my own head. *Just for the summer,* I will insist. I know already she isn't going to believe me. *We will fix up the house, make it as beautiful as it can be, and then sell it. I promise!*

She will say, *Henrietta, sweetie, the island will not let go.*

I will say, *Mama, I have to. I'm so sorry.*

B.B. is grabbing my arm, digging her nails in too tight and pulling me close to her. "I have your word now. No going back." Her smile is replaced by something dark and desperate. Something old that looks like it was nailed to the floor of this house a long time ago.

She lets go of my arm and the smile is back. "You'll see," she says. "By the end of the summer, you will want to stay." I watch her move ahead of me toward the kitchen, skipping a little down the dark hall.

"That's not what we've agreed to!" I holler after her.

In my hand, I hold the yellow slip of paper my father left in the picture frame for B.B. to find. Its tall dark letters do not give away when it was written. Last month? A decade ago? The years in which my father must have watched the quiet eat his daughter up. I feel it too. The stillness of the house. The body part in the quarry, telling us nothing about who it was, only that it *was*. Yet, something about the idea of staying is also intoxicating; it's almost preternatural. Perhaps we are as different as B.B. keeps insisting. Special. And deeper, under all that dreamy noise—the ghosts whispering, *Help us*, and the island whispering, *Stay*, I can hear my own truth, deep in my chest where my ribs curve back in to threaten my heart, and it is not a whisper. My body is screaming, *Run*.

✤ 18 ✤

beatrice

2000

The foot found in the quarry is in the freezer at the sheriff's station, where it waits to be picked up by off-island experts who, Wilde was told, will use their resources—far better than ours, apparently—to tell its age, gender, sexual orientation, sock preferences, and whatever other nonsense they deem necessary. Wilde was chastised for moving it from the quarry even as he explained the procedures he'd followed: pictures taken, notes made, small flags left behind as homage to its original placement. They made him feel small because he's from a small place, and I wondered, not for the first time in my life, why this island preys on sad women when it has a whole country of assholes to choose from.

Despite all the initial bravado and shaming from the off-island authorities, it's now five days later, and the foot still rests in the same freezer where Wilde allows islanders to keep walleye when they've caught too many. While the outside world has plenty of time to be condescending, they are also too busy to pick up the foot of a woman who has not yet been reported missing. There must not be an off-island spouse or mother or employer demanding answers to her whereabouts, so, without the nuisance of an angry relative or friend, other things take priority, I suppose. It makes you take stock, knowing how little importance can be placed on a woman.

Ms. Sonia says it's for the best. She stood right on the front porch of Quarry Hollow and said, "Beatrice, we don't want people digging around, anyway. The woman drowned. End of story."

It took all my strength not to holler at the absurdity of her explanation, since I could tell she didn't even believe it herself. I practically bit through my own tongue to keep from yelling, *Are you fucking kidding me? A drowned body would be a found body.* I should put that shit on the back of a Fowler Island T-shirt: A DROWNED BODY WOULD BE A FOUND BODY.

What really stopped me from yelling at Ms. Sonia was Henrie. Or rather the knowledge that Henrie is part of this mess, and I don't want her to get in more trouble than she or I know what to do with. What pisses me off most about the situation is that Henrie is keeping secrets from me. After all I've done for her, she is just like our father. Doesn't trust me and doesn't think I'm smart enough to figure shit out on my own. How much trouble could have been saved if we'd just spoken truth to each other all along?

On top of my dealing with Henrie's lies, Ms. Sonia has become annoyingly present in my life, unwilling to come into the house but stopping by all the time to ponder things. She yells my name from the front lawn: "Beatrice!" She cups her hands around her mouth as if this is the thing that will amplify her voice enough to get me to come to the front door. I hear her right away every damn time, but I let her shout. Wilde thinks it's mean of me, but I tell him, "Mean runs the world," and he leaves it alone.

Ms. Sonia wants to come into the house and poke around at our stuff—it's easy to see that. She peers in the windows, tips up on her toes to look over my shoulder. I've invited her in—I do it every time I see her at least once or twice: "Want to come in?" My invitations have gotten bolder each time she has declined. She keeps trying to get me to come to the museum so we can "go over things." I persevere, offering new and fanciful invites of my own: "There is a unicorn in the kitchen, want to see?" Other times I go for gross: "The carcasses are really starting to take on their new identities. Want to smell?" Last time I simply said, "I'm planning a big dinner. Family-style. Henrie, Carrie, Wilde, Joshua. Maybe a few others. You'll come?" This time she's the one who shocked *me* by saying, "Yes." Dinner is tonight. We will see if she shows.

Dad used to say that she wanted the house. Wanted to catalog and collect it. Scrape little bits away and label them for her museum. He'd say, "This house does not belong under glass so don't you let that woman take anything out of here that isn't hers." I think about that now, the way my father phrased it, and wonder why I never asked back then, *Which things* are *hers?* If he had to specify, doesn't that mean something in the house belongs to Ms. Sonia? And what would that be? The kitchen faucet, the throw rug in the bathroom, the stupid nailed-down upright piano? I think now she's after my mother. Ms. Sonia knows about the ghosts, the women in the walls. She wants something from them. Once, before I left for college, I was complaining to my father about Sonia always watching me from afar. He said, "She's always imagined you hers."

As if confirming this, just yesterday she pulled me aside and told me I needed to start attending Island Council.

"It's in the bylaws, Beatrice," she says, as if I'd already protested. "A Volt has to be a part of the group."

"Dad didn't attend every meeting," I say with confidence even though I know what I'm saying may not be true.

"Your father did his best," she says.

"What a load-of-crap thing to say," I snap back. It's the kind of things adults say to kids all the time, but I'm not a kid.

"Maybe it is." She blinks three times and clears her throat. "I've invited the new innkeeper to join."

"Wally?" My heart beats a bit faster.

"The redhead. Told me her name was Gwen. You know her?"

"She's been here for months," I say, dodging the question. "Why invite her now?"

"Things are changing, B.B., and you know it." I don't have time to tell Ms. Sonia this is another bullshit thing to say before she's speaking again. "Have you told Henrie that James didn't leave her anything? I mean, islandwise."

I look at Ms. Sonia sharply. I have told no one anything of the sort. I know and the lawyer knows. That's it. How would she know?

"What are you talking about?"

"I'm saying that Henrie has no legal claim to this island, and yet she seems to think it's her problem. Isn't that why she's talking about staying through the summer? Have you forgotten how important it was to your father to keep her off island?"

I think of the husk of my father under the couch in his office. The rustle of it as I shut and locked the door.

"Why the fuck is everyone always worrying so much about Henrie?" I shout at Ms. Sonia and am immediately embarrassed. I might as well have shouted, *Poor me! Love me!* "Listen," I say. "Dad is gone, but we aren't, Henrie and me. Henrie is as much a part of the house as I am. It's our inheritance and we own it together. That's it. End of story."

"Lying to your sister is dangerous, B.B."

"I can't have this conversation with you."

"If you lie to your sister, you're all on your own. Secrets make us lonely, B.B. And weak."

"You're a hypocrite."

She looks shocked. Probably because I've said something she knows is true.

I turned my back on her then. Walked into the house. *Let her follow me*, I thought. *Let her try.* She stayed outside. Stood there for a while, staring at the house like some ineffective burglar.

It will be interesting to see if everyone comes to dinner tonight. Maybe Ms. Sonia will take her meal out in the driveway.

Today, the small sheriff's office is empty, so I do not have to make an excuse for checking on the foot or flirting with Wilde—not that I mind terribly since he's already begun sleeping in my bed, a long muscle of a man that I like quite a lot—but there is something satisfying about walking, unimpeded, through the front door and straight to the back. I open the rust-speckled lid of the freezer, and the cold air rises to my face, bringing with it the stale smell of a past season's gutted fish.

"Hello, Valentine," I say into the dim light. It's nice to say it out loud rather than in my head as I usually do. I check over my shoulder and, seeing no one there, reach in to pull back the blanket. The plastic bag the foot is housed in rustles, and there she is, my sweet girl, graying just a bit.

The finding of the foot and Ms. Sonia's claim that the island has stabilized—apparently it was sinking—has started my brain whirling, pieces of what I know clicking into place. The grave we dug for Dad was filled with water the day of the funeral—I joked we'd have to put Dad in this freezer for a bit—but then the water drained. Gone overnight, leaving a soft dirt pit for the human remains of our father to snuggle in.

Yesterday, I let myself fully think about the sloughed-off skin I found in my father's office the day I found his dead body.

Humans shed millions of skin cells every damn day, but my father was not your average human. He'd left behind his weird to-do list, his dead body slouched over his typewriter, but also a full layer of skin, stretched out on the floor like a dusty Masquerade costume he'd thought better of.

So, yesterday, I went back into his office when the house was empty. I locked the door behind me and took deep breaths, overwhelmed by his books, his smell, his dusty typewriter. My eyes filled with tears, and I let them come. When I was ready, I got down on my knees and pulled the yellowed skin out from under the green sofa. It was brittle, but it stayed of one piece, a slit down the back where, perhaps, he had crawled out—a bit like the shell of a cicada. It was hard to tell, but the shape of a thing was bigger than my father. It had room for four limbs, a head, a torso, but it was larger in grotesque ways too. The arms too long, the fingers short and stumpy like paws. The neck thick and the jaw huge.

With snakes it's called ecdysis and it can happen up to a dozen times a year—the full shedding of skin. It isn't a sign of death, as it was for my father, but rather a sign of a new beginning. Henrie and I used to find those skins in the quarry. They shined crisp and golden near sun-soaked rocks where the snakes liked to bathe lazily in the heat. We'd tell each other stories about wearing the skins as disguises, letting our nature melt into the former experience of that snake until we too were able to slither and slide around the island. So, I did the same, I got down onto the floor, held my breath against the strange smell of my father's skinned layer, and slid inside. I fit my limbs to his, I pressed my face into the oddly shaped snout. Once I was inside, it tightened around me, fit to my body like shrink-wrap. This thing that was once a part of my father started showing me things. I saw what Dad saw—snippets of his life as both savior and monster. What he should have taught me a long time ago. Tortured and torturer.

My family is a part of the island's ecosystem, prey and predator. We survive on a cycle that an outsider might see as grotesque or murderous, but I know now that it is no worse than the snake widening his throat around a still-live mouse or the hawk diving down to snatch up that same snake. We all eat, adapt, eat again, survive.

This foot is my prey, my next step toward a satiated life. The minnow I will hook to catch the bigger fish.

"I'll bring you back if this doesn't work," I say. "And if it does work . . . well then. I'm sorry." I tuck her into the backpack I've brought with me, blanket and all. Next, I shut the lid of the freezer and take a padlock out of my jacket pocket. I feel certain she's been forgotten, but I don't want to risk someone's looking for her and finding her missing. I slide the padlock onto the freezer latch and the key into my bra. At least the padlock will slow things down. If Wilde is the one who busts open the lock to find she is missing, he will cover for me.

Poor Wilde. He is in love with me already. I can tell by the way he sleeps, his breath heavy, his limbs so relaxed that they seem they will sink through my mattress. He sleeps like the dead, pardon the expression, and wakes up looking taller, brighter. I'm not surprised it was so easy to get him to fall for me, to stay with me in the house, but I am a bit surprised by how much I like him. How good it feels to have another live body in the house.

These past few nights, I have sneaked away from Wilde in the night to lie downstairs in the hallway between the front door and the kitchen. The sleeping bag isn't there anymore, so I lie on my back, letting the wood of the floor dig into my spine. I press my right palm to the wall. Sometimes I fall asleep like that and wake up with my body relaxed, my fingers curled, just the tiniest bit of me still touching the wall, but most of the time I talk to the ghosts. To my mother. I tell her I am home again. That I don't know what to do. That I need her to tell me how to save her. She isn't speaking back to me. None of the ghosts are. Not yet. But I know she hears me. It would all be fine, really, if I hadn't caught that look on Henrie's face that I recognize from our childhood. That far-off look she used to get when listening to the ghosts. I try not to dwell on why my mother would speak to Henrie and not me, especially now that the phone call I got on the night of my father's death proves she could speak to me if she wanted to. Maybe if things go right today, all of that will change, and I'll be the sister with the superpowers, the one who frees the ghosts, the one everyone recognizes as the most powerful Volt. Let Henrie be the ignorant and lonely sister.

The island is warm today—midsixties—but the sun comes and goes, the clouds moving in unlikely patterns, as if the island is reaching up to stir the air. My backpack is surprisingly heavy. One little bit of bone and muscle and skin does a lot to weight one to the earth. The plastic rustles as I walk, and I shush Valentine, picturing her toes wiggling, anxious.

The sidewalk is lumpy. Bumping up and down under my feet, cracked spiky, revealing the gritty innards of the island. Bits and pieces of one forced rock. The island sidewalks have always been like this. They erupt in ways that generally indicate trees are nearby, their roots pushing impatiently upward, growing into the track humans have so heavily laid down. This stretch, however, goes down Division, from one end of the island to the other, if not for Fun Land Park cutting it off from the water at one end. From the air, you can see Division and its slim twin of a sidewalk, cutting across the island like a razor shaved the path. The trees here are not prevalent. Pushed back behind the sheriff's office and the subsequent shops and houses. So, why is the sidewalk so disrupted?

I reach a crack that is so wide and thick that the far side of the sidewalk is shoved up so I can just about get my fingers underneath it and lift. I squat down, touching the concrete, so different from the limestone of the island. It's a glued-together thing, hopeful but crumbling. The concrete has lifted itself off the ground and shifted a bit so, if both pieces simply flattened, they would not meet as intended. Between the two pieces is island soil; I poke my fingers down into it. The ground is wet, saturated. But it hasn't rained. I look up to the sky. The clouds tumble and toss above my head, but they haven't let anything go. I shift the weight of the backpack and stand.

Far ahead, down the same lumped-up sidewalk and past where I will turn to get to the house and then the quarry, I see a familiar cloud of red hair. A gorgeous group of curls that can only belong to one person.

Wally and I have a long history to be ashamed of. It was meant to be an off-island story, a series of bad decisions, mostly made by me, but then she up and bought the Island Inn like some sort of stalker. Still, seeing her even from a distance always makes my gut twist. Not that I still have feelings for her. I don't. Not that kind anyway.

I always kept journals. Poetry, mostly. Notes. Observations. Off island, they became whiny. Sad. The kind of bullshit teenagers keep. I started keeping lists. Lists at the back and worries at the front. Lists of movies I'd seen. Books read. Goals for the year. And, of course, I kept a fuck list. An old lover found it and told me it was "a shit thing to do." At the time, I dismissed his disgust. I thought it would be for sure worse to forget whom you'd slept with than to make note of them. Anyway, that criticism worked its way into my head. People I was serious about didn't go on the list after that. Wally was one of those.

"Wally!" I holler. There is soil under my nails and Valentine rustles in my backpack. "Hey, Wally!"

She hears me, pauses, and turns, raises her hand back. She is hesitant. I don't blame her.

I found out she had bought the inn quite by accident—my father told me over the phone, although he did not know what he was relaying. It was quite the on-island uproar, this single, redheaded woman showing up with cash and moving in on a property that the council should have found a way to purchase and keep close. I imagine Wally had a rather cold welcome to Fowler. To her credit, she has told no one about our past or even tried to talk to me until this moment.

I jog so that Wally will see that I'm serious. We've caught glimpses of each other on island before this. I ignored her, purposefully, but now it feels time. Things are falling into place.

When I reach her, I am out of breath.

"Hey," I manage.

"Hello." Quite formal.

Wally is older than me. Her eyes fiercely light gray and her skin pale and clear on her face. You'd never know how thickly freckled her shoulders are, stretching over her clavicles and down to the small of her back. The skin so covered above her ass that it is its own landscape, a continent all its own that I once called Terabithia.

"I'm hosting dinner tonight." I try to catch my breath. "Will you come? Quarry Hollow. You know Henrie and Carrie, right?"

She looks stunned. I don't blame her, and the guilt blooms in me anew.

"Seriously. Family dinner. I want to do them once a week."

"You want me to be part of your family?" She looks incredulous now, like she can't believe my nerve, and I don't blame her. I was not good to her. I did not pay attention, and I acted like I didn't care. I had such a big feeling for her then. Like there was a lump in the middle of me that I couldn't swallow or cough up. It wasn't safe.

"I'm not fucking hitting on you if that's what you

mean," I say, and there is the mean roaring up in me again. Always in there, waiting to ruin. "Listen. I'm sorry. I'm trying to say that I know you need friends, and you and me own part of this island now. Let's be friends if not family. You'll come to dinner, meet everybody. You should be on the Island Council too, you own a business. Ms. Sonia says I have to start going so you should be there too."

"Ms. Sonia?"

"Sorry. Yes. Sonia. Runs the Island Museum. The council."

Wally brushes red curls behind her ear, and I know they won't stay put for more than five seconds. A vein beats blue at her temple.

"I don't like it here, B.B." It is such a simple thing to say but I hear the depth of it.

"Dinner," I say with finality. It's decided.

"Nothing can happen between us again." Her cheeks heat up, the pink of them just a touch softer than the color of her hair.

"I'm with Wilderness now. He's good to me. We want to make a life of it." Then, without thinking, I put my hand to my belly. She sees. Her eyes go wide. Valentine rustles in my bag, reminding me I've stood too long. "I have to go. Six if you want to be a part of things. Bring wine."

I do not wait for a goodbye, but I hear it behind me anyway, stuck in her throat like she has more to say.

Valentine is losing the cool of the freezer, pressing against my back with a warmth that feels like life.

"We're almost there, old girl," I say and pick up my pace.

In the hallway, I take off my backpack and sit on the floor. The wood is warped underneath me.

I lift Valentine out, gently. I unwrap her blanket and open the plastic bag. Her skin needs to touch the wall. I know that. Just as Henrie used to say in the cemetery, contact is important, even to the dead.

It doesn't feel right, touching her. The life I've convinced myself is still in her is less convincing skin to skin. She is cold and plastic, fragile yet stone heavy. I place her carefully so that the sole of her is against the plaster and then lay the blanket over the open stump.

I wait.

Nothing happens. I knock on the wall. I cup my hands around my mouth in a bad imitation of Ms. Sonia and holler into the walls of the house, "Hello!" Nothing.

Here is what I know. The island feasts on female sadness. It licks it up like ice cream. My father was the last male Volt assigned the job of cleaning up the remnants. My dad brought the souls into this house. A kindness or a punishment, probably the latter. It's a fucked-up holy trinity. Then he had daughters. Useless daughters given that he needed a male heir to take his place. But then Henrie turned, surprising everyone, and he sent her away so she wouldn't have to take his place. Then I was left alone, Daddy disappearing into his study more and more, as if Henrie had been the only one who needed him. He thought I was like Ms. Sonia. Like Eileen. Quiet and unobtrusive. Observing and recording, but that's not me. That's never been me. I'm my own big, bad island creation.

When I found his body, both his human form and his island monster skin, I knew I could follow in his footsteps. All I had to do was slither into his shed self, and from that flaked-off, now-dead monster, I learned everything, just as if I'd put his brain in my head. It's how I first saw under the island and how I know the monster is at his most vulnerable when he is deep down there, asleep and connected to his feast. I stayed there, inside the skin of my father, for some time until my skin began to reach for his and the two became one. By the time I rose up off that office floor, stepped out, and relocked the door, my body was aching with the duality of change. I had taken on my father, his skin was now my skin.

Now, I say it into the wall: "O Most Holy Trinity, Mother, Daughter, and Holy Spirit, I adore Thee profoundly. I offer the most precious Body, Blood, Soul, and Divinity in all the tabernacles of the world, in preparation for the outrages, sacrileges, and indifferences by which He/She/It is offended."

Our father did not give us religion. I dated a Catholic once. Loved the legends, the incense, the cathedrals one could find in any big city. If the island is the devil, doesn't that presume there is a god? A heaven, a hell? The logic probably doesn't work, but I thought maybe, just maybe, if I brought the body and the blood to the sole something would click.

It's not fucking working. I gather Valentine. Shove her unbagged inside my backpack, as if this is all her fault. Stupid fucking idea. Stupid fucking house.

I put the backpack on my back and leave.

The quarry pond is calm and clear. Its depth is gorgeous from the height of the cliff. It's a trick, this cool clear view of the water. Just underneath the surface gray limestone lurks in peaks and valleys, a whole mountain range down there hidden by the glint of the sun. The way it nearly blinds me.

I take my backpack off and gently place it on the ground, the sound of the zipper on its track is loud, and I look around. It's midday, a weekday, and the quarry is empty. Henrie and Carrie are packing up their stuff at the inn to move it to the house. It took far less work than I'd thought to get Carrie to stay; we—Henrie and I—just had to say we loved her, needed her. Once she saw that we were both serious about staying, she folded. She's lived her life lonely. It makes her vulnerable.

Wilderness is off trying to determine whether Mr. Cooper should have built his shed on that section of his property or if that is indeed within Mr. Nelson's property line, in which case Mr. Cooper's goat fence will need to be rethought. It is a normal island day, if not for the now-paling piece of bait in my backpack.

I move back into the woods, near the rusty fence the council put in, and find a stick.

I hang the open backpack from the stick. It's a poor excuse for a fishing pole, but the bait is good. I lie on my belly, let the stick reach out over the edge of the quarry. I rest my body on top of the stick, let the weight of me keep the weight of it.

The day is warm, the quarry sucking up the sun in a way that makes me sleepy. Tonight, we will have pasta. Noodles and red sauce. Garlic bread. A big pot of noodles to feed a family of my making. I picture us around the table. My mother is there too, her body translucent but whole. It makes me wish my father could be there, he at one end of the table and me at the other.

Time passes.

There is a swift breeze, and my body is suddenly flipped over, my eyes to the sun, and I squint, unable to see. For a second, I don't know where I am, but then I turn back over, push myself to all fours and look for the stick. It's gone. I move myself to the edge of the cliff, loose rocks slipping out from under my hands. The sound of the splash is normal. The weight of Valentine and her stick going under, but what I see does not match the sound. The pond is thick and black as tar in the sunlight. The darkness is coming up from a deep dark hole and shaping itself into something that looks like ivy. The tendrils of it reach up and wrap around Valentine, swallowing her whole.

"Hey!" I scream down without thinking. The thick syrup stills itself. "Stop!" I watch as it lays its body thin, takes over the whole pool, and then as if shape and substance and gravity are nothing, it thins again, presses itself to the cliff wall, and begins to climb. A shadow of dark that makes me scramble to my feet and stumble backward. The chain link stops me, and I wait, gather my breath.

How do you want me? his voice echoes up from the water.

"As you are," I say.

Watch. He is gleeful. Proud. Eager to show me what he can do.

Twenty-four years on this dumb island, and I'm finally getting to meet the island devil. He is a great big and dripping thing with leathery fins that launch him from the water to flop in front of me on the quarry cliff. The thick bristles that edge his fins, as well as the arms and legs underneath them, make a loud and nauseating stridulation. The chirp of him works to form words in my head. He is a dark shape that adapts with the sun, pulling itself into a tall dark monstrous form, its lips thin and stretched to a cracking red. All-white eyes and a body bending wrong at every joint, bones black and pushing through a layer of pale, veined, pulsing white. I know from my father's skin that this is the scarier version of the monster, the bit he sends aboveground. It is the essence of him.

The tendons in my neck are so tight that I fear my voice will come out a squeak if I try to talk. If I could speak, I'd ask him if my father was scared. If the monster knows my sister. And if he's hungry, will he eat me? Am I not sad enough? His tongue flicks out of his mouth as if to smell me. My heart beats in my chest so loud that I think he must hear it as well.

I step away from the fence to move as close to him as I can.

I feel him inside my skull, his sound making my eardrums vibrate. The taste of blood in my mouth, the rush of adrenaline in every muscle. As he finds his sweet spot, his voice grows stronger.

He tilts his great head in doglike curiosity.

His body pours itself out, like water from a faucet, building back up into a variety of shapes. He becomes pointy, then puddly—a devil then an angel, a gargoyle then an eagle. Shape to shape and back again, smelling, through each transition, like raw meat, something split open and splayed wide. I gag each time, an involuntary response that pleases him. Finally, he grows huge, dragon-size, shifting and inflating into a lumpy and horned creature with round, pupil-less eyes and a long thin nose as sharp as a sword above his raw, red tongue.

Trip, trap, trip trap, trip trap, he says, grinning. *Is this who you want me to be?*

I shake my head. *No.*

I'll gobble you up, I will.

His body moves again, turning himself inside out this time, bursting his bloody insides to the air, his long red tongue lolling off the cliff edge, a slobbery slip and slide that began to grow scales. His head looks like my father, while his body looks like that of a wolf, a four-legged beast with matted gray fur.

Where is your daddy? he asks.

"Dead," I say, trying to keep all feeling out of my voice. Seeing my father's mouth ask this question makes me doubt what I'm doing here. Bile rises in my throat, and he can see that he's upset me. He morphs into something that resembles my sister, and I can't hide my dismay. My knees weaken. I think I might throw up. I swallow, and my throat burns.

And your baby sister. Where is she?

"I'm in charge now," I say. "I wear my father's skin."

He shape-shifts again. His upper half red and muscled, his face angled and topped with devil horns. His lower half a fish tail.

This is how you made me. You and your sister.

"We did not make you," I say, even though he is a nightmare mash-up of our childhood imaginings.

No, you didn't. But you've come today to remake me. You have a deal to propose.

"Forget my sister. Let me serve you. Care for the is-land. Give you a male heir. Two, in fact."

But your sister has already fed me. She has done it more than once, in fact. She can do it again.

"She is sloppy." I think of the foot. Give him the thought. "She has been gone too long."

I can't take it away from her.

I think of Sonia. Her love of me. Her determination to give me her sad world.

"I'm asking you to call to me first. To let me be in charge until I bear you a son."

So be it, he says, as if he's been expecting this all along. I feel the monster part of me growing, a trickling of power from him to me that loosens up my tendons, jellies my bones, and reaches into my uterus, twines itself around the tiny beginnings Wilde and I have made.

We are one, he says, and I feel that I am. *Your babies will be born mine.*

Even as he says it, I feel them more strongly in my belly. Embryos twisting and playing, reshaping them-selves, and multiplying into dozens. I look down at my stomach under my white T-shirt, and I see them. Dark little monsters feeling their power, growing too fast. *For-give me, Wilde. Forgive me babies that will never be*, I think, a thought the devil doesn't catch.

Do you want to hear a story before you go?

I say, *Yes*.

His body begins to melt and move again, his shoulder

blades piercing through his skin. He shrinks himself to my size, to a creature I imagine he thinks will make sense to me but is more horrific for its attempt at a human head, a toothless smile, and limbs too long to be real. His tongue comes out of his mouth, thick as a slug and growing toward me. I stand my ground and the tongue pushes into my mouth and digs to the back of my throat. I am gagging. Choking. Shocked by the pain as he digs out a molar and whips it back into his mouth. Chews thoughtful. I cough and spit blood, but he is back, crawling inside my mouth for another and then flowing downward into my body, taking over every bit of me and telling me his story from inside my belly, where he swims around, gnawing at the edges of my babies. The pain is so great that I fall to the ground, curl up on my side, and black out.

When I wake up, the pain is not exactly gone, but it is distant, and I know he is still inside me. I stay on the ground. I listen to his story as he nibbles. I feel so sad, so lonely, and full of regret. The almost babies in my belly have no chance now. That version of life where Wilde and Henrie and I grow old together raising babies seems more silly than ever. My heart splits in my chest, a dark devil finger spreading the crack open wider, and he laughs as he explains that he feeds off sorrow. *Your pain. Your loss. Your endless grief tastes like candy.*

He whispers about bathing in the bodies of the missing. How he collects their bits and pieces. *The greater their sadness, the longer their flavor lasts.* He has a beautiful under-island nest—I've seen it through my father's eyes, but I try not to let him know this. He describes how good the sadness tastes. He admits he made a mistake when he spoke to my great-great-grandfather long ago. He'd meant to make Seth promise to keep the women coming, to find them and bring them cliffside himself so there would be an endless supply, and not just those so sorrow-soaked that they were drawn there on their own. He didn't need them *all* to be juicy—he just needed them to be. The more the merrier.

But Seth had not made any additional promises, and so he convinced himself that passivity was not murder. Cleaning up the mess left behind was actually responsible, obligatory. If he wasn't responsible for the choosing, or for the moment of death, he need not feel guilty. Nor should he feel shame about passing down his powers to his son or his grandson.

Your father is gone, and you will do better. You will fix this for me, he says.

"I'm giving you my body, my babies. Why would I give you more?" I challenge him.

You are greedy. I feel that now inside you. You are no good at being alone, and this is your kingdom.

"I want more."

He reaches up my throat and into my mouth, extracts another molar, crunches thoughtfully.

I am in a dark place. My body aches but I feel it from a great distance. It is not real to me yet.

What is it you want?

I want a lot of things, but first, I want to hear another story, I say, my voice, like his, a vibration. The sun has begun to sink in the sky, and in the dusk, his body glows. A foul green comes off him, thick as mucus, his pores a million little oozing cuts. *Tell me about the day my mother died.*

And then we will make a deal, he says.

Maybe.

We will.

We will.

When she finally came to me, you were in her arms. She was stubborn, thought she knew everything. Thought she could trick me, negotiate. I'd called to her for months, years. She had no family, an orphan, and if not for your father meeting her when he did, she would have disappeared quite neatly. No one would have cared. No one would have noticed.

He pauses as if that is the whole of it. I try to wait him out, but the silence becomes a frustration, so I shout, "No! I want the whole story." I say it with my full voice so that the quarry can hear, and then he is gone. I am gone. There is only the quarry and a woman. Tall, blond hair, jeans that flare at the bottom, and a white blouse. No shoes. Soft white feet, nails bare of polish but perfect all the same. She is crying, her arms full of baby.

The baby cries too. Wails. I am wrapped in a yellow blanket, one that I know will survive the fall because I had it as a child. Dragged its loosening knit around the house for years.

I can see everything all at once. There is no rusty wire fence. The pond below is clear. The sun high.

"No!" She screams and shakes her head. She rises up on her toes, bounces the baby in her arms. The water below begins to boil. She looks toward the house. The great windowed structure, teetering on the edge of the quarry, and I look too. She is looking for my father, and a thing that I know must be him, is coming toward us. Running down into the quarry, leaping rocks on all fours.

He will be too late. I see her understand this and her feet move forward all on their own even as her upper body leans backward. Her toes grasp the edge, and she begs for it not to happen. She wants to let me go but her arms are locked around me. She has no control, and suddenly I see that something is there within her. A small and altogether new creature. This is not the island devil. Nor is it human. It is the size of a plum and it squirrels around inside her, moving into her lungs, her heart. It glows inside her. Steam rises off her skin.

Little me wails in her arms. The heat inside her grows. This new animal is lit. It's gasoline. Black as charcoal, it beats harder than her own heart. I can see its shape. Its little arms. Its head misshapen. Its claws pierce her skin, talons on either side of her spine.

Her sadness and fear have grown themselves a body, built a life inside her that the island will now consume.

A little meal to be baked and seasoned, carved out like a Thanksgiving turkey. A sad series of events that have shaped themselves into an animal, a weight that shifts from the back of her body to her front. It pulls her over.

I scream, reach for her, but I am ephemeral. A fairy tale all my own.

She goes over with the baby in her arms. Her right palm on the back of my head, a small gesture meant to cushion me from the rocks.

My father is in the water now; he gets to me first. I am even smaller next to his great new shape. He moves to her. His wife. The nasty thing that was inside her has already shattered her rib cage, ripped her open so that it can bob in the water. He holds me to him and wraps his jaws around what is left of my mother, pulls something else from her. A glowing, glistening thing that fattens his throat, and then he is running. Back to the house. Baby screaming in his arms. The troll feasting, gobbling, making great greedy noises that crack my mother's bones.

Is that what you wanted? he asks, and he is sliding out of me, coming out of my mouth in a flow of slick black my body is vomiting, heaving him out, and the pain of what he's done inside me blossoms fresh and new.

He grows tall again in front of me, but I stay low, still curled on the limestone, sobbing.

Is that all? he asks, his arrogance making him grow even darker, taller.

He lets me cry for a while until my throat and mouth

are coated in snot and blood. I dodge my tongue in and out of the hollows he's made in my mouth and cross my arms over my abdomen, curl tighter into myself until the pain of him eases a bit and I am able to answer, *Most of it.*

Once our boys are born, they stay here on island near me. Always near. Never leaving. You may raise them for me, but they must understand that this is a gift. I am their father.

Ahhh, I say. *Is that all?*

It isn't. He takes me quite seriously. *You will feed me until our children are ready.*

I nod my agreement. *There's something else, isn't there?*

You will bring me your sister.

Because he has been inside me, because he has taken over what is growing in my belly, I feel how hungry he is for her. How just the thought of her sad, confused life brings saliva into his mouth, into mine.

⇥19⇤

henrietta

2000

Somehow it is June—two months since I arrived back on island and ditched college. It's 4:30 a.m., and I've been dreaming of ice, the same dream I've had on and off since I moved back into Quarry Hollow. In the dream, I am in bed at the top of the house, as I am in real life, safe on my new mattress. The floors under me are glassy, mist rising up. My bed skates on top of a frozen lake.

I am holding on to the bedpost when something dark appears under the ice. A mass of curling hair and limbs. An open mouth bites at the frozen layer that separates us. It's B.B.

She screams up at me. Her mouth is stretched too wide, her teeth too sharp and pointing in all the wrong directions.

I leap out of bed to dig at the ice. But my fingernails

bend back, tear off. My blood pinks the ice, ravines of
claw marks fill with red, until I break through, one arm
plunging in eager, an animal independent of my body.

My fingers tangle instantly with hair, but it is not
my sister's. I don't know how I know this, but I know it,
and then she is grabbing me, yanking me under. Suddenly, she is me and I am B.B. My ear presses so tightly
to the ice I can hear the cackle of her: "You used to be so
much fun."

I always wake before we are both under. My body is
sweaty from the fight. It took me a couple times of having this dream before I realized that it is part memory. Its
origins creeping back to that last night on the island, in
the house, and then in the quarry. The great big dark
that took over my mind and body. Not amnesia, more
like my brain stored it away as myth. The island must do
this to all of us in some way, create a dark buzz where
there should be clarity. Making it all seem as if it were a
nightmare or a story concocted by confused brains. B.B.
and I made up so many stories. Dreamed so many
dreams. A big fuzzy pile that I mistook for dress-up
clothes. It's still a blurry mess. Just like the night of Dad's
funeral. In the quarry. I did something. Something terrible? Something wonderful? I don't know, and not knowing is horrifying. It means there might be other things
I've done that I can't recall. It means that it could happen
again.

We've been in the house since April, and despite the

dreams and trying to remember what exactly it is that I've done, it's been the best two months of my life. Even now, in the predawn light, with my heart rate still high from the dream, I can feel how miraculously full the house is.

Quarry Hollow has accepted renovations with a graciousness that none of us thought possible. The walls are quiet and accepting of paint and patches. Joshua is here more often than not, and even Ms. Sonia comes inside. Delivering things, helping with small tasks. Mostly to be with my mom, I think.

"Henrie." My sister's voice startles me from the doorway. I didn't hear her come up the stairs, but she's here now, poking her head into my dark attic room, smiling big as the Cheshire cat. She's got her arms wrapped around her torso like she's cold. "You alone?" she asks.

"What kind of question is that?" I blush, thinking of Joshua. "Come here. Cuddle." I pat the bed.

"You're all sweaty," B.B. says, now next to me.

The sky outside is slowly brightening. The sun will be up soon.

"Bad dream," I say.

B.B. snuggles her toes between my thighs, twisting her body so that I have to make room for her head next to mine on my pillow.

"Your feet are ice!" I shout.

"Give 'em a minute. They'll warm up."

"I don't know how Wilde stands you."

"He loves me. He told me last week. Did I tell you that already?"

"Like ten times."

"You and Joshua should have done *it* by now." B.B. elbows me in the ribs, and I elbow her back. "You know what I mean, right? Done *it*. Had *all* the sex."

"Joshua and I are just friends."

"I'm telling you. Now or never."

"Never."

"Liar."

"Slut."

"Every island needs one good whore."

"B.B.!"

"I have other news, but I'm not telling yet. Secret."

"Don't tell me you aren't going to tell me something if you aren't going to tell me. That's so annoying."

"Henrie, Henrie, Henrietta," B.B. whispers conspiratorially, taking both of my hands in hers. The chill of the dream runs through me, but I push it away. We twist our heads on the pillow to look at each other. Even in the dim light, I can see B.B.'s eyes are bright, her hair loose and a little tangled, as if she's been hanging her head out a car window. "I missed my sister."

"I missed you too."

"You ready for a morning swim in the quarry?"

"Right now?" I ask, recognizing the ritual, but thinking of how cozy it is in bed.

"Just you and me. Before everything changes again."

"What's gonna change?" I ask.

"A little bit of everything."

We slip out the kitchen door and onto the porch and into the chilly beginnings of morning. The sky is dimly lit now, the sun burning orange on the horizon. We run across the brief field of knee-high grass that we've promised Wilderness we will let go to prairie, B.B. whooping, hollering to wake the island.

Neither of us has to tell the other to be careful. At the quarry edge, we scramble down the rocks without speaking and are on the stone floor in what feels like an instant. The bottom of the quarry is darker, barely lit by the rising sun, rutted by ash and rock. Low bows of scraggly pines and long, leafy honeysuckle vines scratch at our calves. Despite the terrain, we run, leap, sprint through the predawn light until we reach the water.

B.B. takes off her shoes and dips her feet in. "Too cold!"

I do the same: "Hell no! I'm not going in there."

"Soon, though, we're going in on a daily basis."

B.B. is already lying on her back, looking up at a still-dark sky, and I lie back too, put my head on the crook of her arm. We are quiet, letting our breaths even out.

"Let's stay until the sun is high," I say.

B.B. nods in agreement then says, "He's cute. And he likes you. A lot."

"How can you tell?" I ask.

"Let's just say he never flirts with *me*."

"So, if a man doesn't flirt with you, he must be in love with another woman?"

"Or gay."

"God, B.B.," I say.

"What?" B.B. asks, pretending to be innocent. "I think I love Wilde back, but I haven't told him yet. Isn't he wicked?"

"He's a wild, wiry fucker. I'll say that much."

This gets us laughing. A pulse through both our bodies.

As the laughter subsides, we relax, and I breathe in to capture the smells. Pine needles, limestone chalk, burnt wood, firepits, the sandalwood smell of B.B.'s skin. It all smells like joy, like nothing bad had ever happened or will happen here.

I wake up first. The sky is pink with the rise of the sun, little scratches of color in a light sky. I spoon up closer to B.B. and let myself stay for a few more breaths, aware of my sister's tangled hair under my head. A stone digs into my side below my ribs, and my hip bone feels brittle. The ache of the quarry floor making itself known.

If someone were to find us here—two grown women curled to each other—they would get the wrong idea. We are no longer little girls for whom physical affection is simply considered sweet, but I don't care. On this island we are blood, queens of Fowler. I think of Joshua suddenly. His laugh, the one that bursts out of him when I make a joke, as if I have truly and joyfully taken him by surprise. If he wandered into the quarry and stood above us, would he think us strange?

Joshua's mother has worsened a great deal in a short time. At sixty-five, she'd hoped to retire, but instead her mind is going soft as if she's one hundred, turning into something forgetful and needy. He doesn't like to talk about it, but he's spent more and more time with us at the house.

"Time is it," B.B. says, wincing as she sits up.

"Bright enough that we should be up."

"How long has it been since you slept in this quarry?" B.B. stands slowly with her hand on her lower back.

"Last time I slept out here was with you."

"Really? So long ago?"

I feel a burst of jealousy in my chest. "Are you really in love with Wilderness?"

"Of course. He's it for me for a while. The end all be all. My alpha and omega. You've got a twig in your hair." B.B. reaches across to untangle the twig. The tug of her fingers on me no longer reassuring.

"You sound like you don't really mean it."

"I mean it. You're the one who doesn't mean what you say."

"You sayin' I'm a liar?"

"I just don't get why you are so hesitant to put yourself out there." B.B. puts her hands on my shoulders and smooths them down. "Unless you aren't telling me the truth."

"I don't lie to you," I say to B.B., lying just a little or at least that's what I tell myself. "I love *you*, B.B. That's plenty."

"Forget I mentioned Joshua." She flings her arms in the air. "Forget all of it. We have each other. Always have. Always will. Let's be grateful for this summer! For this island! Here we are. Me and you."

I can't help but smile. Wilderness never stood a chance.

"You think anyone else is awake yet?"

"Probably," I say, feeling that pang of something again. Then I smell bacon fat. Sugar, sweet and thick. A memory I can't quite grab ahold of.

"I've got so much to tell you, Henrie," B.B. whispers. Then louder: "Our lives are gonna change. You wait! You watch!"

"What do you mean?"

"You'll know soon! Morning jog!" B.B. slaps me on the arm, taking off. I follow. My joints cracking, my sight blurring. My sister is far ahead of me, leaping over rocks and laughing. Then she is on the porch of the house, hollering back over her shoulder, "I win!"

The kitchen is dark, especially in comparison to the morning sun outside. The old kitchen, like the rest of the house, is perpetually gloomy despite the window above the sink. I let my eyes adjust, hands resting on the back of one of the four mismatched chairs that surround the kitchen table.

"I'm pregnant, Henrie."

B.B.'s lying. It's not even a funny joke. I laugh like it is, but she just stares at me, solemn. Her body doesn't look any different.

"How pregnant?"

"Too early to talk about," B.B. whispers. With one hand on her belly, she reaches out the other and puts it on my belly, as if the baby could be shared. I take a step back.

"You're happy about this?"

"What kind of question is that?"

"A totally normal one. Does Wilderness know?"

"Oh, sure. I told him the first week we slept together."

"It's not his?"

"It's mostly his."

"What the hell does that mean?"

"I mean, it's my baby too," B.B. answers too quickly. She's being disingenuous but I can't tell why.

She opens the fridge, bending into the cool white box

to pull out handfuls of produce—tomato, onion, spinach, olives, feta—then eggs, juice, bacon.

B.B.'s cooking was always an experiment that ended in more dirty dishes than we previously thought we owned. As I watch my sister pile her ingredients on the counter, I realize this too has changed. She's cooked since we've been back in the house together, and she is organized now, thoughtful, the counters cleaned by the time the food is ready to eat.

"And you actually want it?" I ask.

B.B. pulls a blue bowl out of the cupboard. "Jesus, Henrie. You're being rude. I planned it. Or, at least, I planned not to prevent it."

I feel suddenly so irritated and alone that I can barely stay in the room.

"You're twenty-six," I spit out, as if both our mothers didn't have babies at a young age. "What the hell are you going to do with a baby?"

"Raise it. Here, on island. Boys. More than one. I can feel it."

"Jesus, B.B." Now I feel mad, although I can't quite tell why yet. "You can't *feel* the gender. Or twins. And you don't even know you're really pregnant, do you? Have you been to a doctor?"

B.B. briskly beats the eggs, her smile constant, as if all is right in her world.

"You are not ready for this," I say. My grip on the back of the chair has gotten too tight, as if my body believes it's the only thing holding me to the room, so I release it and blood rushes back into my fingers with a prickly ache.

B.B. slams down the blue bowl. Eggs slosh out the top, viscous yellow liquid stretching down to the counter. "Haven't you noticed how good things have been here for me? For us? I'm raising my babies here, Henrie. With my family," B.B. says, turning to look at me, her voice gone hard and sharp, the same swift slice through the air between us as the knife against the soft tomato.

I understand then that B.B. has thought of the baby, or rather babies, in the same way she is thinking of the omelet she is preparing. Like breakfast, this is something she has made. Something that can be prepared, seasoned. She can add or subtract to control flavor and portion. The omelet a solution to hunger; the babies a solution to the heritage of the island.

My sister clears her throat, then turns to chop off a slab of butter and put it into the already-too-hot skillet. It spits and sizzles, melting straight to a burnt brown that she ignores.

"You're crazy," I say. It is meant as an internal revelation, but it isn't. It's spoken out loud so she can hear it.

She sets the knife on the table, carefully, precisely, and turns to look at me. "I'm taking care of this family. Like I always have. Like I always will. Not like your mother. She could have done this a long time ago and she didn't. She picked herself over everyone else. Had the solution in her goddamn belly and killed it, then left Daddy here to die. And me."

"What are you saying?"

"How did you not figure this out? Carrie was pregnant that summer. She was *pregnant* and everything was happening as it should. She was going to have a boy. Then she disappeared and came back *not* pregnant. That's when your dog—that I gave you by the way—drowned in the quarry pond and you lost your shit and left."

An image of Toast floating in the pond flashes in my mind. His body swollen with water. My breath catches in my throat. I almost ask, *Did I do that?*—but I swallow the question and say instead, "She wouldn't."

"Why not? Just 'cause you're married and have a home and family means you have to have whatever baby gets put up in you? I'm shocked, Henrie. That's not very feminist of you."

"That's not what I meant."

"Oh, also, we're getting married, Wilderness and I," B.B. announces. "Damn, I'm fucking up this breakfast."

Wilderness steps into the kitchen, a tall and deciduous man. "Morning," he says, loping forward and kissing B.B. on the top of the head. "Let me."

B.B. sits down at the table. Resigned, it seemed, to Wilderness taking over. I sit too, more out of exhaustion than from any decision.

"See how he is? Always standing nearby to help. We'll get married here. In the quarry. Next month."

"In July?" I wish Wilderness would leave so I could protest: *B.B., you're crazy. This is not a real plan! A real life.*

"Married?" Joshua asks from the kitchen doorway, his blond curls shooting out around his face. "Who's getting married?"

"Fat with baby over there and me." Wilderness is clearly pleased with himself. Clearly in love.

"When did you get here?" B.B. asks Joshua.

"Just arrived. But, hang on, what are you saying?" Joshua looks astonished, and I'm relieved. B.B. and Wilderness making baby and wedding plans is not normal. It's too sudden.

"I told her to tell you a few weeks ago," Wilderness says to me. "Give you time."

"That would have been nice, B.B. A heads-up would have been excellent. I'm your sister after all. We could have talked the whole 'plan' through from the start."

"Honestly, Sis, it was more fun to 'talk' the whole thing through with Wilde." B.B. rolls her eyes at me.

The shock shifts to hurt.

Then B.B. reaches across the old kitchen table and takes my hands in hers. Her hands are warm from the busywork around the stove. "I wanted to tell you. It was all I could do to keep from telling you."

We stare at each other, unblinking. It's another trick we developed as little girls. We know each other by heart. We know where each other's irises flick from too-pale blue to amber to brown. We always imagined that the patterns of our irises could be fitted together, clicked into place like the gears in a lock, rolled and shifted around, dilated until opened. In staring into those memorized patterns and colors, we learned to recognize ourselves in each other. We could always tell if the other sister was lying just by looking long and hard enough. She is in love—with both Wilderness and these potential babies. I break the gaze first. B.B. let's go of my hands.

"What the fuck was that?" Joshua asks. "Some kind of mind meld?"

I snort.

"Well, that's fantastic! Your news. Right?" Joshua aims a slap at Wilderness's back. "When are you due?"

"Let's see . . . well . . . how long does it take again, Wilde?"

"B.B.!" I say. "You have to take this seriously."

"They say nine months, but it's really about ten." Wilderness nudges me with his elbow and winks. "You're gonna be an auntie."

I realize that we were always going to end up back here. Lulled into something like family. We are dead leaves, trash brought in on the waves of the ferryboats or slipped loose from long-ago Lake Erie shipwrecks. We are the sloughed-off skin of Fowler. The dead weight, the melted glacier. Dead girls rising. If B.B. thinks that anything that comes out of her on this island will be born anything but evil, she is crazy.

"You can't have those babies. Not here," I say quietly, as if it were possible to whisper it low enough for Wilderness and Joshua not to hear.

My sister's face hardens. "Hey," she says, turning from me to Joshua. "If you guys would just get it together and finally fuck, you could get married with us." She says it with venom. So much hate for me in her that there shouldn't be room for those babies, no matter how new or how small or how imagined.

"Fuck you," I say, my face hot with embarrassment.

"Eloping is more our style," Joshua says, so casual and calm, we all turn to stare at him.

"Eggs!" Wilderness announces.

"I'm starving," Carrie says. "What are we talking about?"

"After we eat," B.B. says.

"Sit," Wilde tells Carrie, a command that actually works. He hands out plates filled with eggs and bacon and toast. Everyone is eating as if everything is fine, but I can't do it. I can't even pretend. I feel sick from embarrassment, from my barely begun fight with B.B. Wilderness looks right at me, and I take a tentative bite and nod my yum. I can't taste a thing.

"This is delicious," someone says.

"B.B. and Wilde are getting married, and B.B. is pregnant!" It bursts out of me, a predictable outburst but also unexpected.

"What?" My mom's fork drops to her plate. The clang is loud in the wake of my announcement.

B.B. scowls at me. "Wilde and I are pregnant, so we've decided to get married. In the quarry." B.B. pastes on a smile.

My mom says nothing for a while. I watch her reach up to the back of her head, pull. Her hand comes away with a few strands of hair, but she holds them in her closed palm and tucks her hand under the table. The gesture goes largely unnoticed.

"Mom?" I say, asking her for a verbal response.

I want her to be outraged. To tell B.B. this is impulsive and stupid, but instead, she says, "That's great, B.B. Congrats, Wilde. I can't think of anyone better for my daughter."

B.B. scowls again—she does not like my mother claiming her—but quickly makes her face into something brighter. "July Fourth weekend," B.B. says brightly. "It will be perfect."

The conversation continues all around me. The stupidity of it all seems apparent only to me. The house feels different again. This motley crew of hunched-up bodies feasting. The whispers of ghosts waking in the walls. A fat drip of water hits the center of the table, and I look up. The ceiling boasts a big wet spot that I have not seen before. Above us is my father's office. The door is locked. I tried it once but not again. I should go in there, look around, but B.B. doesn't want me to. She didn't say that, but I could tell. It occurs to me that all our forehead-to-forehead mind melding is bullshit. There are lies between us. Big, monstrous secrets that I never knew were there. Did she?

The edge of the stain on the ceiling is bright and thick. The center is already readying for the next drop: a saliva string of viscous liquid stretches long before breaking from itself and splashing down amid all of us. No one else notices. No one even looks up from their plates.

Joshua and I go on a hike after breakfast. It's his idea, but it feels like mine. I don't want to be around B.B. or my mom or any of them.

"They built a new boardwalk that cuts through the island to the state park beach," he says. "Can I show you?" I don't tell him I've already seen it. "We can walk the beach from there if you're willing to climb over some boulders. It all connects up to the monument."

The monument is a large historical marker that sits at the start of the small piece of island that is owned by the state. The marker announces the deep grooves left by glaciers thousands and thousands of years ago. It makes the Volt family history seem recent and insignificant in a way that I like.

"This walk needs to take the rest of my damn life." I

picture the babies in my sister's belly, swimming around each other, tiny as germs. Their dreams monstrous and bigger than the island.

"I take it the baby thing was a surprise."

"And marriage! She's crazy." I have my camera over my shoulder. I lift the strap over my head so it crosses my body and won't bounce on my hip. We head away from downtown and into the heart of the island.

"Noted. Marriage and babies are crazy."

The island doesn't have many sidewalks. Just the ones out in front of the handful of shops downtown, and even those are too old and lumped up to be truly walkable, so Joshua and I walk in the road—his hands shoved in his pockets so that his right elbow pokes out toward me, brushing my arm every once in a while.

Some of me is here. In the present with Joshua. My body feels his next to mine, flush with his nearness and the knowledge that we have spent nearly no time alone together. Always in the house, painting, eating with the group. The rest of my mind is still deep in the house. Swimming in its rot. All of it seeming as sinister as it had seemed peaceful yesterday. Watching them all eat, leaning over their plates at the same time, with the same eagerness. "What?" I ask.

"You think marriage and kids are gross. I guess I could feel relieved about that. At least for the moment."

"I don't think marriage and children are gross. My sister is not responsible enough for kids. Plus, she thinks she can predict their gender. Pregnant with twin boys! Like she could know that at seven weeks or whatever."

"Well, your sister is in her midtwenties, young but not too young, and she's in love. Oh! And she owns her own home. Seems fairly responsible as these things go. Look," he says and points to an opening in the woods across the street. I can see the planks of a narrow boardwalk winding into the trees. We head toward it.

"She barely knows Wilderness!"

"Haven't they known each other their whole lives?"

"She's been drinking and smoking!" I say it like an *aha*, as if I've caught him in a lie.

"Not really," he says calmly. A half smile on his face. "She quit smoking weeks ago. Pretty impressive actually."

"She did?" I try to remember the last time I saw my sister with a cigarette. At the funeral? She quit, and I didn't notice. "Fine, she quit, but what about last night? She had at least one shot."

"I was just thinking about that." Our feet meet the planks of the boardwalk. They are made out of a pressed plastic, and each section was donated, names etched into them to offer claim. "I don't think she actually drank anything. The rest of us did, but I never saw her drink."

"Fine. It's not weird that my sister is all of a sudden getting married and having babies. It's totally fucking normal."

"Hey. I was trying to cheer you up." Joshua stops walking.

"No, I'm sorry. This day has thrown me off." I look down, the board under my feet says VOLT SISTERS. Joshua walks up next to me to see what I see. Our father probably donated money. Who else would it have been? B.B.? Ms. Sonia? I trace the letters with the toe of my sneaker. "We have matching scars, you know. On our thighs. We did it the summer the divorce was announced. In the Quarry Hollow kitchen with a metal spoon."

"I'd like to see it sometime."

I look up at Joshua, startled. He has a half smile on his face. "Are you flirting with me?"

"Always. You never notice."

There is a pause between us that feels powerful. A *moment deserving of a soundtrack*, I will tell B.B. later if I can bear talking to her at all.

"I notice," I say, and look back down.

We walk the stretch of boardwalk quietly, and I am reminded that the island has quiet spots where the trees are lush and the wildlife thrives in safety. The ground around the boardwalk is soft with moss, and the sunlight rains through the treetops in warm patches. There is nothing sinister here.

Eventually the man-made path ends and the noise of the lake lapping at the shore becomes louder. We walk briefly on a well-trod soil path, then the trees break and

Lake Erie shines proudly, sun glinting off its surface and making us both squint. The water smells clean today. Nothing washed ashore to rot. A boat motors by in the distance.

"My parents are talking about leaving the island early. Mom is so much worse than she was even a week ago. She walked all the way to the quarry before we even knew she was missing. Just walked out of the house. She was waist-high in the pond when we finally found her, and the only reason we even looked there was because Mr. Cooper called to say he'd seen her walking that way. We had to take her back in and get her warmed up as quick as we could."

"I'm so sorry," I say. "I didn't know that happened." I want to ask him only one question: *Are you leaving too?* I hold it in. The selfishness of it too clear.

"Dad thinks he's found a place off island that will take them both. Like a retirement home where he can just live in an apartment, but she can get full-time care. It sounds good, I guess."

We are on the beach now. The sand wet and tamped down under our shoes, the water reaching toward our toes. The beach is narrow, just a strip of land that stretches out on either side of us. I remember it being deeper, even at high tide. People would lay out their towels. Rest far back from the water under umbrellas. The ground feels brittle under my feet, like I could dig through with my toes to its underside. It's an odd sensation, one I wouldn't know how to vocalize even if it were appropriate to bring up right now, but I do take a step back. Then another. Something tells me that I am up on the edge of something from which I could fall.

"I wish I could do more for them. Mostly, I just feel like I'm trying to stay out of the way, which is not why I quit my job and came here. Not at all. If they leave, I can at least help them move."

My heart picks up in my chest. "Will you come back?"

"Do you want me to?"

"You should definitely come back," I say, feeling bold.

"You're saying you want me to stay?"

"I am."

"Then I'll stay." He smiles at me, which puts a dimple in his right cheek. "I like you, Henrie. A lot."

I take Joshua's hand and hold on. His fingers wrap around mine without question and the warmth of us feels right. I think maybe he will kiss me or maybe it's me about to kiss him, but then we don't. Our hands touching is a first, and his words *I like you* echo in my head, so much greater than any other declaration he could have made.

"Come on," I say, dragging him behind me, sand slipping under our feet and kicking up behind us. When we reach the first set of boulders, a property barrier for a house that can barely be seen through the trees on our right, I turn and look at our path across the sand. Our feet have left little holes that have filled with water in our wake.

We climb boulders and push sand until we reach the campground, then twist through the winding road that connects the sites until we are across from the glacial-grooves park. We catch our breath and Joshua reads the signs to himself. Little snippets of information B.B. and I never found much use for. Joshua studies them, tilting his flattened hand midair. It's an almost-unconscious gesture. I've seen him do it when figuring out how much tile we need to buy to cover a floor or paint to brighten the porch ceiling. He is following the path of the glacier, his hand the ice. It is a small gesture—like people who use their fingers to calculate a tip or read interesting lines of text aloud to themselves without knowing they are doing it. I love knowing that Joshua does this. He is thinking it out, marveling at intricacies that would never have occurred to me.

I look around to make sure we are the only two people at the site and then say, "Joshua. Climb the fence and lie down in one of the grooves. I want to take some pictures. I used to do this with B.B. when we were kids."

I expect him to protest. To say, *No, we'll get in trouble.* To say, *What if everyone climbed the fences? What would be left of the grooves?*

Joshua latches on to the fence and hoists himself up and over with no trouble at all. Once over, he keeps to the edges where the grooves are still covered by soil and grass.

"Where do you want me?" he asks.

"Just find a fit for your body."

Once B.B. had convinced me to do it the first time, it became normal to climb the fence every time we visited in order to fit our girl bodies into the rock canals. The rock isn't as smooth as it looks from a distance—it tends to bruise flesh if treated too roughly. The game was to see which of us Volt sisters was better able to fit her body to a groove. The ultimate goal, as B.B. stated it, was to camouflage yourself to the rock. Not so much so that we'd completely disappear to the average onlooking tourists, but enough so that they'd have to look twice, perhaps give a little shriek. Scream for the poor dead girl. *Somebody help!* they'd yell. Or, better still, they'd see me curled there, and I'd be so formed to rock that they'd only point shyly and mutter, *That poor girl. The glacier must have pushed her a long way before she came to rest here on Fowler Island.* They would not weep but marvel. A plaque would be made: SOME YEARS AGO, THE NORTH-SIDE QUARRY FOUNDERS DISCOVERED THE PETRIFIED BODY OF A YOUNG GIRL. IT IS BELIEVED THAT SHE WAS SWALLOWED BY THE GLACIER SOMEWHERE FAR NORTH AND TRAVELED WITH IT FOR HUNDREDS OF YEARS BEFORE GETTING CAUGHT HERE, HER BODY MIRACULOUSLY INTACT.

The game, when played at its best, had always required a bit of mud and leaves caked to my body. B.B. admired me greatly for always being able to locate a spot that wrapped me tight, a semicircle of rock that—once I had placed myself—looked like it had been carved to fit me. B.B. would look on and say admiringly, "It was made for you, Henrie. You were hatched from this island." Back then, I loved it when B.B. would talk about the island as if it had birthed us. I used to love the idea that we were born of the same mother. I don't know if I like it anymore.

Joshua, I can see, has found a circular dip—a spot that looks as if a meteor landed there rather than a slow-sliding block of ice—and he's curled himself inside it. Joshua, although curled fetal, does not look born of the island. Maybe that's because he isn't. He's not a tourist but also not an islander. He can come and go as he pleases. One of the summer people. When his parents pass, he will sell that lakeside house and be free to buy a real vacation home, someplace where the sun shines brightly without humidity and the water is meant for swimming.

He is clearly not a part of the rock, but I realize that's what will make the photograph beautiful. He is wearing a tight black T-shirt and his biceps press at the cloth. His shorts leave his calves entirely exposed, taut muscles keeping his legs in place. I snap a few pictures—some so that the chain link will show, others from above so that it will be as if no barrier existed.

"Gorgeous," I say, as a way of telling him I am finished, and he smiles so wide that I know he's taken it as a personal compliment. Maybe it was.

"I didn't expect the rock to be so cold." He hops back over the fence.

"It remembers the glacier." I think this is a perfectly good explanation, and I also think the picture would be better if Joshua had been naked.

"You're a silly girl," he says. I know it is meant to be endearing, but I don't like being called a girl. "The island doesn't remember the glacier. The rock is just cold because the sun hasn't hit it yet."

"Whatever."

"All things are possible in Henrie's world. The world has no hard-and-fast rules. It's all mermaids and ghosts and photographs."

"You're thinking of B.B."

"Why do you think I don't notice you?" It's his turn to be irritated. "It was charming at first, I guess. Like you're too modest to know that you're amazing, but now . . ."

"Now it's not charming?"

"It still is but it could also be rude."

"I like you," I say, almost too quiet to be heard.

He kisses me, and it feels like we've done it before. Like we know already how we will disappear into each other, like body to glacier. His hands are on my back, his whole body pushing against mine, and it is not enough.

All I can think is *More, more, more.*

-⟡-20-⟡-

sonia

2000

L isten," I say, standing up to face the room. "This morning the shoreline measured the same as it did last week and the same as the week before, but, back in April, we were losing ground. And the whole island, not just the sand but the forest growth leading up to it, was saturated. Like a sponge. And this was a mild winter with very little rain in the early spring. So, there is no logical reason for that extreme change, and please note that we have not gained any of the footage back. The island is smaller, drier, but not regaining size." The room is focused on me.

Wally, who has only recently been asked to stay for the full council meetings, stands at the back. She looks even paler than usual, her red hair chaotic. I try not to notice the lean she takes in the doorway, her hip popping out, arms crossed just under her breasts.

I keep telling myself that my attraction to Wally has everything to do with her being the only other female in the room. But my palms sweat when she shows up. My words come out in a tumble as messy as her hair.

"Is it true she's pregnant?" Jacob asks. He is in the third row and among the youngest in the room. He and his father run the only gas station, probably the most lucrative business on the island.

"Who?" I ask even though I know exactly whom he is asking about.

"Beatrice."

"Yes." I don't look at him. "Early days but yes."

"They stayed with me briefly," Wally adds quietly. "Supernice."

"It better be a boy," Mr. Cooper says, straightening in his chair while his arm rests on his large belly.

I don't like the suggestion that Beatrice is just a baby maker, so I say, "There is no need for a male heir. Not anymore. The land, the house was left to . . ." I pause because I realize I've almost said B.B., which would be a mistake since Carrie and Henrie still think the island was left to both sisters. I've been waiting for B.B. to tell the truth but she hasn't. I don't know why.

Wally raises her good hand and so my pause goes unnoticed.

"Wally?"

"I was planting herbs yesterday." She lowers her hand and places it on her belly. "As I was root deep, I hit water.

Just a big mud pool. Should I not be digging holes? Is it happening again?"

"I'll need to come see."

"So, did I do something? Break the island somehow?"

No one answers. We all feel bad for her, buying when she did.

"You need a history lesson. Come back with me after the meeting, and I'll fill in the blanks." My face reddens again, and I wait for one of the old men to make a snide comment, but no one does.

She nods her assent, and I keep talking, letting the blush settle down to my neck, then shoulders.

"Okay," I say. "I think it's safe for us to say that the island was sinking. Can we agree on at least calling it that?" I look out at general agreement. "I say we come up with a plan for evacuation in case it begins in earnest again."

"I say we all leave now and just leave rowboats tied to the roofs of the buildings so the stupid tourists can survive if they feel like it," Mr. Cooper says.

"Those stupid tourists are the reason you and your businesses have survived."

"Whatever."

"Well." Mr. Weaver picks at something invisible between his teeth. "I say we keep watching the beaches. Check our herb gardens or whatever. When they disappear or fill up with water, we evacuate."

"Islands don't sink," Wally says more to herself than to us. "Does this have anything to do with the missing girls?"

I look at Wally now. Really look. Her red hair a fire around her head and her hands tucked into her armpits. She looks back at me, and for a second I think she is taking note of me as well. My gut flips, a lovely somersault that I haven't felt since Carrie.

No one answers her.

Wally has never been in the museum. After Millie left me the space, a dusty place made of piles and milk crates and scraps of molding paper, I fixed all its cracks, painted the walls, bought used display tables from Island Thrift, and even shored up the bell tower stairs. In my head, it still looks like that. Like a cared-for place with a new shine.

Wally will see something different. The spiderwebs in high corners and piles of books and clothes on the stairway to the loft. The cracked window—blue stained glass interrupted by a long-ago hailstorm—that has not been washed inside or out in years. I smell reheated salmon and onions. Vinegar and the lavender-scented spray I've used to cover it all. I've become more and more like Ms. Millie in the last decade and never even realized it.

"I'm sorry it's such a mess," I say, and find myself

gathering things. Moving piles. It's a useless effort. Clouds of dust erupt in the air.

"It's fine," she says mildly.

It's strange to feel so nervous around someone yet have no impact on them. I set the pile of newspapers in my hands back on the ground. "There is a big table at the back. Let me grab stuff from upstairs and we can spread out there."

She heads to the back of the museum, looking at the books and island maps and trinkets under glass. Her freckled face is placid. Her gray eyes darker than usual and her clothes baggy. It doesn't look like she's been eating. Maybe not sleeping. I shake off the worry. This woman needs information and nothing more.

I clomp up the stairs feeling as heavy as a horse.

"Tea?" I call down, then realize how dangerously close I am to becoming Millie. I shake off the feeling. "How about coffee?"

"Tea," she says, bold certainty in her voice.

Surprised, I plug in the kettle and prep two mugs. The loft is more an apartment than a bedroom. My small kitchen is here, a woodburning stove, my bed. If not for the first-floor bathroom, I could hole up here and survive the flood, a thought I've worked through at 3:00 a.m.

There is something not right about all of them living at the house. A glazed-over joy that's even impacted Wilderness. I tried to talk to Carrie about it first, saying, "This is unlike you."

She looked puzzled, wrinkling her brow and her nose as if the word *puzzled* needed to be pieced apart and then back together. "It's temporary. Besides, Henrie needs me."

I walked away unnerved, as if I was talking to someone who remembers none of their emotional history. That's when I started gathering information. Taking careful measurements of the island and rereading old material from Millie's journals.

I carry two mugs down the stairs, steam in my face and papers under my arms. I have to make several trips back upstairs to gather the journals. Wally waits patiently, tea in front of her, as I dump the last pile.

"I was in love with this island for a long time." She leans back in her chair, hands around her tea. "I knew Beatrice Volt before I moved here. Did she tell you that?"

Beatrice hasn't said a word about knowing Wally—not even as the new innkeeper.

"She didn't tell you, did she? I guess I should be grateful. B.B. is no gossip. We were lovers."

"I had no idea."

"The age difference isn't that great."

"Age rarely matters once you're an adult," I say and then duck my head. My mind immediately went to how old she might be compared to me.

"You're shocked," she says. Her voice is tired.

"I didn't know you had a history with the island." I realize I feel protective of B.B. and so don't want to hear anything bad said about her, so I add, "I basically raised Beatrice for a little while. After her mom died and before Carrie showed up."

"Ahhhh," Wally says, as if she's mistaken my tight expression for disbelief.

"Don't be so quick to think it's sweet. She hates me these days."

"I doubt she *hates* you," Wally says.

"Maybe. Maybe not. I count her as my own regardless."

"Well, I'm the asshole in this story. B.B. was just being B.B. I met her at a coffeehouse. In Boston. She was on a date with some guy, but she looked over at me and rolled those strange blue eyes at me, as if she and I shared a secret. Anyhow, she stayed after he left, and I flirted hard. Did my best work, in fact, but, at closing time, we both went our separate ways."

"Why are you telling me this?"

"It's pertinent, don't you think? To why I bought the Island Inn and moved here and now walk around like a sad sack. And don't you want to know how I lost my thumb? Everyone else does." She tucks a mass of red behind her right ear; it does not stay.

"You don't have to tell me anything you don't want to tell me," I say, but I want to know all of it. Every detail. *I want to know you.*

"You're about to share island secrets with me, right?"

I nod my yes, tired of hiding my blush. I let it rage on my cheeks and neck.

"The next time I saw Beatrice we slept together, and I was smitten. In love. Completely heartbroken when she declared just a week later that we were going to be the best of friends. Thought I'd never recover, but then I met Emma." Wally raises her injured hand as if introducing me to Emma.

"I don't understand."

"I know, you will. But I haven't really told Beatrice all of this, and I'd rather you didn't tell her. It would bother her."

I laugh, a loud awkward bark. "B.B. doesn't talk to me much."

"Well, she used to talk about you when she talked about the island. Man, she painted an amazing picture of this place, although, now that I've been here and the island is—what did you say?—'sinking,' I can see that the charming stories she told were also rather inexplicable and dark. I thought it was just her sense of humor."

"She should have warned you."

"No. It's my fault. Is and was. I didn't tell Beatrice I was planning to buy here. Also, I'm the one who slept with Beatrice again when she showed up one day, sad, and come to think of it, I don't even know what she was sad about. I just wanted to comfort her. At least that's all I wanted at first." Wally pauses. Her turn to flush with color. She touches the stump where her thumb should be. "Anyhow Emma found us together."

"Wait. You mean you cheated on Emma with Beatrice?"

"I did," Wally says, nodding as if this makes her the worst kind of person. "I cheated and got caught. My apartment—not mine anymore, mind you—had this old iron door, heavy as shit. Hard to open but quick to shut. So, I chased Emma out into the hall or tried to, but she pulled the door shut behind her, and it swung closed on my hand. Flattened my thumb. B.B. couldn't get it open from our side. I had to wait half an hour for an EMT to show up and use the damn jaws of life."

"That's a horrible story."

"Mostly just a stupid story. Emma and I were in love. We were planning a commitment ceremony. Anyhow, my thumb was smashed—bone dust and gushy blood stuff strung together with tendons. It hurt so fucking much to lose Emma that the pain of my thumb smashed in that door was a gift. So much easier to deal with. So much what I deserved."

"You are being a bit hard on yourself," I say, sipping tea. It's hot and bitter but I swallow it down.

"I'd been listening to Beatrice's island stories and had been here once or twice as a kid. When the inn came on the market, it felt like destiny. I'm thirty-two. I bought the place. Ditched my life."

"Did you ever try to talk to Emma?"

"Of course. I called and called, but she never would answer. Eventually she changed her number. Just as well, I guess. She wouldn't have taken me back, and how could I have respected her if she did?"

"Part of you must really hate her." I'm thinking of B.B., and all the rumors about B.B. running wild on the island, seducing people then tossing them aside.

"I don't hate anyone. Just myself most of the time. I deserve to die on this rock."

I reach across the table and put my hand on her arm. She lets me.

"I stopped loving Beatrice in that way when I saw Emma's face as she was seeing us. There is just something about Beatrice that makes me not right."

I stare across the room. Light is catching the edge of a cobweb swaying in the window draft.

We sit quietly together.

Eventually I take my hand off her arm. "Thanks for telling me all that. You didn't have to."

"Well, if we get closer, not telling you would start to feel like a lie." She takes a deep breath, sets her tea on the table, gestures at the piles. "What's all this?"

I tell her the story of Seth Volt as Millie told it to me. The devil rising up. Promises made. A house built to look like home but act like a prison. I open my notes. Spread out the pieces of paper I've created. Each one belonging to a missing girl. I've listed the girl's name, the date she went missing, the items found on the cliffs. I haven't found all of them, but I have over two dozen, dating back to Elizabeth Volt herself.

"Holy shit." Wally breathes in shallowly, then out with far more force. She pushes the pages around and begins to read a few aloud and in no particular order.

"That's not even the half of it. There is a ton of folk-lore about Seth Volt. About the house and how Elizabeth sneaked around inside when Seth was gone, nailing shut the windows, bolting furniture to the floor. How she started talking to herself, always mumbling as if there were other people in the room with her. She liked to dig at the walls with her fingers. So much so that Seth had to call the island doctor at one point to bandage her hands—she'd lost fingernails—and when the doctor noticed a chipped front tooth, she confessed to eating the plaster. Her stomach full of lead paint and toxic dust, horsehair between her teeth."

"Yikes," Wally says.

"Fowler has its own rules. It makes people crazy in their own special way. I'll tell you what the last Curator told me when I was still a kid.

"Long ago when Seth's team started work on the quarry, all went well, the rock melting away like butter, until late in the night when the lake found the hole and started rising up. Out of the water crawled something thick and gray and green and slimy as moss on a stone. Its long fin of a tail grew into legs as it heaved itself onto

THE INSATIABLE VOLT SISTERS 347

land. By the time it got to Seth's tent, it looked almost human. Its joints didn't bend right, and it had scales covering its entire body. Oh, and it had grown tall! So tall! Big enough to hover over Seth's tent and block out any light the moon was providing. It smelled like blood and sweat and dynamite. It was the smell that woke Seth. He stepped out into the night too damn stupid to be afraid. He demanded, 'What do you want?' The creature cocked his head and blood dripped from the shape that was his mouth. Still, that dumb-ass man was unafraid. Seth said, 'I'm too tired for this. I'm going back to sleep.'

"Seth turned to go, and the creature stretched out his arm, and as it stretched out, it turned from an arm into something long and skinny and dead gray, a creature all its own. Where his hand had been, he grew two dark eyes and two rows of sharp, dark teeth. The eel curved around to look Seth in the face, then, before Seth could do anything, it pushed its way into his mouth. The creature took a tooth from each side of Seth's dumb head, pulling them out and putting them into his own, crunching on 'em like potato chips.

"Seth, having regained the use of his mouth, screamed at the monster, 'How dare you!' He was angry, but he somehow thought he was gonna be fine. That's how big his ego was. It went on like this all night. The creature reaching inside of Seth to take what it wanted. When Seth was just about empty, he sank to his knees and begged the creature to stop. Our island devil told Seth he'd give him everything he'd taken back except his heart on one condition."

"What was the condition?" Wally asks.

"The devil stood tall and said to Seth, 'If I can't have you, I will have your women. Bring me the weak. The lonely. The ones who will not be missed.'

"Seth asked, 'What will you do with them?'

"And the devil answered, 'I will fill my belly, and when it is full, I will fill their bellies. They will birth my babies, who will walk the island as my own. Until then your firstborn son and their son and the sons of those children will live in the house you make and watch over the island.'

"In any case, Seth agreed, so the devil took all the bone and tissue and blood he'd eaten and barfed it up in one small nugget that he pushed back down into Seth."

"What happened to Seth?"

"Well, the next day Seth woke up near his tent on the ground. His body sore but his vision for the island stronger than ever. He would need a son. He took Elizabeth from her sister that week, and they were married soon enough. She made him a boy, and the island has been passed down from one stonehearted son to another until James."

"This is insane."

"Millie has notes. Drawings, even, of the kind of

demon she thinks lives under the island. She refers to him as *the* Devil—capital-*D* Devil—but I think of it as the troll in that fairy tale with the goats."

"'Three Billy Goats Gruff,'" she says, no spark in her voice.

"Yes. I think there's always been something living under the island, and when B.B. and Henrie's great-great-grandfather came along to colonize, one of the first things he did was blast a big old hole in the middle of it. That became the quarry pond. That troll or devil or whatever came crawling up angry and hungry as hell.

"These missing girls are all young women who have had to overcome something or get past something. And the island found them and ate them. This girl here." I slide my notes across the table. "Off-island newspaper pieces about how, after she went missing, they blamed her boyfriend. He'd been hurting her, that's what her friends said anyway, and I think she came to Fowler on the run. Another girl, Carmen, her mother had just died. Eighteen and she lost her mother. Claudia, here, was twenty-nine and had just been fired by a boss she'd accused of raping her."

Wally sits back. "There is an island troll that eats young women. This is what you're saying to me?"

I do not stop for her sarcasm. I can't. I've never said any of this out loud to anyone, and now that I've started, I can't stop.

"There is a hole at the bottom of the quarry pond that goes all the way to the lake. That's fact. It's not big— maybe twelve inches in diameter—but it's there. And that story about Seth making a deal with the devil has got to have a little truth in it. He built that house so he could keep an eye on the quarry. Feed it, maybe. I don't know."

"The goats make it," Wally says, her voice quiet, but then she sits up straighter, a smile brightening her gray eyes and pushing her freckles higher on her cheekbones. It's so beautiful, it's all I can think of.

"What?"

"The goats. They are a family, brothers maybe. They have to get across, and they outsmart the troll. All three of them. That's what we'll do."

"You believe me?" I ask.

"I have nothing but that inn. Well, that inn and a whole lot of debt. And, when I broke my lover's heart and mutilated my hand, I didn't stay and deal with it. I ran. I ran to this stupid, fucking sinking island—no offense— and pretended I wasn't chasing after Beatrice Volt for love or revenge. I need to stay here. And fight."

Her assessment of herself is said with speed and humor and ferocity. I can see the hurt radiating off her, and I am suddenly scared for her. She is a perfect candidate for jumping.

She reaches her hurt hand across the table to touch me. The same gesture I offered just a little while ago.

"Early on, within my first month on island"—her voice is softer now—"I woke up standing above the quarry pond. I didn't know how I'd gotten there, but I knew I was there to dive in. I'm not sure why I woke up and was able to walk away when so many other women didn't, but I did. I can tell you that I felt something pulling at me. Like physically pressuring me to go over the edge, and that the water looked different. Full of something dark."

"I had no idea," I say. And, by this I mean, *I'm sorry.* All this planning and thinking and worrying about Henrie and B.B. and Carrie, and there is an island of other people that needed me to be paying attention.

"That night, the one when I almost jumped, there was someone else in the quarry. Up on that elevated rock that I've heard you call the Watch Tower. He was kind of standing there, arms crossed, waiting in the dark for me to jump. Like it was no big deal, but when he realized I was seeing him and not going to jump, I swear to God he snarled and dropped to all fours and leapt off that rock like it was nothing. He chased me. All the way back to the inn. I could hear him snarling and huffing. I don't know how I ran faster than him, but I got inside the inn and locked the door. This was before I reopened, so I was all alone and, I swear to you, that thing sat on the lawn all night. Sat and paced and made mumbling, spitting noises as if trying to decide whether to crash through the front door and eat me. At some point, I fell asleep, and when I woke up, it was a sunny island morning, and he was gone. I lock myself in my room at night now. I have a system that isn't perfect, but it would slow me down if I decided to wander again."

"Has it happened again?"

"Oh, no. I've not even woken up trying to get out of my room or anything like that."

"Did you recognize the man?"

"It was nighttime. And he was far away, but I ran into him later, and I know it was him. I don't know how to explain to you why I'm certain, but I'm certain, and it makes sense in this fairy tale of yours."

"Who?" I ask.

"James," she says. "James Volt."

❦21❦

beatrice

2000

It's been nearly three months since I met the devil, and I alternate between moments in which it seems like it never happened and moments when it seems that the seconds in which I am currently living are the ones that never happened. Either way, my changing body brings me back to reality anytime I drift too far off.

I am in the Quarry Hollow kitchen surrounded by my people. It's easy, with so many people around me, to stop worrying about the babies growing in my tummy, how fast they are pushing out my skin, how much they seem to move.

"But it's *not* too hot for soup!" Henrie is shouting in response to something Joshua has said, some niggling comment meant to make her laugh. He loves her. We can all see it. Their argument is playful.

"Joshua's right. It is too hot for soup," Wally offers. "I'm sweating."

The house feels big tonight. The doors seem to hang more loosely on their hinges; the front door is rarely shut. In fact, it swings open on its own, as does the back door. As if every frame in the house has widened to invite more people inside. With the exception of Henrie's darkroom, which she keeps locked, and Daddy's study, which I keep locked, we leave everything that can be opened open. And people come. They stop by. They say hi. They stay for dinner. Tonight, the house is fat with people.

We gather for dinner regularly now. It's our third meal together, but it feels like we've done it a dozen times. We've fallen into a rhythm that is both familiar and familial. Carrie, Henrie, Joshua, Wilde, Wally, and Sonia.

"You'd be sweating soup or no soup," Ms. Sonia, laughing, teases Wally. Flirting? I think yes. There are quiet tensions in this kitchen. So much smaller than they were before we began to gather, but they are here all the same, and the one between Wally and Ms. Sonia is decidedly sexual. I had hoped Carrie and Sonia would hook up again. It would have kept Carrie more distracted, but the house seems to be keeping her plenty preoccupied, so I let it be.

"What can I say? I have an advanced cooling system," Wally says, flirting back. The corners of her mouth lift.

"It's definitely too hot for soup," Carrie offers. She's

sitting to my right, always a little too close for my comfort, as if she intends to never let me out of her sight. She's taken up knitting, a hobby absurd for the summer temperatures, and the thick blue yarn she's learning with is unspooling on the kitchen table, the length of it spilling over and sticking to her bare thighs. "Dammit, I dropped a stitch," she mutters to herself, then looks around at us, as if someone in the kitchen magically knows more about it than she does and will step in and help.

After Carrie and Henrie left the island years ago and it was just me and Daddy in a too-quiet house, I worried I was turning into Carrie. That, even though the connection isn't biological, I was growing into the spitting image of her. Desperate and sad and always walking around like I was exhausted. The house pushing down on my shoulders just as it had hers, like we were the only two people in the world capable of holding up its roof beams. I feared that like her I'd be too afraid to leave the island and also too scared to stay. But then I left for college and graduate school, and it was fine. I didn't have to ditch completely. I came and went as I pleased for years. Dad took care of the island, and I took care of myself. And I realized I don't need the island or any of the people on it. I don't even need my sister. I can stand on my own without anyone else. Henrie can lie to me all she wants. I'll always know more, be more, than her.

"Come on now, people," I offer. "Everyone knows a hot summer soup cools the soul.

"Too bad we don't have freshly knit scarves to go with it."

"Don't be sarcastic, Beatrice Bethany. Meal consumption hasn't even begun yet. Besides, you're one to talk," Joshua says, from where he stands by the stove next to Henrie. "You're baking bread! Wilde, what are you offering, tonight?"

"Frittata. It's super-easy," Wilderness says. "Like an omelet but with a good crust on it. The bread will be perfect with it."

"Thank you, my love," I offer, adding, "He's an amazing chef."

"I'm all right." It's clear by the upward pull on the right side of Wilderness's mouth that he likes the attention, but he is no good with praise, so he quickly busies himself by moving to the sink and filling it with soapy water for dishes. His posture gives away his emotions. His pride and shyness evident in the stretch of his shoulders to the ceiling in one moment and then the slope of them toward the floor in another.

And, like she's read my mind, Henrie asks, "So, when is this supposed wedding?"

My sister is staring at me hard. The question is a challenge that I didn't know was coming. There is an easy answer: Wilde and I decided—or rather I led Wilde to the right answer—but I count a few beats, considering why she is asking, a hint of aggression in her voice. I decide I don't care and answer, "July Fourth. It's soon but also the long weekend so off-island folks can come. Plus, we can pretend the fireworks are for us, can't we, Wilde?"

"They will be for us," Wilderness says, pausing in his washing of dishes to give my shoulder a squeeze. He leaves bubbles behind that Henrie's eyes flick to. *Let them take their time soaking into my T-shirt*, I think. "The fireworks are gorgeous here in a small-town kind of way. They have a barge they fire them from." Wilde's talking mostly to Wally now, but Henrie hasn't been here in over a decade, nor has Carrie. "It's done off the north side of the island, where that old Fun Land Park is. B.B., now that you two own all that land outright, maybe we could open up the parking lot to the public? Let them gather there to watch? When the water is really calm, it works like a mirror, so the fireworks seem to be above and below the island. Plus, I'm in charge of approving the fireworks. I can approve a bigger order this year. Make it more special."

"That's my birthday," Henrie says flatly, any aggression gone.

"That's right," I say, as if I hadn't already thought of that. I remember smeared red icing on too-sweet grocery-store cake. We used to imagine we'd catch the fireworks, or rather the hundreds of little illusions of light they created that danced on the water. I used to tell her we'd gather those pulses of light and fashion them into a birthday crown—pink and green and purple sparkles for her head. We'd watch from the glacial grooves. Lie on our backs in the pockets of the grooves while all the other island inhabitants cluttered Fun Land Park.

"We wanted to check with you, of course," Wilderness rushes in, always trying to make peace. "It's just that it's the long weekend so our friends won't be able to say they can't make it. Would it be okay with you?"

My sister wants to say no. She wants to stop the wedding. Make all of this go away. I keep my eyes on her, dare her to say it's not okay. She's holding her breath now, the soupspoon in her hand and the steam of the pot pressing on her throat, her face. She takes a deep breath and says, "Of course it's okay. I can't remember the last time I bothered to celebrate my birthday. It's not like I'd have anything planned."

"I'll throw you a mini-party," Joshua says, reaching out to hold her hand. "We'll get two cakes. One wedding cake and one birthday cake."

"Excellent. It'll be a crazy mishmash of celebrations."

And just like that there is so much chatter and conversation about babies and weddings and quarry walks that any direct or solitary communication between me and my sister is lost to the commotion. Still, when a drop of something hits the center of the kitchen table, I see Carrie look up. She leans in to whisper to me, "Do you hear that?"

Hearing nothing, I ask, "What?"

"James. Like typewriter keys."

"Shall we go see if he's ready for dinner?" I ask Carrie with a smirk on my face.

She looks at me horrified and drops a knitting needle into her lap. She leaves it there.

No one else has heard this exchange. It's just me and Carrie in a little bubble of communication that feels like it's been created for us by the house. Or maybe I've created it. Maybe I'm that powerful now. I feel that powerful, so I lock eyes with Carrie. Hold them tight.

"That's not funny, Beatrice."

"It's not meant to be, Caroline."

"Why is his office locked? Why won't you let anyone go in there?"

"No one has asked to go in." Which is true. They haven't. I haven't had to do anything but keep the door locked. Easy peasy. "Would you like me to let you in, Carrie?"

I can tell her hands are shaking below my line of vision, so I look down at them. Stare and then lift my eyes back to hers. She tucks them under her thighs in a gesture that makes her seem childlike, unprepared, but then her face changes. She bites the interior of her lip, and the sharp little pain must be strong enough to steady her.

"Sure. Let's go," she says.

"Now?" I ask. She's called my bluff, and I hear the quiver in my voice as soon as it is too late to contain it.

"Yes. Now." She puts her knitting on the table and

stands. "Be right back," she says to the group, but they are all busy eating and serving themselves food. No one cares.

"I have to pee!" I announce, and follow Carrie out of the kitchen.

Carrie stops at the bottom of the stairs, and I see that none of this is actually about wanting to go in Dad's office, or even if it were, she is too scared to see it through. With her hand on the banister to hold herself steady, she looks at me.

"I ran into that lawyer. Dennis something. Your father's lawyer."

"So," I say, but my heart rate speeds up.

"So, he recognized me. Introduced himself. I thanked him for all he's done for my girls." She says *my girls* as a manipulation. I'm sure of it. She doesn't give a shit about me. Not really. "Anyway, I told him I was curious about restrictions on the sale of the house and land. I said Henrie, at least, would want to sell her half. Do you know what he told me?"

"Henrie has not said that she wants to sell," I say.

"He said that none of it was left to Henrie. None of it."

"Huh."

"Why would you lie about that?"

"I have a plan, Carrie."

"That's manipulative, B.B., and I don't like it."

"You don't have to like it. You don't have to be involved at all."

"Beatrice."

"Yes, *Mother*."

I think she is about to tell me not to call her that but thinks better of it. "I love you, Beatrice, but I don't trust you. You aren't making good decisions, and even if you won't tell me what you're thinking, you should tell your sister."

"This is not your business." I feel anger rising in me, an old and childish anger.

"If you don't tell her, I will."

I step forward and force her to stumble back. She sits down hard on the second stair. I tower over her, and I feel that anger mature, rise up in me into something violent. It feels good, this adult version of my old outrage, and I let it bloom, redden my face as I bend down and point my finger in her face.

"Don't you fucking dare," I say. It's a snarl. It comes up from deep in my throat, guttural and full of blood, and I see that she is looking at me in horror. I feel it then. The creature I am becoming, and I wonder if it is similar to what my father was. If Henrie and I would twin in our monstrous shapes. It's the first time I've actually felt it coming on, been sure that the deal I made with the devil wasn't just about my babies but also about my body. The power of it moving through me is fantastic. I breathe.

Slow it down. It is not the time. Calmer, I stay leaned into Carrie's face and add, "Stay out of my way, Carrie. Stay the fuck out of my way."

I stand tall and turn on the pads of my feet, walking back to the kitchen, laughing as I enter the room, ready to eat.

✦22✦

henrietta

2000

On three separate occasions while I was working alone in my darkroom, the house has quaked. It gave a great big, unmistakable shudder, like it was trying to shake water from its back. The first time it happened, I stood in the center of the turret and waited for it to settle. Seconds felt like hours, and when it finally stopped, I ran downstairs looking for someone to confirm that it had happened. They were all outside and no one had noticed a thing.

Summer's spell is breaking, and it's certainly my fault. The house doesn't like what I've discovered, but strangely, in my darkroom, in the attic, I feel safe. No. I don't just feel safe. I *am* safe. Even that third time when the house shook a little longer than before, and afterward, when I pulled back the black plastic from the turret window and saw a long crack in the window glass, I felt somehow that

I'd be okay as long as I was up here, in the attic. It's probably another mean trick of the house, making me feel at peace in this teetering room.

Elizabeth Fowler had the roof fashioned with oak, and the boards softened so they could arch out from the center beam. The beautiful brass bed once belonged to her. It is the one space in the house that she created, so, even though it was her prison, it was also her home. From my darkroom, she could see her sister out on Watch Tower rock. They could signal to each other, sign their love in the air, and that's the piece I'm missing—my sister out in the quarry reaching for me as I reach for her. Instead, she is physically close, but has never felt further away. She prances around half-naked, as if shoving her fast-growing belly in our faces is a way to demonstrate that she has no secrets, but she does.

I've been in the darkroom for hours, spending more and more time in here in these last two weeks. Joshua knocks on the door, and I realize he's been calling my name.

"Call it quits, Hen. We're taking a break. Quarry swim. All of us."

"One minute. I have paper out."

It's a lie. The paper isn't out but the red light is still on, and an image is resting in the fixer, calling for my full attention.

"Henrie." His tone is irritated. I'm disappointing him. I don't think I've done that before, certainly not since we became lovers. The newness of it is enough to pull my eyes off the photograph and realize that the room is stuffy and full of chemicals. My head aches. My fingers are pruned. I don't know what time of day it is.

"I'll be right down. I promise."

"Seriously?"

Have I done this before? Stayed locked in my high place and ignored him? The last two weeks are a hazy mix of days of discovery in the darkroom and nights in bed with Joshua. His body. My body. An education, and it has been glorious.

"Seriously," I say.

A few nights ago, I was lying next to him, sweaty and out of breath, realizing that when I'm with him in the attic, I don't worry about anything else. Caught in the feeling of warmth and ease, I almost told him I loved him. It's slowed me down a bit—this too-close confession— and I've felt ill at ease ever since. I learned long ago that loving people too much put you at risk—the more you loved them, the bigger the hurt when they moved on.

At least whatever happened after my dad's funeral hasn't happened again. There have been no more missing girls since we arrived. No more dark spots in the night that I simply can't remember.

I hear Joshua sigh, then his footsteps going down the stairs. He'd understand if he knew what I've discovered, but I haven't told anyone. Not even B.B. I tell myself it's because they wouldn't believe me, but that's too obviously bullshit. B.B. would believe me in seconds. So why haven't I told her? I suppose I'm afraid she'll stop me, and I know that what I'm doing is important. Essential but also tied, surely, to the tiny earthquakes, an undeniable sign that what I'm doing is destructive. That I am somehow taking us apart rather than putting us back together.

I pull the image from the fixer. The paper still boasting a good quarter inch of shiny white all along its border. In the middle, I've caught another one. Captured by the pinhole camera I made from an oatmeal box—I've made at least two dozen of these cameras in the past weeks. Shoeboxes and cookie tins and mason jars—the latter I coated in opaque black paint. I've got them all over the house now. Positioned on top of still objects so that they can watch the walls throughout the night.

I've told Joshua and anyone else who asks that I'm working on a new project and that the cameras must not be touched. If they are even nudged, the image will be impacted, and I add, I am working on a new show that will depict the island at night. I am practicing in the house before I station cameras all over the island. This has made the questions all but stop. The cameras blending with the other, everyday objects of the house.

A pinhole camera takes patience. Light seeks the tiny hole of the camera and pours itself in, settling onto the paper, the image making a home slowly. So, in a way, it shouldn't surprise me that the ghosts have been seeking them out too, diving in, their images spilling into the containers as they settle into their new homes. The images reflect their journey, the struggle to pull free of the house and settle into the homes I've built for them. Once I saw what was happening, I began building them frantically, out of any object I could find. It seems that as long as the object doesn't leak any light, the ghosts can gather there, one per camera. Their remnants cling to the insides of the containers like dust bunnies, like someone has wished on a dandelion, blown all the beautiful little seeds into the camera, and thrown away the stem.

During the day, I gather the cameras, and they are heavy, sometimes so heavy that I can only bring one up to the darkroom at a time. I make new ones, fresh containers that I fill with a new piece of photographic paper and reposition in the house. The ghosts that still live in the walls chatter now, always in the background of my day, gossiping with one another, anxious to be called out into a new home. I do my best to ignore them. I don't want to be distracted, and B.B. would instantly notice if I listened to them. She's already suspicious of my cameras—the sheer number of them has surely given me away—and I have to get up earlier and earlier in the day to collect them.

At night, lately, when I'm drifting off to sleep, I imagine the house a boat, a big drifting thing. In this world between sleep and wake, when the ghosts are first stretching from wall to camera, I can't tell which way is up and which way is down. The water is all around me, the house swallowed by Lake Erie, lulling me to sleep. In these moments, the house defies gravity, as if there is no up or down. I am floating in time and space.

Under the three turret windows spans a shallow window seat. I considered removing it altogether, so I'd have more space, but it is clearly original to the house, a place Elizabeth surely sat to see her sister, to read a book, to cradle her newborn. I didn't have the nerve to get rid of it, then I realized that if I removed the seat from its base—sawed through the nails holding it in place— I could lift the top, reveal a secret, empty space where I now put my ghost-filled houses. They are there now, calm and cozy in the deep dark, their weight pulling the whole house toward the quarry.

I've caught over two dozen ghosts so far. I'm not sure yet what it means or what I'm meant to do next, but they keep coming so I keep making them homes. The images of them that I capture—faces pushing and pressing and howling—once seemed horrific, but now I see the victory in them. Images of women breaking free, finding a purposeful out. They are triumphant as they find their way into my cameras, pooling themselves up for safekeeping, so I close them back up. Lids on, tape over the aperture, safely tucked in the secret space.

"Henrie!" It's my mom this time. Sent to the bottom of the stairs to holler up at me. "Don't make me come up there, young lady!" I know she's just pretending to be mad, but I also know they are all impatient with me. Even Joshua.

"Coming!"

I hang the photo from the drying rack and make sure the shoebox I've converted to a camera is tightly sealed before I lift the thick plastic that covers the windows to let a little fresh light in.

✦23✦

carrie

2000

B.B. has taken to constantly rubbing her belly. She does it all the time. Sometimes she lifts her shirt up to tuck it under her breasts and then she rubs away, prodding and poking with a pained expression on her face as if it hurts. Her belly is tanned and beginning to round out more than I think it should. I keep resisting the urge to tell her to be careful. Don't push too hard or rub too much. I resist because I know it's absurd. B.B. can't break her belly or hurt the babies by rubbing, but the action of it bothers me all the same. As does the size of her belly. It's been a long time since I was pregnant, but I know her belly is too big too soon, and I'm worried. When I questioned her, asking, "How far along are you exactly?," she accused me of calling her fat, so I dropped it.

I thought time together would help repair our relationship, but now it seems that I know less about both my daughters than ever before. Henrie barely comes out of the attic, and when she does, it's to collect the bizarre handmade cameras she puts all over the house that she won't let any of us touch. She is not eating enough, and she looks skinny and pale. She spends most of the rest of her time with Joshua. He's found a spot in her life, and I suppose I'm grateful for that, but I am lonely and sad and I miss my work, and no one here needs me. Not even Sonia.

I hardly sleep anymore. I lie in my bed and worry, wake in a sweat if I fall asleep at all. I am more muddled with each passing day. Every night I think, *If B.B. doesn't tell Henrie this house doesn't belong to her tomorrow, then I will. I will tell her and then Henrie will leave the island with me, and it will all be okay again.*

I've come down to the kitchen to find coffee, but I've stumbled on B.B. and Wally instead. Wally is on the kitchen table, poking about at the ceiling. B.B. is trying to discourage her.

"I told Sonia I'd take a look at it," Wally is saying, as B.B. swats at Wally's calves with a dish towel. "She's on her way over so leave me be!"

It's a playful conversation on the surface, but when B.B.'s eyes meet mine, I see again that anger she had when I confronted her at the bottom of the stairs.

"Hand me something. A spatula will do," Wally says to B.B. Despite having a houseguest, Wally, here, B.B.

has come down in a sports bra and what are probably Wilderness's boxers.

"Do you think you might put on some more clothes?" I ask B.B., but she ignores me, keeping her eyes on Wally. I'm standing in the kitchen doorway. I've just gotten out of bed myself, but I've still managed to pull on pants and a tank top.

"Morning, Carrie. Did you sleep well?"

"I wouldn't say well. Thanks for asking though, Wally."

"B.B., hand me a spatula."

"It won't be long enough to reach," B.B. says, leaning against the stove, rubbing her belly.

Wally lets out a loud exhale.

"Are you mad at me?" B.B. asks sharply.

"Nope. But I do wish you'd stop rubbing your belly like that."

"Ha!" I say, then cover my mouth.

B.B.'s hand freezes in place, and then cautiously, as if too quick a motion might cause the belly to fall right off her body, removes her hand. I see her skin ripple; a dark thread spreads out just under the surface of her pale belly. It reminds me of a night long ago in the quarry when I stood over the pond and thought about sinking in. It's a veiny dark ink that rises to the surface of B.B.'s skin, then ducks back in, hiding deeper in her center. It's nauseating, that vision. It pulsates before it's gone, and I am so scared for her, for me. *What is happening?*

"You're both just jealous," B.B. says.

"Don't be absurd," Wally says so I don't have to. I've suspected that B.B. and Wally knew each other before this. That maybe there was a breakup at some point. Watching their banter this morning confirms it.

"What's wrong with you then?" B.B. asks Wally.

"Nothing's wrong with me."

"I know you. You won't let yourself be content. Anytime too much good comes your way, you get nervous."

"Excuse me?" Wally puts her hands on her hips and straightens her spine. She towers over us, her rage pointed at B.B., upstaged only by her red hair, backlit by sunlight streaming through the window behind her. She looks like fire.

"Wilde!" B.B. exclaims, and is off onto the next thing.

"Excuse me," he says from behind me. He puts his hand on my shoulder as he moves past me into the kitchen. I put my hand over his hand to say, *Good morning*. He nods his sheepish *Good morning* as he enters the kitchen, but then B.B. is wrapping herself around him, marking her territory.

"What are you after?" he asks Wally. He is a good man, kind enough to give B.B. his full attention before turning to look at Wally, who is still standing on the table.

"I was just gonna poke around and see how delicate this plaster really is."

"It's a nasty spot."

"Yeah, I'm not quite tall enough to reach it."

"I told her not to do it. She's not listening to me," B.B. says.

"Hop down," he says.

Wally does as she's told. I watch as Wilde sweeps one long leg up onto the table, then the other.

"You're like a grasshopper," I say, teasing Wilde.

"Particularly if grasshoppers had a magnificent third 'leg.'" B.B. gives me a little nudge with her arm.

"Beatrice!" An automatic response from me that comes at just the moment Wally says, "Gross," with full disgust.

"B.B.," Wilderness says from his great height, his fingers already pushing on the ceiling. His voice is low and deep, and I admire the way he can warn her with just one word. A bit of a puppy dog is in him, a following of B.B. that I can tell she loves, but something else too. He shuts her down in a way no one else does. "Can someone hand me something I can use to poke at this with? It's pretty wet."

B.B. is wiggling her eyebrows and smirking.

Wally rolls her eyes. "Jesus, B.B."

"What? The babies are making me horny."

"It's the hormones making you horny. Not the babies."

I decide to intervene and move over to the stove, grab a spatula from the metal bin, and hand it to Wilderness.

THE INSATIABLE VOLT SISTERS 375

"Thank you, Carrie. How long has this stain been here?" he asks.

"My whole damn life," B.B. answers.

"That's not true," I interrupt, knowing or rather believing that it must have appeared when James died and B.B. locked his office door, as if something is left of James in that room—his spirit, his unresolved anger, his worry—and it is leaking through the floor as a means of escape. I can barely manage to think that thought through, let alone say it out loud, so instead I say, "I don't remember it from before."

"Seriously, B.B." Wilderness pokes at it with the rubber end of the spatula and then flips it, uses the metal end to poke at the ceiling, and with the first poke there is a loud sucking sound and then a small hunk of plaster hits the table between Wilderness's big, bare feet. A string of moisture hangs between the hunk and the ceiling. It looks like saliva.

"Gross." Sonia's voice makes me jump a little. She's standing in the kitchen doorway with four coffees in a carrier. The kind of cups one gets from the deli at the island grocery—surprisingly good coffee if I remember correctly. I step around the table, ignoring the pulpy mound resting at Wilderness's feet and the string that is now breaking between it and the ceiling.

"Huh," B.B. says, grabbing a spoon from the same metal bin where I got the spatula. Suddenly able to be of use when it is her idea. She moves up to the table and pokes at the lump. "I told you to fucking leave it alone. It's like the Blob. Better make sure it doesn't swallow us all up."

"Don't joke." Sonia looks alarmed. "Hey, how about you come down from there?" she says to Wilde, but she's too late.

What happens next is sudden and nasty. With a noise that can only be described as a tummy grumble, a huge chunk of rust-red plaster comes down. It splashes over Wilderness's head and clunks down on the table. Instinctively, we all take as many steps back from the table as we can. Wilderness scrambles down. The goo of it all sticking to him like spiderwebs. He swipes at it madly, trying to get it off. It's the first time I've seen him lose his cool. I grab a dish towel and toss it to him.

"What the fuck?" B.B. says. Rust red has splashed on her bare belly. Wilderness has it on his face, and a moldy smell has taken over the kitchen.

Sonia hands me the coffees and moves to the far end of the table so she can peer at what is now a large hole in the ceiling. I swear I see her flinch.

"You can see straight up." Sonia's already taken steps back from the table. The house groans, a growl of sorts, and the light shifts above us.

"What the fuck is in that room?" Wally asks B.B.

"It's private, goddammit."

I step forward to look for myself. The floorboards to

the room above are clear. The cracks between the boards are too wide and uneven, as if whatever has moistened the plaster also got to those boards. I have the sudden urge to say James's name, but I swallow. I remember hearing his typewriter the other night at dinner. Maybe at night too? In those times when I was crossing over into sleep? Typewriter keys thundering away. My brain is so fuzzy; I can hardly tell reality from dreams.

"Well, I guess it wasn't a pipe."

"Not a pipe," Sonia agrees.

"We will need to go in that room and see what's happening. This is not good."

"No one goes in there," B.B. hisses.

We all look at her. The others are startled by her ferocity. I am not.

"This is my house. No one goes in."

"I thought it belonged to you and Henrie," I say, poking the bear.

"B.B.," Sonia starts, "this is absurd. You have a huge hole in your ceiling that needs to be fixed."

"No one is going in there," B.B. says, adamant.

"Guys!" a voice comes from the front of the house. I hear the screen door slam. "Where is everybody?" It's Joshua. He sounds out of breath, running through the house to find us.

He stops short in the doorway. His face flushed. "What's going on?"

"Wilde broke the house," B.B. offers.

"Where's Henrie?" he asks.

"In the darkroom," I offer.

"I'm gonna go shower," Wilderness says in his calm way. "You'll need to hire someone to fix that, Beatrice. I think I've done all I'm gonna do."

I look at Wilde. He has it in his hair, on his face. The red of it rests thickly on his right shoulder. It's foul.

"I'll go with you!" B.B. says, noticing for the first time that Wilderness is coated in the muck of the house.

"What about this mess?" I ask.

"Leave it or clean it. I don't care," B.B. says, already following Wilderness down the hallway and upstairs to the shower.

Joshua grabs some paper towels and takes a swipe at the table. He gags a little.

"Hey," Sonia says. "Let's go outside. Drink coffee. Walk away from this mess for a while."

"Fantastic idea," I say, a feeling of dread growing in me, and I think if I don't get some fresh air that I may faint.

Joshua has something to tell us—we can all feel it— but he also wants to get the hell out of the kitchen.

We meet on the front steps—Joshua, Wally, Sonia, and me. The morning is gorgeous. The coffee is strong and black. Things feel instantly better.

"How is the inn?" Joshua asks Wally. He's still trying to catch his breath.

"Strangely empty," Wally says. "It's always been erratic,

except of course for Masquerade weekend, when we're full, but there are usually a few guests. Right now, I have no one. A guest checked out yesterday and I've had three cancellations this week. It's weird."

Joshua is trying to listen to Wally's answer—after all, he asked the question—but his impatience is clear, so I say, "Let's have it, Joshua. What weird shit has happened now?"

"I was just down by the ferry," he says and sets his coffee cup down on the porch step.

"And?" Sonia asks.

"First, I should say that last week I was getting ice cream at the stand on Main, and I overheard Mr. Cooper talking with some other island folks—Weaver and someone else I can't remember—about 'giving up.' Leaving. It was like he was trying to convince them to go too."

"That's not possible," Sonia says. She has gone pale. "Those are Island Council members. They'd have told me if they were thinking of something like that."

"They clammed up pretty fast once they realized I could hear them," Joshua says. "And this morning, just now, the ferry was packed, and I saw several islanders getting into private boats."

"So?" I ask, not quite getting it.

"So, people are leaving. Locals. Not tourists. There was a line of cars waiting for the next ferry. I've only ever seen it that busy on Masquerade, and that's never islanders."

"Those fuckers." Sonia stands. She's angry.

"I want to leave too," I say, trying to lighten the situation, the implications of which don't seem that dire to me. Perhaps everyone is finally coming to their senses.

"Has Henrie mentioned anything?" Sonia asks me, but then thinks better of it and directs her question to Joshua.

"No! I didn't even tell her about the conversation I overheard. It was odd, but not that odd. I kind of forgot about it until now."

"Well, they certainly wouldn't have told B.B.," Sonia says. "Which means they deliberately kept this from me and the Volts. Jesus."

"Why wouldn't they tell B.B.?" I ask.

"No one likes B.B.," Wally says.

My heart hurts for B.B. and I am about to jump to her defense when it suddenly feels like the front porch is shifting under us. Joshua's coffee falls over, dark liquid spills down the stairs.

We all move off the porch, spill like the coffee, but the ground isn't much better. The whole world is moving.

I've been through a small earthquake once in southern Ohio, but I have never felt the earth move like this. This upending of everything is a terrible feeling, like there is no solidity left, nothing to grasp on to. It's rather like being on the ferry crossing the lake when it hits a big wave and, for a moment, you lose your footing, have no sense of where you will land next. I remember how sick I was on the way here, how I sank to my knees in the parking lot. That was so long ago. I sink to my knees now too, dig my fingers into the dirt as if to hold on, but the ground is soaked. Did it rain last night? And as quickly as it started, the earth stills.

"What the fuck?" Wally asks.

I am up and on my feet, running to the house. It looks to have tilted backward, like it's looking up at the sky, leaving a big gap between the first porch step and the ground. The sidewalk leading up to the front door has cracked and zigzagged, looking like an escalator laid on its side. Sonia grabs my arm, pulls me back from the house.

"Henrie! B.B.!" I scream. "Let go of me!"

"Carrie! Breathe. Give it a damn second."

Sonia does not let go of me. Somewhere far off a siren wails.

"Earthquake?" Joshua asks. "Is that something that happens here?"

Inside, I hear B.B. and Wilderness clattering down the stairs. I shake myself loose of Sonia. Try to slow my heart.

Wilderness and B.B. are with us on the front lawn by the time Henrie appears on the porch, face bright red, sweat stains under her arms. She's looking at us oddly, as if trying to guess something. "Did you feel that? The house shaking?"

I run to her, risking the porch steps and the porch

itself to wrap my arms around her for as long as she'll let me. She half-heartedly hugs me back.

"It wasn't just the house. It was the whole island," Sonia says.

"You're dripping with sweat," I say to Henrie, as I release her from the hug. Her sweat is on me now, transferred to the insides of my arms and the crook of my neck above my right shoulder. A thick drop rolls off Henrie's nose and hits the porch boards as if to confirm my observation. It spreads out salty, leaving a ring on the wood. "Let's get off the porch, please." I take her hand, and she listens, following me to stand on the lawn.

"It isn't the first time," Henrie offers under her breath.

"Excuse me?" I have no idea what she's talking about. I look at the others and am relieved to see that they don't either.

"Forget it. I'm going back in." Henrie turns as if to head back inside and up the stairs.

"The hell you are," I say.

"I can't leave my . . . my project in there."

"You can and you will. What the hell is wrong with you?" I am angry now. Really and truly fed up. She may be an adult, but I'll tackle her to the ground if she's going to be straight-up stupid.

"I should check on the station," Wilde says. "B.B., come with me? I'd feel better if you stayed close."

"I'll be fine, Wilde. Don't be silly. I'm staying with my sister," B.B. says, but I notice that even she looks uneasy, as if the earthquake wasn't part of her plan. What is her plan?

He looks questioningly at Henrie. She isn't looking particularly reliable either.

"I've got her," I offer. "Let's stay together. The three of us," I say to Henrie and B.B., and neither objects, so Wilde nods appreciatively before tucking his uniform shirt into his pants and heading to town.

"They kept it from us," Sonia says. "All of us." She is dazed, disbelieving perhaps that her fellow islanders have betrayed her, or maybe, I think more cynically, she can't believe that she's lost control of things. *Your arrogance has finally betrayed you*, I think, and immediately feel bad. I didn't even know I thought Sonia was arrogant. But I did and I do. All that information she keeps. The secrets that have always been just as big as the ones James kept from me. *Do they think I'm a child?*

"We need to leave too," I say, never more certain of anything in my whole life.

"They're evacuating. The council. Everyone. Leaving the island, and no one told us because they knew we'd tell the girls," Sonia says, totally ignoring me. She can't believe she's been cut out of her stupid, secret club.

"They've always been selfish shits," B.B. says, vehement.

"Why would they do that?" Henrie asks. "They wouldn't leave us here. They wouldn't not tell us we were in trouble."

"Don't be naïve," B.B. spits out with certainty.

"Shit," Joshua says.

"This is fucking insane," I say, truly beginning to lose my temper. "It hardly matters who knew what when. That was an earthquake and it seems others knew to leave *before* it hit. The only thing we need to talk about is how and when to get the hell out of here."

"It's okay, Mom." Henrie is looking at me strangely now, as if concerned about my well-being.

"I'm the only one speaking sense—" I begin, but a second quake comes. It's short this time, the island giving us one good shake. The group of us hold still, dig in. We aren't going anywhere yet or maybe ever. I feel true terror as this sinks in and a need to protect my children—B.B. and Henrie—who may not let me protect them at all. I've waited too long.

It's been twenty-four hours since the first earthquake, and the little quakes that have followed have felt more like a slipping under than a cracking apart. It's taken less than a day for the beaches to disappear, the water climbing up to the roads. Anyone who didn't flee the island before is now on their way out. Except, of course, for us—B.B., Henrie, Joshua, Wilderness, Wally, Sonia, and me.

I had to calm down and give up on leaving immediately in order to convince them that we all need to leave together. Wally and Joshua were easy. Wilde and Sonia too with the caveat that they would make sure everyone else was off first. Henrie agreed, and B.B. said she'd go if Henrie went, and only if she and Henrie could say good-bye to the island on their own. B.B. has dragged Henrie away somewhere. They wouldn't tell me where they were going—I'm not sure Henrie even knew—but B.B. said she wouldn't leave until they got this one last thing done. All I could do was make Henrie and then B.B. promise me that they'd be back at the house before the afternoon. I know Henrie was being truthful when she said she'd be back within a few hours no matter what, but B.B. . . . . she was saying what she needed to say to be free of me.

I've spent a lot of my life feeling crazy, feeling alone, but I've never felt this scared or confused about the people around me. What motivates them seems so foreign and absurd when all I can feel is the need to survive. To get the people I love far from here. I can feel the danger of it in my bones; every minute that passes we come close to something terrible, yet when I look up at them, they are calmly planning, maneuvering. It's absurd, but I can't leave Henrie or B.B., not ever again.

I find myself standing in front of the door to James's office, and it's not clear to me why I'm standing here. I can't remember stopping or how long I've been staring at the door, but it feels intentional. A rumble shakes the house. It's slight enough that all I need to do is soften my knees to keep my balance, and it's over.

The door to the office is heavy. I remember that much. It has a lock that keeps outsiders out, but it was always James's temperament that eventually kept us out. I have fond memories of being on the old green couch at the beginning. Little B.B. and littler Henrie playing on the floor in front of me. The strike of James's typewriter keys sounded like hope back then, like ambition. The floor pillared with the books that would no longer fit the shelves. There was always something new to discover. He seemed, at first, so happy to have a second daughter. He'd lie on the floor with her. Marvel at her bright blue eyes. But soon after her first birthday he started drinking more, a bit too much became the norm. He seemed worried. Three women—one of them an islander we knew—disappeared in a short period, and I found him drunk on his green couch, mumbling about how it wasn't going to work. He said, "Once a year would be enough. One life. It's enough. But he's still hungry. Always hungry." I held a cold washcloth to his forehead and asked him what he meant.

"Who are you talking about, James?"

He sobered enough to know I was with him, and he grabbed both my wrists, held them too tight, and sat up. "Let's have another baby, please. A boy. Wouldn't a boy be nice?"

If he'd asked me when he was sober or without holding on to me so tightly that I grew scared, I might have said yes, but as it was, I didn't have to say anything at all for him to sink away from me back into that couch, back into drunk. "Never mind. It's my mess."

After that, he wrote less and fretted more. The books gathered dust and our kitchen cupboards would be bare of dishes because he never remembered to bring them back down. His office smelled like coffee and sweat—the latter, borne of fear and frustration, becoming more and more pungent as the years passed. Henrie and B.B. were always pushing their way in, fighting the mess of their father. Cleaning, organizing, bringing glasses back down to the kitchen. Ever the optimists about his work: "He's writing again! There are pages piled up on his desk!" And books were published, up until about a decade ago. Lovely poems but nothing remarkable. The summer or two before I left, I would sneak in sometimes to look through the piles of his papers. The indent of each letter stamped into the paper like violence, and the pages were more notes about his family tree or the island than anything else. I remember thinking, *If you make the world too small, your art gets too small too.*

Now, as I stand here with my hand reaching toward the doorknob, I see something shift on the other side. A shadow, thick as velvet, slides past. A low growl follows.

"Hello?"

The shadow stops. Holds itself still.

"B.B.? Henrie?"

There is no answer. I step forward. One step. Two. The shadow moves, disappearing. I smell pipe smoke.

My heart is pounding, beating noise into my ears, my cheeks hot, the skin around my nose cold. I take another step forward. Two. I could reach out and touch the skin of the door with my fingertips, but I don't. The sound of typewriter keys being punched begins, hesitantly at first and then frantically.

"James?" I ask.

The typing stops. Footsteps rush toward me on the other side of the door, a gallop, like four large feet on the floor. I jump back. A shadow as thick as tar closes the gap under the door, then one slip of that old typewriter paper glides out from the crack: *Where are they?* The typed words are pressed into paper, the whiteness of the sheet dulled by years, but the ink is black and the rectangle perfect. I step toward it, bend my knees a little, and another sheet pushes out from under the door: *He's coming.* And then another: *You need to find them.* The shadow moves away from the door and the typewriter starts up again.

"James." I say his name. No question this time. "Let me in, James."

I put both palms on the door, and I can smell his pipe. That sweet smell from when I first met him. I rattle the door. It's locked tight. Then the tar of him is back on the other side of the door, and another sheet of paper comes rushing out: *The island is sinking.* Then another: *He's coming for all of you.* Then another: *Where are they? Why aren't you with them?*

I pick the pages up in my hands. They are hot with worry. The indictment in the last typed question is cruel but deserved. I want to say, *Why aren't* you *with them?* But I hold back. I put my forehead to the door instead.

"James, you know I don't know what to do. I never have." Tears well up in my eyes. A big ball of failure and fear and self-pity that quickly turns to anger. I did not ask for this. No one warned me what I was in for when I first moved to this damn place, and once I was here, in all the madness, not a single person told me what was going on. And it's happening again. Here I am. On my own in this stupid house. Sucked back in.

"Asshole!" I scream, and pound both hands on the door.

I did not mean to come back. I did not want to stay. He, whatever is left of him, smashes into the door in response. Over and over. He has no time for my weakness or my anger. The thud of him, it blocks out all else.

Another piece of paper flies out from under the door. And, downstairs, the phone begins to ring.

✦24✦

beatrice

2000

Did Sonia ever tell you what was originally built on this spot?"

Henrie thinks I don't know what she's been up to. That I haven't been one step ahead of her this whole time, waiting for her to tell me the truth about what she's discovered. I know how to pick a lock. I know how to replace a strip of paper in a pinhole camera. Hell, I even know how to develop photographs and slip out of a space without leaving behind a trace of myself. The thing that worries me the most though, more than the rest of it, is that somehow she still doesn't know who and what she is. No matter. I will show her.

Since I met with the beast and settled into my father's skin, I haven't needed much sleep or food—even with the babies growing in my stomach. I can feel my birthright coursing through me every damn minute of every

damn day, and it's wonderful. Gorgeous. Fantastical. I
am capable of anything. How can Henrie not feel that
too?

A week ago, I stayed up all night. I sat in the downstairs hallway with my back pressed to the wall opposite
the stairs. The same spot where I slept when I was here
alone, waiting for my mother to speak to me again, but
this time I sat there with one of Henrie's cameras trained
on the wall. It was amazing to be there the moment the
camera began its work. The hallway plaster taking on
the shape of a human being, a woman stretching forward, reaching, reaching, reaching. I sat close enough to
the camera so it felt like she was reaching for me.

Henrie is walking three paces behind me, and no
matter how much I try to slow down to let her keep up,
she drops the same amount behind. Like she doesn't
trust me. And why should she?

"What spot?" she's asking, impatient. It's possible
she's already asked, but I was too lost in my thoughts to
hear. I'm a little nervous too. What if this plan doesn't
work? What if I should have done it sooner? What if
Henrie refuses to play along?

"Fun Land. Before it was Fun Land . . . well, before it
was Fun Land it was abandoned, but before that it belonged to the Fowlers. Elizabeth and Eileen, to be more
specific. When they started making this place more of a
town, they had a vision for this part of the land. It was
a revolutionary idea at the time."

The asphalt is warm under my sneakers as we turn up Shore Road—the quarry pond is behind us now, and the giant green dinosaur of Fun Land Park peeks out over the large wooden fence around the property. First built to prompt the curious into buying a ticket, the fence was later reinforced with barbed wire to keep out vandals. It now sits lonely, ten unused island acres that house thirty-two nightmarish renderings of primal animalistic scenes, fever dreams of the artist Arthur Williams.

My father was his benefactor. Believed in him and let Arthur use this land to make his garish imaginings, but also to hide what was really there. An entrance, an exit. I knew none of this until I slipped into my father's skin.

"So, before our great-great-grandfather showed up, the Fowler sisters decided to bring this island some life. The church, Main Street . . ."

"I know all that," Henrie says, and I look over my shoulder to see her. She's rubbing her eyes. Her camera is around her neck, and it looks to be bothering her. She keeps rubbing at the skin under the strap. I almost offer to carry it, but there is no way she would let me carry her camera. It's just another thing she doesn't trust me with.

"Jeez, give me a second. They had this idea to build a safe house out here. For women who had nowhere to go. Young women who had lost their parents. Women who had fled their circumstances. It was what they called a 'fresh start' house, and it was set back here in the woods on purpose so that it would be hard to find even if you managed to follow a woman to the island."

"It can't have lasted long."

"It didn't—not in that form—but they did house a few women there. Eileen even traveled off island to spread the word. Quietly, along the coast. She made it as far as Cleveland. That's when Seth arrived. When Eileen was gone. Explains a lot. Anyhow, it is an idea that wasn't popular elsewhere until like the 1970s. Safe houses. That's what we call them now." The earth rumbles under our feet. The beast turning in his ravished sleep.

"I don't remember a building or a house or whatever," Henrie says. "Did you feel that? Another earthquake?"

"No," I lie, but she's putting her hands on her knees and bending over to gulp air. I want to ask, *Why are you fighting this so hard? Why don't you recognize what you are capable of?* I want to tell her, *They say they "saved" you, but they brainwashed you. Dubbed you helpless and hid you away.*

"I don't feel right, B.B."

I move to rub her lower back. "Just a little further."

She straightens. "I'm okay. I got this. Just tell me what we're doing here. I need to get back to Mom. To Joshua."

"I will," I say. "I am." What I don't say: *Choose me this time. Me.*

We've reached Fun Land's parking lot. It speaks to

the ridiculousness of all tourism on Fowler—that this many people would pay to see concrete sculptures in ludicrous colors. Every on-island business is either on the brink of failure or has already failed. Even the once-profitable quarry died too soon. If the island sinks, who will really care besides us? But still the park sits here.

"In a way," I say, "we took over that responsibility. You and me."

"What responsibility?"

We walk until the long neck of the brontosaurus's shadow falls over us.

"Quarry Hollow is the safe house."

"For who?" she asks, laughing in such an awkward way that I know she isn't so far away from understanding. She's got her collection of ghosts.

"Come on, Henrie."

We stop under the shadow of the dinosaur. I look at my sister. She hasn't slept well in weeks, and she looks awful. Weak and tired and sad. I feel a deep pang of regret, looking at her. Am I making the same mistakes our father made?

"B.B., we need to be readying to leave."

"Henrie, I found your cameras. I know what's inside of them." One truth slips out just like that. How many will follow?

She looks at me, straight on. "You left them alone, right?" She is anxious.

"Of course," I say. It isn't a total lie.

"Our family has been taking care of the lost for generations, B.B. I get that now, which means not all of our family legacies are total shit. We can save them. We can let this place go."

"Henrie," I say. I am about to tell her that this is our journey. Our sacrifice. The sad, hopeful look on her face stops me, and I ask instead, "Do you remember coming here as kids?"

"To Fun Land?"

"Yes."

"I do. I remember we liked to sneak in."

"Yes, that too, but do you remember when we used to come to the park with Dad? He'd buy tickets and everything."

"We always begged for ice cream, and he would never let us have it."

"Dad always said, 'Ice cream is so old it's practically turned back into a cow. You don't want that in your body, now do you?'"

"Yes"—Henrie nods—"that sounds like him."

I take a few steps away from her, look around at the parking lot. "Do you remember the last time he brought us? He bought us popcorn that day. Big greasy bags of it. It must have been close to the park closing permanently. He had a fight with Arthur."

The fight started before we'd even entered the park. It was right out here in the parking lot. Dad told us to stay at the entrance, then the two of them walked out into the lot. Their voices were raised. I did my best to distract Henrie, who was eight then, by making shadow puppets with my hands on the asphalt.

Now the parking lot is riddled with weeds, with barely enough clear surface to make rabbit ears if I wanted to. I kick at a pile of stones with my sneaker.

"What are we doing here, B.B.?" Henrie asks. "You still haven't told me." She says the second sentence as if it's only now occurring to her.

I ignore her, turn, and walk along the tall fence, knowing she'll follow.

I crawl through, and the world is darker on the other side, thick with cedar trees. The ground feels cool despite the summer heat, as if abandonment has changed the park's climate. I stand and brush off my knees, pick up my bag. I watch Henrie look around, finger her camera; we've entered another world. A new confidence fills me: *I'm doing the right thing.*

Ahead there is the gravel path—once painted a yellowy gold, it has now faded back to the natural gray of rock—that bisects the entire park. From it, branches of path roll out like red carpets, leading to a variety of sculptures meant to shock and awe.

We'd only been inside five minutes when Dad announced, "B.B., you're in charge. Keep track of your sister." So, we eagerly ran down the paths that day, to the concrete scenes we loved. Each scene had little plaques that told its story. We loved the story part, more than the gruesome structures already falling into disrepair.

"I remember this one," Henrie says now, dragging me down the path to Craig the Crocodile. It's a short path, then we are there, standing in front of a graying crocodile that holds a shark, larger than itself, in its jaws. The shark is limp, clearly dead, its toothy mouth a grimace, its cartoonish human tongue hanging out. It lies next to an empty concrete pool, once painted a rich blue. "Do you remember this?" She is perking up.

"Of course, I remember it." I don't remind her that I spent an extra decade on this island, nor do I offer that I've been coming in through that hole in the fence regularly.

We pass scene after scene. Even the large ones are too small for the fake animals they house. Giraffes that were once caution-tape yellow and would certainly have seemed tall to a child, now just look goofy. Zebras, with reptilelike birds perched on their backs, wear black and white stripes angled to look like lightning bolts. An angry gorilla stands tall, its hands beginning to bend cage bars, its mouth open in a roar that reveals a bloodred tongue.

We come to a wooden bridge that arches over a fake canal. The canal had once been full of too-blue water. Now it's empty, the concrete chipping and the foolishly arched bridge missing a plank or two.

"He let us get the popcorn. I remember that. It was

sprayed with that yellow buttery stuff and thick with salt, the bag transparent with grease. I didn't like it, but I was afraid to throw it away—I didn't want to make him mad." I ate mine, then I ate Henrie's. I remember how the butter lined my mouth, thick as mucus at the back of my throat.

"Did I get lost that day? Did we get separated?"

I keep quiet.

"I remember running. The park was empty, and it was getting dark. Dad had left me with you, and I ran and ran . . . and ran across that little bridge and hid in the lion's cage."

That wasn't how it happened. It was already dark. I led Henrie to the lion's cage—the creature had the head of a lion and the body of a fish—and told her to play dead. Lay her body out by mama lion's mouth. I was scared out of my mind but trying so hard to hide it from my little sister. I helped her fit herself into just the right spot, stretched out so that if the lion came to life, it would take a chunk of her belly first, a big meaty mouthful of Henrie.

"Keep your eyes shut," I'd said. "Just stay here until I get back. No peeking. No moving. Promise?" Little Henrie loved me so much that the promise came easily, and she did exactly what I asked. Guilt blooms in me. She will do it again. Whatever I ask.

I waited until the park was dark—the lights that flanked the park paths flipping off with one great switch at closing. There was one spot we hadn't been to, Henrie and I. I'd made sure we steered clear because it was what our father had been shouting about.

Now, today, we reach it—the well. It sits in a back corner of the park; the gravel path stretches out a weak branch of itself to reach it. Its shiny white has gone dirty now. It's decorated with a pail that hangs by a rope.

"This was the well for the house. If you go a bit further, that's where you can find remnants of the foundation of the house. It burnt down when Elizabeth and Eileen were alive."

"That's terrible. Were there women living there when it happened?"

"Oh no. They'd disappeared long before the fire," I say, dismissive. I don't want to slow down the story I'm here to tell. I've waited too long already. "That day I left you by the lion, I waited. Listened," I say now.

"It was dark, and you were just a kid too. I was like eight, so what were you? Ten at most?"

"It wasn't just that. And it wasn't even that I thought I was gonna get hurt. I just knew. I knew something important was happening. It's taken a decade and us coming back together, here, on island, for me to put all the pieces together." I clasp my elbows and toe at the dirt. "And there was this high whistle, this call coming up out of the ground. I followed the sound and the smell of that sound. Cold, like lake water, like something coming from so far down in the earth that air hadn't touched it yet. It led me to this well. Back then it had a big sign on it that said, 'Make a wish.' I could see the shape of the sign in the dark, but not read the words. So, I hid. I hid in the dark, crunched up in a ball and waited."

"What happened next?" Henrie is deep in my story, believing me. Holding her breath.

"There was a clawing and clattering, like fingernails on a chalkboard, then this big shape crawled out of the well. A mess of a thing. Two great arms that looked more like legs with sharp claws and shoulder blades poking up so high it looked like they'd gone through skin. It had a long snakelike body below the waist. It was dark so I only saw the shape of it. The shape of it as it rustled the water off its back, then it grew actual legs so it could stride across the dark and was gone. I got truly scared because I thought it was headed for you. I ran. Followed the sound of the gravel under my feet and somehow found you. But, when I got to you, Daddy was already there. He had a flashlight and was gathering you up. You know what he said to me?"

"No, what?"

"'Let's go.'"

"That's it?"

"That's it. He carried you home in his arms, and when we got home, he tucked us into our bunks. When he kissed me good night, I smelled that smell again. Cold earth. The deep middle of something."

"What are you saying?"

"You know."

"No, I don't know. How the hell would I know?"

But I can tell she knows something. "I didn't get it back then. I thought of Daddy as one thing and the thing that came out of the well as another. But it was him. Just like it's me," I say and pause to see if she will recognize herself in the story, but she stares at me blankly. "And it's you too, Henrie."

"I don't understand."

But then I see her begin to put it together in her head. Those black spots in her memory, a space when her body and mind became something else. A genetic predisposition that was taken from her.

"Daddy tried to save you from it, God knows why, and Carrie tried to steal it from you. It was wrong what they did to you. To us. Stupid and shortsighted."

"Beatrice . . ."

I can tell I don't want to hear what she's about to say. She isn't letting the truth in yet, so I keep going.

"That well goes all the way through. Through the island just like the quarry pond at its deepest spot. And, unlike the quarry, the well predates our great-great-grandfather."

"How do you know?"

"How do I know what?"

"Any of it."

The island is quiet around us, but a slight breeze moves in to cool my cheeks. It smells of lake water.

"It was Daddy that night, Henrie. He came out of the well."

"Stop!"

"Stop what?"

"Stop your bullshit!"

"I've met him."

"Who?"

"The beast. The troll. The under-island devil. I made a deal with him to keep us safe. I've been down there, Henrie. And I remember that night when I saw Daddy come up the well and put that together with the night he tried to save us from you and you from yourself—"

"That's absurd," she says, interrupting me, "I'd never hurt anyone. Especially not you."

"Henrie," I say. "Do you want to know the best part?"

"No."

I ignore her. "The best part is that when I found your cameras, your photo project, I realized you'd been helping me all along. Even though I hadn't told you. Even though you hadn't told me. We were on the same page. We are made in Daddy's image, but we are better, stronger and smarter. Hideous things can be beautiful too! I love you, Henrietta. It's you and me against the world."

Henrie says nothing at all. She is looking at the well and not at me. I can't tell if she's letting all the things she knows come together or if she is still trying to block me out. She is touching her camera, feeling it as if it will somehow make sense of this for her.

"Just look," I say. "Come here and look in the well. You'll understand if you just look."

"There's nothing there. It's a prop."

"Look again. Look through your camera if it feels safer."

This suggestion gets her attention. She steps forward, takes the strap off her neck, looks through the lens, then presses closer to the well so that her belly touches brick. She stands on her toes. Leans over.

"I'm sorry for this," I say to my baby sister, but I don't give her time to respond. In one smooth motion, I bend at the knees, wrap my arms around her thighs and lift. She goes over easily, headfirst. She barely makes a splash.

⟶25⟵

carrie

2000

I'm holding the phone to my ear when Sonia enters the kitchen. I don't remember getting from James's office door to the phone, but I'm holding a piece of typing paper in my hand, my fist crunching the message on it. Sonia is calling my name, hollering it now from the doorway, but my attention is on the sound of water coming through the phone. It's so strong a sound that I take the receiver away from my ear to see if liquid is about to rush out.

"Hello?" I push the earpiece back to my cheek. There's gurgling, thrashing, and in the fuzz of all the noise, I hear a voice.

"Henrie!" I shout into the phone. "B.B.!"

"Carrie." The voice is female. It is breathless and echoey, fighting to be heard.

"Who is this?"

". . . top . . . the house," she says, the effort clearly exhausting.

"I don't understand," I say, my voice turning to tears.

"You need to push," the woman on the other end of the phone says, and I remember Henrie's birth. Drug-free. A water birth. My body in a huge tub, pushing and pushing and pushing. Twenty-six hours of labor and finally she was born underwater. Her eyes open and staring up at me—we recognized each other immediately. I scooped her up and pulled her into my arms, and she took her first breath of air. A long, deep inhale that set her to crying until I held her to my breast. I remember too that night a decade ago when James pulled us all from the quarry. The monster in Henrie fully violent, almost deadly enough to kill her and all of us. How we gathered around her, put our hands on her body, brought her back to breath.

"We have to go. All . . . us," the woman says, then static takes over, almost blurring out what she says next, "Beatrice . . ." Something in me recognizes the panic, the determination of another mother. Olivia Rose? "Cameras . . ." I do not have time to ponder if this is possible. The line goes dead.

"Wait!" I scream into the phone. No dial tone. No nothing. I hurl it at the wall, and it bounces back, almost hitting me in the face.

"Carrie!" Sonia shouts as she moves toward me. Wilderness is behind her, taking up the entirety of the doorframe. The kitchen table sits between us. The plaster on the ceiling has almost entirely come down, revealing more of the ceiling beams and the underside of the floorboards above. I see movement in the office overhead. Typewriter keys pounding. James still trying to tell me what I need to do next.

"Do you hear that?" I ask, but I don't listen for an answer. Instead, I flatten the paper in my hand. In all caps, it says, *FREE THE GHOSTS*.

"Carrie?" Wilderness walks around the table and touches my shoulder.

"You've cut yourself," Sonia says.

I look where she is looking and see that my palms are bleeding. Four neat cuts where I've dug my fingernails in.

"I don't know," I manage, but I'm tired. I have no words. I crumple the paper before she can read the command on it. "They're in trouble. I think they're in trouble."

"The girls?" Sonia asks, but we are interrupted by a sizzle, a pop, like bacon in a frying pan.

A flash of light follows and then Wilderness says, "Don't touch anything!"

A thin layer of water is forming around my feet. Tiny streams of it at first that quickly turn into rivers.

"This way," Wilderness says. He is pulling me around

the kitchen table to the hallway, where the water deepens up to our ankles.

"I have to go!" I shout, all of it catching up with me. "I have to get to the quarry pond." I scoot down the hall before Sonia can stop me.

The front door swings open just as I reach it, and Joshua steps inside with Wally close behind him, water sloshing in with them. Their clothes are soaked, hair stuck flat to their faces. I catch a glimpse of the world behind them, and it's not one I recognize. The water is up to the porch. The sidewalk gone. The street gone. The tree trunks shorter than I remember.

"Where's Henrie, Joshua? Where is she?" I yell into his face like it's his fault she's out there somewhere instead of with me.

"Isn't she here?" he asks.

"B.B. took her somewhere," I say, and instantly hear the accusation in it, and I realize that I do think this is B.B.'s fault. I'm placing blame on her and have maybe done so for years. "They're in trouble!" I add, changing my pronoun to include both girls. *I will not blame her. I will not. I will be her mother too.* I try to slip past Joshua, but this time I'm not fast enough. He grabs my arm, and Sonia catches hold of my wrist.

A wave of water rushes the front door, pushing up to our knees.

"You can't go out there without a plan," Joshua says, pulling me up the stairs behind Wilderness and Wally.

Sonia follows, placing herself on the stairs between me and the front door.

"The island is sinking," Sonia says. "I thought we had a little more time. I really did."

"You knew this would happen?" I ask, shifting my fear and anger to Sonia.

"No, I mean, maybe. I mean, I told you! Showed you that day after the funeral."

"Really? That's you trying to tell me that we were all going to drown? Jesus, Sonia."

"Stop. None of it matters now. If B.B. and Henrie are together, they'll figure out what to do. We need to get to the third floor. As high as we can," Wilderness says.

I remember the voice on the other end of the phone. She was telling me to get to the attic. I'll be able to see the quarry from the turret windows. The cliffs above the Killing Pond. The girls.

Joshua takes the steps two at a time. The house is rocking enough to throw him off-balance. He holds on to the railing to steady himself and we follow suit.

The attic is empty and the only windows, the best exit if I need to get out and swim to the cliffs, are the turret windows. I rush to the darkroom door, only to see it's padlocked.

A tool belt is on Henrie's bedroom floor. She's left it in a pile of dirty clothes. I rush to it, pull out a hammer and a screwdriver. Wilderness sees what I mean to do and takes the screwdriver from me, inserts the flat end under the clumsy metal that holds the padlock, and pries the whole apparatus off like it is nothing.

The small darkroom smells so strongly of chemicals that I gag, cough. Photos hang from clothes wire, stacks of them sit on shelves. I rip the plastic from the windows. The house is tilting toward the water. The great weight of it easing over the edge of the quarry. I look left toward the Killing Pond—although it is all water now. I see the cliffs, but the girls aren't there. Not yet.

"What the fuck?"

I look back to Wilderness. He's staring at Henrie's photographs. They appear to be of the house. On closer inspection, I see that they are of the walls, dark and bending light in weird ways. Shadowy figures pushing at the middles.

"The ghosts," I say. "They're real." I pluck photos off the drying rack. Faces molding themselves out of the wall. Hands tangled in plaster.

The house rocks under us, leans farther over the edge. We have to steady ourselves to stay upright, as if we are on a ship being tossed by waves.

"What are these?" Sonia's hands are on a small box.

"Henrie's cameras. She's been photographing the—"

"Ghosts," Sonia says. There are dozens and dozens of photos.

"Where are the others?" I ask. "I never see the same

one twice." I don't know why it's important, but it feels important. I look around the little darkroom. Joshua leaves, presumably to look around the attic.

"Open the fucking windows. I need air," Wilderness says as he moves to do so.

"Don't!" Sonia shouts. "Everything stays shut."

"But we'll need to get on the roof," he says.

"Everyone stays right fucking here," Sonia says.

I'm afraid he will insist, but he doesn't. He listens to Sonia.

I nod my support, then look back to the room. I need to find the cameras.

The window seat. I lift up the center board and then the one to its left and the one to its right, and there they all are. Dozens of them.

FREE THE GHOSTS, I think.

Cookie tins, cereal boxes, a cedar jewelry box. I go for a cookie tin, duct tape wrapped around the edges of the lid, meant to keep the light out, I'm sure. It's incredibly heavy, like it houses a boulder. I rip off the tape, and the others step up beside me as I open the lid.

At first it looks empty.

"What's that?" Joshua asks.

Not until he asks do I see it. The bottom of the tin is covered in a fuzz of silver, like dandelion seeds, resting there. It's beautiful, but then the house tilts, and cameras clatter down from the pile and the dust blows up.

"Shut the tin! They'll spill!" Sonia yells, rushing

toward me. I barely keep my hands from getting slammed shut in the lid. "We're going over!"

The house groans. Shrieks.

"Get into the attic! Now!" Sonia shouts, and we do as we're told, slamming the darkroom door shut. We push our backs to the attic wall, and I tilt my head up to look at the curved wood. The center support beam is not so high above our heads. I can hear the windows of the turret groan as the whole of it, this ship of a house, goes over, headfirst, into the quarry.

❧26❧

beatrice

2000

The well pierces straight through the island—an upside-down ice cream cone—so that the aperture opens up as we go down to allow the transition into our more gruesome and inevitable selves. Henrie is ahead of me, tumbling and thrashing her way deeper into the well, but she is refusing to change. Her body remains small and human and frail, pinballing off the widening stone walls. She is ugly in this dim, cold light. Pale and fragile and stupid in her stubbornness. I am beginning to worry. What if I'm wrong about her? Perhaps she isn't made in our father's image. Maybe she hasn't changed since that last time back in 1989 when she was just a kid, untrained and overly powerful. Maybe that time when she tried to kill us all was a fluke, and she isn't the one who has been sloppily fulfilling our father's purpose, but then I see a flash of it. Her skin shines gray then green, and I know I am right. It makes me want to laugh out loud, how right I am.

Soon we will come out the other side—two Volt sisters built in the image of their father and his father and his father before that—and plunge into lake water, and then Fowler will be our night sky, our floating body of dead stars.

Henrie is unprepared, unwilling, and it our father's fault. I used to blame Carrie for every bad feeling I ever had about this family, but it was never her. It was Dad. Sonia even. Those who knew and said nothing, going back and back and back. It must have felt heroic, keeping the island afloat all those years. Very manly to keep everyone but the lonely few safe and to do it all without comment, without complaint. Perhaps the toxicity of our inheritance would have claimed us too if our father had not seen our gender first. Our femaleness a reason we needed saving, the only reason he needed to keep his miserable inheritance all to himself. Would he have loved a son more? Less? It hardly matters, because we were born girls. Lesser. Weaker. They could not cast us as the heroes. They made us Curators or swept us off island, kept us separate as if we needed to be protected from all this, and yet, all the while we were stronger than they'd ever been.

I can smell Henrie's fear—the stink of her too human to be any good to us. The part of me that is monster is disgusted, wants to show off, yell at my sister, *Look what we can do. Here I am, strong as fuck and ready to fight.* There must be some beauty in being the beast. But I try to remain patient. This is Henrie's chance to see herself differently, to break free. To feel all that she's been denied.

Henrie twists, turns, looks up at me for help as she drags her sad fingernails down one side of the cylindrical stone wall. She winces at my change. I grin down to reassure her, bare my beautiful teeth. *Let the change come!* I think, and I'm almost certain she catches the thought.

Drugs and alcohol have never quite been my thing, but I've done them. Tried my share. Changing form feels better than any of it. Better than that first rush of cocaine as it enters your bloodstream. Moves through you fast and hot. Once Henrie feels it, lets it begin, she will want more. More and more and more. She will see what we have, crave it like I do, and then we will do fantastic damage.

She gives up, curls into a ball so that she speeds downward faster, sparking her body open only when we shoot out the bottom and spill into the wideness of the lake. I reach out, grab her arm to keep her from sinking too far, too fast. Her face continues to purple. She thinks she needs oxygen to survive. *Breathe,* I think as hard as I can, but she doesn't hear me. She claws at her throat, digging for air. Her eyes bulge, big enough to fall right out of her head, but then her body fully recognizes this is change or die. Her beautiful anatomy takes over. The monster inside her blooms its skin, flushing out the human, and I let go and watch her transform.

Down here, I discover, even in our monster shapes we resemble each other. I am snaky and strong armed and seal tailed. My hair tangles in thick clots around my swollen head, shooting out seaweed green and gorgeous. Henri is snakelike too with scales that shine silver-green in the dim lake light, and double rows of sharp teeth split her mouth into a wide gouge of a smile. Her blue eyes burn from under a cape of greening hair. Her shoulders are huge, broad and strong, and her body narrows to a muscled flipper much like mine. Her eyes, although wider and set farther apart, still hold her sad little-baby-sister soul. Our hands are huge, webbed between our long, sharp-tipped fingers. Our claws are as long and gorgeous as our teeth. I smile my shark-tooth grin and do a little twirl for her before I point up.

Fowler is above us now. It is buoyed by the disappeared. The drowned and swollen body parts of long-dead women that no one gave a shit about. Underneath the island their legs and hands and feet are amassed in bits and pieces. Their torsos and thighs and torn unidentifiable morsels sag and ripple in the undercurrent of the island. Their mournful faces gape down past us into the deep dark nothing. Eyes eaten out, with tongues floating fat and tasty, attracting fish who have nibbled at their soft edges, tasting at dead taste buds. Frozen in time, their expressions reflect the sorrow of their end point—a screaming and endless pain. Seeing it again, I feel rage. A howling desire to shove the faces of my ancestors into the mess and say, *Look! See! What have you made us do?*

I've been down here twice before. Once as I lay curled on the floor of my father's office, fixed in his skin. That time, I felt what he felt. Saw it for his first time too, and the feeling of responsibility was unbearable.

My sweet father came down here for the first time after my mother jumped. All those years serving the island, but it was her loss that made him brave enough to see it for himself. Maybe he thought he could find the pieces of his wife, my mother, and fix her. Sew her back into a solid and carry her to the hollow of the house.

The man who dove into the well was determined. He'd give his baby girl her mother back. I could feel all that as I dove in him down into the well and found his memory of the sleeping beast. I could feel too how quickly his horror took hold, and his grief instantly woke the beast. The smell and odor of his sorrow even in its maleness so deliciously close that the monster roared and ripped; my father saw the way the beast had sewed himself to the island and its missing women. How the devil and the island had become one inseparable thing.

When I came down alone, did my first dive, I found the same thing as my father—decades of the lost and indistinguishable. Gristle and wispy threads of nerves and veins fraying around the peek of white, white bones. A ghastly puzzle constructed from unmatched woman pieces, and in the middle, the big fat roll of a beast who'd made himself a nest with our losses. All the pieces quilted to his purpose. I, however, did not feel fear or sadness. I felt rage. It made me feel strong. I changed with confidence, and when I was floating under the big ugly bird in his fucked-up nest, I saw only his vulnerability. His big lazy belly ready for bursting. His shut and sleepy eyes. His false feeling of safety. And I knew. I knew that Henrie and I could handle this. Do what all those men before us were too fucking egocentric in focus to deal with.

I want Henrie to see what I see. The island ugly. Its fleshy center weak with satiation.

Henrie, however, is shocked. Even I can smell the fear on her. The beast's stomach rumbles. Henrie pushes herself down into the water, away from the vision above us.

I look at my sister, beautiful in her alternative form. How has she not figured it out yet? That she and I are island monsters. That we are as strong as they come. We are not accidents. We are here to end this. Sisters born stronger than all the Fowlers or Volts combined.

I swim to my sister and grab hold of her neck with one hand. I make her look, raise her face to the bottom of our island bolstered by the heartbroken, the forgotten.

Only, Henrie fights the looking. Fights the seeing. She is monstrous in form, but she is denying herself the sweet power of it, and I realize she has been smashing it down for far too long. I lock my thickly muscled arms around her and push my thoughts into her head.

You are beautiful. Ferocious. You do not need saving. We do not need to run.

I feel the moment she hears me. Her great big body stops fighting mine. Her muscles grow larger, her tail experiments with the water, gives a big push that moves us closer to the beast. I let her go and watch her twist in the water, trying to see her own body from every angle.

Today the beast is thin, needing to be fed. His eyes slit into a half-doze, his mouth twitches, a dog dreaming of food. He is all muscle and scales, translucent skin on his chest and belly so that the pink of his heart and the trails of his veins glow. He is twitching and turning, making the island rattle.

I watch my sister watch him. He shifts, blows bubbles from his long, sharp nose. His eyelids flutter. He sleeps. Henrie moves toward him, floats her way up, a little at first, then a little more, and I become afraid. Of what? I don't know. She turns in the water to look back at me. She is calm. I hold her mind with mine. *See what they did, what we are?*

Henrie nods and we are finally on the same page. I feel a moment of relief as she floats upward, moving toward his belly, his skin stretched tight over the visible contents of his stomach, the remnants of human sorrows consumed over decades. They swarm up and over one another, weaving their own baskets in the monster's stomach. Their desperation keeps them fat and small, slick and shiny as they crawl over one another like maggots. Henri is drawn to them, the hot little gems that nourish him. I don't blame her. They are mesmerizing. They look something like kin.

Henrie moves closer to his belly and closer still. I am amazed by her bravery, her nearness to his razor-sharp claws and teeth. Pride fills me, wrapping its arms around my heart, and part of me reaches out toward my baby sister. I am excited to get up to the surface and finally talk this through with her. To think and plan. But Henrie is in her true self now, and I realize she is not waiting, not for me, not for anything.

She reaches out her talons and grazes him at first. Almost like a caress, and even this draws three distinct lines of blood. His eyes fly open, and then Henrie is roaring, pulling both arms back and plunging deep into the center of him. Her eyes are crazed, her hands thick with the swarm of his insides. His mouth opens wide, water bubbles out, and his body begins to grow. He reshapes himself into something bigger, sharper, just as he did that day on the quarry cliff, and I push myself into action. Move toward him and slice. A huge rip opens, and the little glowing globs slide out, leeching to my arms and going after Henrie.

The devil tears his body from his sleeping spot among the lost. The water is churning with his guts, his body bleeding, flesh flapping open to splatter his insides into our hair, our faces. Body parts scatter, the water around my head fills with soft bits of the dead, their flesh decomposing around me to cloud the water and my vision.

I am blinded. Henrie must be too, but she is diving farther into him, not giving up but digging in, as if she is trying to come out the other side of him. I swim toward her, into the rush of flesh and monster, and I find her middle. Her slippery skin is strong and muscled. I wrap my snake of a body around her waist and try to pull her away from his belly, where her arms are indeed dug in deep, up to her elbows, the center of him in ruins. The little maggoty sorrows are attaching themselves to both of us now. Their swollen bodies hiding tiny mouths that feel like beestings even through my thick, scaly skin. They rip into us, find our sadness, our hurt, and they are growing with it. Their fat little bodies shooting out spidery tendrils, clear as jellyfish. I focus on pulling them off Henrie, but they have wrapped their arms around her, mummifying her while the monster advances.

The sorrows hold Henrie tight, and I see the sad terror that's feeding them in the whites of her eyes. But the monster himself is on us now. His huge mouth opening wide and coming at us both. I move quickly. Slice his eyeball with my open hand, and he misses Henrie, hooks her shoulder with a claw.

I swim clear as he drags her deeper into the lake. He doesn't even know he has her, but she is hooked and can't get free. He is swimming farther down, and I panic.

I am full of loss and regret. That arrogance I had accused my father of lives in me too. I thought Henrie and I could handle this. I thought we had been underestimated.

I am frozen in the water, unsure of what made me confident enough to push my baby sister into this situation, but then I feel our connection click back into place. Our bodies and minds linked. I roar my mouth open, and I dive, pull her free from his mouth. I pull at all the sadnesses suckling on her monster skin, tearing them off her one by one. She does the same for me. Each rip a triumph, but in my focus to get her arms free, a wriggling mass that I've pulled from her hair slides past my lips, tangles around my clamped teeth and floods my throat. I taste self-hatred. Loneliness. A constant weep of weakness. It tastes familiar, like a particular brand of loneliness that I was born into.

I can't stay afloat anymore. It hurts too much. I sink, my belly grows enormous, obscene in size so that it eclipses the rest of me, as if I've swallowed myself whole. I gag, try to vomit up the sorrow, hack and hack until it finds its silvery way back up, but the damage has been done.

Then Henrie is here. Her arms wrap around me as the world goes dark.

We are still under the island when I come to. Just below the Killing Pond. Henrie is pounding at the rock with her arms and her tail, busting the hole wider so we can swim through. Around us parts of the island still fall, sinking. All of it coming undone, and the sorrow in me reignites. The babies in me are many, and each of them is huge. There is no fight left, so I wait, fade back into the black.

When my eyes open again, Henrie and I are floating at the top of the quarry pond. The cave that we once had to climb to get to is at the same level as the water. Henrie is dragging me inside, and its shallowness should be too small for us, but I see that she has changed back to her human form, and I am somewhere in the midst of my change, my arms human and delicate. I feel my face—my cheeks soft and my teeth dull. I sob. Something hurts. Hurts so much that I can't even identify where it starts on my body.

"Shhh."

I realize Henrie is shushing me, a shush that tells me she is afraid to be found.

The pain continues to grow in me, and I see that my lower body does not match my upper. The snake of me is still here, my serpent self stretches out of the cave, my belly swollen and wriggling and then opening up, splitting at my belly button. They spill out of me. Little mole-rat babies—greenish in color with their great troll eyes sealed shut, tiny starts of arms slicing at the air with claws so soft they bend rather than cut. They squeal and snort and smell of decay. I hear Henrie gag, disgusted by what I've made, but some part of me still sees them as mine. I love them, so I try to catch them, cradle their little bodies in my human arms. There are too many, and they are too slippery. One by one I lose them.

Water is starting to slosh into the cave, and blood comes out of me next. Gallons of it. I can't stop what is happening. Somewhere in the water I hear him coming. The devil. Our monster. He smells my sadness. It's my turn.

"He's coming for us, Henrie," I say. "He can have me. I'm almost gone anyway. It's okay."

"Be quiet. Stop crying." She is angry with me.

Henrie pulls me farther into the cave. The pulsing of my body has stopped, and my legs are back. Long white human appendages that hang loosely from my hips. I let her push and pull me; she is trying to hide us at the back of the cave, as if that will help anything. Then I feel him. His big devil mouth on my toes, nibbling. When he bites down, the pain is exquisite, blinding, and I feel how much I deserve it. This grief. This pain. Part of me slides down his throat.

Henrie is screaming. More anger than fear, and I know she will not let him have me.

"I'm sorry, Henrie," I say.

Henrie beats at the monster's good eye with her human hands, but he simply closes his first eyelid, a viscous skin closing over his great pupil to protect himself from her slaps. She is a fly to him, a gnat. He rests his great mouth around my thigh and sips from me, bleeding me for his food, slurping, drinking me in. All the loneliness I grew up feeling. Those years alone on this island, the wanting, the emptiness of it, has been gathered in my veins. He takes it in greedily.

"Listen to me, Henrie. Listen."

"I'm listening." She is out of breath and not listening. Too much of her is still trying to pound at the monster's face. She is not giving up.

"Henrie," I say. I have her attention for a second. "It's okay."

"I'm not leaving you again," she says, and I see that she has felt it this way. The abandonment of me. Of our island. It has been just as painful for her.

"Let me do this," I say. I sit up, shove my whole fist into the monster's eyelid, and his mouth opens a bit, releases its grip around the straw of my leg.

I use my hands to push myself off the rock of the cave and into his mouth.

❖27❖

sonia

2000

There are hundreds of stories about Fowler Island, and I've read them all. Even written a few. Anecdotes, reimaginings, fact and myth, bullshit and horrible truths. It's funny how even when faced with an outlandish life—say a job scrubbing the fact of suicidal women off the surface of a monstrous island—one's brain attempts to filter out the possible from the impossible. I suppose it is a means of survival. To envision a world, no matter how wild, with *rules*.

But here we are, and the Quarry Hollow has tipped right over the edge of the cliff. "Ass over teakettle," as Ms. Millie used to say. An impossible feat, yet it did so easily with a heavy heave and a single, long groan that tore concrete from Fowler soil, as if the structure itself had always been just another sad soul waiting to jump off into the quarry. In a terrible moment in the swirl of it all I knew that the attic—the point of the turret to be more specific—would smash into the island. Limestone would shatter glass and the bowed attic ceiling would splinter inward to flatten us. So I pictured the quarry floor sinking faster, moving down to make room for the poke of the turret, and I focused on it so hard that my mind made it true and we found a softer landing. A bounce as lake water caught us, buoying us into a new world, and for a second, maybe ten, I felt the house's new purpose. A great ship of a building that would carry us to safety. Then the water rushed in.

We were under before I could take a full gulp of air, spinning like clothes in a washing machine. My lungs already burning, I reached for Wally as it all went out of control. It was instinct, and it told me something about my heart. Maybe there is something in the world for me that isn't totally about the island. We found each other's hands, and I warned her—as if there was any kind of warning that would have helped—but the danger came anyway and her head hit something. Our grasp on each other broke. Her red hair floating away from me in the fading light.

I reach out, desperate to grab hold of something in the dimly lit, cold water, and I find the slippery brass bed that has been up here for the life of the house. Screwed into the floor some time ago by Elizabeth Volt. I realize that the bolted windows, the furniture nailed to the floor, were part of a larger plan. A purpose for the house that I had been trained to ignore. All those stories about the crazy sister had taken over. What purpose did a woman serve? None, surely. A madwoman? Even less. Even I had swallowed the lore of a useless Elizabeth, banging around the attic, making no sense. I brushed off all these things as the actions of a hysterical woman. I am no better than the rest.

We are close enough to the surface of the lake that light is still finding its way to us, and I can see now that a good ten inches of space is between what was once floor and the water line.

Joshua and Wilderness find the air pocket at the same time I do. Wilderness takes a deep, quick breath—he has Wally under one arm and tries, failing, to get her to take a gulp of air as well—before he swims for the upside-down stairs. He will get Wally to the surface. Joshua points down and behind me, and I hold my breath, go under again and see that Carrie is at the darkroom door, breath held as she pulls on the doorknob. I go back for air and tell Joshua that I will be in charge of Carrie.

Wilderness, I tell myself, *will know how to get the water out of Wally's lungs and get her breathing again.* I go under, panic growing in my chest. I urgently pull at Carrie's ankle when I am close enough, but she kicks me off. I try again, but she is insistent, tugging at the door, as if she knows something more than I do. My lungs feel weak. I need air and so does Carrie. I make her go first, joining her. Neither of us has much of a choice, and we gulp together, goldfish women, desperate.

We drink the air down in seconds, but it helps, and we get our noses, mouths, and ears above the water long enough for Carrie to say, "We have to get to those cameras."

"What? Why? We don't have time." But I am thinking, thinking, thinking.

As time freezes in that little sliver of air, Carrie grabs my left wrist under the water. There is still warmth in her hand, and it brings back a memory, as if she is sending it to me. A file cabinet at the back of the museum. Long flat drawers that she once helped me sort through. Sketches dating back to Elizabeth. Plans she had commissioned for finishing the attic, a renovation that most islanders thought proved her insanity and Seth's right to keep her close. Along with those are some more artistic sketches, possibly done by Elizabeth herself, although there is no name on them to prove that she drew them. In them the house, this house, floats on the lake. It is upside down. The big boat-shaped attic pointing its great turret of a finger into the deep dark. The three windows of the turret glow like a lighthouse—beams of glittery dust shine out into the lake water. Its foundation floats above the water, poking up in jagged pieces, a bottom row of broken teeth yawning up at the sky. In the sketches, the house is filled with people. Women and children and men standing together, poking their heads up over the floor joists and looking toward the mainland.

"We have to let the ghosts out," Carrie gasps.

She inhales deeply and then is gone, back under, her fingers no longer clasped shut around my pulse. Fear beats in my chest. The girls are out there somewhere, and I am here, losing perspective, balance gone. There is something I should remember. I shut my eyes, tread water, sip air. Calm myself. Think.

Ms. Millie told me many times that Eileen Fowler communicated with her sister every evening—Eileen on the Watch Tower and Elizabeth in her turret. Eileen, who could read minds, had spent every moment she was separated from Elizabeth learning how to send her thoughts into her sister's brain and extract her sister's thoughts. It was Eileen's force of will that kept them close.

So, thanks to Eileen, they could be one body, one set of eyes, when they needed to be. They could watch together from their separate island spaces, as Seth took his new form—the one the devil gave him. Seth galloping on all fours to the Killing Pond to greet the dead body of a once-lonely woman. The devil was there too, but Elizabeth and Eileen could not see him from their separate vantage points. They could only ever see Seth on his exit and his return. When he climbed back out of the quarry, his body was wet, blood on his mouth, still part-monster, his middle swollen, like a snake with his prey still squirming inside him.

Once when Elizabeth had dared to leave the attic—Seth had forgotten to bolt the door—she followed the sounds of him retching. He was in the downstairs hallway, his body convulsing, and Elizabeth could see the thing in his belly push out, punch at his insides until it found a path out of his mouth. What came out wasn't a body. Not a thing that could punch or kick. It was a wave of glittery dust. Wisps on the air like dandelion seeds that gravitated toward the wall and stuck briefly before the house drank them in. Eileen saw it too, pulling the thoughts from her sister as they occurred.

It was written that Seth Volt turned to face Elizabeth. His body still half-creature. He looked a bit broken, and Elizabeth knew then that this was a mess of his making but not one he could control. He knew that now too. He had not defeated the devil, but rather become one himself.

"Elizabeth," he pleaded as his body became human again. He was naked and dirty, blood on his face and neck. He could not get up off the floor. "The island has to be fed or we will drown."

Elizabeth ran from him. Back up to her attic, blocking the door with a chair. She could see the future playing out. Her baby was still in her belly then, and she could see that the horrors would take longer than a generation to stop.

Forehead pressed to glass, calling to her sister for ideas while Seth banged on the door, screaming, "Please. You have to stop me!"

As the sun rose, Eileen and Elizabeth realized the only thing that could be done: "Let the island sink." Whether it happened now or in a decade. The devil, both devils, would have to be starved, and that meant the island the sisters loved would go under.

I swim to Carrie, who is still trying to pull open the door. I put my hands on hers and we pull together, and the water must finally equalize, because the door comes open. The tiny room is filled with water now. The window seat has dumped its contents. Henrie's photographs catch at my limbs, press to my cheeks. Carrie is already holding one of Henrie's homemade cameras in her hands. She is tearing at tape to get the lid free. My lungs are burning again, wanting to be filled so much that I have to remind my brain not to mistake water for air. White spots dance in my peripheral vision.

Carrie has worked lose the lid, and when she begins to crack it open, light pours out. Instant and blinding before it scatters around us like stardust. The water around us fills with stars, and a pocket of air forms around us, growing bigger as we open each container until we are standing in a big bubble of oxygen, our feet on the ceiling of the turret. I keep going, reach forward, pull another camera from the pile, and labor to open it. Again stars. Again light. The turret has become our little ship, a safe space filling with light.

Although it might be my imagination, the house feels lighter, as if it is climbing higher in the water, floating atop the surface of things, steady as a river barge and moving forward. Carrie is pressed to the glass now, no more cameras to pry open, her palms on the window, focused so hard that I am certain she is directing this ship. Her eyes forward, the turret leading us toward the girls.

I place myself next to Carrie. My left hand over her right hand, my other pressed to the glass. If I tilt my eyes up, I can see the surface of the water now. It is daytime above us. The sun is out. Ahead of us are the quarry cliffs, the Killing Pond now indistinguishable from the rest of the watery world, but the flashlight beam we've created reveals the girls inside their old cliffside cave. Both of them. Carrie sees them too and her body jumps a bit. Her excitement and relief something I share. We steer toward them with our hearts and minds and hands. We feel so strong, so powerful, and present, and then we see it. A big dark thing swimming up from the deep. A monster of scales and rot and teeth and open bloody wounds that leave trails in the water. The huge dark body of it—both somehow troll and serpent—is injured. Chunks of it gone. It rises slowly at first, then quickly until it is pointed right at them, and we are screaming, screaming, screaming, pounding at the glass.

The cracks stem from where our fists are pounding, and then little hairs like tree roots shoot up to the sill and down to the top of the frame. The dark shape of a thing reaches the mouth of the cave, nibbling and sucking at

B.B. for just a moment before she slips out of the cave and into the monster. Gone.

The horror is too big. It moves between us, pounding, pounding, pounding. The ghosts push at the windows with us. The glass weakens, and the house moves forward with us in our bubble, propelled now by our panic, our power.

❦28❧

henrietta

2000

My sister is gone. The whole of her disappeared into the foul mouth of that ugly, translucent troll. The rage is in me now, and I can still feel how good it was to rip into the monster—its belly soft as jelly when I pushed my talons inside. All those gnashing teeth and his swollen center was just there soft and exposed, a big pouch of a thing ready to be emptied. This whole island a sadistic ecosystem held up by shame and ugliness. Sorrow and grief. Let it sink if that's all it ever was, but it can't have B.B.

The water has risen higher and the cave, our cave, is almost under. Then there is a beam of light. It comes to me from outside the cave, somewhere under the water. It is bright and full and made up of a hundred tiny beings that float into the cave, twining around me like a warm blanket, telling me that I am strong, telling me not to quit. I recognize them, my ghosts, hundreds of voices humming on the surface of my body.

I stand up and the ghosts unwrap themselves from my body and shoot down into the water, establishing a trail that I can follow. A trail that will lead me straight down into the dark toward the monster. I follow, dive in among them. I hold my human shape and the glittery souls all around me fill my lungs with air, and I think, *This is where it stops.* Below me the devil sinks, a black and bloodied ink of a shape. All these years he's feasted, and we fed him. Fed and fed and fed him. He hid down there, soaking in bodies, when we could have dragged him out into the light and said, *No.* Now we, my ghosts and I, will take the light to him.

I dive down, changing as I go, and think of B.B. weakening inside that filthy beast. As I get closer to the dark froth of him, I see him struggling. His mouth gaping open and closed. His hands clawing at his own throat. Something is poking out the front of him. He's been sliced open from the inside, and the culprit is sticking out of him. He swats at it. I get closer and see that it is my sister's arm. She's alive. I'm filled with hope.

I move quickly. The ghost women get to her first. The light of them, rage, and power warm the water, and I watch as they wrap around B.B.'s arm, soaking into her until they are one with her body. They shoot inside the troll through B.B., electrifying her, making her into a lightning bolt of a girl.

His mouth is now wide open, light pouring out of him, and I know that it is my chance to shoot past his teeth and find B.B.

I dive straight into his mouth; his teeth graze my tail. It's just a scratch but the poison of him is real and the cut burns, flames up my body. I ignore the feeling and move faster toward B.B. I can see her, bright as a firefly, full of ghosts yet still stuck in his throat. I graze the surface of his paling tongue, its cracks and bumps as hot as asphalt in the summer sun, and I push forward into the now-bright tunnel of his throat. I don't hesitate or stop to plan. I just go. The dank tunnel of his throat tries to tighten around B.B., around me, my body fitting to him like he is our quarry-pond cave or a glacial groove. I reach forward, grab my sister. She is too weak and jammed in too tightly to reach back, but the light of the ghosts stays in her, wrapping around my wrist to link us tightly to each other. We are one thing now and I pull. The beast has drunk from her, but her spirit is still there. She's wedged herself tightly inside his throat on purpose, I think, holding on to half of her monster form so that she can be big enough to choke him to death.

Beatrice, keep fighting. Push. She hears me and tenses her shoulders, pushing her upper arms against his throat. The ghosts whisper and groan, their effort clear.

I pull hard and harder still. I will not leave her. Finally, there is a feeling of a pop and space opens up around her, water rushing past, and she is moving more freely. Blood is in the water all around us. I don't have time to find how much is the monster's and how much is B.B.'s, but I taste it, feel its thickness on my eyelashes. I pull B.B. up through the endless dankness of his throat, onto his gritty tongue, past his great teeth, and into the pond water again.

I drag my sister to the surface, holding her as gently as I can. I cannot tell yet if she is still alive. Her arm is missing at the elbow. The wounds look even worse as her monster bits fade. I let mine go as well as we reach air.

The world we surface into is not the one we left. Even the island's sinking was less grim than what I see now. I adjust my sister in my arms, hold her like a baby, and look at the quarry cliffs, which are almost even with the water. The island is sinking more quickly than imaginable, and the quarry, or what once was the quarry, is full of bits and pieces of human bodies, decomposing rapidly now that they are exposed to the light and free of the monster's hungry magic. The air smells of meat left out on a counter too long and I gag, losing the surface for a second and slipping under. Water rushes past my tongue, and the taste matches the smell. Death and sorrow and so many decades of silence. I fight for the surface. My sister limp in my arms.

I swim to the cliff and find the rock with my feet, climb up onto the cliffside. The sun is on my back as I turn to pull B.B. up with me. I work, sweating, crying, until we are at the top. The last of the dry rock of the island underneath us. I look out over the horizon and think I can see the museum's old bell tower still poking up through the water, the tallest island trees greening the surface.

"Henrie Henrie Henrietta," my sister whispers, and my attention is on her. "We did it."

I hug her and she moans.

"It was you and me, baby sister. We got him."

"We had some help, Beatrice." But there is no need to explain. She felt them too. "But the island is almost gone, you're hurt, and we're stranded on this cliff, B.B. I don't know what to do. You look bad." I start crying again, harder than before.

"Do you hear that?"

I shake my head no before I realize that I do.

"Girls!" I hear my name too. My sister's. Voices that I recognize that echo in my rib cage, live in my heart.

"Henrie." The sound interrupts my thoughts. "Look." B.B. points.

I follow her lead and see the hulking shape that must have been there all along. A shape is high in the water. A vessel almost as big as the monster.

It's our house. Upside down it floats, a big hull of a thing bobbing toward us. The foundation sticks up in the air, rebar and chunks of earth still attached. The mossy concrete stretches toward the sky. The first-floor windows float above the surface of the lake, and inside, I see people standing on the ceiling, peering out, searching for us.

"Impossible," I say to myself.

"Possible," B.B. whispers.

I am crying when I stand and wave my arms in the air, my sister resting at my feet. I watch as the ship of our house finds me, moves magically in our direction. It takes another moment to be sure it is my mother and Ms. Sonia I see waving their arms, crying.

Joshua is waving too, next to my mother, and a new rush of feeling floods through me. Gratitude. Love. Others stand with him. Wilderness is there with Wally at his side, and the tears come back as I imagine what B.B. will have to say to him. How we will have to explain that the dream of the babies is gone. I feel weak knowing this is coming. The sorrow moves through me so thick and fierce that for a moment it is all I feel.

The hand of the beast shoots out of the water. It is a big calloused thing with torn pads from fighting. Its claws are still thick and sharp. His body follows, rising until he is treading water between me and my ship. He is badly hurt, his throat ripped wide open. The water around him fills with blood, a red slick on the surface. He is gasping, spurting water from his throat, but rage drives him, and he swings his great ghoulish arm to smack my body, sending me sailing into the air. I see him below me, the top of his nasty troll head and the base of Quarry Hollow, its insides turned to the sky to keep my people safe—their mouths turned up toward me, screaming my name. I hit the surface of the water hard and the world goes quiet. I sink down, down, down, catching a glimpse of the house as I go; the same turret I'd made into a camera watches me now. I imagine it opens its great eye wider before snapping shut around my image.

Sadness sinks me deeper as I imagine that this is the end. We almost did it. The water is dark, the sun blocked by the body of the devil. He swims toward me, his neck split open, and his belly punctured with open wounds, yet he is still here, hungry for the part of me that has given up. I want to let him have it. I want the peace of an ending. Any ending. It doesn't need to be happy. It doesn't have to be right. Just leave my sister. My family.

I can feel his breath on my head. The great sharp teeth orbit my body. He will drain me, and I shut my eyes, waiting for the end.

The water around me begins to warm. I feel it long before I open my eyes, and I know that he should have crunched down by now. Light glows behind my closed eyelids, and when I open them, the world is bright.

Electric, like lightning shattering through a rainstorm, the brightness of it has pushed him back even before it pierces through him, breaking him into pieces. He is squinting, squirming, his face ripples with pain. A hundred little underwater points that glow and flit.

I am in my monster form in an instant. I move in

concert with the ghosts, aiming at his center. The strength of our collective potential is greater than anything he ever planned for. We howl and dive. Bright as lightning. All of us propelled in one direction. A force.

This time, he doesn't stand a chance.

epilogue

It's been five years since the great Lake Erie earthquake, an event that seismologists claim wasn't an earthquake at all, and of course, they are right. The stories about that day are wild—aliens shooting down from the heavens, weapons testing gone wrong—but none of them are as odd as the truth. The Fowler Island monster died that day, and the island went under, shipwrecked at the bottom of that great and eerie water. I helped end it. Swam so hard into that monster that his sharp points and soft organs blew apart, became tiny food for the lake creatures who had so long steered clear of him.

I would have done anything for my Beatrice and my Henrietta—that has always been true—but it was also selfish on my part. I didn't think I'd move on. I expected whatever was left of me to go dark after the troll was dead, so it was a bitter surprise when I woke up in a new place, my soul a little dimmer but still aware. I woke up angry, as angry as I was the day I stood on the cliffs with my baby in my arms. That day I screamed down at the monstrous island. Told it that my daughter and I were done—tired of being scared and fucking furious all the time. Back then, though, I was sad. As sad as I was angry, but I'm free of the sorrow now. The cloying sourness of it is gone.

I've followed the girls south to Gaunt Creek—this small, college town that sits in a sea of cornfields. They have mistaken this town and their new house for a quieter, safer place than it is or will ever be. They think they have finally found peace. And maybe they have, but they do not know how many monsters walk among them as casually as men.

For the first few years, I discovered I could travel between this new home and what is left of Fowler. A tunnel took me back and forth so that I could check on what remained of the island, watch the strong limestone of the Island Inn stay proudly intact underneath the water, fish kissing its windows but unable to get inside. The museum bell tower is a weaker spot. It is the castle at the bottom of a fish tank. Windows and doors are gone. All the recorded history kept there blurred and melted in the cold waters of the lake, a blessing that will keep the mysteries of Fowler safe. The quarry house, of course, brought my babies to shore. Its great attic hull is preserved by the tourism board in Marblehead, a museum of oddities grown up around it of which Fowler would be proud.

Recently the tunnel disappeared, and the earth began to call to me. I resisted for a time, thinking it was the grave beckoning me—a place where I'd be locked up, caged, the weight of limestone on my chest, quieted in a way Quarry Hollow always wanted me to be—but the earth kept it up. It whistled and whispered, so much that I wake up now curled in the deep dark soil with the light of me stringing out into roots. When I'm down here, I feel myself growing, my form has substance again. I am not plant or parasite, or a speck of dirt. I am seed and womb. My essence is hunger, sucking up water and nutrients like air.

I must think of my girls to pluck myself up from this new mission, ripping longer and longer tendrils from the earth and digging upward like a mole when I want the girls. It's begun to hurt, this breaking free. A pain that is almost satisfying—I haven't had a body in a long time.

The others, my sad and ghostly companions for all those years, have moved on, found resting places elsewhere—perhaps they've gone where souls are meant to go—heaven or graveyard or out into nothingness. Perhaps I am the lucky one.

Henrietta is happier now, fixing up this new house with her mother, a house finally that wants to be fixed. Walking to the small-town grocery. Finishing up her undergraduate degree, which was left ragged for a time. Opening an art gallery. She is pregnant—a girl, although she does not know this yet. The baby will be present for the wedding. Little ears not yet formed, but the vibrations of their vows—hers and Joshua's—will be felt all the same. The wedding will be here. They will all attend. Carrie. Sonia. Wally. Wilderness will even come back for it. Their feet will press to the green grass above my head, and I will reach for them without their knowing. Kiss their soles as they press heavily on the front lawn of this not-quite-safe house.

Wilderness is the only one who drifted away. Beatrice took a long time to heal from her island injuries, and she was exhausted and angry and sad from all she lost. She doesn't like to think of it this way, but she misses her ancestry, her heritage, the most. A time when she had a destiny. Power. Now she feels loose, unmoored. Just another woman wandering the earth. Wilde let her push him away, and maybe it's for the best. He is off to find his own life, and Beatrice is working. The college has an archival office, and she is an intern there, learning about how Gaunt Creek was born of the work of women and of freed slaves who crossed the Ohio River from Kentucky, looking for their freedom, a purpose found.

They want to build, my girls, to stretch so that the town grows bigger, more successful. A place to be found. A place that will draw more like them. A bigger school for Henrietta's child. Another restaurant. A town museum.

Greed does not quit with the slaying of one monster. Nor does desire. The need to thrive and expand is by its very nature human. Re-creates whenever and wherever it is allowed. The body remembers and the earth captures the rot. Big shaky patches of land that seem solid, un-monstrous, yet they are sinkholes of secrets waiting to open up and swallow. But this time, it will not hurt my girls. I will be their monster. Their hungry, rooted beast.

I sometimes miss my old self. The infamous Olivia Rose. The queen of an actual island. The birth mother of Beatrice the Powerful. Beatrice the Great. The mothering version of Olivia Rose who thought she could defeat the monster haunting her family by simply confronting it. But that old self is gone, and the missing is fading too, as I find myself underground bathing in my own strength. My limbs grow long and pale, they grow strong, and as I stretch myself out under this town, I do not need eyes to see or ears to hear. I am hungry for the vibrations of townsmen too stupid to know they should shut up.

There are no cliffs to jump from here, but there is the rushing of the river, the steam tunnels that run forgotten under the college, and the sweat and tears of men that find their way down onto the pale tongues of me.

The female body is a miraculous thing. This I know. This I remember. Even as it finds a new shape, it nourishes. Gives and grows. And feeds.

acknowledgments

When I was barely twentysomething and living again in my hometown of Yellow Springs, Ohio, my friend and mentor Susan Streeter Carpenter drove me north to a small and strange Lake Erie island. Reachable by ferryboat, we arrived at a large and neglected house on the edge of an old quarry. We were there to write. It was an annual retreat initiated by two sisters, the wonderful poet Susan Grimm and the prolific fiction writer Mary Grimm. Here, I met a host of dedicated writers—thank you to Mary Robison, Tom Bishop, Tricia Springstubb, Donna Jarrell, Kristin Ohlson, Charles Oberndorf, and Mary Norris for introducing me to this place. I came back that first year with a short story, "Beatrice Was Never Lonely." Although that short story was never quite fit for publication—no clear ending or purpose—it's where I first met Beatrice and Henrietta.

When we moved my family from Rhode Island to New Mexico, I quit my big job (the one that paid real money), and for the first time in my life, I was gifted with time to write. It was wonderful and disturbing—the vast openness of the high desert coinciding with wide-open days. In that space, I found the Volt sisters and their island again. They took over my life for those first three years in the Sandias. I am forever grateful to Daniel Meiser, who gave me the space for this transition and has steadily supported me through it, and to my two brilliant and gorgeous daughters, Violet and Amelia. Your talents and joys, the strength of your bodies, your certainties and truths, amaze me. I love every version of you.

While New Mexico doesn't make an appearance in this novel, the book would not exist without the full support of the wonderful people I met in my first years here: the Meisner family, the Bensons, the Kolbs, Ms. Shelly and her Shucker Bus, Laura Matter, and Barkpit Studios (you know who you are). Thank you, too, to the group that invited me to work out with them at an ungodly hour twice a week, reminding me to smile and laugh during an otherwise very lonely stretch of time: Laura, Shelbi, Renee, Mandy, Felisa, Julie, Kate, Scott, and Alex. For the whole of the Stoerner family, particularly Noah Stoerner, who makes me feel famous every time I see him.

This book is for George Tsakraklides—who read every version twice. His encouragement never faltered. For Mary Carroll Moore: I never want to write anything without knowing your thoughtful edits are just an email away. Thank you to my editor and friend Daphne Durham, who worked hard to make sure this book was all that it could be. Thank you, Lydia Zoells, for seeing it all the way through. Thank you to my agents, Kimberly Witherspoon and Maria Whelan—your advocacy means the world to me. For Jessica Wallis and Eli Nettles—it seems I've known you all my life. For Nancy Fischer, who was in the audience way back when I read the first pages of Beatrice and Henrietta to a coffee shop full of people—afterward she smiled at me and said: "You're glowing." Mandy Minichiello, Anne Griffith (all the damn Griffiths), Katrina Kittle, Alice Carriere, Michael Himelfarb, and Eric Aaronian. To my little brother, and my nephews. Forrest, keep reading and reading and reading. Colin, keep those monsters coming. Thank you to my parents and my hometown of Yellow Springs for raising me to be the way that I am.

My life has been blessed with community—groups of people who give me great strength and inspiration. I am grateful to all of you for the large and small ways you've helped me bring this book to life.